THE SONG OF FALLEN ANGELS

IVY BRANNON

For those who are battered,
but not broken

AN IMPORTANT NOTE FROM THE AUTHOR

They say write what you know, but when I first set out to write this book, that wasn't my intention. I just wanted a little something to get my smut fix, but the more this story took shape, the more of myself I started to see in it. I fought it at first, worried about what people would think of me as my soul bled onto the pages, revealing not just fantasies, but pain and past trauma too.

This book contains heavy topics and themes, which could be upsetting for many readers. In this book:

-There is a **strong anti-Christian rhetoric**. I want you to know this is not to dissuade anyone from religion, or to put you down if you've found peace with one. I only write from personal experience, and my evangelical Christian upbringing left a deep wound that is slowly healing as I deconstruct the beliefs I grew up with. With that being said, I want to state that this is not an attack on *all* Christians. I am honored to know many who are open-minded, compassionate, and truly embody the message of Christ's love. Any negative commentary is not directed at these people, but at the hypocrites who use the guise of God to distract from the darkness in their souls.

-There is commentary on **addiction**. I've lost track of how many of my loved ones have struggled with this, and it's a fight I do not minimize or take lightly. I've witnessed friends lose their lives to heroin, but also celebrated another's anniversary of five years sober. There *is* hope for anyone struggling, and I've listed resources at the back of this book to offer you a helping hand if you need it.

-There is commentary on **suicide**, and characters who have either attempted it, or are contemplating it. This is another topic I don't take lightly. I've personally battled this demon in the dark of the night, and the scars it left, both emotional and physical, are bittersweet reminders that I beat it. That demon still occasionally beckons to me, but we are so much stronger than we realize, and there is *always* something worth living for. You're not alone in your fight.

-There is commentary on **child abuse,** both **physical** and **sexual**. I'm grateful to say I haven't experienced the first personally, but unfortunately that isn't the case for the second. I never planned to write this experience into a book, and I honestly didn't think I should. But my pain needed to speak. It needed to flood out of my aching heart and spill into characters who could help me carry its weight. And they did. Their tears are mine. Their rage and confusion and heartbreak are mine. Their coping mechanisms, both healthy and unhealthy, are mine too. But their healing is also mine. There are resources at the back of the book if you or anyone you know could use some healing too, but I'd also like to share these words a therapist once told me in case someone else needs to hear them like I so desperately did: it was not your fault. It was not ok. I believe you.

-And finally, in this book there are **explicit sexual scenes**. I've included a list of trigger warnings on the following page, but I wanted to briefly touch on this content here too. For years, I considered sex to be dirty and taboo, but now I believe when safe, consensual, and communicative, it can be a place to play, explore, and find freedom. However, one should not consider this book a healthy manual for sex, relationships, or good BDSM practices. Please research and educate yourself if you're curious. There are a plethora of books available to aid you on your journey, and some lovely sex educators out there who would be happy to steer you in the right direction.

Now that you've seen an intimate sliver of me, I hope you can escape into this book with peace of mind knowing these themes are not thrown around flippantly. There's heart here. There's respect here. And don't worry, there's some fun rockstar smut here too.

-Ivy

CONTENT WARNING

The following text contains graphic adult content and is not intended for readers under 18. In this book, you will find the following:

- **pervasive language**
- **graphic sexual content** including: **degradation** (names used: slut, whore, fucktoy, cumslut), **choking, slapping** (buttocks, face), **hair pulling, blood play, spit play, pain play, bondage, forced sex** (consensual), **MMF** scenes, **master/slave dynamic, predator/prey dynamic, CNC, edging, public sex**
- depictions of **depression** and **PTSD**
- discussion of **suicide** (includes graphic descriptions of prior attempts)
- discussion of **child abuse** (**physical** and **sexual**) (includes graphic descriptions)
- discussion of **addiction**
- **anti-Christian rhetoric**
- **violence**

- frequent **alcohol** and **tobacco** consumption
- depictions of **victim shaming** and **parental emotional neglect**

"But who prays for Satan? Who, in eighteen centuries, has had the common humanity to pray for the one sinner that needed it most?"

- Mark Twain

1

I rolled my eyes at the text message and tossed my phone back into my gym bag.

My best friend Kayla clocked the move and arched a brow in my direction as she shouldered a set of dumbbells. "Is it he-who-must-not-be-named again?"

I gnawed furiously at the wad of gum between my teeth. "Yep. It's been three weeks and the asshole still hasn't stopped texting me."

"Piece of shit," Kayla mumbled.

Grunting in agreement, I copied her movements with my own pair of weights.

"You told him to get lost, right?" Kayla pressed.

"Countless times now."

A bead of sweat trickled down my temple. My muscles were screaming at me, still sore from yesterday's workout, but I didn't mind. I liked a little pain now and then, and anything was better than focusing on the cheating ex-boyfriend currently blowing up my phone.

TRENT: I fucked up

TRENT: We can fix this

TRENT: I'm so sorry, please just talk to me

TRENT: We have something worth fighting for

Oh, please. We had a stagnant relationship where I had to beg the man to have sex with me, and when he *occasionally* obliged, it consisted of me on top with no eye contact and his little soldier at half mast.

I'd asked him to go to couples counseling.

I'd tried dragging him on cute dates with me.

I'd purchased an entire nightstand full of toys and accessories that got *my* pulse racing, but when *he* saw them, he acted like I should check myself in to a mental hospital.

That man stole the last eight years of my life. We didn't have jack shit worth fighting for.

I don't know why I stayed for as long as I did. Maybe because it was easy, and we shared a dog, and the rent was decent for Los Angeles. Or maybe it was because I'd been a conflicted 22-year-old when I moved to Los Angeles, and I'd tricked myself into thinking I'd be better off pretending to be someone I wasn't. Maybe I'd shoved down the part of me that wanted to be messy and dark and free in order to embrace being the perfect woman, just like my mom had always pushed me to be. So I'd snagged the perfect boyfriend, moved into the perfect apartment, and practiced a perfect smile to disguise the fact that I felt like an actor playing a role instead of being who I really was. When I'd finally decided I couldn't live that way, I was too far in and felt trapped.

So, in a weird way, I was thankful Trent had cheated on me.

When I'd caught him in bed with the neighbor three weeks ago, it finally gave me the courage to cut the cord, even though that fucker was clinging to it like a leech. I'd told him to pack his shit, but all the old band posters, sports memorabilia, and stinky socks hadn't budged.

Our miniature Australian Shepherd Gracie was the only reason I hadn't blocked his number while I'd been crashing on Kayla's couch. Trent was holding her hostage, refusing to let me see her until I agreed to sit down and talk. He probably figured I'd grab the dog and run the first chance I got. And honestly, he was right. I'd been plotting Gracie's jailbreak for days, but every time I drove by the apartment to snatch her up, Trent's car was in the parking garage, foiling my plans.

"Are you sure you don't want to come with me tonight?" I asked, dropping into a set of goblet squats with a heavier dumbbell.

Kayla puffed a dark ringlet from her eyes and did the same. "Jade, I love you. But I'm not exaggerating when I say I'd rather stab myself in the eye than go to that concert."

I cackled, which made a trio of gym bros glare in our direction. Apparently, chest day was *very* serious, and two women enjoying themselves didn't fit the vibe.

"Come on," I pushed. "It'll be fun!"

"No, it'll give me nightmares. But I applaud you for going by yourself just to be petty."

I snorted, earning another glare from the bros.

The situation with Trent had left me feeling like shit, and I wanted to take a jab at him in whatever way I could. That jab happened to come in the form of concert tickets.

I'd gifted him general admission to see his favorite band for Christmas, and he'd had plans to attend the show with his cousin. I didn't know much about the band besides their name, Legion, and a few songs that Trent played on a loop to get pumped up for the gym. They were a catchy alt rock band with sexy vocals, melodic riffs, and heavy breakdowns, and their sold-out US tour kicked off today with a three-night stint in Los Angeles over Memorial Day weekend. The tickets cost me an arm and a leg, but at the time, my dumb ass thought Trent was worth it. I'd had to take on three extra commissions that month just to make ends meet.

The day of me and Trent's breakup, I'd been storming around the apartment, stuffing my belongings in a duffel bag, when I'd stumbled across the tickets propped on Trent's dresser. I'd considered selling them, but decided against it. Instead, using Kayla's word of choice, I chose to be petty.

My plan was to find a date to the show, look hot as hell, take a ton of pictures hanging on my new boy toy, then post them all over social media to make my ex jealous. Was it childish? Yeah. But it was either this or slash his tires, so I picked the one less likely to end in jail time.

The plan sounded good until it came to the date aspect. It wasn't that I had a problem finding a man; Hinge and Tinder had been very good to me in that regard. The issue was me. I'd spent years in therapy deconstructing my strict Christian upbringing that brainwashed me into viewing sex as a sin, and I was finally freed from a relationship where getting the man to touch me felt like pulling teeth. Needless to say I was a little pent up. I believe *feral* was the term Kayla used the other day. And to be honest? Pretty accurate.

My dates always ended one of two ways; either I scared the men off by being too forward, or we had sex and they ghosted. That would've been fine with me, but only if they'd ghosted me *after* we went to the show. I didn't want a boyfriend. I wanted the sex I'd always fantasized about, and something pretty to look at while listening to good music. Unfortunately, no one had stuck around long enough to give me either of those.

Oh well. At least I was finally getting laid. Even though the sex was still relatively vanilla, it was worlds kinkier than I was used to with Trent. Whenever I used to bring up my ideas to my ex, or show him porn that intrigued me, or read an excerpt from one of the dirty novels I'd devour before bed, he'd usually respond with something along the lines of, "Ew, why do you even like that?" I don't know, Trent. All I know is two weeks ago, one of the personal trainers from the gym choked me during missionary, and it was the closest thing to a religious experience I'd ever had. So you go have lights-off sex with fucking Stacy from 2B, and let me live my life without judgment.

Kayla and I dropped our weights and finished with a set of ten burpees.

"But seriously," she panted, swiping the halo of curls from her face, "you're not going to come back from this thing possessed or anything, are you?"

I huffed a laugh. "They don't actually do anything demonic, Kay, it's just part of their performance."

The other night, after I'd once again tried and failed to lock down a date to the show, Kayla said she'd consider coming, but she'd quickly redacted the statement when we clicked on the band's Wikipedia page.

Apparently, no one knew who Legion was or what they looked like. Instead, the four members wore masks and body paint to obscure their identities, and each was assigned a different persona.

A persona linked to the devil.

Some fan sites even claimed the band held secret, members-only seances and performed Satanic rituals onstage to release demons into the crowd. It was something that would give my religious mother a heart attack if she knew I was attending. Thankfully, we hadn't had a relationship for the past two years, so there was no way of her finding out.

Kayla planted her hands on her hips and attempted to catch her breath as we finished our workout. "Still. Please carry black tourmaline in your pocket and burn some sage when you get back."

I grinned. Kay was a hippie at heart, and one of the best people I knew. The past few years had been heavy, but with unconditional love and healing crystals in hand, she'd helped me carry the emotional baggage every step of the way.

"Don't worry," I assured her. "I'll wear my black tourmaline pendant *and* the obsidian bracelet you got me. It'll be cute with my outfit."

"Oo!" Kayla clapped and bounced on her toes, all paranormal threats forgotten at the mention of fashion. "What are you wearing?"

"White crop tank and a leather mini skirt."

"Hair?"

"I think half up, half down."

I toyed with the damp strands hanging around my face. In the first few days I'd been staying at Kayla's, I'd gotten heated after another screaming match over the phone with Trent, so I'd stomped down to the CVS below her apartment in a fit of rage, purchased an inky, reddish-purple hair dye called Black Cherry, and hacked at my hair with the kitchen scissors to create curtain bangs. After all, what was a bad breakup without a manic makeover? Luckily, it turned out cute. Dark hair made my hazel eyes pop, and the bangs flattered my face shape.

Kayla thought a few seconds longer before nodding again. "Super cute. You'll nab a demon boyfriend, no problem."

I playfully smacked her arm. "For the last time, they're not actually summoning the devil."

"You don't know that! This shit happens! You should see what Reddit says about Florence and the Machine."

I laughed and hauled my gym bag over my shoulder. "God, you sound like my mom."

Kayla chuckled, but her face fell. As we wandered out of the gym, she peeked at me out of the corner of her eye. "Have you talked to her recently?"

"No. Still just getting the occasional 'I'm praying for you' text."

Kayla frowned. "I think she'll come around one day."

I shrugged, hoping the carefree move hid the sadness tugging at my heart. "I gave up hoping for that a long time ago. But that's ok. I don't have any regrets. Besides, you're the only family I need."

Kayla returned my smile and draped her arm around my shoulders. "Amen, sister."

We started in the direction of our cars.

"You down to grab a coffee?" Kayla checked her Apple Watch. "Do you have time? When does the show start?"

"7. Doors open at 6:30."

Kayla stopped in her tracks and checked her watch again. "Where is it?"

"The Palladium."

"Do you have your clothes in the car?"

"No, I'm gonna run home and shower first."

Kayla let out a low whistle and shook her head. "Not if you plan on making it on time. It's 6:15."

"What? No, it's not!" I fumbled through my bag for my phone. "We didn't work out for two hours, did we?"

"Yup. You were in the zone."

And thanks to Trent, I'd been avoiding my phone as much as possible.

"Shit!" I hissed, tapping my cracked screen to see the time defiantly staring back at me. I gestured to my outfit. "I can't go to the show like *this*."

Most of my clothes were still at my apartment, so Kayla had lent me some of hers to exercise in. Not that her matching leggings and sports bra weren't cute, but the baby pink set might get some strange looks in a crowd full of punk rockers and hot goth chicks. Also I smelled like B.O., my face was flushed, and my new bangs were plastered to my face with sweat.

"Just don't go," Kayla offered. "Sell the tickets and put the money towards a security deposit when you find a new apartment. We'll order pizza and watch a movie instead."

My shoulders slumped. "I have to go, Kay. My shoulders slumped. "It's lame, but… I don't know why, I just feel like I have to."

Kayla's eyes softened. "You need to take back some of your power from him."

I sighed and nodded. At times, my best friend knew me better than I knew myself.

"It's ok, I get it." Kayla gave me an encouraging smile and dug around in her gym bag, then tossed me a stick of deodorant and a scented body spray. "Take these. It's my emergency stash. Always saves my ass whenever I go to the grocery store after spin class."

"Thank you." I pulled her into a quick hug before jogging towards my beat up Honda Civic parked at the far end of the parking garage. "I'll tell the demons you say hi!"

"Don't you dare!" Kayla called after me. "I'm serious, Jade, don't invite them in! You're not wearing the tourmaline!"

I snickered and waved goodbye as I clicked the doors unlocked and slipped inside.

2

I hated Hollywood.

Parking was a nightmare, the drivers were insane, and despite flashing the promise of fame and fortune from bright neon lights, the streets were polluted and the buildings crumbling. The whole thing was depressing.

Also I was late, and I hated being late.

It probably stemmed from that Jade-Matthews-Must-Be-Perfect syndrome I'd had my whole life.

In school, I'd been a straight-A student, the star striker on the soccer team, president of student council, and the host of a Wednesday night Bible study after school. I'd been constantly put together and did what was expected of me. I hadn't partied and I'd performed to my full potential. I'd done the right thing, *always*.

Had I wanted to be that person? Hell no. I'd wanted to design posters for drama club and make out with potheads at the skate park. But I didn't. I was too afraid of being anything less than the perfect child.

For years I'd lived in constant fear of a so-called loving God who would condemn you to the fires of hell if you wasted the gifts he gave you, or had sex before marriage, or had the audacity to think a woman should have control of her body instead of the government. I'd been a child who thought for herself and questioned things for as long as I could remember, so from an early age, I was labeled a problem. In response, my mom and stepdad had ruled over me with an iron fist, creating a daughter who was the perfect example of pious obedience.

On the outside, at least.

Inside, I'd been counting the days til I turned 18, went to college, and could finally be myself, whoever I decided that was.

I know it's cliché to blame your parents for fucking up your brain. And in their defense, they weren't responsible for *everything* wrong in my head. There were the typical chemical imbalances and the consequences of my own stupid decisions in there too, but other stuff was one hundred percent their fault. Some big stuff.

Perfectionism wasn't the biggest, but hell, it was a big part of my personality. I liked everything meticulously planned and organized. Typically, the only time I ever liked to be out of control was in the bedroom. There I could shut my brain off and actually let loose. All the voices, worry, and panic were replaced by pleasure, passion, or pain. Nothing else existed for a few precious moments, and it was glorious. I wanted to live in that place of surrender forever.

But I couldn't, because I was *not* currently in the bedroom. I was on a smelly street off Sunset Boulevard, rummaging around in my pocket for a wrinkled ticket. Meanwhile, a mob of religious fanatics stood on the sidewalk behind me, shouting threats of damnation as they picketed the band plastered on the marquis. My mom would've loved them.

"Ah-ha!" I raised the ticket high and slammed it into the hand of an unamused security guard. "There! Told you I'd find it."

Without blinking, the man extended a sharpie and swiped a black X on the back of my hand, proving I was over 21.

"You don't need to see my ID?" I asked him.

He scoffed and irritably motioned for me to move along.

"Rude," I mumbled.

God, growing up was weird. I was confident in who I was now, but also hyper-aware of how my body was changing with the passage of time. Inside, I felt young and full of life and promise, then I looked in the mirror and got confused when I saw frown lines and crows feet forming in my skin. I knew they weren't anything to be ashamed of; they were signs of life, proof I'd laughed and cried and grown wiser with the years, but I often forgot that living in a world that viewed youth as the epitome of beauty. And the fact I was just now in a place where I was living for myself instead of others, doing the things I'd always wanted to? A nagging voice at the back of my mind told me it was too late for that, and too much time had passed me by while I'd been masquerading as someone else.

My brief moment of insecurity was over as soon as I walked past a group of younger women vomiting straight vodka into a trashcan, their night at the show ruined as a result of pregaming too hard. I shook my head and chuckled grimly as I headed for the bar. Thank god I wasn't that young and learning those lessons again. There was plenty of life left to live, and now I was able to experience it with a good head on my shoulders.

The opening act was already onstage by the time I found a kiosk manned by a skinny bartender with a handlebar mustache.

"I'll take an IPA, please," I said.

The man scanned my pink workout set as he grabbed a can from the refrigerator behind him. "Your boyfriend drag you here?"

I'd found one of Trent's old zip-up hoodies on the floor of my car and slipped it on before coming in, but apparently it didn't distract from my outfit the way I'd intended. I hugged the forest green fleece tighter around me.

"No, it's just me."

"You listen to this shit?" the bartender laughed, motioning to the post-hardcore band screaming into the microphone onstage. The lid to the beer popped open with a hiss before its contents glugged into a plastic cup.

I forced a smile. "Yup."

I didn't listen to this shit *specifically*, but I liked rock. Music was an escape for me, just like sex. And like sex, I guess my preferences didn't match my exterior.

I paid the bartender, gave him a decent tip, and was halfway through my beer when my phone dinged in my pocket. When I checked it, I had two new messages.

> TRENT: You can't avoid me forever. Call me, we'll set up a time to chat

> KAYLA: Are you possessed yet?

I ignored Trent's text and went straight to Kayla's.

> Convulsing and levitating as we speak. Super fun. 10 out of 10, highly recommend

> KAYLA: ha ha, very funny. For real though, I'm covering the house in selenite so it soaks up all your bad juju when you get home

> Beelzebub says hi

> KAYLA: Fuck you

I snickered and stuffed my phone back in my pocket. It buzzed almost immediately. I pulled it out again, only to find another text from Trent.

TRENT: Gracie misses you

At that, my blood boiled.

That piece of shit. Trying to use our *dog* to manipulate me? God, the man was the worst. How the hell did I put up with him for eight years?

The text had me so riled up that I chugged the rest of my beer, bought another, then sought refuge in a darkened corner near the merchandise tables where I could drink undisturbed.

The opener's mix was sounding better as they went along, and one song was really catchy. I watched them for a bit, bobbing my head to the beat, then turned my attention to the poster on the pillar behind me. *Legion* was spelled out in white lettering that dripped red blood, while the supporting acts decorated the bottom half of the page in smaller print. I slid my phone from my pocket and snapped a quick picture, then immediately uploaded it to my Instagram story. Lately, Trent had been stalking my social media like it was his job, so I gave it a maximum of ten minutes before he saw it.

A maniacal giggle escaped me at the thought.

"Are you waiting for friends?"

My head jerked up, and I searched for the source of the voice. My gaze landed on a young woman sitting on a stool behind the Legion merch table. One side of her head was buzzed, while the rest of her hair was flat-ironed straight and dyed cherry red. She stared at me with warm brown eyes and a friendly smile, while a glittering spider bite piercing peeked out beneath her full bottom lip.

I raised a finger to my chest. "Are you talking to me?"

"Yeah. I asked if you're waiting for your friends."

I wandered closer. "No, I'm here alone."

The woman's head tilted curiously. "Oh, are you one of their girlfriends?"

"One of their what?"

The merch girl motioned to the band playing onstage. "Are you dating one of them?"

"Oh! No, I'm just a viewer."

"Gotcha." The woman nodded and smiled. "Sorry, you just… I thought you looked a little… Never mind."

I chuckled. "You thought I looked out of place?"

The merch girl flinched. "I suck, I'm sorry."

"No, you don't suck," I laughed. "I *do* look out of place. I lost track of time and didn't get a chance to change after the gym."

"Ah, that makes sense." The woman smiled again. "Well it's cool to see a girl here alone, just enjoying the music for herself."

"Oh, I'm not." I frowned at how that sounded. "I mean, I *am* enjoying it, but I'm not here to enjoy it."

The woman raised an eyebrow.

I sighed. "It's complicated."

"I've got time."

I hesitated, but the warmth radiating off the woman lowered my defenses.

"Ok, so…" I chewed my lip. "My ex-boyfriend of eight years is a piece of shit and cheated on me and now he's keeping me from my dog by refusing to let me see her until I consider getting back together so I wanted to punish him in some little way and Legion is his favorite band so I stole his concert tickets and came here to rub it in his face."

The woman blinked.

I blinked back.

Then she threw back her head and laughed hysterically.

"Oh my god," she wheezed, slapping the table and rattling its contents. "That's amazing!"

"It's stupid," I muttered.

"No, it's not! It's great!" The woman wiped tears of merriment from her eyes. "Seriously. Fuck that guy. He deserves way worse."

"Yeah, well." I shrugged. "What can ya do?"

The merch girl froze at the statement, her eyes flicking back and forth across the surface of the table as she weighed a thought. When she looked up again, her features had twisted into a determined, slightly mischievous expression. "I have an idea."

I opened my mouth to ask what, but before I could, the woman added, "Will you make sure no one fucks with my shit? I'll be gone ten minutes max."

Then she darted away.

A buzzing pulled my attention down to my phone. Another message from Trent waited for me.

TRENT: Did you take my fucking tickets?

I smirked, snapped a picture of the opener, uploaded it to Instagram, and dropped the phone back in my pocket.

The band was on their final song when the merch girl returned.

"Hey!" She beamed as she strode up to me. She was shorter than I'd realized, the top of her head barely reaching my shoulder, but she walked like she owned the place.

"Hey," I replied. "Don't worry, your stuff is safe. I fended off countless foes."

The woman laughed. "Thanks. I'm Veronica, by the way. But everyone calls me Vee."

"I'm Jade." I reached out to shake Vee's hand, but instead, she dropped something into the center of my palm. In the low lighting, I had to squint to get a good look at it.

A rectangular laminate dangled at the end of a black lanyard, the words All Access written across it in block letters.

"Surprise!" Vee spread her arms wide. "Your ex is going to be so pissed!"

I stared at the lanyard in my hand. "Why? What is this?"

"Are you kidding?" Vee laughed. "It's a backstage pass."

"Oh! Cool." I pulled out my phone and snapped a picture, then handed the laminate back to her. "Thanks."

Vee blinked. "Girl."

"What?"

"Jesus, you're so fucking wholesome. It's adorable. Come with me, dude. I'm bringing you backstage."

"Oh!" I blushed at my ignorance. "Oh my god! That's so sweet of you, but it's ok. You really don't have to—"

"I know I don't *have* to. I want to." Vee took my hand. "My ex was a crazy bitch who stole our cats and moved to Florida without telling me. If I could've pushed her buttons like this, I would have."

"I don't want to impose—"

"You're not imposing, I promise. I already checked with the guys and they said it's cool."

"The guys?"

But Vee was too busy dragging me towards the stage to answer. People were already lined up at the barricade wielding handmade signs with phrases like "Hail Satan" and "I love Lucifer" scribbled across them. Some even had fake blood smeared on their skin, and upside-down crosses painted on their foreheads.

"People really go all out for this thing, don't they?" I shouted at Vee.

She looked back at me, her brows arched. "Do you know anything about this band?"

"Not really. I mean, I've read a Wikipedia article and heard a song or two."

Vee chuckled and shook her head. "Well, you're in for one hell of a ride. Pun intended."

She waved at a security guard, motioned to the pass in my hand, and guided me through the black curtains at the side of the stage.

Backstage was just as hectic as general admission, just in a different way. Techs rushed by making last minute tweaks to instruments, assistants and engineers walked around mumbling into their headsets, and Vee and I had to constantly watch where we were stepping so we didn't trip on piles of cables or crash into amps rolling by.

"This way," Vee directed, turning down a long hallway. She barreled ahead to a door at the end with a posted sign that read *Green Room*. Below it was a handwritten addition that stated *Absolutely No Entry Without Permission*.

Vee rapped her knuckles on the door three times.

"Yo, guys!" she shouted. "It's Vee. You covered?"

There was a rustling behind the door, a few muffled voices, and then an answer:

"Come in."

Vee turned the handle and swept her arm in an arcing motion.

"Jade," she said, "meet Legion."

3

Never in a million years would I have imagined I'd be waving at the devil.

But here I was, awkwardly waggling my fingers at four of them.

I also never pictured the devil with rock hard abs, but the wall of muscle currently standing in front of me proved differently.

I wasn't overly tall, but I was slightly above average, and the man directly in my path still towered over me. He was shirtless, dressed in nothing but a pair of low-slung gray sweatpants that exposed a lean stretch of tawny skin. A rose tattoo decorated the side of his neck, and his buzzed coils had been dyed neon pink. But all of that was nearly impossible to see thanks to the metallic red devil mask obstructing the view of his face.

"Don't worry, darling," the man behind the mask cooed, his voice dripping with a thick English accent. "We won't bite unless you ask us to."

I blushed as he ambled past me and continued to mix a white paste in the plastic bowl he was carrying.

"Speak for yourself."

I followed the new voice. This one was American, and I was pretty sure it belonged to the man lying on the far left of the couch. He was also shirtless, with one leg slung over the back of the sofa and his hands behind his head, the position flexing his biceps so they appeared even larger than they already were. His throat, chest, and arms had become a canvas for various colorful tattoos, while his wavy chocolate brown hair had been pulled into a loose topknot. When he sat upright and faced me, I discovered only the bottom half of his face was visible. The rest of his features were camouflaged by a shiny gold ram mask shrouding his face from the nose up.

When he laid eyes on me, the man's lips curled into a wolfish grin. "A few of us bite without warning."

Something in my core leapt at the way his deep, raspy voice crooned those words, but I quickly shoved the sensation down.

"True," another voice laughed.

This one belonged to the man seated on the far right of the couch, who was leaning forward with his elbows on his knees and spinning a drumstick between his fingers. He also spoke with an English accent, and his bleached blond hair had been slicked away from a pair of dark brown eyes. A black cloth mask covered the bottom half of his face, its front adorned with the painted rendition of a wide fanged smile. The studded jean vest over his bare torso was a stark contrast to the casual attire of the rest of the band, and it drew focus to the large dragon tattoo snaking across his tan skin from wrist to shoulder.

"Lucifer here definitely bites," Dragon Tattoo added, kicking the toe of the fourth member's sneaker. "He might even tear out a piece of your soul if you're not careful."

The last man was reclined on the couch in navy track pants, white Nike sneakers, and an oversized gray sweatshirt with the hood pulled over a pair of noise-cancelling headphones. His fingers were interlaced over his stomach, showing off painted black nails and tattoos decorating the backs of his hands. Over his face, he wore a simple, pearly white Venetian mask, its darkened eye slits somehow managing to stare into the depths of my soul.

It was an eerie sensation, four faceless men honed in on you like you were an animal that just stumbled into their den. It instantly set my pulse racing, and the hairs at the back of my neck pricked with the instinctive urge to run to safety. Vee eased the tension when she scoffed and rolled her eyes.

"You really don't have to lay it on so thick, guys. She doesn't care who you are. Like I told you, she's just here to get back at her ex."

Ram Mask leaned forward, mirroring Dragon Tattoo's position with his elbows on his knees. "Now why's a good girl like you doing something like that?"

The mask angled as he looked me up and down, making my skin crawl, but the phrase he purred warmed my blood. He was being condescending, but he'd also uttered two words that, when used together, never ceased to make me weak in the knees.

The Ram's cocky smirk proved he was well aware of the affect his praise had on me. He'd managed to sniff me out like some kink-detecting bloodhound, and something told me he'd purposefully said it to get a reaction. I think I was slowly starting to get this band's *thing*.

Devils. Demons. Cardinal sin.

They'd channeled it into a niche genre of creepy, sexy rock and roll. It was weird, but judging by the sudden moisture between my thighs, it was effective.

Vee seemed unphased by it all and sighed like a frustrated mom dealing with rowdy toddlers.

"They're just messing around, Jade. They can't turn it off sometimes."

Devil Mask set his bowl down and brushed white powder from his fingers before crossing the room to extend his hand to me. "She's right, darling. We're just fucking with you. Sorry to hear your boyfriend's a piece of shit."

"Ex-boyfriend now," I clarified, warily sliding my fingers into his outstretched palm. His fingertips were calloused, and when I peered closer at the slits in his mask, I thought I caught a sliver of gray eyes beneath them.

"Well, I should hope so." Dragon Tattoo stood and joined the devil, flicking the man's horns before slinging an arm around his shoulders. With a charming wink, he added, "They call me Dragon. This is Diablo."

I smiled politely, hoping my cheeks weren't as red as they felt. With their faces covered, there was no way to know if I found the men attractive or not, but something instinctive and primal took over. I was a woman after all, and two impressively fit, half-naked members of the opposite sex stood in front of me, their eyes roving appreciatively over my body like they could see right through my clothes. Anyone else in my place would be weak in the knees too.

My lust-inspired stupor was interrupted when I felt some-one's eyes on me. I dared a peek at the figure on the couch with the headphones. He still sat in the same position, with his legs wide and fingers interlocked, the blank white mask trained on my face. If the intensity of his gaze wasn't so palpable, I would have assumed he was unconscious.

I finally managed to piece together the English language and beckoned to the man. "And you said that's Lucifer?"

"The fallen angel himself," Ram Mask replied. He stood and wandered over to where the other men had gathered around me. He was close enough now that I could see a pair of bright amber eyes shining beneath his mask, and coupled with his broad shoulders and wide chest, it was hard not to ogle him. The only alternative was to keep my eyes fixed on the floor, but my gut told me that was what these men wanted. Refusing to give them the satisfaction of intimidating me, I lifted my chin and challenged the Ram's expressionless stare.

"Who are you supposed to be?"

"The Beast."

I grunted and looked him up and down. "This one's kind of a stretch."

The mask tilted in surprise, and I mentally patted myself on the back for throwing the man off his well-rehearsed game.

"Alright, you boys have had your fun," Vee interrupted, stepping between us. "Will you please just take a picture with her so she can send it to her ex?"

An electronic ding chimed, prompting her to reach into her back pocket and pull out her cellphone.

"Shit," she hissed. "Craig just said he can't find any of the red hoodies in medium, but I swear we had a hundred of them." She shook her head and shoved the phone back in place. "Alright, I've got shit to do. Let's hurry up and—"

"Go." The Beast jerked his head to the door. "We'll take care of your charity case while you're gone."

My stomach dipped.

First off, *charity case*? Fucking rude. Second of all...

Holy shit, was I really going to be alone with these guys? A room full of strangers was daunting enough, but these ones oozed sin. They had taboo tongues and didn't seem to understand the concept of personal space. Or *shirts*.

Plus, they could do god knows what to me because no one knew who the hell they were. It was an unsettling thought, one that had panic surging through my veins, but despite that, when Vee protested, I didn't join in. My eyes stayed locked with those of the Beast, my heart pounding but my gaze unflinching.

Because something else fired in my blood, overpowering my original trepidation.

Excitement.

I wasn't a charity case or some damsel in distress, and even though I melted hearing it, I wasn't a good girl. I was a fallen angel too, and demons didn't scare me. I had plenty of my own.

"Go do your thing, Vee," I insisted. "I can handle these boys for a bit. I get the feeling their bark is worse than their bite."

An unsettling ripple of laughter spread over the men.

Vee raised her hands in defeat. "Alright, suit yourself. I'll be five minutes max." She stepped into the hall, tossing a warning finger at the band as she did. "You four behave yourselves."

The Dragon nudged Diablo with his elbow and snickered. "No promises."

The door shut with a bang, and we were alone.

The Beast immediately whirled on me.

"Alright, cut the act," he barked, taking a threatening step closer. "You may have Vee fooled, but not me."

I glanced at the other men for some kind of explanation, but they stayed silent and watched me like hawks. At least, Diablo and Dragon did. I wasn't sure about Lucifer. He was still motionless on the couch, looking like some creepy porcelain doll in a horror movie.

"What do you really want?" the Beast pressed.

"I think she's a journalist," Diablo muttered. "I can see it now: 'Undercover With Rock and Roll's Bad Boys: A Shocking Exposé.'"

"We don't talk to news outlets," Dragon stated. "You can contact our manager with your questions, and we'll respond via email."

"She's not press," the Beast declared. He slowly circled me, his scrutinizing gaze raking down my body and spreading tingles through my neck and spine. Without warning, he snatched my chin in an iron grip, the rings on his fingers digging into the flesh of my cheeks. I yelped, too surprised to put up a fight. All I could do was blink up at those golden irises and wonder if the sensation I was experiencing was maddening rage or unbearable lust.

Turns out, it was both.

"I think she's with the Jesus freaks outside," the Beast mused, turning my head to the right and to the left as he examined my features. "My guess is they sent her on a crusade to save our poor, corrupt souls from eternal damnation."

I furiously ground my teeth as he manhandled me, but I also had to press my knees together as a shudder of arousal rocked my body. "I'm not with them either."

The Beast scoffed, his thumb skating back and forth across my cheekbone with mock tenderness. "Come on, look at those angel eyes. I know a good little church girl when I see one."

I smacked his hand away, severing the tether of lust that had kept me entertaining his behavior.

"Nope," I snapped. "Looks like you're not as smart as you think you are."

The Beast tensed, but before he could snarl a response, the Dragon interrupted him.

"Hang on." The man's espresso brown eyes squinted in my direction. "Our Beastie's almost right, isn't he? You're a *former* church girl."

Was it written on my forehead or something?

"Yes," I conceded. "But that was a long time ago."

"Why did you leave?"

My stomach lurched as dark memories flooded my mind. I quickly shoved them back down and offered a clipped response.

"Personal reasons."

"You hear that, Lucifer?" Diablo shouted at the figure slumped in the couch cushions. "Looks like there's another fallen angel in our midst."

"I don't believe it," the Beast murmured. He reached up to caress my cheek again, and I muscled down another urge to shiver at his touch. "Just look at this innocent face. This sweet little lamb would be too scared to leave the flock."

My eyes narrowed. "Pretty ironic coming from the guy who's scared to show his face onstage."

The Beast's hand froze, then slowly lowered to his side. "I'm not scared. The mask is a symbol. It's a part of the story we tell."

I puffed a snide laugh, taking sick joy in the way it seemed to piss off the Beast even more. "Sounds like an excuse to me. I think you keep the mask on because it gives you power. Take the mask away, I bet this big bad wolf act goes away too."

"You'll lose that bet," the Beast bit back, his voice low and gravelly. Ignoring the warning in his words, I charged on.

"Oh really?"

"Yes."

"Take it off, then."

"So *that's* what you're really here for. You want a photo of our faces so you can reveal Legion to the world."

Jesus. The man was delusional.

I turned to the other band members and raised an eyebrow. "Is he always this paranoid?"

"Learned behavior, sweetheart," the Dragon said. "Comes with the territory, I'm afraid."

Something tugged at the pocket of my hoodie, and before I realized what was happening, Diablo had pinched my phone between his thumb and forefinger and slid it free.

"Hey!" I blurted, lunging for the device, but the man dangled it over my head so it was just out of reach. "What the hell are you doing?"

"Relax, darling," he cooed. "We'll give it back. But our Beast-ie's raised a good point. You're a liability."

"And you're all insane!" I leapt for the phone, flailing my arms overhead, but Diablo continued to yank it out of the way just in time. Eventually I changed my attack and attempted to haul myself up the man's body like a koala scaling a tree. It did nothing but cause Diablo and Dragon to burst out in laughter.

"I was hoping you'd climb me, but this wasn't quite what I meant," Diablo teased.

"Ok, that's enough. We don't need a lawsuit." Dragon gripped my waist and peeled me off his bandmate. I went limp as I realized my struggle was in vain.

"Relax, sweetheart," he purred in my ear, tightening his arms around my waist, "we just have to make sure you're being a good girl and telling the truth."

"I *am*."

"A good girl?"

I sighed irritably in the hopes it would distract from the flush creeping into my cheeks. "No, I'm telling the truth."

"So you're not a good girl?"

There was no hiding the color anymore.

Changing tactics, I fed into their flirty game with a suggestive smirk. "Sometimes. If a man earns it."

The Dragon chuckled softly and grazed his nose against my ear, sending a shiver down my spine. "Oh, I'll earn it. Just name the time and place."

A tiny whimper threatened to rise in my throat, so I focused on glaring at Diablo to distract myself. As if sensing my eyes on him, he raised a finger, signaling he needed a few more seconds.

"Who's Trent?" he asked, continuing to swipe across my phone screen.

"My ex."

"Who's Gracie? Your daughter?"

"My dog. Wait, are you reading my texts?" I struggled again, but Dragon's grip tightened, rendering an escape impossible.

"She looks good so far." Diablo said. "I just have to check one more thing. Hold on… What's this you were listening to?"

Assuming he'd just opened Spotify, I tried to remember what I'd been blasting during the drive to Hollywood. When it hit me, I squeezed my eyes shut in embarrassment.

"Oh, god. It's a guilty pleasure, please don't—"

But Diablo hit play anyway, and "Fuck Away the Pain" by Divide the Day blasted through the phone speakers.

"Well, look at that." Dragon nuzzled my ear again. "Angel face, but devil thoughts. Hate to say I told you so, Beastie."

The Beast sniffed and toyed with one of his rings. "It actually sounds like you love to say it."

"No need to get all touchy," Diablo snapped. "It's not our fault you can't take a joke."

"Everything's a joke to you two."

"My bad, mate. I'll work on being a brooding prick just for you."

"You have that brooding prick to thank for your three platinum records."

"Oh, it's just him in the band, is it?"

"It's just him writing all the hit singles."

"Because you won't let anyone else touch them!"

"Maybe I would if yours were any good."

The Dragon abruptly released me and darted in front of Diablo. "Take it easy. We've got a lady present. Let's revisit this another time, yeah?"

"Like in another ten years?" Diablo grumbled. But then his mask angled towards me, and his words came out brighter. "Sorry, darling. Pre-show jitters affect us all in different ways."

"In that case, I should get out of your hair."

"So soon?"

"Come on, dance with the devil a little longer," Dragon cooed. He tried sliding his arms around my waist once more, but I fought the urge to melt into him and ducked out of his embrace.

"The gimmick was cute at first, but I'm kind of over it. By the way..." I jerked my thumb towards the man slumped on the couch. "Should someone check to see if that one still has a pulse?"

Still holding my cell, Diablo sidled up beside me. "Lucifer's a man of few words, and good thing too. Got a filthy mouth, that one. We wouldn't want to offend your ears."

I reached for the phone, but Diablo tossed it to Dragon, catching me in a mocking game of keep-away. "I appreciate your concern, but like I told you, I'm no saint."

"Prove it."

The three of us turned to the Beast. He wore that vaguely threatening and ungodly sexy smirk he'd displayed when I first entered the green room.

"Prove you're not a saint," he continued.

"And how would I do that?"

"Kiss me."

My heart skipped a beat. "What?"

"You heard me." The man strode over and positioned himself so we stood toe-to-toe. "I said kiss me."

"No," I stated firmly. I was speaking to him as well as the dangerously curious part of myself that was actually considering it.

"Why not?"

"Because you're an asshole. I'd kiss one of *them*, but not you." I motioned to Diablo and the Dragon.

The two high-fived, while the Beast's faint smile promptly disappeared.

"Their mouths aren't currently available. Only mine is."

"If they took their masks off—"

"The masks stay on," the Beast barked, making everyone in the room flinch.

A wise woman would have removed herself from the situation, snatched her phone out of Diablo's hands, and run for the hills without a second glance back. But I was so goddamn tired of doing the right thing. I craved the dark and the taboo and the exhilarating unknown, and here it was in the form of amber eyes that drew me in like a moth to the flame.

"Just a kiss?" I asked warily.

The Beast's gaze flicked to my mouth. "One kiss."

Nerves and desire fluttered in my chest, but I managed to play it cool and shrugged. "Fine, I'll do it. Unless you're all talk."

"I'm not."

I held my ground as the Beast stepped forward and pressed his body to mine. Something in the air changed. Carnal and compelling, an unseen energy crackled around us, electrifying the space between our lips.

"Go ahead, angel," the Beast urged, angling his mouth towards mine. "Take a bite of the forbidden fruit."

The scent of spearmint and cigarettes on his breath was mouth-watering, his words decadently tempting, but this was clearly a game to him, and I hated losing.

I leaned in, stopped just before our lips brushed, and lowered my voice to a whisper. "Go fuck yourself."

I knocked his shoulder as I pushed past him and started for the door.

In a flash, the Beast's hand whipped out, latched around my wrist, and dragged me back to him. I yelped in protest, but my mouth immediately snapped shut when my chest slammed into his.

"You have no idea the pleasure I'd take in breaking you," he hissed.

I defiantly lifted my chin. "It's cute you think you could. The world's tried, but I'm still here, so take your best shot."

The man sniffed wryly, then looked me up and down like he was seeing me for the first time. My body hummed to life under his gaze, and I became hyperaware of the way I could feel my pulse between my legs.

"I need you to understand something, angel," the Beast said, his voice a low rumble. "You may think this is all fun and games, but playing with fire is only fun until you wind up burned. And believe me, we're more than a burn. We'll engulf you in flames."

I fought the urge to roll my eyes.

"I assume you've heard the stories," the Beast continued. "If not from your fanboy ex, then from the protestors outside. Demons. Rituals. Virgin sacrifices. Maybe you don't believe in all that, and you think it's just an act. Or maybe I was wrong about you. Maybe you *look* like a good little church girl, but you've forsaken your faith and your god." The Beast's eyes darkened. "But you don't know us either. You may think you want to dive into the deep end, but you have no idea what's waiting for you at the bottom. So I'm telling you now, make no mistake… Act or not, onstage or off, with a mask or without, we are not good men."

His ominous warning was drowned out by a strange burst of excitement.

I'd met too many people who claimed to be kind and devout, only to prove themselves as the farthest thing from that. Hearing someone acknowledge and embrace their demons was a refreshing change of pace. Was it a massive, frantically waving red flag? Absolutely. But apparently red was my favorite color.

"I understand."

"Good." The Beast's gaze flicked back to my mouth, and the crackle of energy returned, so strong it overpowered all logic and reason. "Then what's it gonna be, angel? Stay on the safety of the shore, or risk the dive?"

Fuck it.

Just as Eve sank her teeth into the forbidden fruit, I smashed my lips to his.

Every pent up urge unleashed, transforming me into a feral creature that had finally found its match with the Beast. Our tongues feverishly danced while our hands flew across each other's skin, groping and grasping and clawing with vicious desire. Violence and sex collided when he smashed my back into the wall, his hand pinning me in place by my throat while the other pinned my wrists above my head. His mask knocked into my nose and cheekbones as he nipped and sucked at my bottom lip, creating a decadent mix of pleasure edged in pain. I moaned at the sensation and instinctively rolled my hips against him.

Knock. Knock. Knock.

The Beast flew off me, leaving me slumped against the wall in a flustered heap. He hurriedly wiped his mouth and smoothed his hair before calling out.

"Come in."

The door creaked open, and Vee slipped inside.

"Found the sweatshirts," she said, her smile proving she had no idea what had just occurred. "Did we get our photo?"

I opened my mouth to speak, but Diablo beat me to it.

"Yes, we did." He crossed the room and slid my phone into the center of my palm. "I don't think we scared her too bad. Did we, darling?"

I shook my head, still fighting for control of my breath. "No, you guys were... You were... Um..."

"We tend to have that affect on women," Dragon teased, propping his chin on Diablo's shoulder. "Well, sweetheart, you've been an absolute delight. Come back and play with us anytime."

The heated kiss was starting to seem more and more like a fuzzy dream instead of reality. My head spinning, I looked to the Beast, but he was preoccupied with the mixture Diablo had been stirring when I first walked in. He reached into the bowl, scooped out a glob, and swiped it across his chest, shrouding his tattoos in a thick white body paint.

"Thanks for stopping by," he said, not even bothering to look at me. "It's always nice to meet a fan."

Then Vee led me out of the green room, and the door slammed shut.

4

"You good?"

I blinked and looked up at Vee.

I'd been lost in thought again, replaying my time with Legion while the second opener, a pop-punk band called Phantom Spark, took their bows in the distance.

I faked a smile and leaned forward to brace my elbows on Vee's merch table. "Sorry, just zoned out for a second. You need help with anything?"

"I'm alright." She peeked at me out of the corner of her eye. "You sure you're ok? The guys didn't freak you out or anything, did they?"

"No, I'm fine," I muttered.

And I would be. Eventually. Once the twinge between my legs stopped pulsing every time I thought about the Beast's lips, or the Dragon's arms around my waist, or Diablo's playful teasing, or hell, even Lucifer slumped on the couch, watching me with a palpable stare while the others roped me into their games. All I needed was a time to forget. These feelings would dissipate when I returned to my life and had to think about things that actually mattered, like finding a job, and an apartment, and getting my dog back.

"I'm just thinking about all the stuff I have to do over the next few weeks," I said, directing the conversation somewhere else. "I'm kind of broke right now."

"Aw, I'm sorry to hear that. Do you have family that can help you out or anything?"

"Uh…" I ducked my head to fiddle at a loose string at the hem of my sweatshirt. "No, not really. My dad was never in the picture and I don't talk to my mom or stepdad anymore."

Vee pouted. "How come?"

My stomach lurched. "Personal reasons."

"Got it. Sorry, I didn't mean to pry. I of all people should understand some things need to remain secret." She gestured to a poster of the band she was setting up for.

I chuckled a little. "It's ok. But yeah, I'm on my own. So I'm gonna need to find a job before I can move, and there's really nothing out there right now. So it's stressful."

"What do you do?"

"I'm a freelance graphic designer. So I do a lot of movie posters, business logos, book covers, stuff like that."

"Oh, fun. Give me your card at the end of the show. I'll pass it on to the guys in case they want to outsource their next album art. They're pretty private and tend to keep everything internal, but maybe they'll give you a shot. I think they liked you."

I tried not to focus on the memory of the Beast slamming me into the wall with his tongue in my mouth. "Yeah, maybe. They're hard to read."

"I've known them a long time." She grinned and winked. "I can tell."

Suddenly, every light in the venue blinked out.

"What's going on?" I asked, frantically surveying the room. But no one seemed to be concerned about a power outage the way I was. The crowd exploded into a frenzy of wild cheers and rushed the stage.

Vee stepped out from behind her table and came up beside me to watch the commotion in the distance. "It's starting."

I followed her eyeline back to the crowd. People pushed and shoved and whistled and hollered, but nothing seemed to be happening. The entire room was still shrouded in darkness. I turned back to Vee, but she held up her finger.

"Wait for it."

A hiss started on the stage. Thick fog began creeping out from the wings, filling the space and sinking down into the photo pit, past the barricade, and into the crowd. It resembled the foreboding mist amusement parks use during Halloween.

When nearly all of general admission had been filled by a dense white cloud, a distorted guitar chord rang out, sending the crowd into another bout of hysterics. The sound rippled across the venue, hitting me all the way in the back where it sank into my chest and rattled my bones.

Gradually, a light appeared.

It was small, shining up from behind the drum set like a ray of morning sun. In the darkness, while everyone had been distracted by the fog, a stagehand had come in and arranged a black backdrop with a simple white pentagram on it, as well as a microphone stand front and center. The unseen guitar shifted to a different chord, still heavy with reverb. The sound continued to dance inside my chest, making the hair on the back of my neck stand on end like it sensed the presence of a higher power.

Almost as if my thoughts had conjured him, a figure appeared, and a reverent hush swept over the crowd.

Fists at his sides, he strode towards the microphone at center stage, his movements slow, methodical, and confident. He was shirtless beneath the sheer black robe draped over his shoulders, and every inch of his skin was encrusted in thick white paint.

Even if he hadn't been wearing that gold ram mask, I would have recognized who he was just by that cocky smirk on his lips. Lips that seemed to tease me as they pressed against the mesh of the microphone screen. Fans swarmed the barricade, trying their best to remain quiet, but the room was so silent that their eager whispers and emotional squeals may as well have been screams.

Unfurling one of his fists, the Beast reached out to grip the mic stand, his gold rings flashing in the spotlight as his fingers curled around the metal.

I'd never wanted to be a microphone so badly.

The man had everyone in the room, myself included, breath-lessly waiting on his next move. His power was undeniable when his lips parted to utter a single word:

"Kneel."

In unison, the crowd fell to the floor, unconcerned about the filth and grime. They only had eyes for their master, and eagerly awaited his next order. But instead of a command, the Beast opened his mouth and began to sing in a rich, raspy baritone.

Give in to me, swallow your fear

Surrender your soul and lend me your ear

As he was singing, shadowy figures appeared at the sides of the stage. They moved the same way the Beast had, unhurried and unbothered as they took their places. They'd also disguised their skin entirely with white paint, except for the Dragon, who had his arm tattoo on display for the world to see as he took a seat at his drum set.

Diablo sauntered onstage after the drummer, guitar in hand. He was dressed in a black tailored vest and trousers, which proved an eerie combination when paired with his devil mask. On the other side of the stage, Lucifer had traded his athleisure for ripped black jeans and a leather jacket. White angel wings had been painted on the back, and it hung open to reveal his bare, paint-streaked torso. No longer trapped by a hood, a mop of shaggy black hair toppled over the forehead of his white Venetian mask.

The Beast pulled the microphone from the stand, hauling its cord with him as he approached Lucifer.

Breathe in the darkness, abandon the light

Taste the temptation, join in the rite

On the last word, the Beast reached out, opened his fist, and slid his hand around Lucifer's throat.

My stomach flipped at the memory of him doing the same to me not thirty minutes before.

When the Beast pulled his hand away, it revealed a smear of crimson on Lucifer's skin, the result of a handful of fake blood he'd been hiding.

The Beast backed away from Lucifer and headed for Diablo on the opposite corner of the stage. The guitarist struck another chord I felt deep in my core, and the sensation only amplified when the Beast looped the microphone cord around Diablo's neck and dragged him closer. Diablo didn't fight the movement, and instead melted into him, causing a handful of whistles and screams to pepper the crowd.

Come to me sinner, drink of the potion

Dive in deep and choke on devotion

The Beast freed Diablo and returned to center stage. There, he wiped the remaining fake blood down the center of his chest, jangling the gold pendant hanging around his neck. At first glance it looked like any normal rosary, but when I craned my neck forward, I saw the crucifix on it was upside down.

Symphony of chaos and desire

Join with me, set your soul on fire

Burn for me… Burn for me…

The Beast's voice grew louder as he uttered each lyric with more conviction. The Dragon twirled his drumsticks between his fingers, and Diablo tightened his grip on the neck of his guitar.

The singer raised his hands high, bringing the crowd to their feet.

Burn for me… Burn!

A row of floodlights ignited at same time the Beast screamed the word, Dragon slammed into his cymbals, Diablo struck his strings, and Lucifer launched into a driving bassline. The crowd roared to life, joining in with the Beast's head banging, starting mosh pits, and throwing themselves against the barricade, eagerly reaching for any piece of the band they could get. The Beast obliged a few of them as he crooned the chorus, grazing their fingertips with his own, resting his hand on their heads, even going so far as to lick the cheek of a latex-clad blonde in the front row.

I'll be your ruler, you're mine to command
Make you burn with desire at the touch of my hand
No turning back, get lost in the sound
Let the angels all weep, we're eternally bound

Legion had the crowd enraptured, and for good reason. The song felt like they'd harvested your darkest desires and fashioned them into a melody. It conjured passion and adrenaline and set your pulse racing without you realizing it was happening. I caught myself leaning forward on my toes, like something was tugging at my heart, beckoning me into the music itself. Was it the result of a demonic invocation by the sinful creatures onstage? Or was it just some damn good rock and roll?

I shook my head to rid it of the thoughts and refocused on why I'd come here in the first place. I wasn't here to get starry-eyed by four guys with a god complex. I was here to get even.

I slid my phone from my pocket, snapped a few photos of the band onstage, then swiped the screen open so I could choose one to upload to Instagram. But when I clicked on my recent photo gallery, I gasped.

"Oh, shit!"

"Right?" Vee shouted over the noise. "They're pretty good!"

"No, it's not that. It's…" I hesitated, then stuffed my cell back into place and shook my head. "Never mind."

There was no way I could let her see the photo I'd just stumbled across on my camera roll.

It was an image of me pinned against a wall, too wrapped up in the Beast's kiss to notice Diablo snapping my picture.

5

"You *what?*"

I clapped a hand over Kayla's mouth and peeked over my shoulder at the table behind us.

"Keep your voice down!" I hissed.

It was a miracle Kayla and I had managed to get a table at the popular brunch spot across the street from her apartment. I'd gotten to bed late, too busy replaying the events of the night for sleep to find me quickly. Images of that performance, those men, and that mind-blowing kiss kept me awake, and it was only made worse by me staring at the photo on my phone.

The Beast's broad back was mid-flex as he pinned my wrists above my head with one hand and the other caged my throat. His tongue was entwined with mine, and both of our hips eagerly angled into each other, the expression on my face one of blissful surrender. Looking at the image thrust me right back into the moment, and it took every ounce of willpower in me not to grab my vibrator from my duffel bag and use it on the lowest setting so Kayla didn't hear the buzzing from her bedroom.

Somehow I'd resisted, and managed to fall asleep sometime around six. Kayla shook me awake at nine, threatening a meltdown if she didn't get mimosas and a full report ASAP. So I'd begrudgingly rolled off the couch, threw on a bra, and shuffled over to the trendy cafe.

When I removed my hand, Kayla lowered her voice to a whisper. "You and the lead singer *kissed*? How the hell did that happen? Where were the other guys?"

"In the room watching," I muttered, a flush spreading through my cheeks.

Kayla's eyes looked ready to pop out of her head. "I'm sorry, *what?*"

I shushed her and glanced at the table behind us again, but they were taking photos of their clinking glasses instead of paying attention to our conversation.

"Wow. Ok. We're gonna unpack *that* later. But go back to him kissing you. How did that even happen? I thought they wore masks."

"They do." I slipped my phone from my pocket, checked over my shoulder for prying eyes, then swiped open the screen to reveal the photo. Kayla gasped and snatched it from my hands for closer examination.

"Holy shit!"

"Yeah, it was weird," I admitted.

"No, holy shit he's *hot!*"

"Yeah, and he fucking acts like it. They all do. They flaunt it, and it's obnoxious."

"What do you mean they flaunt it?"

"Like when they talk, it's just pure sex. And onstage they choke each other and lick girls' faces and shit. It's *weird.*"

Kayla leaned back in her seat and sipped at her mimosa. "Good weird?"

"No," I replied a little too fast.

Kayla cocked an eyebrow.

"I mean…" I groaned and rubbed my eyes. "Yes? Maybe? I don't know! It was confusing. It was… it was…"

"Weird." Kayla flashed a Cheshire Cat grin.

I glared at her. "What's that face?"

"Nothing, it's just... You like weird, don't you?"

"No."

Kayla tossed her head back and laughed. "Ok, little miss kinky."

"I'm not *that* kinky!"

"Well you ain't exactly vanilla. I know you've just started experimenting so you might not think that, but trust me. I see into that deliciously twisted psyche of yours. If you met someone who didn't judge you and wanted to help you explore, I think you'd surprise yourself."

I sipped at my mimosa and considered her words. I could pretend all I wanted, but deep down I knew she was right. There were loads of things over the years that had piqued my interest, things that would send my straight-laced mother into a coma if she knew I thought about them. Even though I'd deconstructed my upbringing, sometimes I still couldn't shake that judgmental voice at the back of my head.

Be pure. Be Perfect. Behave. What would people think? What would *God* think?

I believed that voice was a liar, but it still gnawed away at me when I least expected it. Like now, when I couldn't even admit to my best friend that I got insanely hot and bothered by a man masquerading as Satan while three of his demons watched.

My phone buzzed, knocking me from my thoughts. One glance at the screen found Trent's name polluting it.

"Ugh." Kayla wrinkled her nose when she saw the message. "He's psychotic."

I nodded in agreement, but scanned the text anyway.

TRENT: how was my fucking concert?

Kayla read over my shoulder and nudged me in the ribs. "Send him that picture of you and the band guy."

I cackled and batted her away. "You're horrible."

"I'm serious!" Kayla's eyes lit up with glee. "You'd ruin his whole year! Hell, he may even keel over right then and there! Then you could scoop up little miss Gracie and flee to wherever you want."

"Wouldn't that be nice."

I mindlessly scrolled through my emails, looking for any commission requests but only finding spam.

"I need to work soon," I mused out loud. "My bank account is scary low. At this rate, there's no way I'll be able to afford a new apartment."

"Maybe your mom could lend you some money." Kayla's eyes went wide as she realized her mistake, and she smacked a hand to her mouth. "Oh my god. I'm so sorry, my brain was on autopilot. I completely forgot."

I tried to smile, but a hollow pit opened in my stomach like it always did at the mention of my family. As if reading my mind, Kayla leaned forward and squeezed my hand.

"Hey. I just wanna say I'm proud of you."

I blinked in surprise. "For what?"

"For being brave and putting yourself first. I mean, look at you! You went to therapy, cut out toxic family, left a shitty relationship. You're doing things that scare you but make you happy, some of that including weird kinky sex stuff—"

"Hey!" I laughed, smacking her arm. "I haven't done any weird sex stuff yet!"

"*Yet.*" Kayla lovingly patted my hand. "I can't wait for you to find someone who appreciates your crazy. They're gonna unleash a monster."

My cell buzzed again, and I rolled my eyes. "Goddammit, Trent, I'm going to kill—"

But when I looked down at my phone, an unsaved number lit up the screen.

> UNKNOWN: Hey Jade! It's Vee Hernandez. It was great meeting you last night! Really hope you weren't traumatized by the whole thing lol

"Oh shit," I mumbled. "It's that girl I told you about."

"Aw, cute!" Kayla peeked over my shoulder. "You guys exchanged numbers?"

"Yeah, she asked for my card and said we should hang next time they were in town."

I saved Vee's number in my contacts, then got started on my reply.

> It was great meeting you too! Thanks for being so awesome. Your plan was a success, the ex is pissed lol. And I'm only a tiny bit traumatized, don't worry. I'm stoked to get drinks with you next time you're in town!

Vee responded almost immediately.

> VEE: About that... wanna come to the show tonight?

Kayla smacked my shoulder so hard I choked on my mimosa.

"Ow!" I yelped.

"Say yes!"

"What happened to the fear of me getting possessed?"

Kayla waved away my comment with a flick of her wrist. "That was before some bun daddy with a six pack pinned you against a wall. I think that's worth the risk. I'll just cover you in every crystal I own."

I snorted a laugh and tapped at the keyboard.

> Is there another red hoodie emergency you need help with?

> VEE: haha no you were just cool is all. Life on the road gets boring and you make friends wherever you can. I'm sure the guys would like to see you too, they said you were chill

Kayla smacked me again, this time harder.

"*Ow!*" I snapped.

"Oh my god they were talking about you!"

I rolled my eyes. "Kay, it's not that deep. The conversation probably went something like, 'hey that girl didn't act crazy, did she?' And they were like, 'no, she was chill.' The end."

Kayla wasn't listening. She'd perched her chin on my shoulder and was drumming her acrylic nails against the table-top. "What are you gonna say? Are you gonna go?"

I thought for a few seconds, warring with myself. That feral thing inside me woke at the thought of being in the same room with those devils again, but I let my logical side take over and reminded myself that just because I went, it didn't mean I would see them again. I *would* see them perform though, a thought that caused an eager twinge between my legs.

"Well?" Kayla pressed.

I bit my lip, weighing the choice a few seconds more before typing.

> Can my friend Kayla come?

Kayla gasped in horror and tried to snatch the phone out of my hands, but it dinged with a response before she could.

> VEE: You're both on the list. See you tonight

6

"Relax, you look fine," Kayla reassured me.

I'd told her the same thing when she'd stomped out of her room an hour prior and insisted she wasn't going to the show because she had nothing to wear. Now she was standing beside me in a black slip dress, Doc Martens, and about fifteen crystal pendants.

I nervously smoothed the front of my mini skirt, which I'd paired with a cropped vintage tee and beat up motorcycle boots to be more comfortable.

"I *am* relaxed," I lied.

I felt comfortable in my outfit, I was having a good hair day, and my winged eyeliner turned out symmetrical for once in my life. It wasn't my appearance that was stressing me out, it was *theirs.*

Everywhere I looked, there was a poster or t-shirt emblazoned with those four masks, and every time I saw them, I was rocketed right back to last night. The longer the memories swirled in my mind, the more I craved another taste of the forbidden fruit.

Huffing a flustered exhale, I attempted to shake the thoughts from my head and looked around for the bar with the shortest line. Instead, I glimpsed Vee and a heavy-set man with a mustache unloading tee-shirts from a plastic bin.

"Vee!" I called, grabbing Kayla's hand and dragging her behind me as I made my way through the crowd.

"Hey!" Vee greeted us with a wave. "You made it! I didn't know if you would. We heard protestors shut down a few of the streets."

I fought the urge to roll my eyes at the mention of the fanatics packing the route to the theater, screaming doomsday prophecies and thumping Bibles against passing car windows. "It was fine. You just nudge 'em with your car a little bit and they get out of the way."

The man stacking shirts behind Vee snorted at my joke. Vee pulled him forward and clapped him on the back.

"Jade, this is Craig. Tour manager, roadie, and most importantly, one of my oldest friends.

"Nice to meet you." The man shook my hand, sounding gruff but smiling brightly. He instantly made me think of a big teddy bear.

"I'm Kayla," my friend interjected. "Thank you so much for having us."

Vee lit up at the sight of her. "Our pleasure. Are you a fan of Legion?"

"Not in the slightest. I'm only here because Jade promised to pay for my drinks all night."

Vee flung back her head and laughed. "Love the honesty. Well, we're happy you're here."

"Speaking of drinks, do either of you want anything?" I asked. "We're headed to the bar."

"Oh! Here, I have vouchers." Vee slipped a handful of tickets from her back pocket. Each was inscribed with the words *one free drink*.

"I have a ton of them," she added as I opened my mouth to

protest. "Please take them, or I have to give them to the band. You'd be doing me a favor."

"Oh my god, you're so nice," Kayla exclaimed.

Vee winked at her. "Just because I work for the scary guys, doesn't mean I'm scary too."

Kayla giggled and coyly ducked her head.

"Tequila or Whiskey?" I asked, backing towards the bar.

"Whiskey ginger, please," Craig replied, pressing his hands together in prayer position. "Thank you, kind stranger."

"Margarita," Vee tacked on.

I nodded and pushed through the crowd, Kayla following close behind.

"You didn't tell me Vee was cute," she hissed in my ear as we dipped into a nearby line.

"You think? You should make a move, then. She's single."

"Nah, I'm in my self love era," Kayla replied. But she was looking wistfully over her shoulder at the merch table, and Vee was glancing her way too.

"Well, let me know if the era comes to a close. I've got her number if you want it."

Kayla just chewed the inside of her cheek and stared down at the scuffed toes of her Docs.

The line moved as a trio of goth girls at the bar cleared, and the man in front of us stepped up. He readjusted his beanie and ordered two bourbons on the rocks, then reached into his pocket to grab two drink vouchers. The movement jostled a carabiner on his belt loop full of keys and an ID card with *crew* written in all caps. He accepted the drinks, nodded to the bartender, and turned, nearly colliding with me in the process.

"My bad," he muttered.

"It's ok," I giggled, my voice involuntarily high-pitched. With pale skin, green eyes, a nose ring, and a tattoo under his right eye that read *sinner*, he was obscenely hot and exactly what my wet dreams were made of.

The man blinked back at me and frowned before brushing past. I groaned and slid my drink card to the bartender.

"You'd think at my age, I'd have learned how to flirt by now."

"You can't blame yourself," Kayla replied. "Trent stole your 20s. Those are vital years for coming into your sexuality. You're just getting a little bit of a late start."

I sighed and glanced over my shoulder at the merch table. Hot crew guy was busy chatting with Vee, but he briefly glanced my way. My stomach flipped and I immediately averted my gaze back to the bar.

Once we'd tipped the bartender, we made our way back to the table with our spoils and passed off the drinks to their respective owners. Hot guy had disappeared, and the opening act still hadn't taken the stage yet. Craig explained that it had something to do with them getting to the venue late due to the protestors.

"Does that happen a lot?" I asked.

"Oh yeah. And you'd think a band being problematic would be a negative thing, but that's not really the case. The more fuss people make, the bigger the band gets. Each rumor that circulates increases their cult following. "

Kayla fidgeted with the straw in her drink. "So it's all just rumors then? The whole demon-summoning thing?"

"Maybe, maybe not," Craig replied ominously.

Kayla paled.

A buzz prompted Vee to check her texts. What she found made the smile disappear from her face. "Huh."

"What is it?" Craig looked over her shoulder to read the message. He frowned, and his eyes darted to me.

Vee tucked the phone back in her pocket and nibbled at her lip piercings. "Hey, Jade? That was Legion. They heard you're here, and they want to see you."

My heart sank to my stomach, and my mouth went dry, making it impossible to offer a reply. Kayla answered for me.

"She's down!"

I whipped my head to her, but all she did was smile back with eyes as wide and innocent as a fawn.

I licked my lips and cleared my throat, forcing myself to think of something besides *oh fuck oh fuck oh fuck.* "Can Kayla come too?"

"Nope," Kayla blurted, furiously shaking her head. "Kayla will not be coming. I'm still not sure they aren't going to possess me."

"So you're sacrificing your best friend?" Craig clicked his tongue in mock-disapproval.

"She's tough, she can handle it."

I glared at Kayla, but telepathically sent the message, *I'm freaking out.*

My friend simply grinned. I could practically hear her repeating the words she'd said at brunch.

You're doing things that scare you but make you happy, some of that including weird kinky sex stuff.

I quickly pushed away that last part. The guys probably just wanted to talk, nothing more.

Despite the mental pep talk, anxiety ate away at my stomach while heat pooled between my legs.

"I can stay here with Kayla while Craig takes you back," Vee offered. "Wouldn't want the demons to get her."

Kayla blushed at Vee's teasing, and I forced myself to nod before I could overthink any more than I already was.

After one last panicked glance at Kayla, who simple mouthed the words *bun daddy,* I followed Craig into the crowd. Lust, fear, and excitement roiled within me as we headed for the barrier, the barrage of conflicting emotions engulfing me in a daze. By the time rational thought finally broke through the chaos in my mind, we'd already arrived backstage at the green room door.

"Wait!" I blurted as Craig raised his fist to knock.

Craig froze and arched an eyebrow.

"Um…" I gulped and looked to the right then to the left, desperately searching for a way out. When I found none, I sighed. "I need you to be honest with me. I know you can't say much, and I'm not trying to get you to spill anything, but as a *woman*, I have to know… Am I safe with these guys?"

Craig's gaze shifted to the floor, and he chewed his lip as he considered his words. When he looked up again, his eyes were earnest.

"If you say the word, they'll stop. You don't need to worry about that, I promise."

I breathed a sigh of relief.

"But…" Craig's eyes iced over again, reigniting the flicker of panic in my heart. "I'm not going to lie to you and tell you these are good men. So do with that what you will."

Then he turned and knocked three times.

When the door opened, it revealed the Beast staring back at me, his gold ram mask reflecting the light from the hall and turning his eyes to molten lava.

"Hi, angel," he purred. "Miss me?"

7

His voice was deeper and raspier than it had been last night, presumably from the amount of screams included in their songs, and it was by far one of the sexiest sounds I'd ever heard. I shifted my weight in an attempt to disguise the fact it instantly made me wet. Before I could utter a response, the Beast slid a hand to my nape and hauled me into the room.

"Thanks, Craig," he called, kicking the door shut.

When we were inside, I smacked his arm away.

"Hands to yourself, asshole," I snapped, ruefully rubbing the back of my neck.

The Beast balked slightly and folded his arms over his chest. "You've changed your tune since last night."

He was wearing his black joggers again, but tonight a burgundy sweatshirt had been zipped over his bare torso, obstructing the view of his muscles and the tattoos etched across them. My feral womanhood wanted to yank that damn zipper down with my teeth, but I wrestled my lust into submission and scanned the room.

"So what's up? Vee said you boys needed to see me?"

Diablo and the Dragon were huddled together on the couch,

Diablo tuning his guitar while the Dragon scrolled on his phone. Both of them were dressed in sweats and baggy graphic tees, the eerie masks their only accessories. At the other end of the room, Lucifer was in the process of pulling on the shredded black jeans he wore on stage, buttoning them just below the low-slung waistband of his briefs. He didn't have bulging biceps like Diablo and the Beast, and his abs weren't quite as whittled as the Dragon's, but he was long and lean, and the vast assortment of patchwork tattoos peppering his body made him more than easy to look at. I quickly averted my gaze before I got caught drooling.

The Beast casually ran his fingers through his hair. "We just wanted to see what you thought of the show last night."

Diablo set his guitar aside while the Dragon clicked his phone shut and tossed it onto the coffee table. All masks were facing me, squeezing all the air out of the room.

"You want my honest opinion?"

They nodded in unison. It was terrifying and weirdly hot and so confusing I had to raise my eyes to the ceiling to focus on forming words.

"It was interesting."

"Cop out," Diablo coughed into his fist, prompting the Dragon to bust up laughing.

"Tell us what you actually thought," the Beast commanded.

"Unless you're too embarrassed to admit how much it turned you on," the Dragon teased.

He was right, but my pride could never in a million years let him know that. So instead, I laughed like it was the funniest thing I'd heard all day.

"Sure, let's pretend a raging god complex is hot."

The Beast chuckled and examined his rings. "Three platinum records would prove it is."

"Three platinum records proves you're talented musicians and songwriters. There's passion in your music. Every emotion sits right on the surface. Whether it's anger or heartbreak or sex or violence, you make people feel it, and your shows give them a place to play in it. I don't know any other bands who do that. *But...*" I met the Beast's stare, refusing to make myself small for any man. "I'll be honest, the mix was a little off in places. And if you weren't so busy trying to fuck the girls in the front row, some of those high notes wouldn't have been so pitchy."

Dragon and Diablo stifled their laughter.

"Also, what's with that backdrop?" I continued. "I get you're trying to be in-your-face about the whole demon thing, but it's too simplistic for the quality of show you guys put on. At the very least, make the pentagram look like it's dripping blood or something. But if I were you, I'd put something else on there as well. A goat's head, or some other esoteric symbol. Or make your own sigil that's a combination of all your different characters."

Tense silence settled over the room.

Finally, Diablo cleared his throat. "That's... not a bad idea, actually."

The Beast huffed and shuffled over to a bar cart in the corner of the room where he ripped open a bag of spearmint tea with his teeth and tossed it in a cup of hot water. "Sure, let's fix what's not broken. We've been successful because we've done our own thing all of these years, but you're right. Let's listen to some random girl who's not in the industry and not a fan. That's a great idea, Diablo."

"Who said shit's not broken?" the guitarist mumbled.

"There's nothing wrong with evolving," Dragon added.

The Beast dropped a glob of honey in his tea. "You back anything Diablo says. Try having an original thought for once."

"Oh, fuck off," Diablo barked. "You're just miffed because you got shot down and now you have blue balls."

To dig the knife of rejection a little deeper, I strolled over to the two men on the couch, nestled between them, and smiled sweetly up at the Beast. Diablo clicked his tongue and playfully knocked me under the chin with his knuckles.

"I see how it is. We're just pawns in your sick twisted games."

"And we're absolutely here for it," the Dragon purred, draping an arm over my shoulders.

The Beast sighed irritably, set his tea aside, and picked up a bottle of whiskey instead. Lucifer immediately joined him, and the Beast poured them each a double shot.

"It's not *entirely* a game," I protested. "Like I said yesterday, I would've much rather kissed one of you two."

"We can arrange that," Diablo crooned, sliding his free hand onto my knee. I rolled my eyes, but didn't push him away.

"No, we *cannot* arrange that," the Beast snapped. "You know the rules. Masks stay on."

The light around Diablo and Dragon seemed to dim.

To try and lift their spirits again, I flicked one of the devil horns on Diablo's mask. "So do these things ever come off, or do you sleep in them too?"

"We don't take them off around anyone but our crew."

"How do you… Never mind."

"How do we fuck?"

He enunciated the last word so much I felt it in my core.

"We could give you a demonstration," Dragon offered, adding fuel to my fire as he leaned forward and nuzzled my earlobe. It sent a shiver down my spine the same way it had the night before.

"You two go ahead," I teased. "I'll watch."

Dragon chuckled and slid his hand to my opposite thigh, mirroring Diablo. "Oh, is that what you're into? Watching?"

"I like the idea."

"I like *you*."

I rolled my eyes again, but a blush crept into my cheeks.

At the bar cart, the Beast and Lucifer downed their whiskeys and mumbled among themselves. The Beast snickered and returned to his tea while Lucifer poured himself another shot.

"So what *are* you into?" Dragon pressed. "What turns you on?"

My stomach dipped. "Excuse me?"

Diablo leaned in closer, his hand inching up my leg. "You heard him. We want to know what makes these delicious thighs shake."

I readjusted in my seat to try and hide the fact his words made my insides twinge so hard my body jerked. "That's a broad question."

Lucifer and the Beast wandered over to sit across from me. The energy in the room shifted from playful and lighthearted to something that thickened the air and made it feel like every atom in my body was vibrating. All of a sudden, I became acutely aware of the fingertips brushing my skin and the moisture growing at the apex of my thighs.

"How about this?" the Beast suggested, settling back in his seat and lifting his tea to his lips. "How about we say a word, and you tell us the first thing that comes to mind?"

I arched an eyebrow. "You want to play word association right now?"

The corners of the Beast's lips tugged upwards. "I really do."

I glanced at Diablo, then Dragon, then at the statuesque Lucifer, whose white porcelain mask was glued to my face.

"Alright, fine." I straightened my shoulders. "Who's first?"

"Me," the Beast declared.

"As usual," Diablo sighed.

Ignoring him, the Beast continued. "First word: music."

"Soul. Next?"

"Rock and roll," the Dragon threw out.

"Sex."

I flinched at my accidental slip, but hey, this was the game. They wanted an instinctual response, they got one.

"I like how you think, angel." The Beast's arrogant grin finally made an appearance as he flicked his wrist to the rest of the band. "Someone else go."

"I've got one," Diablo said, his hand sneaking a little further up my thigh. I made no effort to stop it. "How about Dragon?"

"Fantasy."

"Oh?"

"You know, like Lord of the Rings and stuff."

"Oh."

"And how about Diablo?" the Dragon asked. His hand slipped up my leg to the same level as his guitarist's. I pretended not to notice.

"Diablo…" I tapped my lip with my index finger. "Hmm… Spicy. Like the Taco Bell sauce."

The Dragon grunted with disappointment.

"What about the Beast?" the lead singer asked.

"Pig."

Dragon and Diablo got a kick out of that one.

"And how about Lucifer?" the drummer asked, wiping tears of merriment from his eyes.

"Beautiful." I glanced at the smooth white porcelain mask slumped in the seat parallel to me. "He was supposed to be the most beautiful of God's angels, wasn't he?"

"So says the mythical book." Diablo's hand traveled higher. "Next word: tease."

"Fun."

"Blindfold."

"Also fun," I laughed.

"Restraint," Dragon added.

"Surrender."

"Pain."

"Release."

I blinked in surprise at my last response, my shock only

doubling when I realized the question had been asked by Lucifer.

"Sorry…" I shook my head. "I, uh… I meant to say bad."

The Beast chuckled and shook his head. "You're full of surprises, angel. I think we could have some fun with you."

"So much fun," Diablo whispered in my ear, his hand drifting dangerously close to my most sensitive places. I caught his wrist and held it still.

"You guys really love pushing boundaries."

"Don't you?"

I opened my mouth to argue, but promptly shut it when Dragon's hand moved from my leg to my arm, where he began trailing his fingertips across my skin in slow sensuous strokes.

"Come on, admit it," he urged. "You like seeing how far you can push yourself. Haven't you ever held your hand over an open flame because you were curious how long it would take before it started to burn?"

For some reason, my gaze flicked to Lucifer. His attention was fixed intently on me, and before I processed what I was doing, I'd eased my grip on Diablo's wrist.

"I… may have done that once or twice," I murmured.

"You like that rush, don't you?" Dragon insisted. "You like treading the line of what's right. What's *good*."

He finished the word with a nip to my earlobe, dragging an accidental moan from my lips. I tried to recover by clearing my throat.

"Just so we're clear," I stated in the firmest voice I could muster, "I'm not some groupie who's going to let you bend her over this couch."

"Why not?" Diablo asked, his fingers toying with the hem of my skirt.

"Because I don't know you."

"You've never fucked a stranger?"

"Not one whose face I couldn't see."

"What if I told you we're all devilishly handsome under these masks?"

"I'd say prove it."

Diablo clicked his tongue. "Now where's the fun in that?"

"It's exciting, don't you think?" the Beast chimed in, leaning forward in his seat. "Without a face as a distraction, you could focus solely on pleasure."

Lucifer nudged him.

"Sorry," the Beast laughed. "Or *pain,* If that's more your speed. You'll get along with our fallen angel, then. He's got some rough edges, but I think you like it a little rough. Don't you?"

Suddenly, I'd never felt so on display.

"Imagine getting out of that overactive brain of yours," the Beast continued. "Imagine completely letting go of control and becoming nothing but an obedient fucktoy whose only purpose is to be used."

His lecherous words made my head spin. How did he know I had an overactive brain? Or fantasized about letting loose exactly the way he'd described? And how the hell was I supposed to form a rebuttal with Dragon's breath on my neck and Diablo's fingers mischievously slipping under my hem again.

I caught the guitarist's hand and wrenched it off of me in the nick of time.

"That sounds like a deliciously twisted version of heaven, but unfortunately it's not realistic." I stood and readjusted my rumpled skirt. "I'm a grown up. I have a life. We aren't all lucky enough to live in a haze of rock and roll fueled lust 24/7."

"We could take you with us," Diablo suggested. "Pack you up with the equipment, treat you like our little pet."

The Beast let out a hungry sound that was more animal than human. "She'd look good with a collar around her neck."

A carnal twinge shot up my center, forcing me to press my knees together.

"She's got a bit of an attitude though," Dragon mused. "She'd need to be taught some manners. I don't know if she could take it."

"She could take whatever you gave her," I snapped. "But that doesn't change the fact that she doesn't know you, *or* what you might have, so her bags will remain unpacked."

"We're squeaky clean, darling," Diablo said, sounding slightly offended.

"And again, I'd ask you to prove it."

"Done. What else is stopping you?"

I released a shaky exhale and raised my eyes to the ceiling. "Hypothetically, if money was no object and everyone was healthy, then sure. I'd love to pack my bags and go on some weird, slutty vacation with you freaks. Happy?"

The men just stared.

Eventually I cleared my throat and clasped my hands in front of me. "So, is that all you needed? Can I go now?"

The Beast shrugged. "I was hoping to bend you over that couch and fuck you senseless, but if that's not on the table, yes. You can go."

My cheeks turned beet red, but I wasn't sure if it was from arousal, embarrassment, or homicidal rage.

I whirled and stomped for the door. "Thank you."

"The correct phrase is thank you, *Master*," the Beast called after me.

"Over my dead body," I threw back.

The door slammed shut behind me, and I whirled to press my back against the wood, my heart pounding like I'd just stepped off a rollercoaster. And just like a rollercoaster, I had such a rush that I was tempted to turn around and do it all again.

"Are you alright?" a voice asked.

I looked up to find a man with a guitar slung over his shoulder, his expression etched with concern.

"Yeah, I'm fine." I straightened and smoothed my hair. "Sorry, just catching my breath."

The man's gaze scanned my disheveled outfit, then flicked to the green room behind me. His eyes widened and he nodded knowingly. "Ah. I see."

"No, I wasn't..." I flushed at what he was insinuating. "They're just friends. Friends of a friend, actually. It's not what it looks like."

"Hey, no judgment." The man raised his hands and beamed at me, his teeth so white against his tan it almost hurt to look at him. "I'm Chase, by the way. My band Phantom Spark is one of the openers for Legion."

Recognizing him as the lead singer, I shook his hand. "Jade. I caught the end of your set last night. You guys were really good."

"Thanks." Chase held onto my hand a little too long before letting go. "It wasn't our best, though. First night of tour is always a little rocky because you haven't ironed out the kinks yet. We're still feeling out the crowd, too. Since we're a little softer than Legion, I don't think people know what to make of us."

"I'm sure you'll figure it out. Seriously, you guys are good. The fans will realize that eventually."

"I hope so." Chase smiled, then jerked his thumb over his shoulder. "You wanna come hang for a bit? Meet the rest of the guys?"

"I should get back to my friends."

And away from this door before I lost control and ended up over that couch, which called to me louder the longer I stood here.

"All good." Chase stuffed his hands in his pockets and dipped his head. "It was nice meeting you, Jade. I'll see you around."

"See ya," I called after him.

I hesitated a few seconds more, my gaze darting between the green room and the hall. The two should have had flashing neon signs above them that read, "The Wrong Choice" and "The Right One."

But Jade Matthews always did the right thing.

So she took a deep breath, squared her shoulders, and walked away.

8

Kayla was snoring.

She'd had four margaritas with Vee, and the two of them had laughed and flirted all night while I'd stayed slumped in the corner. They'd periodically taken breaks to check on me, and I'd always don my most convincing smile to reassure them I was fine before sinking back into my mind.

The interaction with Legion had me reeling. I told myself to shrug it off, but every moment played on a loop, every touch still heated my skin, and every word they'd said still echoed in my mind. I couldn't let it go, because at the root of it all, I was afraid.

I was afraid because I'd meant what I'd said.

If all the pieces fell into place, if it was safe and healthy and I was offered an opportunity to disappear into some debauched fantasy world with rock and roll's bad boys… Hell, I'd do it in a heartbeat. Perfect, put-together Jade Matthews would burn every morsel of morality to become four strangers' plaything. Not forever, obviously. But it sounded like the perfect escape from my current shit-storm of a life.

What went so wrong with me that something like *that* sounded good? No, it was beyond that. It got me *wet*. When

Kayla and I had gotten back from the concert, she'd immediately passed out, but I'd locked myself in the bathroom, jumped in a scalding hot shower, and touched myself to the image of me and Legion in various filthy scenarios.

Now I laid on the couch, mindlessly scrolling Netflix in an attempt to locate anything that would distract me from my own brain. After throwing on a random comedy special, I picked up my phone and clicked through my texts. Trent's thread had grown even more unhinged since I'd been at the concert. His most recent attempt at manipulation was just a string of old photos of the two of us and Gracie entitled, *I miss this.*

Hikes, holidays, brewery visits.

My heart twisted at the images, but not from missing my ex. It ached for the glazed look in my eyes as I feigned joy even though I'd been incredibly unfulfilled.

I sighed, set my phone aside, and shut my eyes, relaxing into the murmur of the TV. I'd just started to doze off when a buzz caused me to peel one eye open and peek at the screen.

UNKNOWN: T.B. has sent you a document: "Jade Matthews - Please Review And Sign.pdf"

Blinking sleep away, I sat up. My thumb hovered over the link as I weighed the risks of opening a spam text, but curiosity got the better of me, and I clicked.

A legal document popped up in a separate browser, entitled *Contract of Employment.*

"What the hell?" I mumbled.

This Agreement is made by and between Jade Matthews ("Employee") and Legion, LLC ("Employer"). This Agreement is made on September 2nd, 2023.

In consideration of the promises and of the mutual covenants and agreements contained in this Agreement, the parties hereby agree as follows—

"What the *hell*?" I repeated, pinching the screen to zoom in closer. The words shocked me so much I couldn't process full sentences, but I fixated on certain phrases that expressed the gist of it.

Opportunity of employment.

Employee shall provide employer with intimate physical contact.

The entirety of the employer's U.S. tour.

A sum to be determined at a later date.

A safe word to be determined upon signing.

I don't know how long I stared at the document in shock, but I eventually huffed a laugh of disbelief and rage. Before I had the chance to second guess myself, I stabbed my finger into the *call* button at the base of the number. The line picked up after two rings. A voice raspy from singing and screaming answered on the other end.

"Hi, angel," the Beast said, his words dripping with amusement.

I clambered off the couch and slipped out the sliding glass door to the patio so I wouldn't disturb Kayla. "I hope you're all having a good laugh."

"I don't know what you're talking about."

"Oh, fuck you," I spat, fighting the urge to slam the door shut behind me. "Seriously, dude? Is your life really so pathetic that you have to mess with random women to feel something?"

"Again, I don't know what you're talking about." There was less joy in the Beast's voice now. Clearly the word *pathetic* hit a nerve, so I decided to use it again.

"Well, I hope you pathetic emo frat boys had a good laugh, but this is childish, so lose my number."

"We're not joking."

I froze.

Pretty sure I blacked out for a few seconds, because when I blinked, the Beast's voice was speaking, but I had no idea what it was saying.

"Sorry." I cleared my throat. "Could you repeat that?"

"I said we're not joking. You gave us your demands, and we're meeting them. We're waiting for our medical records to be faxed over, which we'll then forward to you. We'll provide room and board for the entirety of tour, and we've already had our accountant set aside a sum of money—"

"What the fuck?" I muttered, mainly to myself. I pulled my gaze from the outline of the city and rubbed at my eyes. Maybe I'd fallen asleep and I was dreaming. That had to be it. Because if this was reality, it was *crazy*. Legitimately crazy.

"You're not doing this." I laughed. "You're absolutely *not* trying to hire me as a live-in prostitute."

"I think they prefer the term sex workers."

"Sorry," I snapped. "You're not trying to hire me to be your live-in *sex worker*."

"We are."

"What the *fuck*?" I repeated, my voice growing increasingly high-pitched. A neighbor's light turned on, and they peeked through the blinds to see what the commotion was. I faced away from them and lowered my voice.

"I'm a graphic designer, asshole, not an escort."

"You told us what it would take to get you to do it. So here we are, giving it to you."

"Yeah, but—"

"Did you lie earlier?"

I thought back to that green room a few hours before. I'd been hot and bothered, but in that moment, I'd spoken from the heart.

"No," I mumbled, a strange wave of shame rushing over me. "I meant it. But—"

"But what? What's stopping you?"

"I... I need to find an apartment."

"We'll pay you enough that you can have your choice of places after you get back."

"I need to work."

"We'll pay you enough that you won't have to think about work for months. Besides, you're a freelance artist, aren't you? That means you do most of your commissions on a personal tablet or laptop, right?"

I frowned. That was true. I could work from anywhere, which was half the reason I stayed freelance. I wanted the freedom to go where I wanted, when I wanted, and with who I wanted.

"Looks like you've run out of excuses, angel. Now the only thing standing in your way is you."

I licked my lips. My heart was pounding so hard I worried it might crack a rib. "You're… you're joking."

"Why is this so hard to believe?"

"Because it's crazy!" I barked. Another neighbor's light turned on, but I didn't care anymore. The world was spinning and I felt like I was on the verge of a panic attack. "If you guys are bored, you have crowds of hot girls flashing their tits at you. Why not ask one of them? You probably wouldn't even have to pay them."

"Where's the fun in making someone worship you if they already think you're a god?"

I scoffed. "Sorry to burst your bubble, but I won't be worshipping anyone."

"But you want to." The Beast's voice lowered an octave, morphing into a shiver-inducing rumble. "You want to get on your knees for us. You want to debase yourself and do things you'll never be able to admit to another human being. I bet you've never wanted anything more."

I gulped and squeezed my knees together. My traitorous pussy had started to ache the second he mentioned getting on my knees, and it was making all rational thought fade into the background.

"Why?" I asked again, my voice hoarse. "Why are you doing this?"

Silence stretched across the line so long I thought the Beast may have hung up. Just when I was about to click my phone off, there came a heavy sigh from the other end.

"A couple reasons. Some of them you already touched on. Yes, I'll admit we're a little bored. For ten years we've had to stay secluded on the road to keep our identities a secret. We have each other, but we don't always get along. And we do have, as you mentioned, a crowd of women flashing their tits at us, but we have to be careful. Fuck the wrong groupie and she's threatening to make your life hell if you don't reveal your identity to her, then you have to line her pockets to keep her quiet."

That scenario was explained with far too much bitterness for it not to be personal.

"We've sold our souls for fame and fortune," the Beast continued. "We have everything we've ever wanted, but it's sucked the life out of us. If this ship is sinking, we might as well have some fun on the way down."

"You want to escape your life too," I murmured.

Another stretch of silence.

"Yes, we do."

I took a deep breath and let it out slow as I ran my fingers through my hair.

"I see you, angel. You've been wanting to play with your demons, now they want to play with you too. Sleep on it. Our last show in LA is tomorrow night. If we don't receive a response by then, the offer is off the table."

There was a *click*, and the line went dead.

9

I needed my dog.

Gracie wasn't an official emotional support animal, but she might as well be. When all the shit was going down with my mom and stepdad, I was an absolute wreck, but Gracie's snuggles and loving kisses could always bring me back to earth.

Seeing her was worth facing my ex.

I'd left a note for Kayla to find if she woke up from her alcohol-induced sleep apnea, threw a hoodie over my t-shirt and pajama pants, and hopped in the car. My old apartment was only twenty minutes from Kayla's, but with the clock reading 3:22 AM, no one was on the road and I got there in ten.

I pulled into me and Trent's tandem parking spot in the garage and leapt out, taking the stairs two at a time until I got to the second floor. I jammed my key into the lock, not even trying to be quiet as I threw open the door. I didn't give a shit if I woke Trent up. I only cared about one thing, and after two alert barks and a flurry of nails tapping against the laminate, her mottled black and tan coat came into view.

"Hi Gracie girl!" I squealed, falling to my knees and reaching out my arms. Gracie leapt into them, squirming and yipping with such joy it immediately made my eyes sting. I kissed her head over and over while her tongue lapped at my tears.

"I'm sorry," I whispered. "I'm so sorry I've been gone, sweetie."

"What the fuck? Why didn't you call?"

I looked up to see Trent scowling in the doorway.

My ex was someone most girls would feel lucky to snag. He was 6'2", blond, a former pastor's kid and D1 athlete, and he had a solid job climbing the corporate ladder. When I was on speaking terms with my mom, she'd always ask more about him than me, and she'd constantly rave to her Bible study about "the nice man Jade finally settled down with."

But that "nice man" had always found subtle ways to cut me down or belittle me. Towards the end of our relationship, I hadn't even wanted to share anything with him anymore because I he'd make me feel so horrible about it. Not to mention the boring-sex-every-three-months situation we'd had going on. So needless to say, watching him shut the bedroom door and shuffle into the living room stirred up zero emotions besides resentment.

"You ignore my texts for almost a month and now you show up out of the blue?" he huffed, lowering onto the couch. He reached out his hand to Gracie, but she continued to nestle into my chest.

"This is still my apartment," I snapped. "My name is on the lease, I can come and go as I please."

Trent shrugged. "I'm just saying it's inconsiderate. So is stealing someone's concert tickets."

I tossed my head back, a slightly crazed cackle tearing from my throat. "Wow. *Wow.* You really want to talk about *that* right now? First off, *I* was the one who bought those tickets—"

"Yeah, for me!"

"Second of all, you know what's *inconsiderate*, Trent? Cheating on your girlfriend with fucking Stacy from 2B."

Trent sighed and rubbed the back of his neck. "I told you I was sorry about that. I was going through a tough time, I made a mistake."

"Oh, were you?" I sneered. "What's the matter, did they discontinue your favorite protein powder? Is your favorite team on a losing streak? Is that why you didn't touch me for *years*?"

"I touched you!"

"When I forced you to!"

Trent rolled his eyes. "God, you're being so loud right now. You're gonna wake the neighbors."

Sensing the looming explosion, Gracie jumped off my lap and ran to her crate in the corner.

"You know who was going through a tough time, Trent?" I shrieked, stalking over to him. "*Me.* I went through a lot of shit over the past few years, and I could have really used the support of my boyfriend."

Trent stood too. I could tell he was angry, but he reined it in and tried a different tactic. Feigning compassion, he slid his hands around my waist. "Babe, I *did* support you. When you started going to therapy and all that shit came out about your childhood, I didn't leave you. I stayed."

The most terrifying type of anger is the kind that silences the world around you, trapping you in a swirling tunnel of all-consuming fury. In that moment, your blood runs cold and nothing else exists beside rage primed for action.

I stood in that place, shaking so hard from holding back that my teeth chattered. But when I spoke, my voice was calm, soft, and sweet as sugar.

"You *stayed*?"

"Yeah." Trent shrugged. "A lot of guys wouldn't have stuck around if they heard their girl went through something like that. But I didn't hold it against you."

A stunned laugh squeezed from my lungs. "You didn't *hold it against me*?"

Finally noticing the unhinged gleam in my eyes, Trent released my waist and stuffed his hands in the pockets of his sweatpants. "Well, yeah. I mean, it's a lot for someone to hear. Like, I just see you different now—"

Another laugh ripped out of me. "Oh, I'm *sorry*. Did my trauma ruin your perception of me? Whenever you talk to me, is that all you see?"

"Kinda, yeah. And I'd really like you to adjust your tone, it's making me feel very unsafe."

A floorboard in the bedroom creaked, and Trent went as still as a statue. My head whipped towards the sound, then slowly swiveled back.

"Who's here?"

Trent scoffed. "What? No one."

A tense beat followed before I lunged across the living room.

"Jade, don't—"

I cranked the handle and flung the bedroom door open, coming face-to-face with fucking Stacy from 2B attempting to stealthily slip on her jeans. She was wearing nothing but a thong and one of my old t-shirts, stretched tight across her massive tits.

"H-h-hey, Jade," she stuttered, tucking a bleached-blonde curl behind her ear. "This isn't what it looks like."

The simmering rage came back with a vengeance.

I turned to Trent, my hands repeatedly clenching into fists at my side. "There is not a string of words I can think of that will fully encapsulate what a piece of shit you are."

Trent opened his mouth to protest, but I flung a damning finger in his face, effectively stopping him. "You're too thick to understand it, but I am *not* my past. I may not exactly know who I am or what I want yet, but I know for a fact it's not this."

I stomped past him and scooped Gracie into my arms, giving her a squeeze and a kiss before setting her down and digging my phone out of my pocket. "Since I'm tainted already, why not add some more shit to the pile?"

"Jade, you're overreacting—"

"I'm going on a vacation," I cut him off, tapping at the screen. "Take care of Gracie. I'll send you money for her food, but when I get back, we're getting as far away from you as possible."

"What are you talking about? Where are you going?"

I hit send.

In the other room, Trent's phone chimed.

When he eventually looked at it, he'd see a photo of me and a man in a mask pressed against a wall in the midst of a life-altering kiss. I shoved my cell back in my pocket and stormed out the door, flipping my ex the bird before slamming it shut behind me.

That asshole hadn't even noticed I'd dyed my hair.

10

Once again, I looked out of place. But this time it was on purpose.

I was dressed in a gray blazer and matching slacks, which I'd paired with a black bustier and sky-high pumps, while my hair was pulled back tight in a claw clip. It screamed hot-CEO-who-will-impale-you-on-her-stiletto, which was exactly what I was going for.

That morning, I'd sent a single text to the Beast:

A contract negotiation is required

To which I'd received a response within seconds.

UNKNOWN: You're on the list

Now venue doors had just opened, and Craig the tour manager was leading me through the gathering crowd. My getup garnered a slew of odd looks, but I kept my chin lifted high.

If these fuckers wanted to *hire* me, I'd show up like it was a goddamn job interview.

As Craig and I headed backstage, I clutched my portfolio to my chest. My hands were shaking from the nerves, but I set my jaw and focused on putting one foot in front of the other. Crew members' heads swiveled as I passed, following the pointed clack of my heels as I strutted towards the green room.

When we arrived at the closed door, Craig knocked three times. A few seconds passed before it creaked open, revealing the Dragon on the other side. He blinked in alarm when he saw my outfit.

"Holy shit." His eyes roved appreciatively over my body. "You look—"

"Thank you for meeting with me," I interrupted, blowing past him.

"You guys good?" Craig asked, raising a skeptical eyebrow in my direction.

"I think so." The Dragon squinted at me as I clomped past Lucifer, who was pouring two whiskies for himself. "We'll ring if we need you."

Craig dipped his head, gave me one last wary glance, then shut the door to give us privacy.

"Have a seat, gentlemen." I beckoned to the sofa and settled into the armchair across from it. It sat me directly in the Beast's eyeline. He was already sprawled on the couch, his knees wide and his lips quirked upward in an amused smirk.

"Whatcha got there?" he asked, nodding to my leather binder. He sounded like he was talking to a child, which made it easy to ignore his question and stare pointedly at the other men.

"Once you've all obeyed, we'll begin."

The Beast chuckled and leaned forward. "The dirty secretary act is cute, angel, but we're the ones who tell you to—"

I cut him off with a raised hand. "Drop the act. No games this time. This is strictly business."

A muscle in the Beast's jaw ticked, and his fingers curled into fists, their rings flashing in the overhead light. A slurping sound intercepted our attention. We both turned to see Lucifer faced away from us, downing his drinks in their entirety before readjusting his mask and shuffling over to the couch. He had his hood up and his headphones on, but when he sat next to the Beast, he pulled them both off, smoothed his shaggy black hair, and interlocked his fingers over his stomach. Diablo and Dragon followed suit.

"Thank you," I said, tersely dipping my head to the men when they were all settled. I pulled out my phone and laid it on the coffee table in front of us, hitting record in the voice memo app I'd cued up beforehand. "For legal purposes, this conversation will be recorded. Any objections?"

Four masks hesitated, but eventually shook no.

"Excellent." I leaned forward and handed Dragon the leather-bound folder on my lap. "This is my portfolio. Inside you'll find an assortment of my past work."

He and Diablo flipped through the pages, while Lucifer and the Beast exchanged glances. I answered their question before they asked it.

"I'm a graphic designer," I stated firmly. "I have two bachelor's degrees, years of real world experience, and a never-ending list of references. I'm a professional, and therefore, I'll be treated as such. If you want me to come onboard, you're going to commission a piece of my artwork. It can be used on merchandise, posters, whatever you want, but it *must* be used."

Diablo and Dragon let out identical stunned laughs. The Beast irritably sucked his teeth. Lucifer just stared.

"Any other demands?" the Beast sighed.

"Yes. As previously stated, I'd like a clean bill of health from each of you—"

My phone chimed.

"That would be Craig," Diablo said, motioning to the cell. "He was told to send our records once this meeting started."

"What else?" Dragon asked.

"I'm allowed to say no whenever I want—"

"Absolutely not," the Beast snapped. "That defeats the purpose. A slave doesn't get to refuse work. You'll have a safe word you can use in situations where a hard limit is reached. It'll be honored, but you can't deny us."

I pursed my lips. "You clearly don't understand the female anatomy. Sometimes things happen, like maybe we're bloated or have really bad cramps—"

"If there's a valid reason like that, obviously you can say no. We don't want you to be miserable."

I blinked in surprise. "Really?"

"We said we're not good men, but we're not evil," Dragon said with surprising tenderness. "Granted, some of us may be slight sadists..." A glance at Lucifer. "But we don't want you doing any of this if you're not going to have a good time."

At that, I relaxed slightly. It was a relief hearing that mutual pleasure was the goal, not just theirs.

"I'll have a good time as long as there's consent."

Dragon nodded and gestured to the band. "We're all in agreement there. Is there anything else?"

I thought for a few seconds, my cheeks heating as a surge of vulnerability came bubbling up to the surface. "Degradation is fine, but no negative comments about my appearance. I spent enough years hating myself, I won't tolerate someone preying on any remaining insecurities."

Diablo leaned forward, bracing his elbows on his knees. Even though the devil mask obscured his features, I could still sense the earnest expression behind it.

"You're stunning, darling. And if anyone ever tells you different, I'll break their fucking teeth."

His words had my cheeks heating for an entirely different reason now, and I quickly looked away in the hopes he wouldn't see. "Thank you. Do either of you have anything you'd like to add?"

"Yes." The Beast folded his arms, his biceps straining the sleeves of his plain black tee. "No drugs."

Lucifer shifted in his seat.

"Oh." My brows pinched together in confusion. "Ok."

"Is that gonna be a problem?" the Beast pressed.

"No. Sorry, I'm just a little surprised is all. You've got the whole sex, drugs, and rock 'n roll thing down, so I thought you'd be party animals."

"Sex and rock 'n roll, yes. Alcohol, yes. But no drugs. Not even marijuana."

"Sometimes I take edibles for sleep—"

"Leave them at home."

I scanned the men, taking note of how their energy had darkened. "Alright. I can do that."

The Beast nodded and continued. "Next thing: at the end of that contract I sent you, there's an NDA. When you sign it, you're confirming that you won't repeat anything you see and hear, not even to family."

I chuckled grimly. "Well I don't speak to my family, so you're safe there."

"We're being serious. If you breathe a word to anyone, we'll destroy you. Understood?"

The intensity in his voice reconfirmed the gravity of my situation, and I grew serious. "Understood."

"On that NDA, beside your name, there will be a line where you'll write your safe word. Choose one you won't forget, not even in times of pain or distress. If you don't say it, we don't stop."

I nervously picked at a hangnail as I considered. "What if I'm gagged?"

Diablo eagerly rubbed his hands together. "Oh you like to be gagged, do you?"

Dragon smacked his thigh. "Remember this is *business*."

"Right. Sorry."

The Beast pulled us back on track. "If you're unable to speak, we'll check in with you."

"Promise?"

"Promise. Lastly, we'll pay you a sum of 15,000 dollars—"

"Holy shit," I blurted, then clapped a hand over my mouth to keep any other shocked responses contained.

"As I was saying, we'll pay you 15,000 dollars for your…" He eyed the phone recording on the table. "*Commission*. It'll be wired to your bank account on the final day of tour, when your work with us has been completed. If, for any reason, you decide to break the contract and leave before then, you won't receive a dime."

I pulled my hand from my mouth. "Even after all that work, I'd get *nothing*?"

The Beast shrugged. "Those are our demands. Take it or leave it."

Chewing the inside of my cheek, I weighed everything, including the state of my own heart.

Did I *really* want this?

It was impulsive and reckless. If I went down this path, it wasn't just deconstructing my upbringing. It was setting fire to everything I'd been raised to believe was pure and good and proper. Jade Matthews could no longer pretend she was perfect. She'd officially be a fallen angel; dark, depraved, and undeniably fucked up.

But deep down, no matter how far I'd run or how hard I'd fought it, I'd always known that. Now I just had proof.

Because the truth of the matter was I *did* want this. Desperately.

I took a deep breath and let it out slow, making peace with myself and my decision. "It's a deal."

The Beast reached into a bag beside the couch, pulled out a stack of paper, and dropped it onto the coffee table, while Dragon produced a ballpoint pen. He tossed it to me while I was in the process of stopping the recording and scanning the medical paperwork Craig had sent over. The men were all free of infection, but the names in the upper right hand corners of the files had been blurred out.

"Wait, how am I supposed to know these tests actually belong to you guys?"

"We'll show you the originals after you sign."

"No way." I tossed the pen onto the contract and sat back, barring my arms over my chest. "I need to be sure you're not using somebody else's paperwork. I'm not signing if I can't see your names."

"Well that's not going to happen, so you'll just have to trust us."

"How about instead *you* trust *me*?"

"Looks like we're at a standstill," the Beast bit back.

Tense silence settled over the room. Diablo and Dragon fidgeted in their seats, the Beast glared at me with fire in his eyes, and Lucifer remained as still as a statue, the Venetian mask still trained on my face. *God*, what was he even doing under that thing? Sleeping? I bet they'd all lose this weird power trip if I ripped those goddamn masks right off—

"Your faces," I said, sitting up straight.

"What?"

"That's how we can prove we trust each other." I took turns looking to each man individually. "If you show me your faces, I'll sign the NDA without knowing for sure if these are your records."

The Beast adamantly shook his head. "No. Absolutely not."

"Why? I won't know your names, and I'm not going to take a

picture. There's no way I can hold it against you if I back out before signing."

The Beast ground his teeth and glanced at the other members of his band. Apparently Lucifer *wasn't* sleeping, because he lifted his hand and beckoned for all of them to lean in close. When they did, the four spoke in hushed tones for a good five minutes. I grew antsy in my seat in the meantime, my mind flip-flopping between giddy anticipation and second-guessing everything.

Finally, the men returned to their original positions.

"Not good enough," the Beast declared.

A pang of disappointment cut through my chest.

"We also need *you* to prove you're someone *we* can trust," he added.

My eyes narrowed. "And how would I do that?"

The Beast's lips curled into a grin. "This is a job interview, isn't it? As your potential employers, we'd like to see you're capable of performing the duties required of you."

When his meaning clicked, indignant rage flared through me at the same time my insides clenched with desire.

"I told you, I'm not fucking you without the tests."

"I didn't say you had to fuck us." The Beast's smile stretched wider. He extended an arm, motioning to the four of them.

"Choose your god, angel. Then get on your knees for him."

11

I was hit with a rush of humiliation, fury, and unbearable arousal.

I attempted to readjust in my seat to ease the pulse that started between my legs, but the seam of my underwear rubbed against my rapidly swelling clit, and I was forced to clear my throat to keep from uttering a soft moan.

"You can still get sexually transmitted infections in your mouth, you know," I stated, my words clipped in order to disguise my conflicting emotions.

The Beast shrugged, a whisper of a smile still on his lips. "This is our compromise. Get on your knees, or get out."

A chuckle sounded from behind Diablo's mask as he stretched his arms wide, draping one over the back of the couch and the other across Dragon's shoulders. To my simultaneous horror and delight, the drummer's gaze shifted to the apex of my thighs like he could somehow see what was happening there. I fought the urge to check and make sure there wasn't a wet spot forming on my slacks.

"Fine."

The word sounded like it came from someone else's mouth, but it had come from mine.

The Beast interlocked his fingers behind his head. "Then who's it gonna be, angel?"

"And choose wisely," Diablo added. "You want to showcase your best work."

The Dragon stifled a laugh.

"Oh, and angel?" the Beast crooned. "Be sure to do as the Bible commands. Prostrate yourself before your lord."

I frowned. "What does that even mean?"

"*Crawl.*"

This time, Dragon couldn't contain his laughter.

My cheeks went red, but I rolled my eyes to feign indifference. This really was just a sick game to them, wasn't it? I was just a slutty little toy for them to amuse themselves with. The thought infuriated me as much as it turned me on, but it also had my competitive spirit roaring to life.

If these men wanted to play games, then I'd choose the one who'd shown the best sportsmanship so far.

I set my sights on my target, whipped off my blazer, and slid to the floor. I shifted to my hands and knees, the carpet under my palms rough from years of wear and tear. Moving into a crawl, I kept my face down so I wouldn't have to look at the masks trained on me, but I didn't have to see them to know they were watching. I could feel their stares fixed on my swaying hips and the cleavage spilling from my shirt, giving me a strange sort of high. Realizing I had the power to capture the attention of four men sent a shiver of adrenaline through my body, increasing the intensity of my aching core. I tried not to dwell on the sensation and instead focused on the task at hand.

When I arrived in front of a pair of white sneakers, I slowly looked up at my chosen demon.

A fallen angel, just like me.

Lucifer still didn't move, even when Diablo reached over to ruffle his hair.

"Lucky bastard."

"Unlucky girl," Dragon snickered. He leaned forward to stare down at me over his knees. "You don't have a safe word yet, so if you need mercy, tap on his thigh three times. Understand?"

My gaze darted between him and the blank white mask looming above me. "Am I going to need mercy?"

Instead of answering, Dragon nestled in beside Diablo. "Good luck."

The ominous air of his words set my heart racing even more than it already was.

Attempting to rein in my breath, I rose to my knees and slid between Lucifer's legs, which stretched wider to make room for me. My hands shook as they came to rest on his thighs. He was wearing sweats again, but I could feel the warmth of his skin radiating up from under them.

I was nervous and excited and *god* why was this turning me on so much?

In the distance, the opening act took the stage, the bassline pulsating through the floor and into my body. It matched the pace of the ache inside me, which only worsened when I set my eyes on the outline of Lucifer's cock. I glanced up at him again.

"Sorry, I just want to make sure you're ok with this?"

Beside him, the Beast let out a gravelly laugh.

"This whole thing was his idea, angel." He leaned forward to stroke my hair before cupping my chin and giving it a taunting shake. "Now be a good girl and open wide."

My pussy clenched at his words, but I irritably tugged my face from his grasp. "I'm not talking to you."

The Beast just grinned and angled himself to get a better view of what I was about to do. I returned my attention to Lucifer and raised an eyebrow.

"You should teach these guys how to shut up every now and then."

The white mask bobbed up and down in agreement. I chuckled a little and refocused on the bulge in front of me, tentatively inching my hand forward until the flat of my palm rested at the center. It twitched beneath my fingers.

"So as I was saying before we were so rudely interrupted…" I began running my thumb back and forth across the mound. "Are you sure you're ok this?"

The mask dipped in a silent yes, and in one swift move, Lucifer lifted his hips, hooked his thumbs in his waistband, and yanked his sweats down.

I blinked, suddenly hypnotized by what now lay in front of me. He was bigger than I thought, and he wasn't even fully erect yet. The shaft was pale pink and thick, with a vein running down the center and the tip already plump with blood flow. My mouth instantly began watering at the sight of him, and I had to shift my hips in an attempt to relieve some of the pressure forming in my core.

"Having second thoughts, angel?" the Beast teased.

His smug tone snapped me back into my body.

I licked my lips and slid my fingers around the base of Lucifer's cock, unable to encircle it fully. "Just admiring."

"You'll have an entire tour to drool over our cocks. But we've got a show to play tonight, so hurry it up."

I refocused on the object in my hand and slowly leaned in, pausing just above the head. Hovering my lips over the sensitive skin, I could smell the faint scent of Lucifer's body wash mixing with his own musk. It immediately flipped a switch in me, shutting the world off like a light and silencing the anxious chatter in my brain. Keeping my gaze glued to the eye slits on the mask, I bent, sucked Lucifer into my mouth, and swirled my tongue, savoring his salty tang. He didn't say anything, but his chest rose and fell faster as he continued to engorge in my hand.

"This is the best day of my life," Diablo mumbled, leaning his head on Dragon's shoulder while they both watched me work.

Feeling their attention only fueled me. I transitioned down to Lucifer's shaft, dragging my tongue up and down the silky length while gently kneading the tip with my hand. Lucifer readjusted in his seat, but seemed otherwise unaffected.

"You're such a tease, angel," the Beast said. "Give him what he really wants."

I would have mouthed off at the Beast's unsolicited advice, but I desperately wanted a reaction from the man I was on my knees for. Swallowing my pride, I accepted the Beast's coaching and sucked Lucifer farther in.

"That's more like it," the Beast purred.

My gag reflex engaged, and I moved to pull Lucifer from my mouth, but his hand whipped out, grabbed a fistful of my hair, and forced me down again. I squirmed against his hold, choking and sputtering on his length.

"Come on, open your throat."

It was a voice I'd only heard once before, when it had uttered a single word the night before.

"Open you throat for me," Lucifer repeated.

One hand slid down to my neck and squeezed, while the other stayed in my hair to hold me in place.

I focused on the muscles fighting the intrusion and urged them to loosen. Begrudgingly they obeyed, and Lucifer slipped deeper in. It felt like he was hitting the space behind my collarbones. The sensation was foreign and uncomfortable, but I liked it. It was only a brief moment in time where I could experience the thrill of pushing my body to the edge. A thrill that was only heightened when Lucifer let out a noise that was half moan, half growl.

"*Fuck* yes. That's a good girl."

He began to pump in and out of my mouth, stretching the

muscles of my throat even more than they already were. My body jerked as I fought the need to retch.

"Come on, you can take it," Lucifer urged.

I dug deep and focused on keeping my throat relaxed as Lucifer fucked my mouth faster.

"Fucking hell, she looks good like that." Diablo's voice was thick with lust.

"Such a good little slut," the Dragon added.

Their words gave me strength, and instead of letting Lucifer control the pace, I bobbed my head as fast I could. Eventually my gag reflex couldn't take the strain anymore, and I jerked upright, panting for air. A string of saliva dripped from my chin, dropping onto my chest and soaking my shirt.

"Tapping out already?" the Beast taunted.

Fiery rage turned my blood to molten lava. I braced my hands on either side of Lucifer and leaned in close.

"Fuck my face until you see tears," I demanded.

Needing no further bidding, Lucifer's hands slid around my neck and dragged me back down.

His pace became punishing, with furious grunts accompanying every thrust into my mouth. My pussy clenched in time with each drive as pleasure and pain formed an intoxicating cocktail so intense that moisture beaded at the corners of my eyes.

"That's right," Lucifer hissed, "let me see those pretty eyes cry."

I retched, but focused on Lucifer's ragged breaths to power me through. They became more and more desperate, and soon he ripped free of my mouth. Gripping my hair again, he dragged my head back and pumped his cock with his hand until he released a long spurt of cum onto my outstretched tongue. When he'd finished, I licked him from my lips and moaned my appreciation.

A glance at the Beast found his mouth hanging slack, and

judging by the way Diablo and Dragon were as still as statues, they were just as stunned by my performance.

Basking in the melody of Lucifer's satisfied pants, I sat back on my heels and swiped my sleeve across my mouth. "There. A deal's a deal."

Dragon was the first to move.

He peeled himself off of Diablo and lifted a hand to the fang-adorned mask covering the bottom half of his face. Slowly, almost shyly, he hooked his index fingers around the elastic and pulled it down.

The man had a face painters throughout history would have used as their muse. Strong bone structure, a jawline sharp enough to cut glass, and perfectly defined lips created an individual so beautiful he seemed better suited as a statue in a museum than a drummer in a rock band. His smile was self-conscious, like he didn't know how gorgeous he was, and his big brown eyes were kind yet wary. He nervously combed his fingers through his bleached hair, slicking them away from his face.

Following the drummer's lead, Diablo raised his hand and yanked off the red devil mask. The grin beaming back at me was contagious, and lit up a pair of gray-blue eyes that contrasted beautifully with his tawny skin. Long dark eyelashes highlighted the mischief in his gaze, his pink buzzcut the cherry on top of his playful aesthetic. Unlike the Dragon, he knew very well how attractive he was, and when he caught me gawking at him, he bit his plump bottom lip and gave me a cheeky wink. I blushed and directed my gaze to the remaining two members.

A few more seconds passed before the Beast moved. He begrudgingly slipped his fingers under the gold ram mask and hauled it upwards. The man underneath was annoyingly handsome, with chocolatey shoulder-length waves and a sunkissed complexion. His square jawline had already been on display, but now I could see it was coupled with broad, defined cheekbones that gave his face a rugged edge.

At first, I didn't think Lucifer would take off his mask. He waited so long that even his bandmates grew antsy. But eventually his fingers found the Venetian mask and lifted.

Holy shit, I recognized him.

He had pale olive skin, green eyes, a nose ring, and a tattoo under his right eye that proudly displayed the word *sinner*. I'd run into him at the bar last night, but with no mask and a beanie covering his messy black curls, there had been no way to know. His beauty took my breath away just like it had then, and words failed me.

But luckily, I didn't need words.

I pushed myself to my feet and wandered over to the coffee table where a stack of papers waited for me. I found the ball-point pen, flipped to the back page, and signed my name with a safe word beside it.

When I looked up again, Diablo had his phone out.

"One more thing," the guitarist stated, tapping at the screen.

Within seconds, my own phone dinged. Curious, I picked it up and glanced at the message. It was a photo from an unknown sender. Hesitantly, I swiped open the screen, and a gasp leapt from my throat.

The text I'd been sent was a picture of me, taken from Diablo's point of view, in the middle of giving Lucifer the world's sloppiest blowjob.

"What the fuck?" I screeched. "I didn't say you could record any of that!"

"Consider it collateral." The Beast crossed to the table and gathered the contract, his expression cold. "If you breathe a word about us to anyone, or if you fail to follow through on the job you've been hired for, this picture goes viral."

Dread hollowed a hole in my stomach.

"We warned you," the Dragon said gently. "We're not good men."

"Fuck you," I spat.

"Don't worry," the Beast chuckled. "You will."

Lucifer tucked himself back into his sweats and hauled his headphones over his ears. "Welcome to hell, angel."

12

Luca Serino. Dante Ramos. Callum Sherwood. Donovan Davies.

Those were the names on the clean bills of health that had been forwarded to my email, and I stared at them so long they went blurry in front of my eyes.

I barely remembered leaving the green room and driving home from the show. I'd been in a strange kind of daze, my body still humming with a mix of adrenaline, lust, and humiliation.

Who the hell was that person in there? It sure wasn't Jade Matthews. Jade Matthews would never get herself into something like this.

Maybe my body had been taken over by a succubus or some sex-starved alien. It was a harebrained idea fit for a Sci-Fi themed porno, but it seemed more likely than perfect Jade Matthews giving a blowjob to a faceless stranger while his friends watched. That couldn't be who she really was when she abandoned her fear and embraced her dark desires.

Could it?

I tried not to dwell on the answer, even though the embarrassingly damp spot on my panties was a constant reminder of the truth.

When I'd gotten back to Kayla's apartment and began stuffing my belongings into my duffel bag, reality set in. And with it, panic.

A voice in my head kept screaming over and over that this was completely insane. And dangerous. I'd watched enough true crime documentaries to know that these men could very well be cleverly disguised serial killers, and this might be the last time my friends would ever see me alive. So even though it broke the rules of the NDA, I'd told Kayla everything when she got home from work a few hours later.

"What the *fuck*?" she screamed at the top of her lungs.

"Shhhh!" I hushed, chucking a pillow at her. "Your neighbors will hear!"

"I don't give a fuck if they hear!" Kayla leapt up from the couch and wildly flailed her arms as she paced the room. "When I told you to find someone who appreciates your crazy, this is not what I meant!"

"I'm being responsible about it," I argued. "They've been tested, and we all signed a contract agreeing to terms and a safe word—"

"A safe word?" Kayla's eyes bugged out of her head. "What the fuck are they planning on doing to you?"

I chewed my bottom lip. "Well, I don't know the full extent—"

"Jesus!" Kayla flopped on the couch beside me and buried her head in her hands. "This is insane, Jade. Like actually insane. Like I should call the loony bin insane."

I sheepishly picked at a piece of lint on my pants. "I know, ok? I know it's messed up, and weird, and wrong. But that's exactly why I want to do it. I've always been so *good*. You know very well there's a part of me that's dark and twisted, and if I never get to take that out and play with it, I'm worried I'll regret it forever."

"I get that you have some shit to work through after every-thing you've realized about your childhood, but—"

"That's not why," I snapped, making Kayla flinch. I felt bad, but she'd touched a nerve, and the day had been such a roller-coaster that I didn't have the energy to keep a dam on my emotions anymore. "I'm sick of people treating me like I'm frag-ile. What I went through didn't break me, ok? It tried, but I'm stronger than that."

Kayla's eyes softened. "I know you're strong, Jade. But some-times repressed trauma makes us act out in weird ways—"

"I'm not acting out." I lifted my chin. "I want this, Kayla. I want to avoid my responsibilities for a little while and focus on embracing a part of me I've silenced. I want to be with men who aren't freaked out by the things I want. I want to be around people who don't see me as broken."

Kayla's full lips parted like she was about to argue, but after searching my expression, she shut her mouth. We both sat in silence for what felt like an eternity, until finally Kayla huffed an exhale and shrugged.

"I just don't want to see you get hurt."

I clicked my tongue and slipped her hand into mine. "I know. That's why you're my best friend."

Kayla scooted closer on the couch and took my other hand, peering at me with earnest, no-nonsense eyes.

"You sit down with them and communicate hard limits," she demanded. "And if any one of those fuckers crosses them, I will personally hunt them down and sacrifice *them* to Satan."

A snort of amusement escaped me, and I nodded. "Ok."

"And you keep your location turned on and text me all day, every day."

"Ok."

"And bring your crystals for protection."

"I will."

Kayla sighed in defeat and dragged me into a fierce hug.

"I don't like this," she whispered.

"I know. But I'm doing it."

"I know."

We pulled away, and Kayla managed a half smile. "Now get fucked. Literally."

13

During the Uber ride to the venue, I wasn't sure if I was shaking from anxiety or excitement.

It felt like I was wholly alive for the first time in my life, which meant I was experiencing the full range of human emotion all at once. Apparently it translated poorly on my face, because the driver asked me three times if he should pull over because I was going to be sick.

I managed to get my nerves under control by the time we arrived at the venue and pulled into the back alley. Crew members were in the process of rolling gear boxes up the ramps into the trailers hitched to two black tour buses. I spotted a head of cherry red hair among them.

After thanking my driver, I shouldered my duffle bag and jogged towards Vee. She and Craig were dragging a bin of t-shirts up one of the ramps when I joined them.

"Jade! Hey!" She brushed off her hands and leapt off the trailer to pull me into a hug. "I heard you were joining us on the road."

"Yeah, it was a last minute thing."

"Let me introduce you to the rest of the team. You've already met Craig."

I shared a sheepish smile with the tour manager and contract liaison. With that cherub-like face, I would have never assumed he would help facilitate the things he had.

"Jade, this is Eric Chao, Legion's sound engineer." Vee beckoned to a skinny man with short black hair and glasses who was coiling cables and packing them up with the microphones. He waved, but otherwise paid me no mind.

"And finally, we have Marcus. He's one of the guitar techs and unofficial security."

A burly, mountain of a man who'd been organizing boxes stepped forward and extended his hand. It nearly swallowed mine whole, it was so massive.

"Welcome aboard, Jade." He spoke in an English accent identical to Diablo's, his broad white smile popping against his dark skin.

"Thank you. I'm happy to be here."

"And that's everyone besides the drivers," Vee said with a shrug. "We're a small crew."

I frowned, my gaze shifting to the other bodies milling around the buses. "Then who are the rest of—"

My words fell flat as I looked closer at the remaining roadies.

Baseball caps and beanies disguised their hair, baggy hoodies and long sleeved tees covered up their bodies, and badges that read *crew* dangled from carabiners hooked onto their belt loops. They were far from their stage personas, but it was them.

Legion was still hiding their identity, but this time in plain sight.

The Beast and the Dragon, Luca and Callum respectively, were leaning against the back wall of the venue, talking in hushed tones and sharing a cigarette. Across the way, Diablo, or Donovan as I now knew him, was checking something on his guitar. Beside him, with his hood up and headphones on in typical Lucifer fashion, Dante was packing away his bass while he puffed on a cigarette of his own.

"I thought you weren't going to say hello, angel," Luca said, letting a wisp of white smoke trail from his lips and drift into the night. "My feelings were going to be hurt."

I donned a condescending smile. "Well, saying hello wasn't part of the contract."

The lead singer threw the cigarette to the ground, crossed to me in two strides, and gripped my elbow to draw me in close.

"Keep your voice down about that," he hissed.

I attempted to wriggle free, but he was too strong. "You crew doesn't know?"

"Craig does. The rest probably assume, but we don't know who else could be listening." Luca glanced warily at the back door of the venue and gestured to the badge on his keychain. "The rest of the bands on the package think we're techs. If your job *and* our identities came out, we're fucked. Do you understand what I'm telling you?"

I finally managed to wrench my arm out of his grasp. "Wise up and shut up."

"Exactly." The scowl remained on Luca's face as he turned to his real crew. "I'm gonna show Jade to her bunk. You guys good here?"

"Yeah, we're basically done." Vee waved us away. "Is she on the crew bus?"

"Nope. Ours."

Vee blinked in surprise, then glanced at Dante. He stared at her pointedly, taking a long drag of his cigarette before exhaling smoke through his nose. The two must have shared a silent language, because Vee's eyes went round with realization and she nodded.

"Got it."

"Dante, Cal, Dono," Luca called, jerking his head to the bus to signal for them to follow. As we went, I could faintly make out

Marcus snickering to himself and mumbling, "You five have fun."

His suggestive words set me on high alert. Was the band cashing in on the promised services *now*? How was this supposed to go? Was I just supposed to lay there while four men stood in line and took turns? Fuck, that was kind of hot but also weird and oh *god* why had I agreed to this?

I let the knowledge that there was a safe word in place calm my nerves as Luca opened the door. He beckoned me inside, and I made my way up the steps into my home for the next three months.

I immediately came face-to-face with a balding man slumped in the driver's seat chugging a Red Bull.

"This is our driver Randy," Luca said, coming up behind me. "He's been with us ever since we started."

Randy wiped his mouth and smashed the can against his knee, causing the "I love mom" tattoo on his bicep to flex. "I don't see nothin' and I don't know nothin'."

"It's true," claimed an English accent, and Callum's head popped up behind Luca. "Randy is a vault of secrets."

Their meaning was clearly communicated: Randy would be hearing everything we did on this bus. I frowned at the thought of some random hillbilly listening in on my intimate moments, but as if reading my mind, Randy piped up again.

"Don't worry, kid. I've seen some shit in my day. Nothin' surprises me and nothin' excites me."

"Nothing except one of these." Luca pulled a pack of cigarettes from his pocket and extended it to the driver.

Randy made a noise of disgust and spat a loogie out the window, but snatched up the box anyway. "Hadn't had a smoke in twenty years before I met these fuckin' assholes. They're a bad influence."

I glanced at the man behind me. "Yes, they are."

Luca's smirk didn't hold a shred of shame, only pride.

"Move." He nudged the back of my leg with his knee, nearly knocking me off balance. I walked forward, but made sure to go as slow as possible.

"The layout goes front lounge, bathroom, bunks, back lounge," the singer explained, pointing to the spaces as he said them.

The front lounge felt surprisingly roomy for being such close quarters. There were brown leather sofa seats on either side with blacked out windows behind them, and a TV in the upper corner that was hooked up to an Xbox. At the far end was a counter and kitchen sink on one side, with a tiny dining room table on the other, its vinyl surface the same wood paneling as the walls.

The rest of the band filed in behind us. Dante gruffly shouldered past me and plopped down on the sofa, where he grabbed one of the Xbox controllers and began swiping through game options.

"The only ones who sleep here are us and Craig," Donovan added, shimmying past me far more gently than the bassist had.

"Wait, you're not expecting me to sleep with Craig too, are you?"

"The agreement you made was between *us*, not him." Callum slid onto the sofa beside Dante. "Besides, Craig is astronomically gay."

"Oh. Never mind then."

"You're in the junk bunk," Donovan called from further up the bus.

"I'm sorry, the *what*?"

"The junk bunk," the guitarist repeated, hauling several backpacks, laundry totes, and a sack of sneakers from one of the bottom beds. "We have one spare bunk. All our extra shit usually goes there, but now it's yours."

I winced as he brushed grit off of a balled up sleeping bag. "Yay."

"The back lounge also has a bed," Luca chimed in, propping

his hand on one of the cupboards above me. We were so close I was practically in his armpit, and I tried to take a step away from him but ended up nearly toppling into Callum's lap.

"The back lounge is probably where you'll be doing the majority of your work," Luca added with a wink.

"You sure know how to woo a woman, don't you?" I grumbled, elbowing him in his annoyingly perfect abs as I brushed past him. With a grunt, I swung my bag into my assigned bunk and turned back to the men. The weight of their stares still caused that same electricity it had before, but the expectation hanging over my head dampened my lust.

I crossed my arms and lifted my chin high. "So what now? You guys gonna flip a coin to see who goes first?"

"We can if you want," Donovan said with a shrug. "Not really my style, though."

"I have an idea," Luca stated. "I'm sure you're curious about your new employers, right?"

I scanned his seemingly earnest expression and nodded.

"Then how about we play a game to get to know each other?"

"Actually, yeah. That would be nice."

"Great."

Luca smiled and lowered onto the sofa opposite Dante and Callum. Donovan joined him while I remained standing, awkwardly hovering in the center of the aisle like the new kid at school who didn't know which table to sit at during lunch.

I cleared my throat. "So how did you all meet?"

"Not so fast," Luca interjected, a devious smirk creeping onto his face. "*This* is the game: we answer one question in exchange for one article of clothing you take off."

Dante immediately tossed aside the controller so I would be his sole focus.

Hit with a sudden wave of insecurity, I tightened my arms around myself. "You're disgusting."

Luca shrugged. "We're going to see you naked eventually. Might as well get it over with."

I rolled my eyes. "Wow. You're making this whole experience so romantic, thank you."

He adopted that infuriating smirk again.

"Fine," I snapped, my cheeks heating. "Let's play."

I lifted my foot, ripped off my sneaker, and chucked it in Donovan and Luca's direction. The latter caught it just before it whacked his guitarist in the teeth.

"How did you all meet?" I asked.

Luca tossed my sneaker into a small garbage can in the corner. "A concert."

I glared at him and stomped over to retrieve it. "Care to expand on that?"

"That's another question."

With a furious grunt, I ripped off my other shoe and handed it to Donovan. He responded by whacking Callum in the shin with it.

"Will you expand on that, please?"

"Cal and I had just moved here," Donovan explained. "We'd packed up everything and come to the City of Angels in pursuit of fame and fortune. One night, we met these two assholes at the Roxy, got piss drunk, and the rest is history."

I considered his words, then pulled off my sock and dropped it onto Callum's lap. He immediately hurled it in Donovan's face.

"Where did you move from?"

"London," Callum laughed.

"South of London for me," Donovan added.

I gestured to Luca and Dante. "And what about you two?"

Wordlessly, Dante extended his hand. I sighed and handed over my second sock, but it was Luca who answered my question.

"We grew up in San Diego."

I scanned my body for another copout, but found none. Setting my jaw, I peeled my tank top over my head, revealing my bra underneath. I kicked myself for wearing an old Target bra instead of some lacy thing from Victoria's Secret.

"Have you ever done this before? Hired someone to do this, I mean?"

I tossed my shirt to Callum, who caught it and folded it in his lap.

"No," he replied. "We've talked about it, but we never pulled the trigger. It never felt right."

Which meant it felt right with me.

A rush of warmth threatened to melt the ice around my heart, but I shoved it back down. A glance at my shorts brought me back to reality.

Slowly, I unfastened the button, hooked the waistband with my thumbs, and wiggled them down my hips. The men's unflinching stares prickled on my skin and made time slow to a crawl.

When the denim finally dropped to the floor, I tried to speak loud and proud like before, but my voice came out as a whisper.

"What do you want to do with me?"

Donovan's head angled to get a better view of my backside. "The better question is what do we *not* want to do with you?"

I was shaking as bad as I'd been on the car ride here, and I couldn't resist wrapping my arms around my abdomen to try and hide some of my body.

"I'm serious," I said. "This whole thing is... Well, it's exciting, don't get me wrong. But it's also terrifying. So I'd like to know what I can expect from you all. Sexually, I mean."

The men stared so long, I wasn't sure they'd answer me. Dante was the one who finally broke the silence.

He leaned forward and pointed at Donovan and Callum. "They're sugar." He gestured to himself and Luca. "We're spice."

"That didn't answer my question."

Dante shrugged and picked up the video game controller again. "If you have more questions, you know the price."

I glanced at my bra and panties, then the other three men, expecting someone to stand up for me.

Nobody did.

"Game over," I declared, snatching my shorts off the floor. "I'm going to bed. *Alone.*"

I stomped down the hallway, threw open the sliding door to the bathroom, and locked myself inside.

14

I was chopped liver.

At least, that's how Legion was treating me.

But maybe that was a good thing. I'd made it very clear I didn't want anyone touching me tonight. I just didn't think they'd take that to mean they should completely ignore me. When I finally emerged from the bathroom and changed into my pajamas, my new roommates made no effort to even look my way, let alone have sex with me. Part of me still expected them to even after I'd said no, and I'd retreated to my bunk to cower and wait for one of them to come and collect. But no one ever did.

It was a relief for my conflicted spirit, but it also left me antsy and a little confused. Had my impromptu striptease showed the men everything I had to offer, and they found it lacking? While I was in the bathroom, had they been regretting this whole thing the way I was?

The bus ambled down the interstate, the typically traffic-heavy stretch of road deserted thanks to the late hour. Despite the time, the majority of us were still awake.

Dante was still playing video games in the front lounge, the blaring rap in his headphones so loud I could hear it from where I'd holed up in my bunk. Beside him, Luca and Craig were involved in a game of cards at the kitchen table. Donovan was the only one sleep had managed to find. He'd crawled into the bunk above mine an hour ago and was now snoring with an arm bent over his eyes and a long leg hanging over the side to dangle in my space. I tried to follow his lead and get some rest in the hopes tomorrow felt significantly less uncomfortable, but the man sounded like a goddamn lawnmower. It was impossible to tune out. Plus my bunk still smelled like stinky sneakers, and I was worried my hair was taking on the scent too.

Donovan twitched in his sleep, his heel jerking backward to hit the eReader in my hand and knock it into my face. I sat up in a huff, accidentally whacking my head on his bunk in the process. I sucked in sharply at the pain, ruefully rubbing my scalp as I maneuvered past his leg and stumbled into the walkway.

I slipped into to the bathroom to splash water on my face, then caught my reflection in the mirror. The oversized tee and checkered pajama shorts I'd changed into weren't an especially sexy ensemble. After years in a stale relationship, stained sleep shirts and tattered bottoms were the extent of my nighttime wear. If I'd had more time to prepare, I would have gone out and bought something cuter.

"Looking cute wasn't part of the contract," I muttered bitterly to the girl in the mirror. "You're a body to them, nothing more. That body doesn't need to be perfect."

Shrugging off my insecurity, I turned out the light and exited the bathroom. I started for my bunk again, but noise in the back lounge caught my attention. I tiptoed towards it and peeked through the crack in the sliding door.

Callum was sprawled on the L-shaped sofa that filled the room, a blanket draped over his lap and his eyes half shuttered as he watched a TV on the wall. The LED screen flashed red and blue across his face as a dissonant soundtrack and pitiful screams played over the speakers. He looked relaxed and comfortable, the picture of peace despite the eerie background music. The space seemed much more alluring than a stinky bunk or lounge full of strangers, so I knocked at the door and slid it open fully.

When he saw me, Callum bolted to an upright position. "Hey."

I hesitated in the doorway, fiddling with the drawstring on my shorts. "What are you watching?"

"Some cheesy slasher film from the 80s. They're a guilty pleasure." He snatched up the remote and clicked it so the bloody images disappeared, and a home screen took their place.

"It's ok, you don't have to change it."

"Nah, it's fine. Don't want you to think you've gotten mixed up with a bunch of psychos."

"Ironic considering it's been mentioned multiple times that you're not good men."

Callum chuckled and rubbed the back of his neck, making way for another round of awkward silence as he looked anywhere but my face.

"Everything ok out there?" Callum eventually asked.

"Yeah. I'm just not really used to sleeping with a lot of noise."

Callum scrunched his nose. "Dono?"

"Yeah."

"We probably should've warned you about him."

"Probably. That alone would've been enough for me to say no to this whole thing." I offered a playful smile.

Callum's eyes lit up at my timid attempt at teasing.

"Oh, yeah?" he asked, a grin twitching at the corners of his mouth. "That would've done it? Not ominous warnings or sex slave contracts?"

"No, definitely the snoring."

Callum let out another chuckle. Before silence set in again, he ran a finger through his hair and scanned the lounge. "Um… Do you maybe wanna watch something?"

My stomach did a silly little flutter like a teenager who'd just been asked to the movies by a cute boy. Reminding myself I was a grown ass woman, I pushed the feeling down and slid the door shut behind me.

"Sure, that'd be nice."

Callum nodded and scooted to his left, giving me a wide berth on the couch. I frowned as I lowered into the space he'd created.

"I don't bite, you know," I mumbled, gesturing to the gap between us. "You're all treating me like I have the plague."

He averted his eyes and toyed with a loose string on the hem of his blanket. "Sorry."

Nerves getting the better of me, I blurted out the thoughts that had been gnawing at me.

"Are you guys not down anymore? I mean, I know I don't look like a swimsuit model or anything—"

"Oh, fuck." Callum's eyes widened. "No, it's… Shit, I'm so sorry. We should've said something. That's got nothing to do with it. You're gorgeous. Believe me, we're all chomping at the bit for a turn with you."

"Really?"

"Are you fucking kidding me? Look at you!"

My stomach did a somersault. Maybe the checkered pajamas were sexier than I thought?

"It's just…" Callum sighed. "No offense, but from the moment you set foot on this bus, you've looked ready to vomit."

"You sure know how to sweet talk a woman."

"Fuck, I didn't mean… Not in a bad way… Shit, I'm sorry."

With his graceful, sculpted features and the intricate tattoos etched into his skin, the Dragon typically looked like an impressive work of art. But now the art was flustered and blushing. It had a little crack in it, no longer some untouchable masterpiece in a gallery, but something *real*.

And really fucking cute.

"What I *mean*," Callum went on, "is we're giving you space to process everything. While you were in the bathroom, we made a pact that nobody touches you until you make the first move. But as soon as you get with one of us, it's a free for all."

I blinked in surprise. "That's pretty thoughtful for a bunch of not-so-good men."

Callum turned his attention back to the TV and clicked through movie options. "See, it's *that* shit that has us worried. You talk like you don't believe it's true. If you knew what we've done, I'm not so sure you would've gone for this."

Warning bells went off at his words, inciting another wave of anxiety as a million worst case scenarios flooded my mind. I liked a bad boy, but how bad was too bad? At what point did a sordid past switch someone from tortured and brooding to full-fledged psychopath?

"Can I know what exactly makes you bad men?" I asked warily.

"Besides all the depraved things we're going to do to you?"

Fear flew out the window, immediately replaced with arousal. It only worsened when a cheeky grin spread over Callum's face to reveal an adorable pair of dimples. He tossed the remote into my lap.

"We have to keep *some* secrets, sweetheart. Can't have you getting too close. Don't want you falling in love."

I snorted and nestled into the sofa. "Well, you don't have to worry about that."

Callum faked a pout and eased in beside me. "Rude."

I laughed and gently smacked his thigh, which turned out to be rock solid underneath those baggy sweats of his. "It's nothing personal. I just…" I hesitated as vulnerability rose to the surface.

"I'm just numb, I guess. I think I have been for awhile. I feel like the piece of me that's capable of love is missing, like it died somewhere over the years. Either during my last relationship, or maybe even before that. I mean, as a kid I'd been a hopeless romantic. I'd played princess and dreamed of my wedding to Prince Charming just like all the other girls. But all those starry-eyed dreams left with my innocence."

An image of a cornfield flashed across my mind. I hurriedly shoved the memory down and shrugged. "Anyway. What I'm trying to say is, I think I'm broken."

Callum stared at me with a sad smile. "You're gonna fit right in. We're a band of broken."

A weight lifted from my chest, and I breathed a sigh of relief as I hiked my legs up to sit cross-legged. My knee came to rest against Callum's, but neither of us moved.

"So is there *anything* you can tell me about yourselves?" I asked.

Callum raised his eyes to the roof of the bus as he considered. The t-shirt he'd changed into after the show smelled like fabric softener, and his hair was clean from a shower that had washed him free of all the stage paint. His fresh scent was cozy and calming, reminiscent of linens billowing on a clothesline in the summer breeze, and I found myself leaning further into him to get another whiff.

After a few moments of pondering, Callum met my gaze. "Luca likes coffee."

"Coffee?"

"Yeah, he's obsessed. Every city we hit, he goes on a mission to find the best espresso. If you ever want to push his buttons, just bring him something sweet from Starbucks."

A devious giggle rose in my throat. "Good to know."

"I bet it is." Callum reached over and knocked my chin with his knuckles. "Don't think we can't see that little brat inside of you in need of taming."

Heat pooled at my center. "What would that entail exactly?"

Callum hesitated, his eyes flicking to my lips. I thought for sure he was about to lean in to kiss me, but after a long beat, he turned away.

"God, you're confusing."

"How am I confusing?"

"You've got one hell of a poker face. I can never tell if you're eager or scared."

I considered before letting another sliver of vulnerability shine through. "To be honest, it's a mix of both."

Callum nodded thoughtfully. "Well how about I put your mind at ease?" He extended his pinky finger and waggled it. "I promise not to fuck you 'til you're begging for my cock. Deal?"

The playful move was a stark contrast to his crude words, and a small laugh of surprise bubbled out of me. Maybe these *were* dangerous men. And maybe they were, in Callum's words, planning on doing depraved things to me. But at least they respected consent. That was something I hadn't always experienced, even from men who would be considered more honorable according to the so-called righteous God they worshipped. *Those* were the true demons, not men who were pinky-promising not to touch me without my say so.

I looped my finger with Callum's and shook. "It's a deal."

His dimples made another appearance as he grinned. Our gazes held, neither of us moving to unhook our hands.

"So Luca's a coffee snob," I said. "What about Dante? He's hard to get a read on."

Callum grunted. "Yeah, get used to that. Half the time, me and Dono don't even know what's going on with him. He only really talks to Vee, Luca, or Craig. But let's see…" He chewed his bottom lip while he thought. "Dante loves music more than life itself. I've lost track of how many instruments he can play. He writes and records all the stuff on the album. Pretty sure the man thinks in sheet music."

"I guess that explains the ever-present headphones."

"Well, yeah. And external noise drowns out the internal."

I frowned. "What do you mean by that?"

"Never mind. It's nothing."

I studied his features, trying to piece together the meaning behind his solemn expression. These men were four beautiful but insanely complicated puzzles, and something told me trying to figure them out was going to become my new obsession.

With Callum unwilling to expand, I got us back on track. "Ok, so coffee and music. What about Donovan? What does he like?"

"Besides making people laugh?" A fond smile spread across Callum's lips. "He's a massive anime nerd."

I laughed and scooted closer, still keeping my finger entwined with Callum's. "Really?"

"Yep. Bastard's tried to make me watch Attack on Titan about fifteen times."

"Aw, I love Attack on Titan!"

Callum groaned. "Oh, god. Don't tell him that. He'll never talk about anything else."

"Noted." I pointed the remote at the TV, tapped a few letters into the search box, then hit *enter*. The theme song for Attack on Titan blasted through the speakers as a set of animated credits flashed across the screen.

Callum sucked his teeth and gave me a sideways glance that was as amused as it was annoyed. "I walked right into that one, didn't I?"

I donned my most angelic smile and tossed the remote in his lap. "And what about you? What can you tell me about yourself?"

Callum surveyed the lounge, searching for inspiration. His eyes landed on our interlocked fingers, and he jerked his chin to the ink on his forearm. "I've designed all my own tattoos."

I angled him towards the glow of the TV in an attempt to better see the dragon winding up his arm. "You drew this?"

Callum nodded, eyes sparkling with pride. "I've done most of Dono's too, and inked them myself. But this guy was the first. Got him the day I turned 18."

"It's amazing."

The creature's scales were hyperrealistic, and its face so detailed you could almost feel the emotion in its eyes. Though it roared with fury, if you peered closer, you saw it was close to tears. "What made you pick a dragon?"

Callum's skin pebbled beneath my fingertips as I lightly traced them over the lines of the tattoo.

"Dragons are usually docile," he explained. "They prefer to be left alone, and are harmless until you fuck with them or the things they treasure. Then the fire comes out, and they destroy everyone responsible for their pain."

I peeked up at him. His eyes had taken on a melancholy, far-off look. There was clearly a story there, and not an especially happy one by the look of it, but when he met my gaze, Callum wiped his expression blank and shrugged cooly.

"Plus, it looks badass."

I chuckled. "So when can I have the rest of the tattoo tour? I'm sure you have more."

"I do."

Arching an eyebrow, I gestured to his body with a flick of my wrist. "Go on then."

With a knowing smirk, Callum peeled off his shirt and whipped it to the cushions behind me. He leaned back so the images etched across his torso were on full display.

The man was truly stunning, and a massive ego would have been completely justified, but instead, he went from confident to bashful when my fingers made their way to the rendition of a rose on his hip.

"This is beautiful," I murmured, lightly grazing my fingers

over the complex petals. "Is this the same design Donovan has on his neck?"

"Mm-hmm." Callum's voice was composed, but more goosebumps had broken out across his skin.

I considered it karma for the way he and Donovan had teased me in the green room the night before.

"You two seem really close." My fingers slipped a little lower down his hip.

"Mm-hmm."

"Did you know each other before you joined the band?"

Callum's breath hitched as my fingers brushed the waistband of his sweatpants. "We met when we were sixteen."

"Did you go to school together?"

When my fingers brushed the elastic on the sweats, air hissed through Callum's teeth. "I think you've learned enough about me. Now it's my turn."

Without warning, Callum flipped over and pinned me to the couch. I gasped at the movement, but he lowered his face to mine and playfully nudged my nose with his.

"I'm not going to fuck you, remember?" he whispered.

Those breathy words did more for my sex drive than my ex ever had.

My body swelled with heat as Callum relaxed between my thighs, his arms framing me on either side. I wanted to grind myself into him, but I muscled down my lust and tried to think of anything but the bulge I felt in his sweatpants.

"Where are you from?" Callum asked softly.

"A small town in rural Ohio."

"When did you move to LA?"

"A little over 8 years ago."

Callum angled his head, brushing a feather-light trail across my cheek with his lips. "Do you like it?"

I shut my eyes as his mouth moved to my earlobe and down the side of my neck. "Yes and no. I like that there's always something to do, but the traffic is horrible and I wish there was more rain."

Callum migrated to the crook of my shoulder, where his lips caused a shudder as they skated across my collarbones.

"And do you like this?" he breathed.

I'd never nodded so fast in my life.

"Yeah?" There was a smile in Callum's voice. "You like teasing, huh?"

He pushed himself forward, putting pressure on the sensitive area at my center and forcing me to grit my teeth in order to stifle a moan.

"And what about what Luca did to you? Did you like him being rough with you that first night?"

Callum drove forward again, bearing down harder. This time I couldn't keep quiet, and a soft groan slipped out.

"Yes," I panted, my hips instinctively following his motion. "Yes, I did."

"And did you like when Dante fucked that pretty face until you cried?"

My pussy clenched at his crude words, forcing me to bite my lip to keep from whimpering.

Callum moved his face to the other side of my neck and continued to brush his lips across the delicate skin. "And this? Does me whispering filthy things in your ear get you wet?"

He finished the question with a light nip to my earlobe, forcing me to buck beneath him. It only added to my torment as the pressure increased on my clit.

"Yes."

"Good to know." In the blink of an eye, Callum rolled off me and refocused on the TV. "So Titans are like giant zombies or something?"

Dumbfounded, I lay splayed on the couch, my brain taking a few seconds to catch up.

"What?" I asked, still breathless.

Callum gestured to the show.

I scoffed. "And you say *I'm* the tease."

A mischievous smile sneaked onto Callum's face, inspiring one of my own.

Game. *On.*

15

I peeled myself off the couch cushions and settled in close, mirroring Callum's innocent expression. I let my hand rest on his thigh while pretending to be focused on the anime in the corner.

"So what do *you* like?" I asked. "Besides being an unbearable tease, of course."

Callum's hand floated to my thigh too. "I'd rather show you instead of tell you."

"I want a preview. Like watching a trailer before the movie comes out. Please?" I slipped my hand further up Callum's thigh.

The drummer's hand slid to the same place on mine. "I like pleasure."

"No shit."

"Let me finish." Callum fidgeted slightly as my hand inched higher. "I like giving pleasure. Lots of it. Sometimes so much of it that it becomes punishment."

My thumb brushed the area where his hip and leg connected, and Callum's hand copied my movements, prompting my insides to clench at his proximity to my increasingly aching clit. I was thoroughly wet now, and if Callum moved his fingertips just a few centimeters to the side, he'd feel what he was doing to me.

"And what's your preferred way of dishing out this pleasure?" I asked, praying he felt like demonstrating.

Callum peeked at me out of the corner of his eye. The air tightened between us, and his hand twitched, but he held back from crossing the line. His words replayed in my ears.

Nobody touches you until you make the first move.

The standstill we'd found ourselves suddenly made sense. He was waiting for me to prove I wanted this. And *god*, did I want this.

My hand slid higher, connecting with the erection tucked into the waistband of Callum's sweats. He leaned his head back and groaned in appreciation, then reached his hand exactly where I wanted him to. I gasped as Callum's middle finger slid under my shorts, parted my slit, and dipped inside me.

"Fuck," he hissed. "Look at you already so wet for me."

I attempted to knead his swelling cock over his pants, but he curled his finger, pressing lightly on my G-spot, and my eyes fluttered shut as I basked in the sensation. My hips instinctively rolled into his movements, driving him deeper.

"Is this a good enough preview for you?" Callum slid another finger inside me, and I let out a moan. "You asked what I like, so here you go. I like doing this. Over…" Another curl of his fingers. "And over…" Another. "And over."

Tension built in my core with every stroke. Callum leaned in close and buried his face in the crook of my neck so I could clearly hear the husky words he muttered against my skin.

"And just when you think you're done and can't possibly experience any more…" He picked up his pace, making my inner walls clench. "I like to do it all over again. Then again. Then again. Until you're convinced you can't take anymore. And then, I do it one more time."

I raced closer and closer to a climax, my breath dissolving

into shallow gasps, but just when I saw release on the horizon, Callum pulled his fingers out of my panties, rolled off me, and returned his attention to the TV. The rest of the band probably heard my indignant yelp, but I didn't care.

"What the fuck?" I wailed.

Callum adopted an innocent expression that was truly Oscar-worthy. "What's wrong?"

I tackled him in a kiss as my reply.

Callum's tongue swept into my mouth, lapping mine at the same eager pace I ground against him. His fingers tangled in my hair as he mumbled against my lips.

"Tell me what you want."

Lust was making my vision fuzzy, causing the glow of the TV to highlight Callum's hair in a halo effect. He was a beautiful archangel indulging in forbidden earthly desires, and it was the most erotic and sacrilegious thing I'd ever laid eyes on. It eradicated all doubt in my mind that I wanted this.

I was all in.

"You," I replied without hesitation. "I want you inside me."

Callum's body trembled from restraint. "You remember our promise?"

I promise not to fuck you 'til you're begging for my cock.

"If you want it," Callum continued, "beg for it."

"For the love of god, Callum, fuck me!"

"What's the magic word?"

"*Please!*"

"That's better." He pulled his sweats down, yanked my shorts aside so roughly the seam ripped, and slammed me down onto his swollen cock.

My palm smacked flat against the cabinet behind Callum's head as I gasped at the pressure. He groaned in agreement, holding me in place as I adjusted to him.

"Show me how you like it," he demanded, reverently running his hands over my breasts and stomach. "Do exactly what it takes to get yourself off. I want to see exactly what it takes to make you come."

His words caused another flex of my inner walls, which Callum must have felt because he tosses his head back in ecstasy.

"This cunt is fucking heaven," he muttered.

His sinful words set my body in motion, and I rolled my hips forward and back. I experienced every inch of him, slowly at first, letting the pleasure accumulate into an overwhelming ache low and deep. Then I picked up speed, and my eyes drifted shut as my hand found its way to my clit. I'd started to rub circles around the sensitive bead when someone else's hand joined in.

I opened my eyes to meet Callum's gaze.

"Let me do it," he insisted, sliding his thumb under my fingertips.

I nodded obediently and leaned back, bracing my hands on his knees so that my body was open for him. He continued the pattern I'd set before, drawing a stuttering moan from my lips.

"More pressure or less?" he asked.

But his touch was already perfect, and made my insides quake in record time.

"Just like that," I managed, shutting my eyes again to focus on the feeling. Combined with the pressure of his cock driving into me, the result was almost immediate. My heart rate skyrocketed, the pleasure swelled, and the noises leaving my mouth became more desperate. The promise of release shone on the horizon again as my body raced towards a climax.

"That's it," Callum urged, increasing the speed of his strokes. "Come on, you can do it."

"Oh, god," I cried as the tension knotted.

"Come for me, angel," Callum panted. His free hand flew to the base of my neck to steady me as my body began to shudder. "Make a fucking mess."

His words snapped the cord, and the knot exploded, unraveling me from the inside out. I clapped a hand over my mouth to smother my scream of ecstasy, shaking so much from the rush that I probably would have vibrated right off Callum's lap if he hadn't held me in place. When the fit of pleasure had ceased, I collapsed forward onto Callum's chest. He carefully maneuvered out of me and planted a kiss on the tip of my nose, then brushed the hair from my eyes.

"I'm so sorry," he whispered.

My brow furrowed. "What are you sorry about?"

Guilt colored Callum's expression. "I... wasn't entirely honest before."

"Well, shit."

I jumped at the new voice, instinctively snatching the blanket and hauling it over my body like that might somehow hide what Callum and I had been doing. My head whipped around to find Luca, Dante, and Donovan silhouetted in the doorway. How long they'd been standing there watching us, I had no idea.

"Alright," Luca sighed, rummaging in his pocket. "Everybody pay up. Fucking Draco Malfoy over there is the winner."

Callum frowned and sat up, fumbling in the dim light for his shirt and tugging it over his head. "You know I hate that nickname."

"You all took *bets*?" I snapped.

"I wouldn't call it a bet, per se," Donovan snickered. "More like a cash incentive."

While I grappled for words, Dante stepped into the room and slapped a hundred dollar bill in Callum's palm. Luca followed suit, then Donovan, who ruffled the drummer's hair.

"I knew you could do it."

Despite his $300 win, Callum looked far from happy. "Jade, I swear I wasn't going to try anything, but then you came in and—"

"All of you get out," I barked, hiking my knees to my chest and pointing to the door. Humiliated tears pricked at my eyes.

Luca sniffed. "It's *our* bus, angel, you can't—"

"Get the fuck out!" I screamed.

Callum immediately leapt from the sofa and shoved his bandmates out the door. When he passed over the threshold, he glanced back at me over his shoulder.

"We warned you. We told you we weren't good men."

Then the door shut, and I sank into a miserable heap on the floor.

16

I was woken up by a slamming door and the obnoxious whirring of a blender.

Groaning, I sat up and squinted at my surroundings, my eyes still blurry. Last night, I'd rattled off a long text to Kayla about having second thoughts before crying myself to sleep, where I'd been plagued with horrible nightmares.

It was always the same one. It was only flashes of images, but I'd always wake up screaming or crying. I'd assumed it was just a random dream until I'd started therapy a few years ago. Part of me wished we hadn't dug so deep in those sessions. Then I never would've discovered that those images were memories I'd buried long ago. But as much as I wanted to forget them, they served a purpose. If I'd never learned the truth, I would still be in contact with the people responsible for them.

The recurring nightmare reared its head whenever I was stressed, which meant last night it played on a loop. Only this time, it was accompanied by another memory. One at rockbottom, sitting in a bathtub holding a bottle of pills, screaming at the top of my lungs as the pain of the past weighed too heavy on my shoulders.

I swiped my disheveled hair out of my face and rubbed my eyes. The dark memories disappeared back into my subconscious while my last interaction with Legion resurfaced. My cheeks heated, but I muscled down my discomfort. There was no reason to be embarrassed. I wasn't the asshole here, *they* were.

Hardening my expression, I stood, hauled open the lounge door, and stepped out. I immediately bumped into Callum, who was holding a smoothie in one hand and grabbing his headphones from his bunk with the other. In the kitchen behind him, Donovan was sipping an identical beverage and watching us out of the corner of his eye. The two men were shirtless, dressed only in athletic shorts and sneakers.

Callum's face drained of color when he saw me. "Hey! Um… How did you sleep?"

"Fine." I brushed past him and rummaged through my own bunk for a change of clothes. I felt Callum hovering, but didn't look at him.

"Jade, I'm really sorry about last night. I shouldn't have agreed to Luca and Donovan's game. I swear, I wasn't even planning on making a move, but everything happened so naturally and—"

"I don't want to talk about it." I turned back towards the lounge, but Callum blocked my way. For a moment I almost melted under his sad puppy dog eyes, but I dug deep and tersely motioned to the room behind him. "Excuse me. I need to get back there."

Callum sighed and stepped aside.

"Dono and I are going for a run," he called after me. "We go every morning if you ever want to join."

"K," was all I said before closing the door.

I could faintly make out Donovan murmuring something about giving me space before their voices faded and the front door slammed again.

I took my time getting ready, using the time to put a little extra effort in my makeup and give myself a pump up speech. I hadn't really thought about it before, but I understood now that these next few months would require a level of mental toughness. It was daunting, but I could handle four bullies in masks. I'd overcome far worse.

When I finally emerged, the bus was silent. The bunks were empty, which gave me an opportunity to snoop and get a glimpse into the men they belonged to.

Craig and Luca had bottom bunks like me, both with extra pillows for comfort and pictures stuck to the walls. I assumed Craig's photo was of his boyfriend; the image was the two of them with their arms around each other, while a hand-written letter entitled "Happy Anniversary, Baby" was pinned beside it.

The three photos on Luca's wall didn't contain him. One was of an older woman, her hair gray and her eyes shining with the wisdom of the years. She was making pasta by hand, and had flour up to her elbows and dusted across her wrinkled cheeks. In the photo beside it, she was in a near identical position, with a younger woman by her side. The woman was my age by the looks of it, with wavy brown hair and sad amber eyes that held the weight of the world. There was also a man in the photo standing behind the women, his arms barred in front of him as he observed them working, but his face had been cut out with a pair of scissors.

The third photo seemed out of place. It was tucked away in a corner apart from the others, almost as if it had slipped and fallen. In it, a little curly-haired boy who looked around three-years-old was mid-laugh. He was perched in a woman's arms, but her head had been cut out too.

I moved on to Donovan and Callum's upper bunks, the two parallel to each other and already filled with an assortment of fairy lights, artwork, and funny notes to each other. The doodles in Donovan's bunk were all anime characters, drawn by Callum according to the signature, while the drummer's bed was filled with ethereal-style drawings or hyper-realistic sketches. On Donovan's wall, front and center, there was a single photograph of a young woman. The two looked so similar I assumed they were related somehow. In the photo, she was balancing a set of toddlers on her hips, one twin dressed in blue and the other in pink.

Dante's bunk, diagonal from mine, had nothing in it except a sleeping bag.

"¡*Levántate, pendejo*!" a voiced shouted as the bus door flung open.

I whirled to Vee bouncing up the steps into the front lounge.

"Oh! Hey, Jade. Sorry, that wasn't directed at you. I'm here for my cousin."

"Your cousin?"

In response, Vee kicked a mound on the sofa. I jumped as it grunted and moved. A tattooed hand with chipped black nail polish poked out to flip her the bird.

"Seriously. Wake up, Dante." Vee yanked the blanket off Legion's bassist and balled it up. "It's only the fourth day of tour. We need to start off with good habits."

"Too late," Dante grumbled, grabbing his headphones from where they were wedged between the couch cushions and slipping them over his ears. "I'm hungover as fuck."

"Typical." Vee wandered over to a cupboard, rummaged around inside, and pulled out a bottle of water and some aspirin. She popped the cap and shook two into her palm, then delivered them to her cousin. "Take a shower and put something in your body besides nicotine, please."

Dante simply stared at her, snatched a packet of cigarettes off the kitchen table, and dragged one out with his teeth.

"Jade, you wanna grab breakfast?" Vee jerked her head to the door, and I gladly followed. Dante didn't even look at me as I passed.

We stepped out of the bus into sunny 80 degree weather.

"Where are we?"

"San Jose." Vee pulled out her phone and started searching for nearby cafes. "Doors open at seven. Then tomorrow we head to Portland, followed by Seattle. The guys didn't share the route with you?"

I shook my head. "We haven't really talked much."

Performed sex acts? Yes. But talked? Not really.

"Alright, well there's a West Coast leg of tour, then a week break back in LA before we head to the East Coast." She paused for a moment, chewing the inside of her cheek as she considered her words, then turned to me. "Hey, I just want to say I wasn't in on this whole thing."

"What whole thing?"

"You and the guys. When I introduced you, I wasn't trying to set you up or anything. I was genuinely trying to help you mess with your ex. I had no idea it would turn into... well, *this*."

I sheepishly ground the toe of my sneaker into the asphalt. "Yeah, I didn't either."

"I've gotta ask, though..." Vee weighed her words again, then took a deep breath. "Are you sure about this? I mean, the guys are... Well, they've got some baggage. And as a woman, I feel it's really important for me to check on you and your needs. So... Are you ok? Blink twice if you need help. I can take you somewhere these psychos will never find you."

I laughed. "You can rest easy. I'm of sound mind and body, and doing this of my own accord. I'm just sowing my wild oats, I guess. And we all have baggage." I flinched as last night's dream flashed back into my mind.

"Well if and when the guys' bags get too heavy, I'm here for you." Vee grinned and squeezed my arm. "It'll be nice to have another girl around."

Our intimate moment was interrupted when the door of the bus banged open and Dante shuffled out, hood up, headphones on, and a lit cigarette in one hand with an energy drink in the other.

Vee jabbed her finger at the can. "That is *not* what I meant when I told you to put something else in your body.'"

Dante finished the drink in three chugs, then tapped his headphones. "Sorry, can't hear you."

He blew past us, headed towards the bustling street.

"*Adónde vas?*" Vee called after him. When he didn't respond, she sighed and turned back to me. "I gotta go with him. I'll catch you later."

She jogged after her cousin, yelling something at him in Spanish, which he continued to tune out.

Another shout reached my ears, but this time it came from behind me. When I turned, I discovered Luca striding down the street from the opposite direction, his phone to his ear and a steaming paper cup in his hand. He was barking at someone on the other line, but when his eyes met mine, he lowered his voice and turned the other way so I wouldn't hear.

Donovan and Callum rounded the corner, passing their lead singer, both of them glistening with sweat from their run. The guitarist was mid-phone conversation too, only his call was through video chat. A woman's voice spoke on the other end, a heavy South London accent coating her words.

"Thank you for calling," Donovan said, his smile stretching so wide it crinkled his eyes. "Seriously, Em. It means a lot."

"Yeah, well. Have to make sure you're not dead every now and then."

Despite the unenthusiastic statement, Donovan continued to beam. "Can I say hi to the little ones? Just for a bit?"

"They're asleep."

That dampened Donovan's spirits. "Already? It's only 6 o'clock there."

"They're kids, Dono," the female bit back. "They go to bed early."

"Can you at least turn the camera around so I can see them?"

"I've gotta go. Got friends coming around. I'll ring you another time, yeah?"

"Alright." Donovan nodded sadly, but tried to remain upbeat. "Give the kids a kiss for me. Tell 'em Uncle Dono loves them."

"Uh-huh."

"And Em? I love you—" A beep signaled the line had gone dead. "Too."

Donovan cleared his throat and approached me, chuckling grimly. "Siblings, am I right? You got any, angel?"

"No, I'm an only child."

"Me too," Callum chirped, smiling wide.

I was still annoyed by what he'd done last night, so I didn't return it. He tried to smooth things further by adding, "You look really nice today, by the way."

"Thanks," I mumbled, toying with the hem of my top.

Donovan slung his arm over Callum's shoulder and leaned in close. "Come on, darling. Don't hold last night against Cal. He's sensitive."

Callum responded by punching Donovan in the stomach, knocking the wind from his lungs.

"We dragged him into the challenge," Donovan explained when he'd recovered. "Sometimes me and Luca start squawking at each other and take things too far. Cal got caught in the cross-fire. Besides, you can't be too miffed. Judging by the sounds we heard, you two had a great time."

I sighed, forcing any remaining shame out of my system. I had no doubt we'd all be seeing and hearing each other's intimate moments throughout the duration of this tour, and the sooner I got over how foreign it all felt, the sooner I could accept that the concept actually turned me on.

"You boys can play your little games, just fill me in on what they are. That way I can put a horse in the race too." I shrugged.

"If I'd have known money was involved, I would've made you work a little harder. Not sure what you did was worth $300. Maybe $20 at best."

Donovan laughed so hard he snorted, while Callum irritably sucked his teeth and narrowed his eyes.

"Go ahead and run your mouth, sweetheart. We'll see if you're singing the same tune when I tie you down and make you come so many times you forget how to speak."

Even if I was a little annoyed at him, my body was not, and my pussy thrummed to life at the image he painted. Callum started for the bus, but Donovan hung back to whisper in my ear.

"Careful, angel. He's not lying. And after he follows through, when you're lying there wet and used, whimpering like a needy little whore, you'll get me for round two."

He landed a smack to my ass and jogged after Callum.

Jesus. It was only ten in the morning and I already needed a drink.

17

I spent the rest of the morning jumping around to different cafes and breweries, claiming I needed to get some work done on my laptop.

That "work" was really just cyberstalking my new employers.

I paid for access to a website that ran background checks and inputted each man's name. Thankfully no mugshots came up. After that dead end, I got to work Googling all the men individually.

The Brits were practically wraiths. A search of their names turned up nothing online, not even social media. I did find a few photos of them on a Legion subreddit, though. Fans had snapped pictures of them during load-out with the caption, "Holy shit, Legion's crew is just as hot as they are!"

Luca and Dante were almost invisible, but not quite.

A search of "Luca Serino - San Diego, CA" produced a handful of articles and sports databases, and after a few clicks, I pulled up a picture of a high school soccer team. At the center of the crowd, proudly holding a shiny trophy overhead, was a 17-year-old Luca. Ironically, he'd played the same position I had when I was in school, only by the looks of it, he was significantly better. Articles mentioned him getting approached by college scouts as early as his sophomore year, and after digging some more, I found photos of him during that time. In all those articles, the captions also mentioned the name of the young man pictured passing Luca the ball: Dante Ramos, a promising forward who'd disappeared from the team after their first state championship at 16.

A phone call from Kayla interrupted my stalking session, and when I answered, she claimed she was ready to drive up from LA and steal me away. Somehow, I talked her off the ledge. She wanted details of everything that had happened with the guys so far, but I kept things vague, not just because of the NDA in place, but also because I didn't want to scare her. My best friend said she supported my freaky side, but I was worried if I told her too much, it would stress her out even more. So all she got was, "the drummer and I fooled around a little," and we moved on.

It was around one in the afternoon and I was halfway through a burger and fries when a text lit up my phone.

UNKNOWN: I'm adding you to a group chat with the guys. Save our names. We need to be able to contact our fucktoy whenever we want

I made a noise of disgust, but I also had to clench my legs together at the nickname. The bossy tone of the text was unmistakable, and I changed the contact to Luca's name. When I'd finished, my phone dinged again.

UNKNOWN: Hi Jade! This is Callum

A new ding.

UNKNOWN: And this is your future husband

A smile accidentally crept onto my face, and I saved the two as Callum and Donovan.

A fourth ding.

LUCA: Waiting on you, Lucifer

A fifth ping. The restaurant was starting to give me strange looks. I ducked my head and turned the phone on vibrate before checking the message. The unknown number had sent nothing but a middle finger emoji.

I saved Dante's name, expecting that to be the end of it, but my phone continued to buzz.

CALLUM: Have you eaten? Dono and I are gonna grab food here in a sec. You're welcome to come with

LUCA: Soundcheck at 3:00. Be back at the bus before then

DONOVAN: Not really necessary for her to be there for that, is it mate?

LUCA: I like to keep an eye on my investments

CALLUM: So is that a no to the food?

DONOVAN: Loosen the reins cowboy. Your hands have to be hurting from how tight you're holding them

LUCA: If you have something to say to me, be a man and say it to my face, not over a fucking text

Dante has left the group

Luca has added Dante to the group

"Jesus," I mumbled. "It's like a soap opera."

> Already ate. I'll be back before 3. My
> sentiments exactly, Dante. All of you please
> stop blowing up my phone

I tossed my cell onto the table and returned to my lunch, but after a few seconds, it vibrated again. It wasn't a text from the group chat, but a new feed with a single person.

> CALLUM: You're welcome to hang here with us
> during the days, btw. You don't have to
> stay away

I chewed the inside of my cheek. He was clearly trying to make amends for last night, which I appreciated. Regardless, I waited a good minute before picking up my phone and answering with the truth.

> I just don't really feel like being fucked or
> fucked with right now

The drummer replied instantly.

> CALLUM: Dono knows you're upset, he won't
> push it. Dante's a zombie today. Can't speak
> for Luca, but he typically gets dialed in before
> shows. And by dialed in, I mean he turns into a
> control freak and only cares about making
> everything perfect

Luca and I were sounding more similar by the second.

> And you?

> CALLUM: I learned my lesson. Paws off

> CALLUM: ... Even though you were fucking
> amazing. Gonna be dreaming about that angel
> pussy for weeks

An unintentional blush crept into my cheeks, and I nibbled at my thumbnail as I considered my next text. I finally lowered my walls slightly and decided to give the dog a bone.

> Only dreaming about it?

CALLUM: Unless you want to make my dreams a reality…

> I'll think about it

CALLUM: pleeeease

> Now look who's begging

CALLUM: hahaha

CALLUM: This tour is gonna be fun

> It'd be more fun if I'd won $300 dollars too

CALLUM: Take it. Feels like blood money now anyway

> No, you won the game fair and square

CALLUM: We're playing a new game now. The money is hidden somewhere in your duffel bag. When you find it, you win

I sat back in my chair, tempted to be touched by the sweet gesture, but I quickly reminded myself of my situation in order to keep my feet firmly planted on the ground.

This was just business.

And they were not good men.

18

When I made it back to the bus, Dante and Luca were sitting outside, puffing on cigarettes and muttering to each other while Dante mindlessly strummed his bass. When he saw me approaching, he flicked his smoke to the asphalt, ground his sneaker into its glowing cherry, and and stood.

"We'll try working through the rest of the chords later when everyone's asleep."

"Hey," I greeted them, purposefully ignoring the lead singer and focusing on Dante. "How's the head?"

"Fucked up."

He pushed past me, the brush off making my blood boil. If I was trying to behave, I would have bit my tongue and continued my attempt at killing with kindness. But hell, this whole thing came about because I wanted to *misbehave*. So I abandoned my polite facade and faced the bassist's retreating back.

"Hey, you're welcome for that blowjob the other night, asshole."

My words didn't quite have the desired effect, because Dante simply raised his arm overhead to give me a thumbs up and disappeared into the venue.

I turned back to Luca.

"Damn," he chuckled. "The angel's got some bite today."

"Submissive in the bedroom, not in life." I plopped down beside him. "What's his deal, anyway?"

"Don't worry about it."

I rolled my eyes. "I get it. You're brooding and mysterious. You've built a career off that. But you're going to have to open up eventually."

Luca shook his head so fast I thought he might get whiplash. "That wasn't part of the deal. We hired you for your body, not your company."

"Wow. How are you single? With lines like that, women should be falling at your feet."

"Women *are* falling at my feet every goddamn day." Luca leaned in, amber eyes narrowing. "I'm just being honest with you, angel. If you want pretty words, I better be getting paid for them."

We stared at each other for a few tense seconds, but I couldn't figure out if the tightness in the air was from hatred or unfulfilled desire.

"Jade?"

I broke Luca's gaze in search of the voice. My eyes landed on a bright white smile, beachy curls, and boyish good looks.

"Chase! Hey!" I waved and stood as the lead singer of Phantom Spark strolled over to us. Luca rose too.

"What are you doing here?" Chase laughed, shaking his head and opening his arms to pull me into a warm hug.

"I booked a job with the band," I said, peeking at Luca over Chase's shoulder. "I'm going to be designing something for them, and they wanted me to come on board to get a sense of their vibe."

Luca nodded in approval of the lie, but for some reason, he still looked annoyed.

Chase pulled away, keeping his hands on my waist as he

beamed at me. "Well, I'm happy you're here. Now we can finally hang out."

"Yeah, I'd really—"

"Hey, man." Luca stepped between the two of us and extended his hand, intercepting Chase's attention. "I don't think we've met yet. I'm Luca. I'm a tech on Legion's crew."

"Oh, hey." Chase offered a polite smile, which Luca didn't return. "I'm Chase."

"Cool." Luca's head tilted to the side, and his brows nudged together as he feigned innocence. "Are you supposed to be back here?"

"It's cool, dude. I'm the lead singer of Phantom Spark, so I can kinda do whatever."

Luca's jaw twitched with contained rage, but he managed to pull off a laugh. "Really? Huh. Weird, I thought all the bands on the package signed a contract that said they'd stay out of Legion's space."

Chase tucked his hands in his pockets. "Uh… We might've signed something like that. But it's almost soundcheck, so I gotta do my job, you know?"

"Yeah." Luca smiled, but there was no joy in it. "Except it's *not* almost soundcheck for you. It's almost soundcheck for *Legion*. Everyone else is called at 5, so they can stay out of Legion's way."

Chase stared at Luca a few beats longer before peeking at me. I shrugged helplessly.

"Alright, you caught me." Chase raised his hands in defense and chuckled. "I was just trying to make friends."

"Clearly. You're also in violation of a contract."

"I was being *friendly*," Chase stated, an edge coming into his voice. "I don't how many tours you've been on—"

"A few." Luca's smile remained, but it was growing more pained each second.

"Dude, all I'm saying is tour can be tough, and camaraderie helps."

"And all *I'm* saying, *dude,* is you're breaking the rules. I'd hate for Legion to find out about this. It's only the fourth day of tour, you don't want to ruffle their feathers so soon."

Chase's mouth clamped shut, and his gaze shifted to me. I sighed in defeat and averted my eyes to the dirty asphalt.

Despite the verbal spanking, Chase donned a grin as he backed towards the street, headed for the openers' buses on the opposite side of the venue. "My bad. Won't make the mistake again. I'll catch you later, Jade."

"Bye." When he'd gone, I whirled on Luca. "What the hell was that?

"I knew I didn't like that guy," he grumbled to himself. "I should've stood my ground when Donovan pushed to have that fucking band."

"Chase is actually really nice. That was completely uncalled for."

Luca scoffed. "He's not nice."

"And how would *you* know? You're a fucking asshole."

The singer's eyes flicked to me, the intensity in them making my breath catch. "I'm good at reading people. How do you think I could tell you'd be down for all this?"

"Lucky guess."

A chuckle grated out of Luca's throat that had no right sounding so seductive. "Nice try, angel. But face it. I see you." He took a step forward, setting my senses on high alert and prompting every hair on my body to stand on end. "I see the darkness you hide behind that perfectly crafted mask. I see how much you're fighting your true desires, because they're messy and fucked up, and you're not ready to admit that you are too."

Luca was close now, and he lightly skated his fingers down my arm, making the skin pebble. "I see the way you war with yourself, because you hate being objectified, but it also turns you on." He pushed his face nearer, his lips caressing the shell of my ear as his voice lowered to a whisper. "I see how bad you want to submit to me."

I hurriedly shoved him away, sending him stumbling back a few steps. He laughed and shook his head.

"Yep. I see you, angel. Crystal clear."

"Great. Then you'll be able to see this." I flipped him my middle finger, then stomped towards the bus.

"Stay away from the other bands," Luca barked after me. "You belong to us, not them."

I slammed the door so hard the windows rattled.

19

"Motherfucker," I grumbled, furiously scrubbing my eraser against the page.

I was hunched in a corner of the packed venue with my sketchbook, trying to get inspiration from the band onstage, but watching Legion's performance only turned me on or pissed me off. Currently, it was the latter.

I attempted another design, a creepy tree dangling a juicy forbidden fruit, but it ended up looking more Nightmare Before Christmas than badass rock band. I grunted in frustration and ripped the page out, crumpling it into a ball before chucking it into a nearby trashcan.

Legion started up their fifth song of the night, and the crowd went wild, devolving into a writhing mass of jumping and moshing to the fast-paced melody. The band's energy shifted too, and they traded their typical unhurried sensuality for aggressive physicality that riled the crowd even further.

Everyone was digging into their wells of primal aggression, and the scene caused an eager chill to break out across my body. I wanted to keep stewing on the words "you belong to us, not them" like I had been all day, but as the floodlights danced across the band playing into their base instincts, my fury was doused by arousal. It was dangerous how these men could impact me. I had a good head on my shoulders, but when these guys got me going, reason seemed to fly out the window.

"You boys are trouble," I mumbled to myself.

"Talking about me?"

I turned to find Chase standing behind me, observing my drawing. He was sweaty from the set he'd just finished, but that crowd-pleasing smile was still present.

"Maybe," I teased. "Good job tonight."

The singer shrugged. "Nah, I was late on a few of the choruses."

"You really need to learn how to take a compliment."

Chase chuckled and rubbed the back of his neck. "I think I just have trouble taking compliments from beautiful women."

I wrinkled my nose. "Ugh. How many times have you used that cheesy line?"

"Not a line. Just being honest." Chase's wide smile disappeared, and concern filled his eyes. "Hey, I just want to say I'm sorry about earlier. I didn't mean to step on that guy's toes. I was seriously just trying to make friends."

"I know. Luca's just..." I frowned as I tried to think of a fitting description.

Luca's a cocky prick? An asshole? A confusing, complicated, utterly infuriating caveman I wanted to strangle at the same time I rode him?

"Luca's a little protective," I finally settled on.

"I can see that." Chase warily glanced over his shoulder. "Is he so protective that he wouldn't let you grab a beer with me and my band?"

"Probably. But he's not here, is he?"

Chase's grin made a reappearance and he jerked his head towards the door. "Come with me, then."

I followed him out to the parking lot where the rest of the

openers were camped out in front of their buses. Chase introduced me to each by name, then brought out an extra camping chair so I could sit with them. I was supplied with a cold PBR from a nearby cooler and regaled with tales of past tour shenanigans. It was a playful, warm environment, worlds different than the atmosphere on Legion's bus.

We were having such a good time that we didn't realize Legion had finished their set until the show was over. Throngs of concert-goers poured out of the venue, and Spencer, Phantom Spark's drummer, jumped to his feet.

"Shit, we gotta get in there and sign autographs at the merch table. It was great chatting with you, Jade. We'll see you around."

The rest of the band jogged towards the doors, but Chase remained behind.

"You're not going?"

"I will in a sec." He rummaged around in his pocket and pulled out a small tin. He lifted the lid, revealing a lighter and several joints lined up in a row.

"I get nervous talking to strangers sometimes," Chase said, popping one of the hand-rolled sticks into his mouth and lighting it. "This helps."

An earthy cloud of marijuana puffed from his lips, and he politely held out the tin to me. I shook my head.

"I'm ok, thanks."

"You sure? It's good stuff. A buddy of mine grows it."

"I'm not much of a smoker. Plus, I'm pretty sure there's a rule against it." I raised my eyebrow in a silent reproach. Chase just laughed.

"What Legion doesn't know won't hurt them, right?"

I tried to smile, but it came out more like a grimace.

"You sure you don't want any?" Chase asked, pulling the joint from his mouth and extending it to me.

"No thanks."

"Come on, just a little hit."

"Really, I'm good."

"What if we shotgun it?"

Suddenly there was a flash of movement, and someone grabbed my wrist and yanked me backwards. I yelped in surprise and pain, but my mouth snapped shut when I realized who'd taken me hostage.

Luca must have just gotten off stage. He was still wearing his body paint, and underneath the mask, I could see his amber eyes narrowed into enraged slits. Chase stiffened at the sight of the Beast and moved to tuck the joint behind his back, but he was too late. The Beast tore it from his hand and hurled it onto the asphalt before thrusting a threatening finger in his face.

"Next time I put it out on your fucking skin."

Then he spun on his heel and dragged me back into the venue.

When we made it to the green room, Luca kicked open the door and tossed me inside like a rag doll. I stumbled forward, almost losing my footing, but Donovan swooped in and caught me before I did.

"What the fuck?" Donovan barked, turning away so his shoulder blocked me from Luca's view.

"I told you that band was bad news," Luca snarled, lifting his mask and tossing it onto the couch. "But no, you insisted we bring them on."

"What did they do?" Callum asked. He and Dante were in the process of scrubbing the white stage paint off their skin with baby wipes. Luca's fury eased slightly as he glanced at Dante, a flicker of worry taking its place.

"It doesn't matter," he snapped, whirling on Donovan again. "They're pushing their limits. This exactly why I don't trust you with this stuff. If this whole tour goes to shit now, it's your fucking fault."

That ignited something in Donovan. He released me and

stood tall, his usual carefree demeanor morphing into something darker.

"If this tour goes to shit, it's got nothing to do with me. It's because of you and him." He jabbed his finger to Dante on the last word. "You can be as psychotic and controlling as you want, but *that* fucker is a ticking time bomb, and we all know it."

"Fuck you, Dono," Dante muttered before tugging on a hoodie and swiping a bottle of vodka from the counter. Not bothering to find a cup, he collapsed on the couch and took a swig.

"Guys, this really isn't the time or the place," Callum stated. "Maybe Jade should go back to the—"

"I'm not done with her," Luca interrupted, side-stepping Donovan so he could fling a finger in my face. "What the fuck did I tell you about staying away from the other bands?"

A small part of me wanted to cower in fear, but something else had been rattled awake. Something that sharpened her claws and eagerly bared her teeth at the scent of a fight.

"You can't tell me who I can and can't talk to. That wasn't part of our agreement. I'm not your prisoner. You rented my pussy, not my affection."

Luca was shaking with restraint, his hands repeatedly balling into fists at his sides. "And I paid good money for that pussy. If the other bands want a taste, they can scrounge up the price themselves."

"If you don't have a shitty personality, you don't need to pay for sex."

Luca scoffed. "You think I *need* you? I could have anyone I want out there. I brought you on for convenience, not necessity."

I examined my fingernails. "If you say so. You seem pretty desperate right now, though. It's a little pathetic."

Luca lunged for me, but Donovan stepped in and shoved him backwards.

"Take ten," he barked, his broad shoulders flexing as he

squared off against the singer. "I'm not in the mood to beat your ass tonight."

I held my breath, certain Luca was going to smash a fist into Donovan's jaw, but the singer eventually cracked a grin and backed up. "You're right. I do need to cool off. I'll decompress in my favorite way."

He spun, snatched up his mask, and tugged it back on before storming out of the green room. After a few seconds, Dante stood from the couch and shuffled after him.

"Where are you going?" Callum asked, watching the bassist hook his crew lanyard on his belt loop.

"Don't know yet," Dante replied.

"I'll come with you."

"I don't need a babysitter."

The door banged shut, but Callum sighed and pulled a beanie over his hair. "Yeah, you do."

He shot me an apologetic wince and darted after his bassist, leaving me and Donovan alone.

20

"Sorry you had to see that," the guitarist said, wandering over to the sofa and sitting with a heavy sigh. "I can usually keep my head with that twat, but he's in a special mood today."

I lowered onto the cushion beside him and propped my fist under my chin. "There's a pretty big rift between you guys, huh?"

"You could say that again." Donovan gingerly rubbed his eyes. "We've always butted heads, but it's just gotten worse since..." He frowned and trailed off, then shrugged. "It's just gotten worse over the years."

"Well, it can't have been all bad. Something must have drawn you guys to each other originally."

Donovan's eyes glazed as his mind drifted to a distant memory. "We were just kids back then, all running from our own demons. When we collided, we latched onto each other for survival. We needed each other then, but sometimes you outgrow people."

I sat with his words, then replayed the memory of the phone call with Luca when he'd proposed that fateful contract to me.

"Luca told me you all needed an escape," I mused. "He said if this ship was sinking, why not have fun on the way down?"

Donovan tensed like he could sense my next question.

"Bringing me on… Was it just so you could end on a good note? Is the band breaking up?"

Donovan stared at the floor, searching for a way out of the conversation, but he found none. Eventually he hung his head and huffed another sigh. "Nothing's official yet, but we all feel it. So I'll just come out and say it… Yes. This is Legion's farewell tour, and you're our goodbye present. Honestly, that's probably why Luca's been acting so mental. He's terrified of what'll happen to Dante without the band, but Cal and I can't keep setting ourselves on fire to keep someone else warm."

I hummed at the analogy and readjusted in my seat. "Well, what would you do if the band breaks up? Would you go back to London?"

Donovan shook his head. "Nah. Not the best memories in that city."

"How come?"

Donovan averted his gaze and picked at a piece of lint on the sofa. "Like I said, we all have our demons. Besides, I don't come from the best area."

"No?" I tilted my head and squinted at him. "But you sound so fancy."

Donovan tossed his head back and laughed. "You clearly don't have an ear for accents. I'm from a shit part of London. Rough areas make rough kids, and I was no exception. I spent my childhood running from the cops and watching my friends bleed out from bullet holes."

My heart sank. "Oh my god, I'm so sorry."

Donovan shrugged, but there was pain behind his eyes. "I needed to have the piss scared out of me so I'd get myself sorted. And it worked. I cleaned up my act when I was fifteen, got a job at a local music shop, found God, then promptly lost him when I met that Draco Malfoy-looking motherfucker at a church picnic."

Happy someone was finally opening up to me, I leaned closer. "You met Callum at church?"

A fond smile chased away the remaining sadness in Donovan's expression. "Yeah. And don't let the innocent act fool you, he was a terrible influence. He always cracked jokes during prayer so I'd bust up laughing. Of course, I was always the one who got blamed for it. I was also the one who got blamed for luring him into a coat closet and snogging him senseless, but for the record, that was his doing too."

I blinked, panic and guilt hitting me like a brick. "Oh, fuck. I'm so sorry, when he and I hooked up I had no idea you guys were—"

"Relax, darling," Donovan laughed, patting my knee. "You didn't do anything wrong. We're more openminded than that. I love Cal to pieces. He's my best friend, my partner, and I mean it when I say I'd fucking kill for him. But back in the days of that coat closet, we quickly realized we didn't match up in some important areas. That didn't change our feelings for each other, but we didn't want to force the other into things they didn't want to do. So we kept *us*, and opened up the option to add others."

I nodded, slowly putting together the puzzle. "So you're technically together, but you—"

"Prefer fucking other people."

My face flushed. "Got it. And Luca and Dante, are they together too?"

"They may argue like an old married couple, but no. Both straight as a board."

"Good to know." I nestled into the couch and hugged my knees to my chest. "So back to the band breaking up. If London's off-limits, would you and Callum stay in America?"

"Yeah, we bought a little place on the beach in Malibu a few years back. Cal would probably get an apprenticeship in a tattoo shop somewhere, and I'd focus on my photography."

"Photography?"

"Yeah, I take pictures."

"I noticed." I glared at him in reference to the scandalous images he'd snapped a few days prior.

Donovan tried to disguise his cheeky grin, but his twitching lips gave him away. "Sorry, darling. It's not my fault you're so beautiful. I'd love to get you on film one day. We could do a boudoir shoot, and you could give it to me as our wedding present."

"I'm sorry, *our* wedding?"

"If the band breaks up, then my visa expires, and I'll need a green card."

I laughed. "So citizenship is all I'm good for?"

"And nude modeling."

I playfully smacked his arm. "Not sure Callum would approve of our nuptials."

"I'll divorce you in a few years, then marry him."

"Deal."

We shook hands, Donovan's grip lingering a little too long. It wasn't uncomfortable, though. In fact, it uncovered the flirty part of me that the events of last night had humiliated into hiding.

I skated my thumb across his knuckles. "Thank you for coming to my rescue earlier."

"Of course. I hate that aggro shit. Did enough of it as a boy."

I nodded and looked away. Out of the corner of my eye, I caught Donovan's head tilting as he examined me closer. "But you like it, don't you? It turns you on."

I fidgeted, feeling so on display I may as well have been naked. "Callum said I had a good poker face…"

"Cal's shit at poker."

I laughed again, then focused on picking at my nails so I

wouldn't have to make eye contact. "Damn. Then… Yes. It pisses me off, but it also makes me fantasize about that aggression coming out in other scenarios."

"Ah." A mischievous smile lit up Donovan's face. "So getting tossed out of heaven wasn't enough for this fallen angel, she wants to be tossed around in the bedroom too."

A pulse shot between my legs, his the statement.

"People treat me like I'm fragile," I explained. "Emotionally, or physically. But I'm not. I fall apart sometimes, just like everyone does, but I can handle more than people think. I want to be treated like it."

Donovan's eyes sparked with lust. "I'll make a mental note."

I bit my lip. "So now that you know a little of what I'm into, can I know what you like?"

"I could tell you." Donovan's hand slid onto my thigh, causing a tingle to spread through my leg and up into my belly. *"Or* I could show you."

Bang!

The door to the green room flew open without warning. Thinking fast, Donovan twisted towards me, burying his face in the crook of my neck to disguise his identity. The intruders stumbled in, lip-locked and lost in a haze of lust, and my stomach dropped when I caught sight of who they were.

The Beast looked up from a female companion to grin at me, his eyes sparking behind his mask.

"Excuse us. We need the room."

"What happened to fucking knocking?" Donovan shouted from my shoulder. "My mask's not on!"

"Sorry, we got carried away." To make his point, Luca caught the woman's face in his hand and dragged his tongue up her neck. Her corresponding moan of appreciation sent a complicated wave of emotion crashing over me. It was made of humiliation and fury, but jealousy led the charge.

Donovan sighed irritably. "Just hand me my mask, will you?"

"I'll get it," I offered.

I crossed to the counter directly behind Luca and the starry-eyed fan who was suckling his neck. I reached out and pinched Donovan's mask between my fingertips, then smiled at the woman.

"Can you close your eyes, hun? Just for a second while Diablo puts his face on."

The girl giggled and nodded, then turned her back to us. But instead of passing off the mask to its owner, I pushed the girl out the door, slammed it behind her, and locked it.

"This'll just take a second," I shouted through the wood.

Her cries of protest were drowned out by the rage buzzing in my ears like a swarm of bees. I faced Luca again.

"What the fuck is this?"

He shrugged. "I'm decompressing in my favorite way."

"That's not what I'm referring to." I stepped forward so our faces were close. "*I* can't have anyone else, but *you* can? That's bullshit."

"The Beast plays by his own rules." Disdain dripped from Donovan's words as he walked over to us and snatched up his mask. "Haven't you figured that out yet? It's his way or the highway."

"Not anymore." I lifted my chin, my eyes still glued to Luca's. "I'm making a new rule. If you don't want anyone else touching me, you can't touch anyone either."

Luca scoffed. "That wasn't part of the agreement."

I leaned in further so that he could feel the heat of each carefully enunciated word. "Get the girl to leave, or I swear to god I'll fuck every last person on this tour."

"Then I send you home without a dime," Luca countered. "And that lovely picture of you choking on Dante's cock starts circulating the internet."

"We signed a contract, remember? I've already fooled around with half your band. As far as that document's concerned, I'm fulfilling the responsibilities of the job. If you send me home now, you'd be guilty of unlawful termination, and if that picture of me gets out, it'll count as retaliation. That's not gonna go well for you when I take your ass to court."

We shot daggers at each other for what felt like an eternity. Finally Luca sniffed, squared his shoulders, and yanked open the green room door.

"Bus call got moved up," he told the woman waiting patiently outside, a convincing pout playing into his ruse. "Sorry. Send me a DM on the band's account, ok? I'll hit you up next time we're in town."

The woman shot me a death-glare, but she eventually shuffled away with her head hanging. Luca turned back to me.

"Happy?"

"Ecstatic."

We continued to glare at each other, the tension only broken when Donovan snickered.

"Fucking hell," he muttered, starting for the door. "I think it's safe to say you underestimated this one."

I shot Luca a sweet smile as I followed Donovan out of the room. The singer stayed behind and sulked until we set off for Portland.

21

We drove overnight, and when we woke up, we'd made it to Oregon. The landscape outside the window had transitioned to lush hills and forests, while the sun hid behind a thick layer of gloomy clouds.

I spent the morning watching the world pass by in a green blur. I hadn't slept much, too distracted by Donovan's snoring and the anger still wafting off Luca. Even when he'd been fast asleep in his bunk, I'd kept a wary watch on him. I kept expecting him to storm over to me at any second, grab me by the collar, and demand I perform the duties I'd been hired for. Which, to be honest, sounded as sexy to me as it did terrifying. But Luca never made a move. He would occasionally murmur things to Dante, but otherwise kept to himself.

Once we arrived in downtown Portland and parked at the venue, everyone went their separate ways. Craig and Dante wandered off to find food, Luca muttered something about needing coffee, and Donovan and Callum laced up their sneakers in preparation of their morning run. My mind was all over the place, and usually a trip to the gym would help relieve it, but unfortunately I was stuck in a frat house on wheels. A run sounded like the next best thing, and the Brits had been the kindest to me since I'd been here, so I hesitantly asked if I could join them. Callum nearly leapt out of his shoes he was so excited.

We set off at a leisurely pace so we could take in the city and still have enough breath to chat. The men continued to be fairly guarded, but the longer our blood was pumping, the more they opened up. I learned that both Callum and Donovan's parents had died when they were young, just like my biological father had. Cal had gone to live with his grandma while Donovan and his older sister Emilia moved in with family friends. Em didn't approve of Donovan's sacrilegious job and frequently let him know it, while Callum had purposefully kept his ailing nan in the dark for fear of the same. They cracked jokes about their pasts, but I could tell by the way their eyes hardened when they spoke that it still hurt to some degree.

We'd gotten so caught up in the conversation that we ran for over an hour. By the time we got back, we were all looking forward to a shower and a nap, but a vicious shouting match inside the bus kept us hovering in the parking lot outside. I recognized Luca's gravelly, barking tone, but I'd heard the second voice so few times it took me a moment to place it.

"Sounds like Dante finally snapped," Callum mumbled.

As if on cue, the door flung open and the bassist stormed out, his features twisted in fury. With dark bags under his eyes and tousled hair, he looked like he hadn't slept much last night either.

"Trouble in paradise?" Donovan asked.

Dante rolled his eyes and fumbled in his pocket for a lighter and cigarettes. "I'm being smothered, man. I can't fucking breathe. I've gotta get out of here, or I'm gonna lose my shit."

"Why don't you come running with us sometime?" I offered.

I hadn't even meant to say the words, they'd just slipped out. All three men turned to look at me, just as surprised by the question as I was.

"It might make you feel better," I added. "Activity always helps me."

Donovan threw his head back and laughed. "Lucifer's not really cut out for physical activity, darling. The man breathes more nicotine than oxygen."

I thought about the images I'd discovered of Dante and Luca playing soccer in school, but kept quiet so I wouldn't reveal that I'd been checking up on them.

"Thanks, but I'm good." Dante took a long drag of his cigarette and exhaled an aromatic cloud into the air. "Can never seem to go fast enough on foot. Everything still catches up."

He pushed past me and slid on the headphones he had draped around his neck. "Do yourselves a favor and stay away from Luca. The baby mama's on a warpath, so now he is too."

Callum and Donovan's eyes went wide.

"Dante!" the drummer snapped. "Shut up!"

I blinked. "Luca's a father?"

"That's not our story to tell, sweetheart. You'll have to ask him."

"It's a simple yes or no question."

"And we've taken a vow a silence." Callum glared in Dante's direction. "At least, that was the agreement."

The bassist sniffed and flicked ash to the ground. "Whatever. Fuck that guy."

He popped the cigarette back between his lips and continued on towards the street, but Donovan called after him.

"Where do you think you're going?"

"I told you, I can't breathe," Dante shouted back. "For fuck's sake, just let me be alone for five goddamn minutes."

Donovan glanced at Callum, who shrugged helplessly. "It's your turn."

The guitarist growled in frustration and jogged after Dante, who greeted him with a barrage of furious insults once he'd caught up.

Callum came up beside me as I watched them go and frowned at the figures in the distance.

"I know you want to understand us, angel. But even after ten years, we still don't understand each other. So if you'd like to get through the next few months with your sanity intact, I suggest coming to terms with what this as soon as possible."

"And what is this exactly?"

"A shit show with a killer soundtrack."

22

I sat in on soundcheck that afternoon, happy to have background music accompanying my next attempt at a design. It also meant I was be able to spend time with people besides the hot mess express that was the band. Everyone outside of those four men seemed so normal. Craig was quiet but kind, and Marcus had hilarious stories about when he was a bouncer at a club in London. Eric stole me away from my notebook at one point to show me how to program lighting cues, and Vee was so easy to talk to that I could easily imagine her being a part of me and Kayla's friend group.

The friendliness and normalcy of the crew made Legion all the more confusing. They were surrounded by good, grounded people, but they were a hurricane of emotion, creating chaos wherever they collided. Whenever they would clash, spitting and clawing and hurling insults, the crew didn't even bat an eye. Their expressions weren't worried, but more tired and sad, like they'd seen this movie before and hated how it ended.

The rift between the band was palpable until the music started. Then they sank into the songs, escaping into melodies and riffs until any trace of anger or resentment dissolved. They didn't just play; they felt the music, breathed it. Onstage they weren't at war. They were brothers, their souls so in tune it made your heart ache in want of something similar.

As soon as the music cut out, though, they rocketed back to reality. Luca barked something about everyone being a half-beat late, Donovan and Callum voiced their true feelings to each other in private whispers and hushed laughs, while Dante simply set aside his bass and stormed off the stage.

I was seated on a stool at the empty venue bar, mindlessly scribbling in the corners of my notebook, when Dante joined me. He still hadn't seemed to warm up to me yet, but I appreciated the distance. It had given me time to watch him.

There was something haunting about Dante. With his pale skin, sunken cheeks, and the dark shadows under his eyes, he had a face worthy of a Tim Burton film. But he wasn't a frail, whimsical creature. There was a grittiness to him, something hardened and volatile that might explode at a moment's notice and demolish everything in its path. Despite that, I was drawn to him. I didn't know why, but I desperately wanted to find out.

"You guys sounded good," I greeted him.

"Tell that to fuck-face," Dante replied.

"Sorry, which one is fuck-face again?"

Dante pushed himself onto the bartop and swung his legs over to the other side. When his feet landed on solid ground, he pulled his headphones on and began rummaging through the liquor bottles.

"Are you allowed to be back there?" I asked, scanning the venue for prying eyes.

"Such an angel," he muttered. One hand latched around a bottle of spiced rum while the other grabbed a nearby plastic cup. "Tell me, angel. What went so wrong in your life that you agreed to this harebrained scheme?"

"What went so wrong in yours that you got the word *sinner* blasted on your face?" I bit back.

I wasn't sure what I expected, but it sure as hell wasn't Dante bursting into laughter.

"Too much," he finally answered, pouring an alarmingly large shot for himself and grabbing a second cup for me.

"Same," I muttered.

"Well, cheers to us."

Dante passed me the drink and raised his own before downing it in two gulps. I sipped at mine while he poured himself another.

"You want to elaborate?"

"Nope."

Another shot.

I sighed. "Not gonna lie, this whole mysterious rockstar act you guys've got going on is getting annoying."

"You try living in seclusion for ten years, then add someone else to the mix. It's fucking weird." Dante poured himself a third drink, but his movements slowed as his mouth curved into a frown. "You don't know the shit we've been through. I've been followed home from shows. Callum had his number leaked online. Fans took Donovan's fingerprints off a water bottle and ran them through a database to try and get his name. Luca's had someone blackmailing him for years, all because they want to see his face. You try letting people in after all that."

My walls lowered ever so slightly. When I'd accepted that contract, I was under the impression these men were sex-craved deviants, ready to ravage me whenever they saw fit. But now they were looking a hell of a lot like people who were just as tormented and desperate for release as I was. I don't think Dante had meant his words to be profound, but they made my heart twist with compassion all the same.

"That can't have been easy for you guys," I mumbled. "I'm sorry, I didn't know."

"There's a lot you don't know," Dante murmured into his

drink. He stared at the brown liquid, his frown deepening before he tossed it back.

My phone buzzed, interrupting me before I made a snide remark about Dante's alcohol consumption. I liked a little day drinking just as much as the next girl, but three shots in under two minutes seemed excessive, especially if you were playing a show in a few hours.

Whatever. Not my circus, not my monkeys.

I grabbed my phone and checked the text on the screen, expecting it to be Trent or Kayla. My breath caught when I saw the message.

> MOM: Phil and I miss you. We're willing to forgive all of this if you repent

Nausea punched me in the gut, and my fingers went numb, forcing me to drop my phone to the bar with a clatter.

Dante looked up from the fourth drink he was pouring and raised an eyebrow. "You good?"

"Yeah," I croaked. It felt like someone was squeezing all the air from my lungs with an icy grip, but I painted a smile on. I turned my phone face down, finished the rest of my drink, and gestured to the one in Dante's hand. "Can I?"

He hesitated, eyes narrowing suspiciously, but eventually slid his cup my way. As soon as I took the drink, he snatched my phone from its resting place.

"Hey, give that back!" I snapped, flailing for it, but Dante ducked just out of reach.

He stared down at the message on the screen, his brow furrowing. "Uh-oh. What did you do, angel?"

"I didn't do shit," I hissed, catching the phone, but Dante held firm.

"That's not what mommy thinks."

"And that's why I don't talk to her anymore."

"What happened?"

"None of your business." I finally ripped the phone from his hand and jammed it into the safety of my back pocket. "If I don't get to know about your lives, you don't get to know about mine."

I packed up my sketchbook and pencils and hopped off the barstool, giving Dante my back as I set my sights on a more private part of the venue.

"Catholic school."

I paused, then slowly turned back to Dante. He was leaning a hip against the bar, his eyes glued to the label on the bottle of rum.

"Luca and I met in Catholic school when we were kids. He was the class clown and I was shy, so the nuns paired us up to balance each other out. He latched on like a leech and I've never been able to get rid of him."

I clutched my notebook to my chest and tried to analyze his expression, but it remained a puzzle. "How come? You seem pretty good at pushing people away."

"Yeah, well he's stubborn." Dante absentmindedly scratched at the black polish on his thumbnail. "He liked having someone he could talk to, and I liked that he never made me talk back." He sighed and reached into his pocket in search of his cigarettes. "Now talking is all anyone wants to do. It's so goddamn loud, but people won't stop talking."

A lighter clicked, and a cloud of tobacco filled the air between us. When it cleared, the emptiness behind Dante's stare had lessened.

"There you go. You know a little bit about my life. Now it's your turn." He propped his elbows on the bar and took another drag of the cigarette. A tendril of smoke drifted from his lips as they curled into a taunting sneer. "Tell me. What made this perfect little angel fall from grace?"

I swallowed hard, my head dizzy from the smoke, the buzz of the alcohol, and the pain of the past threatening to claw its way back in. I leaned in to match Dante's stare, yanked the cigarette from his lips, and plopped it into the bottle of rum.

"This is a non-smoking venue."

I spun on my heel and stormed out, praying no one would notice the tears pricking at my lashes.

23

The band was in a foul mood after the show.

Luca was berating everyone for messing up timing, but Dante got the brunt of it.

As someone who wasn't a musician, I hadn't noticed his mistakes. But apparently, no one was pleased with the bassist's performance that evening, and his slurred words explained why. Load-out turned into a war zone of hurtling shouts, swears, and threats of violence, so I retreated to my bunk and put in my headphones in an attempt to drown it out. When I drifted off to sleep, the stress of the day worked its way into my psyche, and my recurring nightmare reared its ugly head again.

Stalks of corn.

The snap of a twig.

A scream for help that no one could hear.

I woke with a gasp, my heart nearly pounding out of my chest. I frantically searched my surroundings for a threat, but when I recognized the interior of the tour bus, I breathed a shaky sigh of relief and wiped the sweat from my forehead.

I was safe. It had been a memory, nothing more.

I gulped air until my heartbeat slowed to a normal rate, then took another look at the bus. Load out was over, and we were on the road again. Donovan and Callum had taken over the back lounge to watch a movie; from my bunk I could see the two of them laying in a heap on the couch, their legs propped up and Callum's head resting on Donovan's chest. In the front lounge, I heard Craig chatting on the phone with his boyfriend, while Luca grumbled things to himself as he tapped at his laptop.

I craned my head so I could see the final member in his bunk. To my surprise, his eyes were already on me.

As per usual, Dante's headphones were jammed over his ears, a heavy metal melody blasting so loud I could make out its thumping beat and guttural screams. With his head propped on a pillow and his arms crossed, Dante stared at me with an expression I'd never seen from him. It wasn't empty, angry, or mocking like he'd shown before. Instead, he looked wary, but curious. He jerked his chin in my direction, a silent question I interpreted as, "Are you ok?"

I swallowed and nodded, forcing the final remnants of the dream back into the recesses of my mind.

Dante's brows pinched together as he studied me, his searing green gaze so intense I had to fight the urge to look away. He eventually beat me to it. He shook his head like he was ridding his mind of something and rolled onto his side away from me.

I stared at his back until sleep came calling again.

The next morning in Seattle, I once again joined Callum and Donovan on their morning run. The sky was overcast and a light drizzle rained down, but the cool weather/cardio combination was a perfect refresher from the night prior. Callum and Dono began to seem more like their happy, playful selves, and in turn, my trepidation from the past few days melted away. The men hadn't tried to make a move on me since the first night Callum and I hooked up, even though they'd frequently made their attraction known with cheeky comments, flirtatious touches, and lingering stares. Their ragged breath created a seductive symphony in my ears, and the dusting of rain and sweat across their skin made my imagination soar. I decided halfway through the workout that I could absolutely get on board with being physical with these two. Had they acted like idiots before? Yes. But they also made me laugh, and were sexy as hell. I was still a little nervous since I didn't know what exactly they had in store for me, but maybe the unknown could be exciting if I just had the guts to embrace it.

"Alright." Donovan clapped his hands together and rubbed them eagerly as we approached the tour bus. "Protein shake, then showers."

I nudged Callum. "Is he a guitarist or a personal trainer?"

"He's a tyrant," the drummer replied with a sigh. "I can't tell you the last time I had some chips and a pint."

"You're denying the man chips?" I cried.

Donovan whirled and flung a finger at Cal. "Don't let this one paint me as the villain. He wants to look like a fucking god, so I get him there."

"You two look amazing." I sneaked a peek at their rock hard backsides. "I think you can afford to cheat every now and then."

Cal glanced over his shoulder and grinned. "I look amazing, huh?"

The adrenaline pumping through my veins fueled my confidence, and I gave him a sly smile back. "So amazing I wish that bus shower was big enough for all of us."

Both men stopped dead in their tracks and faced me, lust blazing in their eyes.

"It might be tight, but we'll fit," Callum said, his voice a low purr.

"Don't worry, darling," Donovan added with a wink. "We'll make sure you're wet enough."

I laughed and rolled my eyes, but subtly squeezed my knees together.

Before any more suggestive words could pass over our lips, the door to the bus swung open and Luca trudged out. Without so much as a "good morning," he pulled his hood over his head and brushed past us.

"Dante's just waking up," he said in passing. "Craig's doing inventory with Vee, so I need you to watch him until I get back."

He continued on towards the street, its sidewalks already bustling with morning foot traffic. I watched him go, then turned back to Callum and Donovan.

"Does that man even know the word please?"

Donovan sighed. "He stopped saying please a long time ago."

"Just another day in the life now," Callum added with a melancholy smile. "Looks like that shower's gonna have to wait, sweetheart."

He and Donovan entered the bus, but I hung back. After a few seconds, I spun and jogged after Luca. I caught a glimpse of him through the crowd, striding purposefully with his hands stuffed in his pockets. I finally managed to catch up when he halted at a stoplight.

"Hey," I greeted, falling in beside him.

His head jerked up at the sound of my voice, his expression a mix of alarm and anger. "What do you want?"

"Coffee." I smiled innocently. "That's where you're going, right? You find a new coffee shop in every city?"

Luca's brows nudged together, either from surprise or irritation that I knew his routine. He faced forward again and glared at the light like that would somehow make it change faster. "Go back to the bus. I'll bring you something if you want it that bad."

"No."

Luca's eyes snapped back to me.

I shrugged. "I want some fresh air."

"And *I* want to be alone."

"We can be alone together."

"That defeats the purpose."

"You won't even know I'm here, I promise. I won't say a word."

I mimed zipping my lips shut and throwing away the key, then pointed at the stoplight, which had changed to green over the course of our conversation. Luca sighed and stormed across the street with me hot on his heels.

We walked for about ten minutes, Luca puffing on a cigarette and pouting the whole way. Eventually, the smell of roasting coffee beans and fresh pastries hit us, and a lively cafe on the corner of a trendy block of the city came into view. Luca tossed his cigarette butt into a nearby flowerpot and entered the building, not bothering to hold the door for me. I glared at the back of his head through the glass as it shut, then yanked it open and stomped in after him.

The mid-century modern interior was classy, yet sleek and simple. The moment he was inside, Luca's demeanor completely changed. The tension drained from his shoulders, and his chin wasn't lifted with its usual smugness. Instead, he seemed at ease, and even donned a smile when he inquired about the day's specials. When he began eagerly discussing Colombian versus Ethiopian beans with the barista, it felt like I was looking at a different man entirely. His eyes lit up with passion, the skin around them crinkling as he laughed at a joke the employee cracked. Until now, I'd never noticed the handful of tiny freckles dotting the high points of Luca's cheeks. I guess I'd always been too heated around him to ever stop and really see him.

Luca ordered a double espresso, then jerked his chin in my direction. "She probably wants a pumpkin spice latte or something like that."

I had to bite my tongue for two reasons. One, because his condescending tone had me fighting the urge to kick him. Two, because he was absolutely right, and I hated that he could read me so well.

I pointed out a salted caramel latte on the menu, but when the barista turned his back, I exchanged it for my middle finger to flip Luca the bird. He just smirked, paid, and went in search of a table.

We claimed a spot in the corner by the window, and when the baristas called out our order, we collected our spoils and settled in. The excitement in Luca's face rivaled that of a kid at Christmas, and it was so cute, I almost forgot what an ass he'd been. I was quickly reminded when Luca lifted his espresso to his lips, blew steam from its surface, and grumbled, "Stop staring. It's annoying."

The asshole was back.

Suddenly inspired, I lifted my mug and slurped at its contents. I was pleased to see it got the reaction I was looking for, and Luca's face contorted with disgust.

"Really?" he asked flatly. "You said you were going to be quiet."

I smacked my lips. "No, I promised I wouldn't say a word. I'm not saying words." I started slurping again, but Luca caught my wrist in his hand.

"Stop." He said it low and soft, but an unspoken warning dripped from the word.

My arousal jolted awake, like it always did when I was in close proximity to Luca, but I wrestled it into submission and yanked my arm free. "Fine. I'll stop."

"Good."

"*If* you talk to me instead."

Luca grunted and scanned the cafe like he was looking for an escape. "For fuck's sake, I can't get a moment's peace."

"I don't have to talk." I nodded to the mug.

Luca's eyes narrowed into slits, and we stared at each other until I couldn't remember the last time I'd blinked. Eventually, a slight smile sneaked onto Luca's lips.

"Ask me nicely," he said.

"Ask you nicely to talk to me?"

"Yes."

I warily squinted at him. This man always had some sort of trick up his sleeve, and I was certain now was no exception. Regardless, I clasped my hands in my lap and cleared my throat.

"Luca will you sit and have a normal conversation with me for once?"

"I said ask nicely."

"That was nice!"

"Not nice enough." Luca motioned to our feet. "You know the drill, angel."

When I realized his meaning, my cheeks flushed. "You want me to get on my knees in a crowded cafe?"

"I always want you on your knees."

My cheeks flushed for a different reason now. "What the hell is wrong with you?"

Luca shrugged cooly and took a sip of his coffee. "You don't have to do it. You're right, it would be pretty embarrassing. I'm used to the attention of a crowd, but you? Little Miss Perfect?" He let out a wry chuckle. "God, that would probably be traumatic for you."

My hands instinctively clenched into fists. "There you go again, acting like you fucking know me."

"Then surprise me."

"You think I won't do it?"

The lead singer chuckled, the sound as sexy as it was infuriating. "Angel, I *know* you won't do it."

My heart began to pound, and I sneaked a peek at the cafe. Slurping my coffee in front of a crowd was one thing, but kneeling in front of a man, debasing myself just to ask if I could speak to him? Luca was right, it would be humiliating. And degrading. And shameful.

So why was I suddenly so turned on?

Before I could second guess my instincts, I leaned forward on my elbows and matched the singer's smug grin. "I'll get in your favorite position and ask nicely. But on one condition."

"What's that?"

"You have to say *please*."

Luca blinked in surprise, and my pride swelled at the scent of victory. But the celebration was short-lived. Luca's hand whipped out, wrapped around the back of my chair, and dragged it around the table so I was positioned beside to him. The screech of the wooden legs against the floor echoed through the cafe, cutting through the hum of chatter to draw everyone's attention our way.

I was mid-protest when Luca leaned in, caught my jaw with his free hand, and pushed his face so close I felt his breath on my lips.

"Angel," he said quietly, his voice a seductive threat as he punctuated each word. "Get. On. Your. Fucking. Knees." His mouth moved to my ear and grazed the delicate skin. *"Please."*

I had no control over the full-body shudder that whispered word caused. Still, I couldn't let him win.

Casually, I lifted my napkin and let it flutter to the ground.

"Oops," I giggled before slipping out of my chair and dropping to my knees. I made a scene of fumbling for the cloth, mumbling only loud enough for Luca to hear, "Can I have a normal conversation with you over coffee?"

A mixture of amusement and frustration washed over Luca's face at my discovery of the loophole. Not one to take a loss lying down, Luca shook his head.

"You didn't say please."

I snatched up the napkin. "Please."

"Please, *Master*."

"Don't push your luck." I returned to my seat and brushed grit from my knees. "There. I did it."

"Good girl," Luca crooned. He smiled to himself when I unintentionally bit my lip at the praise. "Not exactly what I had in mind, but I'll give it to you. What do you want to talk about?"

"Dante."

Luca's face fell. "No."

"I'm not stupid. There's an obvious rift between the band. I don't know if Dante's the one who caused it, but he's certainly not helping it."

"That topic's off limits," Luca snapped. "We butt heads, but even Cal and Dono agree we don't discuss Dante."

Trying to hide my disappointment, I chose a different attack. "Alright. You can tell me about your kid, then."

Luca's shoulders tensed. "Who told you about that?"

"Dante."

He hissed an expletive through is teeth and ran his fingers through his hair.

"We either talk about your bassist," I pressed, "or your kid and your ex. It's your choice."

"Can't we just talk about coffee?"

"I don't really care about how dark roast differs from light. I care about the people I'm surrounding myself with for the next couple months." I pushed my mug aside and leaned forward. "Listen. You've made it very clear you didn't hire me to be your friend. I know I'm only a distraction so you don't murder each other before tour's over. I just want to make this experience as enjoyable as possible for all of us, and for me that means knowing you all a little deeper. I'm ok with not being your friend, but I'm not ok with being a stranger. The stranger was the man in the mask, but that mask is off now."

Luca sat as still as a statue, staring at the tabletop like the grooves in the wood spelled out the words he was searching for. After awhile, he sighed and shifted his gaze to the window.

"She's not my ex. It was a one time thing."

A heavy pause followed, stretching so long I wondered if Luca had decided not to continue, but eventually, he did.

"She was a fan at the Richmond date a few years back, a girl I singled out in the front row. Afterwards, I had Marcus find her and bring her back to the green room. I flirted with her a little, then one thing led to another. It was quick, and I kept the mask on, like I always do in those scenarios."

The image of him stumbling in with the female fan at the San Jose date flashed into my mind, sparking an irrational pang of jealousy.

"We hooked up and I didn't think anything of it." Luca frowned and absentmindedly toyed with one of his rings. "A month later we got a DM on the band page. The message said, 'pay up, asshole' with a photo of a positive pregnancy test."

"Holy shit," I mumbled.

"Yeah." Luca sniffed wryly. "She said she'd waive the child support if I sent her a picture of my face. The Beast in his true form, as she described it."

The singer shrugged and took a sip of coffee, but it didn't disguise the pain in his eyes. "I told her to fuck off. Said I'd pay whatever I needed to, but she'd never see my face. She's been trying to take me for all I've got ever since. She keeps raising her rate, and when I fight back, she threatens to go public. So I give her what she wants no matter the cost, financially or emotionally."

Now I knew why he'd been so against taking off his mask the day I signed the contract.

"Are you sure the kid's yours?" I asked. "Have you done a paternity test?"

"No." Luca fidgeted in his seat. "I asked for one, and she said she'd set up an appointment. But if I did that, then she'd see my face, and my full name would be on the lab report."

"What about a home test? I'm pretty sure they have those. Can't you do it yourself?"

"She won't send me a DNA sample." Luca downed his coffee like it was a shot of liquor and wiped his mouth. "Believe me, I've thought of everything."

I leaned back in my seat and huffed a slow exhale. "What does your family think?"

Luca's expression grew even darker. "I don't speak to my family anymore."

"Why?"

"They're embarrassed of me."

"Being the lead singer of one of the most successful rock bands in the world is something to be embarrassed of?"

"When you're a family of strict Catholics, yes. You think my little Italian Nonna goes to mass and brags about the grandson who screams into a microphone about sex while pretending to be the devil?"

"I guess not."

I may want to smack the man sometimes, but it was starting to be painfully obvious that Luca and I shared similarities. We were both perfectionists. We both had a competitive streak. And now this.

"I'm the black sheep of my family too," I muttered, picking at a crumb on the tabletop. "Last time I spoke to my mom in person was two years ago. I believe one of the things she said as I walked away was, 'Satan has his claws in you.'" I sighed wearily. "So I guess I'll be seeing you in the fires of hell."

Luca cracked a grin. "At least we'll have good music."

We laughed a little, and for a split second, life seemed normal. There were no contracts. No masks. Just two people connecting in a coffee shop, finding a hint of sweetness in the bitterness of the past. But then Luca's phone rang, and the moment was shattered.

"Shit." Luca eyed the screen. "It's the label. Hang on a sec."

He hit a button and lifted the phone to his ear. "This is the Beast."

I couldn't hear any distinct words from the man on the other end, but his slick, car-salesman-like tone was evident.

"Tour's good. Entirely sold out. I think next time around we'll have to move up to stadiums... The what? ... Oh, the protests. I thought you said they weren't a big deal? No publicity is bad publicity, right? ... Fuck 'em, let them cry about it. We're not cancelling shit. ... The next album?"

Luca's expression fell, and he pushed back from the table to create slightly more privacy. I was still able to get the gist of the conversation.

"No, we don't have a single off of it yet. ... I'll get it to you when I can... Yeah, I know, I just don't think that deadline is realistic... I don't know, ok? We've got a lot going on and... I realize that, but... A single isn't a priority right now and neither is an album, ok? We're just trying to get through this tour. If you're not happy, then fucking drop us."

Luca smashed his thumb into the end button, shoved the phone back into his pocket, and stood.

"We're going," he barked, stalking towards the door.

Normal was nice while it lasted.

24

The shows in Seattle and Spokane were the same as Portland; Dante drank too much, Luca turned into a whirlwind of rage, and Donovan and Callum pulled even farther away from them both. But even the two Brits began to feel the strain, and they started randomly bickering about minuscule things. I clung to Vee the majority of the time, or Eric in the sound booth, and I even went so far as smoking cigarettes with Marcus and the driver Randy so I didn't have to be in the bus while four men screamed at each other inside. I spent the rest of my time texting Kayla or trying to draw up designs like I'd been hired to, but the only images I could conjure on paper were instruments in a burning heap.

By the time we got to Bozeman, Montana for the start of two days off, all of us were beyond ready for a break. We arrived at an upscale hotel with a view of the mountains in the early morning, and we all retreated to our separate rooms for some much needed personal space. The label hadn't calculated my presence when booking the accommodations, so I was without my own room, but Callum kindly offered to give up his and sleep in Donovan's.

I spent the day at the hotel gym, running and lifting weights until my brain stopped chattering so loud. I tried to nap too, but the recurring nightmare reared its head, and images of a corn field and a bottle of pills in a bathtub kept me from attempting again.

Part of me expected to hear a knock on my door at some point. I assumed I'd open it to find someone cashing in on the deal I'd struck with the devil. Antsy with anticipation, I perked up any time I heard footsteps outside the door, then wilted when they walked away. I thought it was insecurity that made my heart heavy, but after digging deeper, I realized it was disappointment.

Over the past few days, I'd found myself thinking more and more about being with each man. Callum and I had already hooked up, and it was wonderful. I don't think I'd ever experienced foreplay so fun, and I'd definitely never come that fast. I was too prideful to admit it to any of the guys, but I was chomping at the bit to have him again, especially now that I'd gotten to know him better.

Donovan was so similar to Callum that I assumed being intimate with him would be a similar experience; effortless and comfortable, with lots of laughter that morphed into moans. He was so tall he'd completely envelop me, making it feel like nothing else existed in that moment except us.

And if Luca was the one who came to the door? God, I'd be unhinged with Luca. Even when he pissed me off, I couldn't deny the pull between us. I wanted to scream at him as much as I wanted him to fuck me senseless, and it was driving me insane. My mind raced with the possibilities of what might happen if we finally gave in and released whatever the hell it was we were holding back. Would we murder each other, or break the bed?

Even Dante had crept into my thoughts. There was something behind those tortured eyes of his, something I couldn't quite put my finger on. It was something dark, and made my own darkness perk up in recognition. Maybe this was just the classic tale of the moth drawn to the flame. Maybe I was drifting towards a painful lesson that would leave me broken in the end. But maybe I didn't care. Maybe I wanted to burn.

God, I sounded crazy.

I decided to research symptoms of Stockholm Syndrome in the morning, then turned off the TV, brushed my teeth, and crawled into bed.

Alone.

25

Sleeping in a queen-sized bed after a week of a cramped bunk can work wonders for someone's mood.

I slept a solid ten hours and woke feeling refreshed and rejuvenated. I bounded out of bed in the morning and threw on a sports bra, shorts, and tennis shoes before heading down to the hotel's free continental breakfast. We had another day off in Montana, and I was going to make the most of it. My plan was to start with a hearty meal, then I'd hit the gym for a workout that would get my legs shaking, since apparently no man was going to do it.

When I got to the lobby, I stopped in my tracks when I discovered Luca already there. He didn't notice me, too busy scribbling in a notebook while a plate of eggs, sausage, and fruit sat on the table in front of him. His shoulder length waves were pulled back in a top knot, and he'd shaved his face and trimmed his undercut. His only accessories were his tattoos, his typical rings missing from an ensemble made up of gray sweatpants and a tight white tee.

I scanned the rest of the space, but no one else from the tour package was there. They were probably still sleeping, or had already gone into the city to explore. Warily watching Luca out of the corner of my eye, I slid into line and began loading up my plate, but he still didn't see me. With his brows pinched over his eyes as he focused on the words he was writing, he looked oddly normal. Still ungodly hot, but he could have been any regular Joe enjoying breakfast in a hotel lobby.

A good night's rest had put the fire back in my soul, and I decided that toying with Luca would be a fun addition to my day's activities. I grabbed two paper cups and filled them with the burnt-smelling lobby coffee before topping them off with cream and sugar. Then I turned and pranced over to Luca's table, plopped down in the seat across from him, and slid one over to him.

"Sorry, they didn't have pumpkin spice. I know that's your favorite."

Luca blinked at the milky liquid swirling in the cup, then looked up at me. I wasn't sure if he was grimly amused or tempted to commit a homicide.

"If you think I'm putting that in my mouth, you're insane."

"I've said that before." I used a fork to stab a grape off his plate. "Whatcha working on?"

Luca closed the notebook and set it aside. I thought he'd say something snippy back, but he only sighed and rubbed his temples. "Lyrics. The label wants a single to promote the next album ASAP."

"Is there even going to be a next album?"

At that, Luca's face hardened. "What did Donovan and Callum say?"

"No one needs to say anything. You told me yourself this is a sinking ship. Everyone can see you guys are miserable."

Luca opened his mouth to argue, but eventually sighed and looked away.

"Hope is a funny thing. Even when you think it's gone, a

spark stays behind." He shrugged. "But it's still early in the tour. Ask me next week and I might have a different answer."

"Jade!"

I looked over my shoulder to see Chase crossing the lobby towards us. I smiled and waved, prompting Luca to grunt his disapproval. My head whipped back to him.

"Play nice," I demanded.

Chase plopped down at our table before Luca could reply. "So how was it spending the night in a bed after a week on the road?"

"She loved it," Luca answered for me, hinting I spent said night with him.

I kicked him under the table.

Chase turned to Luca and blinked like he was seeing him for the first time. "Oh hey, Luke."

"Luca."

Chase nodded and propped his elbows on the tabletop. "Right. My bad. You're one of the techs for Legion."

"Yup."

"How do you like it?"

"Love it. Best job in the world."

"Really? That's surprising."

"Why do you say that?"

"I don't know. They just seem so… " Chase raised his eyes to the ceiling and chewed his lip as he considered his words. "Intense."

God, if he only knew.

"They're passionate about their job," Luca replied, adopting the measured tone of a diplomat.

"That's a nice way of putting it," Chase chuckled.

The smile stayed glued on Luca's face, but his eyes narrowed into a glare. "I feel like there's more you want to say."

"I dunno man, I just don't get all the insane secrecy. I understand they've got this whole gimmick going on, but not even introducing yourselves to the other bands on your package? That's crazy."

"They want to keep their identities a secret," Luca countered. "What's so bad about that?"

"It's just rude. We're all family out here on the road."

"Maybe they already have their family and they don't need to bring anyone else in."

"They brought *her* in." Chase jerked his thumb in my direction.

"She's a talented artist who's creating something that captures a carefully crafted brand," Luca bit back. "She's invaluable. But other bands are only prying eyes and gossiping mouths. The more people who know their identity, the more likely that identity is to get leaked."

Chase's cheery demeanor melted as he motioned to me again. "So they don't trust their peers, but they trust some random girl? That's messed up."

"What's messed up is that you've disrespected Jade twice in the last ten seconds by diminishing her worth and conveniently forgetting her name now that she has nothing to offer you. I suggest you apologize to that *random girl*, or you'll have to cancel the rest of your shows because your face has been beaten to a pulp."

Both Chase and I stared at Luca in shock. His calm demeanor was an eerie contrast to the violence in his words and the ice in his stare.

"Jesus, even Legion's crew are psychos." Chase pushed away from the table and stood, offering me his hand. "Let's get out of here. Me and the boys are gonna hit up a few breweries. These aren't the kind of people you want to surround yourself with."

I blinked up at him, then peeked at Luca.

"Thank you for your concern," I finally said. "But I'm not some damsel in need of saving. I can handle myself just fine."

Chase balked, making me wonder if it was the first time a woman had ever told him no.

"Whatever," he mumbled, spinning on his heel. "Don't say I didn't warn you."

I watched him disappear out the front doors, then turned back to Luca. "So threatening to beat the shit out of someone is your idea of playing nice?"

"Fuck that guy," Luca hissed through gritted teeth, still watching Chase's retreating form. "No one goes after what's mine."

"Are you referring to me or your band?"

"Both."

His gaze flicked to me and held, making my heart pick up speed. When I found the strength to break the spell and look away, I cleared my throat and stole another piece of fruit from Luca's plate.

"I still don't see why you care if someone else touches your toy. It's not like you're using it."

"Is that what you want, angel? You want to be used?"

My stomach dipped at his seductive tone, but I feigned indifference and shrugged. "Why else would I be here?

"Emotional masochism."

"Maybe a little of that too."

I dared to meet Luca's gaze again. His eyes were glazed with lust, thickening the air the longer we stared at each other. Unable to resist the pull of his gravity any longer, I leaned forward and lowered my voice.

"Tell me, is the devil ever planning to come and collect?"

After a pause, Luca slowly leaned in too. He stopped when our faces were mere inches apart, his stare never breaking from mine. "The devil always takes what he's owed."

"Doesn't look like it."

In one quick move, Luca's foot slid between my sneakers and

kicked my legs apart. I gasped in surprise and gripped the table to steady myself.

Luca shook his head and mockingly clicked his tongue. "God, look at you. You're just desperate for my cock, aren't you?"

My cheeks flushed, and I nervously scanned the lobby to make sure no one had overheard his words. But Luca didn't seem to care if they did. He moved his hands under the table to alight on my knees. My breath hitched at his touch, but I didn't pull away. Instead, I licked my lips and pretended I was unenthused by his fingertips, even though they were firing every nerve and pleasure receptor in my body.

"I'm just making an observation," I cooed. "For a bunch of sex-starved demons, you're pretty bad at having sex."

Luca chuckled, but his hands showed no amusement and roughly wedged my legs further apart. I pressed my lips together and shot the room another wary glance. My heart was pounding, the sensitive spot between my legs twinging along with it. I didn't want anyone to see what was happening below the table, but I also didn't want it to stop.

As if reading my mind, Luca inched his hands further up my thighs, so slow and subtle that no one would notice but me.

"I've warned you about that bratty mouth of yours, angel."

I rolled my eyes. "Oh please, what are you going to do?"

"Fill it."

"Again, I hear a lot of talk but don't see any follow through."

It was a blatant lie. Luca's hands had traveled up most of my inner thighs and were nearing their apex, a fact he reminded me of by raking his nails down the tender skin. I had to bite my cheek so I wouldn't let out a moan.

"Such a needy little slut," he purred. His fingers continued their journey, increasing the pressure in my core. "Admit it. You're aching to have my cock inside you."

Yes.

"No." I matched his smirk with one of my own. "Couldn't care less."

"How many times have you fantasized about me taking you against that wall the night we kissed?"

Twelve.

"Zero. Haven't thought about it again."

"You're a terrible liar." Luca's fingers were dangerously close to my clit. "How far do you want to push this, angel? I'm used to a crowd of onlookers, but I'm not sure you could handle it. Especially not the one that would gather to watch me finger-fuck you into submission."

Jesus. He wouldn't go that far.

Would he?

Would I let him?

Luca teased the hem of my shorts, making me wriggle in my seat. I was unsure whether it was from trying to get away, or trying to rid my body of the maddening desire pulsing through it with each brush of his thumb.

"I don't lose," I warned him.

"Neither do I."

Luca's index finger maneuvered under the hem of my shorts, making my breath catch. Our stares still hadn't broken, but there was more intensity in our eyes now. It was as if we were both asking each other if we were really doing this, if we were finally going to cross this line and face the consequences, whatever they might be. Or maybe that was just me projecting onto the situation. Either way, I knew what I wanted.

I quickly scanned the room for peeping toms, then returned my attention to Luca, adopted a look of angelic innocence, and spread my legs wider as an invitation. A tense beat passed, then a hungry smile spread across Luca's face. His hand moved forward.

Bzzzz.

Both of us exhaled sharply when the singer's phone vibrated

against the table, breaking the enchantment and rocketing us back to reality. We simultaneously sat back in our seats as Luca cleared his throat and checked the screen. With a heavy sigh, he lifted it to his ear.

"What's up, Vee?"

I sipped at my coffee, trying to focus on the taste instead of the wet spot in my shorts Luca had been milliseconds away from discovering.

"I saw him last night when I checked on him before bed." Luca's expression darkened. "Have you asked Craig?"

To give him some privacy, I checked my own phone.

> TRENT: I'm gonna burn all your shit

> KAYLA: Ok be honest, should I go for Vee?

> MOM: I know you'll find your way back to us. Today the Lord reminded me of the parable of the Prodigal Son...

"Well, when was the last time you saw him?" Luca sat up straight, his brow furrowed with worry. "Why didn't you check on him first thing this morning?"

I gave up pretending to be busy and set my phone down. Luca was growing increasingly agitated.

"Have you tried calling him? Maybe he got drunk last night and he's just sleeping it off... Yeah, I'll go look... Ok, see you there."

Luca hung up and immediately bolted for the elevators. I hurried after him.

"What's going on?" I asked.

Luca repeatedly smashed the "up" button like that would somehow make it go faster. "Nobody knows where Dante is."

"Is that bad?"

The elevator arrived and we darted inside.

"Dante's never alone." Luca repeatedly prodded the twelfth

floor and stepped back to watch the numbers creep upwards. "Things happen when he's alone."

"What kinds of things?"

"Bad things." He crossed his arms, anxiety transitioning into anger. "Why the fuck is this thing so slow?"

"I'm sure Dante's fine," I assured him. "He's probably just sleeping in."

"Dante doesn't sleep." Luca checked his phone, then slapped his palm against the button again. "Fuck! Come *on*."

When the elevator jerked to a halt and the doors opened, Luca raced down the hall like he was being chased by the devil himself. I had to sprint to catch up to him.

We skidded to a halt in front of a door at the end of the corridor, where Luca began furiously pounding on the thick wood.

"Dante, open up!" he barked.

No question, no greeting. Just a single demand that echoed through the hotel.

When the door didn't budge, Luca hammered his fist against it, rattling its hinges.

"Dante!" he shouted. "Open the fucking door!"

"Hey!" Vee's voice cut through the building tension. She raced up behind us, sheer terror written on her face. "Did you find him?"

Luca continued to pound against the door.

"Vee, what's going on?" I asked, my heart beating in time with his fists. "What's wrong?"

"We can't find my cousin." Vee frantically wrung her hands before trying Dante's number again on her cell.

"But why is that—"

"Fuck!" Luca exclaimed.

Vee and I followed his gaze to a puddle of water expanding beneath the hotel room door.

"Oh, god." Vee clapped a hand over her mouth. "It's just like last time."

Her statement sent Luca into a frenzy.

"Dante!" he screamed, unaffected by all the people poking their heads out of their rooms to see what the commotion was. "For fuck's sake, Dante, open the goddamn door!"

"He was doing ok," Vee muttered to herself. "He wasn't great, but he was ok. He was supposed to be ok…"

Luca began slamming the heel of his shoe against the door, and the only thing I could think to do was wrap my arm around Vee's shoulders and pull her in tight. The hinges on the door creaked, and the wood groaned against Luca's force.

Without warning, the door flung open, and Dante stumbled out.

His curls were mussed and matted, while dark bags decorated the skin below his bloodshot eyes. He swayed on his feet, blinking at the light in the hall for a few seconds before focusing on Luca in front of him.

"What?"

If his movement and speech weren't enough, the scent of him alone informed everyone what he'd been up to. Being within two feet of him was like sticking your nose in a bottle of vodka.

"What the fuck?" Luca panted, his chest heaving. "Why didn't you answer?"

Dante slumped against the doorframe. "Didn't hear."

Water continued to pour out of the room behind him, soaking the carpet beneath our feet. Vee released me and pushed past Dante, and within a few seconds, the flow of water slowed. When she returned, she couldn't look her cousin in the eye.

"Bathtub was overflowing," she muttered.

At that, Luca's face went pale. "Jesus."

"I forgot about it," Dante said with a shrug. "My bad."

"Bullshit," Luca snapped. He was shaking, but I wasn't sure if it was from rage or residual panic. "I thought you were good!"

"I *am* good," Dante slurred. "I just forgot, ok?"

"It's ten in the morning and you're drunk," Vee cried. "You're not fucking good!"

At that, Dante's eyes darkened. "Fuck off."

He tried to slam the door, but Luca shoved his foot in the way.

"You've lost the privilege of being alone."

"I'll stay with him," Vee offered, her voice still wavering.

"No." Luca pried the door out of Dante's hands. "I will. I never should've trusted him anyway."

"Fuck you," Dante spat. It was then his gaze landed on me, noticing me for the first time. He huffed a grim laugh. "Ever wanted to know what hell looks like, angel? Get a good look."

Before Dante could say anything else, Luca shoved him into the room and followed behind. He caught my eye just before the door shut, a wordless apology in his pointed stare. Then a battered slab of wood closed between us, and he was gone.

Vee inhaled a shuddering breath and patted my hand.

"Come on, I'll take you back to your room."

From the look on her face, she needed it more than I did, so I didn't protest. We walked to the elevator in silence, but when we filed inside and pressed the button to my floor, I turned to her.

"What just happened?"

Vee rubbed her forehead. "We're a private bunch. We don't talk about—"

"Anything!" I blurted. "And it's tearing you all apart."

The doors opened to my floor and we stepped out.

"I know. It's just…" Vee thought for a few seconds before setting her jaw. "Alright, fine."

Taking my arm in hers, she led the way to my room, walking slow so we had time to speak.

"My cousin hasn't had the easiest life. He was a good kid for awhile, but over the years, he started having some behavioral issues. It was little stuff at first, like he'd set things on fire or carve swear words in the church pews. But then in high school, it escalated. He started stealing my mom's painkillers and got kicked off the soccer team because he was always high. Luca's always tried to protect him, but he couldn't seem to protect him from himself. When the guys met Dono and Ca, and their music started taking off, certain things became more accessible to them. Money. Girls. Substances. And don't get me wrong, I'm not going to pretend to be innocent. We all took part. But Dante liked the drugs a little too much. For a few years, it was fine. It wasn't a problem as long as he was in a good place mentally. He was the life of the party. But if he *wasn't* in a good place…"

Vee stopped in front of my door and hung her head. "Well, one night we found out just how dark things were inside Dante's head. He used to disappear all the time to go get high, so when we couldn't find him, we hadn't thought anything of it. But walking by his hotel room one night, we noticed a puddle." Her words were strangled, and tears filled her eyes. "We had to call the front desk to let us inside. When they did, we found Dante passed out in a tub with a razor in his hand."

Air whooshed from my lungs. The picture she'd painted of Dante's past looked eerily similar to my own. The memory of sitting in an empty tub and sobbing over a bottle of pills flashed across my mind.

"Luca dragged Dante out," Vee continued. "I was a wreck, but he told me to call 911 and applied pressure until the paramedics showed up."

"I'm so sorry, Vee," I breathed, shaking my head. "I had no idea."

"Yeah, they don't like to talk about it. We didn't even tell Callum or Donovan right away, they found out on their own. And to be honest, I don't think they've ever forgiven the others for keeping it from them." Vee shrugged and forced a pained smile. "But that was years ago. Dante got off drugs, and Luca made us all swear we wouldn't bring any around to tempt him."

"Why didn't you ban alcohol too?"

"My cousin needs some form of outlet or he'll burn the world down. He has music, but shows are only a small part of the day. So we let him have one vice, and we all take turns making sure he doesn't relapse." Vee slumped against the door. "I get why he resents us. Really, I do. It has to be humiliating having your friends and family treat you like a toddler they're babysitting. But we do it out of love. The night we almost lost him, I got a glimpse of what life would be like without him in it, and I never want to experience it again. If that means he has to hate me, then so be it. At least he's safe."

I leaned against the wall next to her. "He's lucky to have you."

Vee shrugged and examined her chipped nail polish. "No, he's lucky to have Luca. He's fought tooth and nail for my cousin, ever since they were kids. He's given so much of himself to keep Dante afloat, I'm worried there won't be anything left of him pretty soon."

All of Luca's outbursts and barked demands made a little more sense now. All of this on top of what was happening in his personal life? Hell, if that was me, I'd be an asshole too. It didn't excuse Luca's behavior, but at least now I understood it.

"Anyway," Vee sighed. "I'm sorry you got roped into this. I know this isn't what you signed up for. But could you do me and Luca a favor? Don't mention this to Callum or Donovan."

I frowned. "This affects them too, though. The band is a family, they need to know what's happening."

Vee shook her head sadly. "They haven't been a family for a long time, Jade."

She squeezed my arm and retreated down the hall, leaving me alone with my warring thoughts.

26

I was distracted for the rest of the day. I'd find myself zoning out during my workout, absentmindedly wandering the halls of the hotel, or drawing random scribbles in my notebook instead of working on a viable design. I wanted to check on Luca and Dante, but I knew my presence probably wouldn't be welcome. There were two men I knew I *would* be welcome with, though.

Once evening hit, I showered and made my way down the hall to Donovan and Callum's room. I was still struggling with Vee's request not to tell them what happened, and wasn't sure if I was going to honor it or not. Regardless, I wanted to see them. They always managed to brighten my day, and I desperately needed a little sunshine after the events of the past few hours.

I stopped in front of their room and knocked, and after a few seconds the door opened, revealing Callum in the doorway. He was dressed in a tee shirt and black jeans, but his hands were covered by latex gloves.

"Hi." He beamed and beckoned for me to enter. "This is a nice surprise."

"Yeah, I was bored and wanted to see if you guys want to grab dinner."

"Sure. We can go as soon as I'm finished with Dono's tattoo." Callum waggled his gloved fingers and led the way further into the room. Donovan was sitting on the edge of the bed in nothing but a pair of gym shorts, one leg rolled up to expose his bare thigh. A partially finished image was freshly engraved in his skin, a tattoo gun and ink resting on the desk beside him. Even though he was in the middle of a video chat with his sister Emilia, he smiled and waved at me as I followed Callum in.

Donovan winced slightly as Callum knelt in front of him, took up the tattoo gun, and brought the needle to skin again. "Em, I was thinking of finally coming for a visit after this tour's over. Maybe around Christmas?"

"We're pretty busy that time of year."

"Alright, then how about I fly you all out in the new year? You could stay with me and sip cocktails on the beach while I teach the kids to surf."

"We'd stay with you and Callum?"

He kept his eyes glued to his work, but Callum's shoulders tensed at the mention of his name. Donovan glanced at him briefly, a flicker of worry in his eyes.

"Yeah, we bought that place in Malibu together. Remember?"

He was met with silence. The longer it stretched, the more Donovan's smile dimmed, and the more uncomfortable Callum grew. Finally, Emilia cleared her throat.

"It's late. I have to get to bed. Lizzie's got ballet in the morning."

Donovan frowned. "I thought she had ballet on Wednesdays."

"Good night, Dono."

"Right. Yeah, good night. I love you. Thanks for chatting."

"Uh-huh."

"Give my love to the kids—"

There was a beep, and the line went dead.

Donovan tossed his phone onto a nearby pillow and ruffled Callum's hair. "Don't let it get to you, babe."

"Never do," Callum mumbled, glaring at the section of shading he was working on.

I lowered onto the bed and watched Callum work until the silence grew too heavy, and Donovan reached out to squeeze my knee.

"I know you want to ask and don't know how, so I'll beat you to the punch."

Callum peeked up at him, and Donovan gave him a small, sad smile back.

"Not everyone's as open-minded as us, angel. To a lot of people, love has to be one way. They can't accept terms like bisexual or pansexual, even if it comes from their own family." Donovan met my gaze and offered a weary shrug. "My sister's been like this since the day she caught me and Cal snogging in that coat closet. I know things may never change, but I love her, and I'll never stop trying to show her that."

My heart twinged at the pain behind Donovan's eyes, but it soared at the strength and hope in his smile. I slid my hand into his and wove our fingers together.

"You're pretty amazing, you know that?"

Donovan's face fell and he ducked his head. "Not quite, darling. I've made a lot of mistakes. I just don't want this to be one of them."

He shared a moment with Callum, who gave him a slight nod and returned to the image he was working on.

"Now that's enough of that. To what do we owe the pleasure of such a beautiful woman's company?"

Donovan's vulnerability was making it difficult to lie. He'd trusted me enough to be honest with me, so I had to do the same.

"Vee told me about Dante," I stated.

The tattoo gun clicked off.

"Why would she—" Callum began, but after searching my face, his expression grew solemn. With a sigh, he hung his head. "It's getting bad again, isn't it?"

I looked away and toyed with the hem of my tee shirt. "I don't know what he's typically like, but I know Luca was really freaked out."

"Shit," Donovan mumbled, catching Callum's eye. "Looks like you were right."

"Told you." Cal set the tattoo gun aside and ripped off his gloves. "I swear, death brought us together and death is going to tear us apart."

Donovan smacked his shoulder and hissed a warning.

"What do you mean, death brought you together?" I asked, my brow furrowing.

The two exchanged glances before Donovan adopted a charming smile and knocked my chin with his knuckles. "No need for you to worry your pretty little head about that, darling. You've dealt with enough today."

I wanted to argue, but found myself grateful for the distraction after the day's events. I playfully batted his hand away.

"Do you always have to be so mysterious?"

"This is what you signed up for. Better get used to it."

"It made more sense when the masks were on," I mumbled, watching Callum gently blot the excess ink from Donovan's thigh before bandaging it with translucent film.

Looking at each member of Legion, you'd assume they were rough, tough, and incapable of any form of intimacy. But seeing Callum and Donovan now completely changed the narrative in my brain. They exchanged delicate caresses and cheeky smiles, and understood the other's thoughts and feelings with nothing but an expression. Something about their bond made me feel a strange sense of homesickness. My whole life, I'd craved something like what they had, and after years of nothing remotely close to it, somewhere along the way I'd convinced myself that what I wanted was unobtainable. But seeing their comfortability, openness, and easy intimacy, I saw that it *was*. It ignited a spark of hope in my soul that I hadn't felt in a very long time.

Clocking my stare, Donovan slid his hand onto my knee. "You know, we could always put the masks back on if you'd prefer."

It was the same silky, seductive tone he'd spoken in the first night we'd met, and it made my stomach flip the same way it had then.

"I'm alright," I replied. "If you had a mask, I couldn't do this."

I leaned in and popped a kiss on Donovan's cheek. When I pulled back, his hand whipped out and caught me by the jaw, stopping me. We stared at each other for a few beats before the corner of Donovan's mouth tugged upwards in a soft smile. Slowly, he leaned in and pressed his lips to mine. They were warm and pillowy soft, and made my stomach roll with butterflies. When Donovan broke away, his eyes were still closed to savor the moment.

"God, I've been wanting to do that since the moment I saw you," he breathed.

A flush crept into my cheeks. "Really?"

"Yep," Callum answered for him, still kneeling at our feet. "We even talked about it that night."

"You did?"

"Mm-hmm," Donovan mumbled, opening his eyes to stare at my lips like he craved another taste. "We went home and stayed awake talking about all the filthy things we wanted to do to you."

My blush intensified. "What did you come up with?"

The men exchanged glances, and a devilish smile spread over Callum's face. He turned back to me and sidled forward so that he was kneeling between my legs instead of Donovan's, his hands planted on either side of me.

"We could tell you," he murmured, his voice low and husky, "or we could show you."

My blood heated. "Both of you would show me?"

"Would that be alright with you?"

The muscles low in my belly clenched eagerly, but I played coy. "Give me a preview and I'll decide."

Donovan chuckled and sat back, bracing his hands on the bed behind him. "So demanding. I think we're gonna have to teach this one some manners, Cal."

"I'm counting on it." Callum began massaging my thigh, relaxing the tight muscles and making it difficult to keep my appreciative moans silenced. "Now, where were we?"

Donovan watched us closely as he continued his story. "That night you showed up in the green room, you took our breath away."

"But I'd just come from the gym," I muttered.

"Doesn't matter. You're radiant in any situation. Are you going to let me finish, or do you want to keep interrupting?"

I pressed my lips shut.

"Good girl," Callum crooned, his hand sliding a little higher and causing a twinge in my core.

Donovan readjusted on the bed, angling his head so he could better view Callum's activity. "When Cal and I got home, you were all we could talk about. We sat on our patio overlooking the sea, brainstorming all the positions we'd like to get you in."

I readjusted in my seat in the hopes it would disguise my growing arousal. "What positions?"

"I believe I mentioned something a little like this." Donovan nodded to Callum wedged between my legs. "Only when I described it, you were wearing significantly less."

Any nerves were overshadowed by a rush of excitement and anticipation. I licked my lips and spread my legs wider. "Show me."

Callum landed a quick rap on my thigh. I jerked at the sudden sting.

"Where are those manners?" he reprimanded. "Ask me again. *Nicely.*"

I rolled my eyes, earning myself another smack. I gasped as pain morphed into a jolt of pleasure.

"*Please* show me," I conceded.

"That's better."

In one swift move, Callum hooked his thumbs in my waistband, yanked my shorts down my hips, and tossed them to the floor. The seamless thong I was wearing offered no protection as he settled between my thighs and pressed his pelvis against the tender flesh.

"Something like this?" Callum asked Donovan without breaking our gaze. His chest began to rise and fall faster, and the bulge in his jeans hardened slightly, increasing the ache in my core.

"Exactly like that." Donovan propped himself up on his elbows to watch us. "I told Cal I wanted to see him on his knees just like this, grinding his cock against you as he kissed your neck. His mouth sinking lower and lower..."

Following along with Donovan's words, Callum dropped his head to the crook of my neck and planted kisses across my skin. When he rolled his body against mine, my lips parted to release a breathy moan. Beside us, Donovan chuckled.

"That feel good, angel?"

Basking in the sensation, I nodded.

"Should I keep going?"

When I nodded again, Callum peeled himself away from me. "Use your words, sweetheart."

I let out an indignant huff at his absence, to which he responded by smacking the inside of my thigh the way he had before. It stung, but it also shot a pang of adrenaline through my body that increased my building arousal.

"Manners," Callum scolded, extending his index finger in warning.

Flustered and frustrated, I instinctively nipped at his finger. He yanked it out of reach just in time, a rumble of laughter resonating in his chest.

"Oh, you're in for it now." He looked to Donovan and raised an eyebrow. "Three?"

"I was thinking five."

"Five it is."

"Five what?" I asked warily.

Callum only smiled and slid further down my body. When he reached my hips, he hooked my panties and pulled them aside. His breath puffed against the delicate skin, making me squirm as the ache inside screamed with need.

"Cal here is going to do what he does best," Donovan replied, maneuvering behind me so his chest was pressed to my back. I sank into him, using him as leverage to push my hips towards Cal's teasing mouth. But Callum grabbed hold of my thighs and dragged them wide, pinning my legs to the mattress.

"While he's doing that," Donovan continued, nuzzling my ear so I could clearly hear his whispered words, "you have to count."

Callum lowered his face to my thigh and lightly grazed his lips across the skin, making me shiver.

"All I have to do is count to five?" I panted.

Donovan laughed and slid his hands around my waist. "Not quite, darling. You have to count how many times you get close to coming."

Without warning, Callum dipped his head, connecting his mouth to my clit. I jerked from surprise and pleasure, but Donovan tightened his grip to hold me steady.

"*Close* being the operative word," he added, his hands traveling up to massage my chest. "You're not allowed to come until we hit five, and after that, only when you have our permission. Do you understand?"

I tried to speak, but Callum swept across a sensitive spot with his tongue and drew out another moan. Donovan kissed my cheek.

"Come on, angel, find those words. You wouldn't want Cal to stop, would you?"

"No," I managed. "Don't… don't stop. Please. I understand."

"Good girl." Donovan kissed me again and turned his attention to the man between my legs. Callum's face was buried in me, but from the way the sides of his eyes crinkled, I could tell he was smiling up at us while his mouth worked.

"God, you look sexy like that," Donovan muttered.

Callum lifted his head just enough to speak. "Are you talking to me or her?"

Donovan laughed and let go of my chest to thread his fingers through Callum's hair. "Both."

With a tug, he guided Callum back down.

Donovan hadn't been lying. Callum was *really* good at this. He watched my expressions and the way my body moved and adjusted accordingly. Soon the room filled with my heavy breaths and stuttering groans, while Donovan kissed and caressed and coached me closer to a climax. He seemed to read my mind when he nipped my earlobe and whispered, "Remember to tell us when you're close, angel."

"Ok," I panted, "I'm close. I'm gonna come. I'm gonna—"

My breath hitched as the tension raced to a head, but right at the last second, Callum pushed off the mattress and stood, bringing an end to the promise of ecstasy. I cried out in protest, to which Callum silenced me with another smack to my inner thigh.

"What number was that?" he demanded, his tone uncharacteristically gruff.

"One," I whimpered.

"That's right. Four more to go. Your turn, Dono."

"Fucking finally." Donovan slid out from behind me and traded places with Cal, who swiped a strand of hair from my face as he settled in.

"You taste like fucking candy," he murmured, nuzzling my neck before wrapping his arms around me the way Donovan had. I opened my mouth to reply, but was distracted by a pair of hands landing on my thighs, their fingers calloused from countless nights working the strings of a guitar.

A low, hungry groan rolled in Donovan's throat as he knelt and spread me wide, staring at my body with such reverence I may as well have been a painting in a gallery.

"Fucking hell. Just look at you," he said through gritted teeth, like it physically pained him to hold back. "You're not an angel, you're a fucking goddess."

His praise made my cheeks go red.

"She makes a man want to speak in tongues, doesn't she?" Callum added.

"She sure does."

Donovan bent and dragged his tongue up the length of me, ass to pulsating clit. I jerked again, but Callum held me steady.

"Stop squirming, or I'll have to tie you up," he hissed in my ear.

"You sound strangely excited about that." I gasped with pleasure as Donovan's tongue found my entrance and drove inside.

Callum huffed a dark laugh. "I'm not always as nice as I seem."

"You don't seem very nice right now," I countered, trying not to wriggle as Donovan's pace quickened. "I don't know if I can hold off four more times."

"You can, and you will."

"And if I don't?" My hips lifted, increasing the pressure of Donovan's mouth.

"If you disobey, then you don't get my cock." Callum lazily

raked his nails up my torso. "And you wouldn't want that, would you? You want to be filled and fucked tonight."

"God, I love it when you talk dirty," Donovan muttered, face still buried in my heat. The tension slowly built again, but I knew I could inch a little closer to a climax before having to put an end to this bliss.

"I think you're getting a bit rusty, Dono," Callum teased. "Pretty sure I had our angel's legs shaking by now."

"Just playing with her before the finale."

Donovan released my legs so he could bring his fingers to my center, then slid one inside me while his thumb massaged my clit.

"Oh fuck," I gasped, reaching up to grip Callum for support.

The delicious intrusion created the perfect amount of tightness, and when Donovan repeatedly curled upwards, hitting my G-spot, my eyes practically rolled back in my head.

"Already so fucking wet," Donovan mused, shaking his head. "You're gonna be dripping by the time you take my cock."

I responded with a string of desperate whimpers as the pleasure raced to a head. I was tempted to let it run its course, but Callum had been right. I desperately wanted to get fucked.

"Ok, ok!" I cried out, clenching my teeth in an attempt to hold back. "Two!"

Donovan immediately pulled his hands away, leaving me trembling as the build up of energy went stagnant. A deep ache formed from the lack of release, so intense it was almost painful. There was no time for it to dissipate before Donovan reached out again and started up with the same motion. I was so sensitive I nearly shrieked at his touch.

"Wait, no!" I shrieked. "You're gonna get me too fast!"

"That's the point," Donovan said, increasing the speed his fingers were moving. "Come on, you can do it. Give us three."

His urging pushed me to my peak almost instantly, my frantic pants transforming into a pitiful, "Three."

Donovan pulled away. I was left quivering as my insides screamed for deliverance from this purgatory of pleasure. My tormenter smiled and sucked my arousal off his fingertips, then stretched his arm out to Callum for him to do the same. The sight was enough to evacuate every morsel of pride from my body.

"Please," I whined pitifully, "please, just let me come."

Callum and Donovan switched positions again, the latter hauling me further onto the bed so I could comfortably rest my head on his lap. "Can't do that, darling. You need to learn your lesson."

"I have, I promise."

"No amount of begging is going to save you." Callum pulled off his shirt and lowered to his knees where he smacked the insides of my thighs again, guiding them apart. "Keep these spread."

"He's sexy when he's bossy, isn't he?" Donovan reached forward, hooked my knees, and hauled my legs to my ears so I was fully exposed. "How's that?"

"Much better." Primal hunger fired in Callum's eyes. "God, that's a pretty cunt." On his last word he slid a finger inside me, making me clench around him and groan at the pleasure.

"I can't wait to fill the rest of these holes," Donovan whispered, his breath tickling my ear. Every sensation was heightened, which made the return of Callum's tongue to my clit nearly unbearable. Donovan continued to speak as Callum's finger and mouth worked in tandem.

"It won't happen all at once, though. At least, not tonight. We're going to work you up to that, make sure you're nice and ready. Does that sound good?"

"Mm-hmm." I was incapable of saying anything else. Nothing existed in my mind except pleasure, which grew more consuming each passing second.

"How about us taking you together? Callum in your ass

while I fill up that gorgeous cunt of yours? Does that turn you on?"

"Mm-hmm."

"Give me four then."

I'd nearly forgotten my punishment, too busy racing towards the desperate orgasm at the finish line. I caught myself just in time.

"Four!" I gasped, twisting the sheets in my fists. "Fuck, this is four!"

Callum's face surfaced. He was smiling, his lips slick and glistening. "That was a close one, angel. Better be careful. You still want to get fucked, don't you?"

God, yes. It wasn't just my pussy that was aching now, but everything belly button and below. The need was agonizingly deep, and the only thing that would be able to satiate it was currently straining against Callum's jeans. Donovan was getting hard too; I could feel him swelling and twitching beneath me. If he was as big as he felt, I may have trouble walking in the morning, but that was a risk I'd happily take.

"Your turn," Callum stated, tearing off my soaked thong and tossing it onto the bed. Donovan picked up the panties and looped them around my wrists, yanking the fabric tight enough that I grunted in discomfort. He planted a kiss on my knuckles as his apology.

"You finish her off," Donovan insisted. He grabbed my face and gave it a taunting shake. "I made this one a promise. I told her you'd have her whimpering like a needy little whore before she got me for round two."

"Well, we can't have you going back on your word, can we?" Callum leaned forward so he was looking down at me. "You're going to give us one more. Then maybe, *maybe*, we'll decide to have mercy."

It was amazing how he could flip the switch so easily, going from fun and lovable one second to dominant and commanding the next. I nodded obediently, and he straightened. One hand moved to my clit, where he repeatedly swiped his thumb across the hypersensitive skin, while the other drifted to the button on his jeans. With a twist, the material unfastened, then the zipper. Callum's pants slid off his hips, followed by his boxer briefs. When we'd hooked up on the bus, it had been too dark to see him perfectly, but here he was in all his glory. If anyone looked the part of an angel here, it was him. The intricate artwork decorating his skin rippled as his muscles moved beneath it, and a strand of white blond had fallen in front of his eyes, which he swiped out of the way before taking hold of his stiff cock. He began stroking himself, continuing to work me at the same time.

"You have no idea how badly I've wanted to be buried in this cunt again," he said, almost to himself. "Do you have any idea how perfect you feel, angel?"

I pressed my lips together to smother a desperate moan as Callum removed his thumb from my clit and replaced it with the head of his cock. He tapped himself against the delicate skin a few times, causing shockwaves of pleasure. Behind me, an appreciative groan rolled in Donovan's throat.

"You know how many times I've relived the memory of you stuffed full, grinding and dripping all over this fat cock?" Callum slid the tip lower, notching it at my opening. I instinctively pushed my hips forward to try and guide him in, but received a punishing slap to my thigh.

"I said one more," Callum snapped.

"Please," I cried. "*Please*, Callum, just fuck me. I'm begging you."

"Greedy little slut, aren't you?" Donovan said, pressing a kiss to my temple. "Be a good girl and give him what he wants. You can do that, can't you?"

Callum continued to tease his way up and down my slit. He'd press in just enough to make my inner walls clench, only to slide out and swirl circles around my swollen clit.

"Just one more," Callum urged, increasing the speed of his taunting. "Hold off a little longer, and you'll get your reward."

I was so goddamn turned on I wanted to cry. Pleasure and pressure built deep and low, gearing up for a devastating snap. My breath caught as it neared its peak, and my body wanted nothing more than to topple over. But something had unlocked in my mind, something that wanted to please.

My hands curled into fists as I focused on holding back, the thong digging into my wrists further with the movement. I inched closer to a climax.

Closer.

A little further.

"Five!" I blurted at the last second. "Stop! Stop, this is five!"

Callum pulled away, dragging a defeated whimper from my lips with him. My body quivered like electricity crackled through my veins, the tension frantically stuck in search of a way out.

Donovan awarded me with a passionate kiss. "Such an obedient little slut for us."

"You did so good, angel," Callum added, massaging my thighs with gentle, loving strokes. "I think you earned a reward."

"I think so too." Donovan smiled down at me. "Do you want to come?"

My body prickled with anticipation. "Yes, please."

"Look at those good manners." Callum smirked and dropped to his knees. "Don't hold back, sweetheart. I want everyone in this hotel to hear you scream."

27

Donovan hauled me up so my back was pressed to his chest and nuzzled my ear with his nose. "How do you want to come? From his tongue or his fingers?"

I bit back a whimper as Callum dragged his nails up the insides of my thighs. "Both?"

"God, you're a greedy little thing," Donovan teased. "Think you can handle her, Cal?"

Callum scoffed. "Please. I've been praying for one like this."

He dipped his head, touching his lips to my tender flesh, at the same time Donovan planted kisses along my neck and shoulders.

"Remember you have a safe word," he murmured against my skin, "but try to push through if you can."

"Push through what?" I panted, crying out from the jolts of pleasure Callum's tongue caused as it rapidly flicked my clit. "I already took my punishment."

Two unnerving chuckles escaped both men.

"We didn't say we were done with you," Donovan stated. "Pleasure can be a punishment too."

With that, Callum slid two fingers inside of me. I gasped

and tried to reach for something to hold onto, but my wrists were still bound with my thong. Seeing my struggle, Donovan raised my arms and looped them around the back of his neck, leaving his hands free to slide under my shirt and squeeze my breasts.

"Fucking hell, you two look amazing," he muttered, his hands continuing to explore my body but his eyes glued to Callum's activity between my legs. "Go on, Cal. Make her see God."

"Oh, fuck," I blurted as Callum's fingers pumped faster. "I'm getting close."

"We didn't say you could come yet."

"Please," I shouted, unconcerned about who might hear me. "Please, can I come?"

"Hmm… I don't know. Should we let her, Cal?"

A muffled "Mm-hmm" answered, and I'd never felt so relieved.

"Alright, you heard him. Come for us, angel."

Their permission was the final thing I needed to topple over the edge. I couldn't have held back even if I wanted to. Callum's punishing pace propelled me to my peak, and an explosion of ecstasy tore through me. If Cal hadn't gripped my thighs like his life depended on it, I probably would have seized right off the bed.

Callum didn't wait for me to finish riding the waves of bliss. I was still vibrating when he stood upright, lined up with my center, and firmly drove himself in. An involuntary cry of plea-sure leapt from my mouth, but Donovan craned his head to smother it with a kiss.

"That's right, sweetheart," Callum hissed through clenched teeth, swiping his thumb repeatedly across my clit as he smashed his hips forward again and again. "Come all over that cock like a good little slut."

My orgasm dragged out, making me shake and shudder until

the pleasure finally transitioned to satisfaction. But Callum still didn't let up, and satisfaction morphed into overstimulation.

"I didn't say you were done coming," Callum growled. He kept up his pace, pounding into me with a fury I'd never seen from him. At first, the pleasure seemed used up and impossible to conjure again, but sensation gradually returned my body, this time more intense. I tried to pull away, but Donovan held me still.

"Come on, angel," he demanded. "You can give us one more, I know you can."

The pleasure was so consuming I was practically hysterical. Another orgasm tore through me, causing me to deteriorate completely, and my body's only response was to release every emotion at its disposal. I collapsed on the bed in a crying, shuddering, giggling heap, but Callum and Donovan weren't phased.

"You did so well, sweetheart," Cal praised, his cock still twitching inside me.

"You took him perfectly," Donovan added, swiping my bangs off my forehead before doing the same to Callum. "God, I could watch the two of you all day."

"I know you could," Cal laughed. "But now it's my turn."

He bent and pressed a kiss to my cheek, then Donovan's, before sliding himself out and flopping onto the bed beside me.

"I... I don't think I can," I panted. "I can't come anymore, I'm too tired."

Donovan chuckled and took Callum's place between my legs. "Challenge accepted."

I looked to Cal for help, but he was propped on his elbows, looking at us with lust in his eyes.

"You can do it," he urged, slowly stroking himself. "Show him what a good girl you were for me."

I sighed in exasperation, but his words reawakened my appetite.

Donovan reached into his shorts and pulled out his length.

He was long, straight, and thick, and just the impressive sight of him made my inner walls clench. My exhaustion forgotten, I eagerly squirmed towards him. He took hold of my hips and teased my entrance with the swollen head of his cock.

"Jesus," he breathed, pressing in just enough to make me gasp before pulling out again. "Look how fucking wet you are for me."

I wriggled closer. "Stop being such a tease."

"But it's my favorite thing." Donovan continued to toy with the sensitive skin. "And I think you secretly like it."

"I'd like it more if you just fucked me."

Donovan fully sheathed himself inside me, forcing me to cry out in surprise.

"Like that?"

"Yes," I groaned, hooking my heels behind him. "Fuck, you're big."

Dono pumped his length in and out of me, slow and deep, his stare never breaking from mine. Our breath synced as our bodies rolled in tandem, and before I knew it, the pressure was building again.

"Are you going to come again?" Donovan asked.

I nodded fervently.

"Me too." Dono's pace quickened. "Come with me, angel."

The world faded away, leaving me lost in knee-weakening pleasure until I toppled over the edge. Donovan followed suit, thrusting into me as far as he could as he released. Decadent warmth spread through my core as he filled me.

"Jesus Christ," Donovan huffed, running his hands over my chest and torso in awe before looking up at Callum. "I think I slipped in and out of heaven there for a second."

"Told you." Cal was still pumping his length in his fist, his movements increasing with his breath as he neared a climax of his own.

Instinctively, I craned my neck towards him, and he hissed a curse of appreciation before dipping his cock in my mouth. I sucked lightly and moaned at his taste, which pushed him to his limit. Cal groaned and grasped the back of my head, holding me there until cum spurted across my tongue and down my throat.

"God, you're perfect," Donovan said, leaning down to lap any remnants of Cal from my lips, then claiming me with another kiss.

"Agreed," Callum ruffled Dono's hair and flopped back into the pillows. "So. Dinner?"

"Let's order in," I replied, shakily hauling myself up to snuggle into the crook of his arm. "I'm going to want round two pretty soon."

Donovan lifted his face to the ceiling and shut his eyes. "Lord, I don't know what I've done to deserve this creature, but thank you."

I laughed and reached for the tv remote buried in the rumpled comforter, saying a similar prayer in my mind.

28

The next day, bus call was 5 AM. It was an eight hour drive to Cheyenne, Wyoming, and the guys wanted to get there with plenty of time before soundcheck.

I groggily shuffled out of the hotel with Callum and Donovan, who carried my bag for me and dressed me in one of their oversized hoodies. I felt Luca's eyes on me as we arrived on the bus, but when I glanced at him, he ducked his head and continued replying to emails on his phone. Dante sat slumped beside him, the bags under his eyes darker than normal. It looked like he hadn't slept in days. All of us took turns dozing off over the course of the drive except for him. He did nothing but stare at the wall, arms crossed and headphones blasting. Donovan and Callum didn't say anything to him, but thanks to their sideways glances and the overall sense of unease clouding the bus, it was obvious they knew what had happened. I found myself watching Dante more and more, wondering if he could feel everyone's eyes on him and hear their unspoken thoughts, or if he really was as numb as he looked.

By the time we reached the outskirts of Cheyenne, everyone was fully awake and caught up in their own activities. Craig and

Callum were playing video games, Luca was hunched over the table attempting to write, and Donovan had pulled out his camera to snap photos of me, who he'd fondly started referring to as his muse. I tried to sit still for him, but my gaze continued to drift to Dante. He'd barely moved since we'd first piled onto the bus, and no one had bothered to say a single word to him.

"Is he ok?" I finally asked, lowering my voice so only Donovan could hear me.

He followed my line of sight to the man on the couch. "Yeah, that's normal. He goes somewhere else sometimes."

I frowned. "It doesn't look like it's a very good place."

"Probably isn't, darling. But what can you do?"

The shutter clicked as Donovan snapped another photo. His words set my mind racing, and after a few more snaps of the camera, I stood.

"Where are you going?" Donovan asked.

Ignoring him, I walked over to my bunk and grabbed my headphones. Then I made my way back to the front lounge, slid into the seat beside Dante, and tapped him on the shoulder. He jumped slightly, like my touch had woken him from a long slumber. His head swiveled to face me, and he lifted one of his headphones off his ear.

"What?"

"My playlists are feeling a little stale." I extended my earbuds. "I was wondering if you had any recommendations? Maybe you could show me a couple songs."

Dante blinked again, the warily glanced at the other guys on the bus like this was some kind of trick. But they looked just as surprised as him. A few tense beats passed before Dante slid his headphones off completely.

"Not sure you'd like my stuff."

"Try me."

Another moment of silence.

Finally, Dante grabbed my headphones and slid the cord into

place. I popped in one of the earbuds and settled in beside him, letting my shoulder rest against his. He peeked down at it, his brows inching together in confusion, but he shook his head and returned his focus to the phone in his hand.

"What do you normally listen to?" he mumbled, scrolling through Spotify.

"My tastes are all over the place. How about you just play what you were before? Pretend I'm not here."

Dante's thumb hovered over the screen as he considered. Finally, he slid the free earbud in place and tapped play. The uptempo guitar intro of "Locked in My Head" by Fit For A King blasted through. I bobbed my head to the beat, subtly watching Dante out the corner of my eye. The lyrics spoke of being at war with your own mind, and I got the feeling they weren't just words to him. The songs that came next only painted a more detailed picture: another song by Fit For A King, "Shattered Glass," followed by "O.K?" from Picturesque, and finally, The Devil Wears Prada's hauntingly melancholy "Louder Than Thunder." The slow song was a stark contrast to the ones before it, and it sang of the longing for inner peace and a desperate desire to quiet the mind. The pattern in the songs was evident, and for the first time since I'd met him, I got the tiniest glimpse of who Dante was when the mask came off. Not the Lucifer mask, but the emotionless one he wore each day to keep everyone out.

The sensation of someone watching me pulled my attention across the bus. I caught Luca staring at us, a ghost of a smile haunting his lips. He dipped his head to me, then returned to his notebook. He didn't speak, but the message was clearly communicated:

Thank you.

The moment was shattered when the bus lurched to a sudden stop, sending all of us flying. Dante and I toppled into a heap on the floor, where he instinctively wrapped his arms around my waist.

"You ok?" he asked.

"Yeah," I grunted, pushing myself off his chest to sit upright. "What the hell just happened?"

Luca was already stomping towards the front of the bus.

"What the fuck, Randy?" he shouted.

"Ain't my fault," the driver barked back, "it's them goddamn Jesus freaks!"

Callum emerged from the back lounge and helped me to my feet while Donovan raised the blinds.

Since the windows were tinted, they couldn't see us, but we could see them clear as day.

A line of around fifty protesters curled around the front of the bus and down the side, waving signs depicting scripture verses and messages like "burn in hell."

"We're a God-fearing place," a blonde woman shrieked, her voice shrill enough to penetrate the bus walls and pierce our ears. "The devil is not welcome here! We cast you out, demon!"

"Run them over, Randy," Dante grumbled, grabbing his phone from the floor and yanking the headphones out. He handed them back to me before crawling into his bunk and facing away from us.

"Slow and steady," the driver replied, putting the bus in gear. "Just like always."

The bus crept forward at a snail's pace, which caused the mob to grow even more agitated and claim they were being attacked. I jumped as someone chucked something at the window, causing a loud *bang* to echo through the bus.

"How often does this happen?" I asked nervously.

Luca sighed and returned to his seat. "We get protesters everywhere, but it's usually only this bad in the rural areas."

Another object bounced off the bus.

"I think it's great," Donovan chirped. He pulled his camera

forward and snapped a photo of the commotion outside. "Keep it up, assholes. The more you hate, the more money we make."

His lighthearted words calmed my nerves, and I relaxed further when Callum sat down beside me and slid an arm around my shoulders.

"Don't be scared," he said, pressing a quick kiss to my temple. "You're safe. They can't touch you."

"And if they did, they'd have to answer to us," Luca added.

There was an ominous air to his words, and when I peeked at his hardened gaze, I realized they carried a very real threat.

A wry chuckle puffed from Donovan's lips as he reviewed the photos he'd just taken. "That's the first thing we've agreed on in a very long time."

Despite our early start, thanks to the mobs of protestors we continued to encounter on the outskirts of the city, we arrived for soundcheck an hour and a half late. The boys immediately ran inside to rush through their set, while I hung back and camped out with my sketchbook on the steps of the venue. Protestors had already gathered across the street, doing their best to form a roadblock to keep concertgoers from lining up, while a handful of law enforcement officers were trying to wrangle them. For some reason, the shouts of protestors harmonizing with the melody of the music wafting out of the venue unlocked the creative part of my brain. I was flooded with the most inspiration I'd had in weeks, and my pencil flew across the pages in front of me like it was possessed. A graphite landscape took shape, populated by throngs of awe-inspiring angels with wings outstretched in fury. Fire spewed from their mouths, transforming into arrows as the flames arced through the air. Several had already burrowed into the back of a beast, whose form I was still in the process of fleshing out. So far, it had scaly skin and feathered wings that curled around its body in an attempt to shield it from the assault.

"Babylon the Great!"

My head jerked up at the voice, and I scanned the sidewalk in front of me. A squatty woman had broken free of the police and stood at the foot of the steps I was crouched on, repeatedly jabbing a poster board with "John 3:16" written in glitter glue into the sky.

"Babylon the Great," she repeated, her beady eyes narrowed on me. "The Mother of Harlots and the Abominations of the Earth!"

I blinked and looked around, then tapped my chest. "Are you talking to me?"

"Fallen!" The woman screeched, flinging a damning finger my way. "Fallen is Babylon the Great! She has become a dwelling for demons and a haunt for every impure spirit."

My face flushed at her words, but I wasn't sure if it was from humiliation or rage. Her tone resembled countless sermons and reprimands I'd experienced growing up, the most recent of which had severed me and my mother's relationship. Hearing the woman now made it feel like my mom was the one condemning me instead of some crazed stranger.

Choosing to excuse myself from the drama, I closed my notebook and stood, but the woman wasn't finished.

"For all the nations have drunk the maddening wine of her adulteries," she shrieked. "The kings of the earth committed adultery with her, and the merchants of the earth grew rich from her excessive luxuries."

"Give it a rest, lady," I snapped, starting back towards the buses in the parking lot. "No one here is going to buy your bullshit."

"I'll pray for you, child!"

Those words made me freeze.

"I'll pray for you" was the last thing said to me as I stormed out of my family's rural Ohio home and slammed the door behind me. It was a deceivingly innocent phrase, but it was too often twisted, corrupted, and used as a weapon, like it was in this moment.

Without thinking, I whirled and faced the woman.

"Please do," I stated. "I'm gonna need it. The vessels of the devil sacrifice a virgin onstage every full moon, and tonight I'm the lucky winner. Hail Satan."

The woman's face drained of color, and I triumphantly spun on my heel and stomped back towards the bus parked in the side alley.

"Troublemaker."

I followed the voice and caught a glimpse of Chase striding towards me, a backpack slung over his shoulder.

"You're going to rile these people into a frenzy," he teased, falling in step beside me. "What would your employers say?"

I shrugged. "Honestly they'd probably thank me. They say no publicity is bad publicity."

Chase rolled his eyes, but nodded. "Sure. How's all that going by the way? Everything still good?"

My mind flashed with images of the panic outside Dante's hotel room, followed by the intimate night with Donovan and Callum. "Yeah, it's all pretty normal."

"You figure out who they are yet?"

I stopped in my tracks and faced him. "I'm sorry?"

"I'm just curious if you know who they are. Everyone talks about it. There are even whole Reddit threads dedicated to cracking the case. Hell, I even tried bribing their crew into telling me, but they wouldn't budge."

I tried to smile along with him, but the hair on the back of my neck pricked defensively. "They don't want anyone to know who they are, Chase. You should respect that."

"And I think they should respect the bands they bring out by trusting them with their secrets. Don't you agree?"

I sighed and stuffed my hands in my pockets. "I don't know, I really can't comment."

"Don't tell me you drank the Kool Aid too." Chase's head tilted as he analyzed me. "Wait a minute… Are you being tight-lipped because you know who they are?"

"What? No."

"Come on, just tell me. I promise I'll keep it to myself."

He extended his pinky finger, but I didn't take it. "It seems like *you're* the troublemaker here, not me."

Chase laughed. "Relax, it's not that serious. We've gotta have some fun out here on the road. You look like you could use some fun."

"I'm having plenty of fun."

"You'd have more with me though." He shot me a suggestive wink.

The creak of hinges interrupted us, and I glanced at the back door of the venue. Legion's crew filed out, followed by the guys in their masks. A gold ram's head locked onto me and Chase, who hissed an expletive under his breath.

The Beast broke apart from the group and stormed over to us, but before he could open his mouth, Chase raised his hands in defense.

"I'm sorry, I know I'm not supposed to be back here. I swear I'm leaving. I just wanted to give Jade something." He brought his backpack forward and unzipped it, then reached in to pull out one of the Phantom Spark t-shirts sold at their merch table. "I feel bad about what happened at breakfast yesterday. I think some of my words got misconstrued. Either way, I wanted to give you this to say sorry."

He handed me the shirt and backed away, giving me another wink. "Plus I think you'd look pretty cute repping my band."

When he turned his back to us, the Beast snatched the shirt out of my hand.

"Hey!" I snapped. "Give that back!"

He held it just out of my reach, but pushed his face close to mine and lowered his voice, his words soft but his eyes dark and dangerous.

"If I see you wearing this, I swear to god I'll rip it off and gag you with it."

Fury drummed in my ears, and I leaned in so our lips were inches from each other. "Is that supposed to deter me?"

Luca sniffed wryly, his gaze dropping to my mouth. It felt like the moment that first night we met, right before he kissed me with such ferocity you would have thought it was his last act on earth. I barely breathed waiting for his next move. My heart ached with hope, while other parts of me ached in hope of something else. His lips were a drug I'd been craving since the first hit, his touch a high I couldn't stop reliving. Our games had been infuriating and addicting, but I needed an ending. I needed to *win*. I needed to unleash the Beast and have him consume me mind, body, and soul, which wasn't something I'd fully realized until Luca stepped away, tossed me the t-shirt, and left me shivering with pent up desire.

"Careful, angel," he warned. "That tongue of yours is going to get you into trouble."

"Promise?"

Luca hesitated a few seconds longer before spinning on his heel and filing into the bus after the rest of the guys. I had to pace the parking lot for ten minutes before I trusted my raging hormones enough to follow.

Thanks to our late arrival at the venue, Dante didn't have enough time to get nearly as fucked up as usual, so the show went off without a hitch. Despite the resistance from the God-fearing folk of Wyoming, the turn out was great. Legion had another sold-out show under their belt, and the crowd was one of the best so far. The high energy was contagious, and even though they were playing melodies and lyrics they could recite in their sleep, I swear Legion's smiles shone brighter that evening.

Despite the good night, which was made even better by fooling around with Callum and Donovan in the back lounge after the show, my psyche decided to torture me with another nightmare.

Stalks of corn.

The snap of a twig behind me.

A scream for help that no one was around to hear.

Fear, confusion, and guilt, then a bottle of pills in a bathtub.

I jerked awake from the dream, panting for air. Something wet trickled down my cheek, and when I reached up to feel my face, I discovered I'd been crying in my sleep. My heart raced like I was being chased, and I whipped my head around to check my surroundings, reassuring myself that I wasn't. I'd crawled into my bunk after Callum and Donovan passed out, even though they'd groggily asked me to stay and cuddle all night.

Craning my neck, I found Luca and Craig fast asleep, but when my eyes lifted to the bunk diagonal to mine, I discovered I wasn't the only one awake.

Headphones in place, Dante stared at me with the same strange expression he had the other night. It was a look of curiosity, tinged in sadness but clouded with caution. Our eyes met and Dante blinked twice, like he too was waking from a dream. He jerked his chin to me in a silent question.

Are you ok, it seemed to ask.

I licked my lips and attempted to calm my breathing before dipping my head.

Yes.

Dante nodded and averted his gaze, adjusted his headphones, and rolled away from me. I tried to do the same, but for some reason my eyes stayed glued to his back. My heart ached, but it wasn't from the pain of the past. It ached because it desperately wanted to be understood, and though no one had ever come close, something about Dante made it feel like he could.

With a shaky inhale, I mustered my courage, turned, and fumbled through my bunk until my fingers landed on my phone. Squinting at the bright light of the screen, I swiped it open and tapped the Spotify icon. After scrolling through a few of my curated playlists, I found the song I was searching for: "Bad Dreams" by Faouzia.

I clicked the song's sharing options, then opened a new text thread with just Dante and pressed send. Out of the corner of my eye, I watched his bunk light up as my message arrived on his phone. He lifted it to see who'd texted him, pausing for a few seconds before sliding it open and tapping on the link. I watched him like a hawk, trying to read his thoughts through body language alone, but he remained a closed book. Eventually, enough time had passed that I knew the song was over, but Dante still hadn't moved or responded. It shouldn't have made my heart ache more, but it did.

With a sigh, I rolled over and shut my eyes, silently kicking myself for showing even a sliver of vulnerability. Sleep managed to come calling again, but just when I was starting to nod off, my phone buzzed. Peeling one eye open, I glanced at my screen.

Dante had hearted the message.

29

Kansas reminded me of home.

It was the open spaces. Nothing but fields and plains and vast emptiness as far as the eye could see. Ohio had a few more lakes and trees, but the two had the same rural Americana feel. Driving through the state immediately had me irritable and on edge, and not even Donovan's playful banter could snap me out of it. The only thing that helped was drawing.

I scribbled frantically in my notebook throughout the bus ride to Wichita. I caught the guys watching me in their peripheral vision, but they wisely kept their distance. I was in no mood for games or petty arguments. I needed a release, and the only thing that was offering it was pencil and paper.

Caricatures of monsters and demons began to fill up the pages, their sinister eyes peering through cornfields and snarling in the pews of churches. I even tried to change veins and work on the piece I'd started in Cheyenne, but all I could add was a giant puddle of blood pooling beneath the unfinished beast. I barely said a thing, but my emotions were warring inside me, and by the time we arrived at the venue, I was exhausted from the battle. I had even less patience for the meaningless bickering swirling around me. By the time I was curled on the green room couch, listening to Legion's nightly display of animosity, I was at my breaking point.

"Watch your timing on Corruption, Callum," Luca said without looking up from the text he was furiously punching into his phone. "If Dante's not keeping up, you need to adjust."

Cal opened his mouth to speak, but Donovan beat him to it. "It's not Cal's fault our bassist can't do his fucking job."

I glanced up from my notebook to peek at Dante, who was without his headphones for once and seemed to be regretting it immensely. He frantically paced the room like a caged tiger, his fingers drumming his thighs to the beat of the opening act's first song.

"No," Luca bit back, "but it's Cal's job to adapt to the rest of us."

Again Callum attempted to speak, but Donovan cut in. "He wouldn't have to adapt so much if you stopped making excuses for your boy over there."

Luca tossed his phone to the cushion beside me and whirled on Donovan. "And maybe you should let *your* boy speak for himself every now and then."

"Fuck you, don't turn this on me!"

"I'm just stating facts."

"You want facts? Alright. No amount of nitpicking or controlling every little thing is going to change the massive fuck-up Dante's become—"

Before Donovan could finish, Luca shoved him roughly, making him stumble back a few steps. The guitarist's eyes immediately iced over and his hands curled into fists. He charged Luca, but before the two clashed, Callum darted between them and held Donovan back.

"Try putting your hands on me again, motherfucker!" Donovan barked.

Luca tauntingly spread his arms wide. "Come on, big man. Let's see what you've got."

"Enough!" I shouted, slamming my notebook shut so hard the clap echoed through the room. Four pairs of eyes shifted to me as I shot to my feet, stormed to the door, and yanked it open. "I get you have issues, but if you can't handle your emotions like adults, then stop making it everybody else's problem. Go jump in the mosh pit if you want to hit each other so bad."

Luca and Callum blinked in surprise, but Donovan was still shaking with rage.

"With all due respect, angel," he hissed through gritted teeth, "it's best you stay out of our business."

"You guys *made* me your business." I stubbornly crossed my arms. "This shit may be normal for you, but it clearly hasn't helped anything over the years, so we're trying a different way. *My* way. Now what's it gonna be? Shut up and sit down, or get out and get hit?"

A dark chuckle puffed from Luca's lips, and he shook his head. "I don't know what gave you the idea you were suddenly the boss—"

"I'm down."

We all turned to Dante. He was already hooking his crew lanyard onto the belt loop of his jeans and tugging a beanie over his hair.

"We don't need to get ready until Phantom Spark goes on," he added. "Plenty of time to do some damage."

I glanced at the others. Callum had started pacing nervously, Donovan's glare was boring into the side of his lead singer's head, and Luca was just staring. I shrugged and followed Dante out of the room.

When I caught up, I fell into step beside him. "This suggestion wasn't really directed at you, you know."

"Why not? It was a good idea. Those guys have fantasized

about beating the shit out of me for years. I'm sure it'll feel good to finally make it reality."

Dante pushed past a security guard, who had stopped a trio of drunk girls from sneaking backstage in an attempt to meet Legion. Completely unaware of who had just walked by, they didn't even glance Dante's way.

We emerged in the packed venue and looked around. The floor was already a writhing mass of bodies, all screaming and singing along to the band onstage. Dante craned his neck to see the crowd better, mapping out the best way to get to the rowdy mosh pit at its center.

"Why do you let them talk about you like that?" I shouted over the noise. "You always just stay quiet. Why don't you defend yourself?"

"Because they're right." Dante's attention remained fixed on the crowd. "Believe me, I'm well aware I'm a piece of shit."

"You say that like it's unavoidable."

"Some people are just broken, angel. And they always will be." He motioned behind us. "That's what I've been telling that one for years."

I glanced over my shoulder. Luca had joined us, with Donovan at his side, their faces solemn.

"Just like old times, boys," Dante muttered, cracking his neck to limber up.

"No face shots," Luca stated, looking pointedly at Donovan. "I still have to sing tonight."

"And watch the hands," Donovan retaliated. "We have instruments to play."

The singer and guitarist nodded curtly before pushing into the crowd. Dante moved to follow, but I instinctively caught his wrist.

"Wait!"

He tensed at my touch, but didn't pull away. I wasn't sure exactly what I wanted to say or do. All I knew was the idea of him and the rest of the guys being knocked around with violent fists made my chest tight with anxiety.

"Be careful," is what I feebly settled on.

Dante blinked down at my fingers on his arm a few seconds longer before maneuvering out of my grasp.

"Go back to the green room," he ordered. "This isn't the place for you."

I bristled, but he disappeared from sight before I could get another word in. I raised to my tiptoes in an attempt to watch his progress through the crowd, but it had swallowed him whole. Lowering back to the floor, I nervously chewed at my thumbnail and waited. For what, I didn't know. A riot? A murder?

Muscling down my anxiety, I set my jaw and straightened my shoulders. There was only one way to know for sure I hadn't unleashed three psychopaths on the world, and it sure as hell wasn't standing here on the sidelines. After taking a deep breath, I dove into the sea of people.

"Excuse me… Sorry… My bad…"

I grunted my apologies as I shouldered my way through the mass of skin and sweat. Everyone was too enraptured by the music to pay much attention to me. The closer to the center I came, the more the crowd buzzed with energy. Bodies packed together like sardines in a can, movements became more gruff and erratic, and I quickly realized that Dante had been right. This really wasn't the place for me. There was nowhere to run, it felt like there was limited air to breathe, and every time someone got too carried away and knocked into the surrounding onlook-ers, the movement rippled into the rest of the crowd and jostled all of us along with it.

I inched closer to the pit until I'd joined the boundary. Squinting at the mob in front of me, I tried to pick out three familiar faces. I eventually found them on the other side of the circle, using their bodies as weapons against those around them. The stage lights transitioned from blue and purple to a disorienting strobe effect, making it seem like every flailing limb around me was moving in slow motion.

Rising to my tiptoes again, I craned my head to try and catch another glimpse of the guys, who had disappeared back into the madness. A burly bald man suddenly flew in from my left, bashing his shoulder into my side and knocking me into the ground. A few of the onlookers in the boundary rushed to help me up.

"Are you alright?" a pierced, purple-haired woman asked, brushing grit off my back.

"Yeah, I'm ok." I rubbed my eyes, trying to get my bearings, but the strobe was still making it difficult to see clearly. Before I realized what was happening, the bald man barreled in again, bashing into me even harder than he had before. I fell to the floor with a grunt, then cried out as he trampled my fingers.

"Hey!" The purple-haired girl shrieked after him, "We look after each other in here, asshole!"

She stooped to help me once more, but the man circled back and hurled himself into her this time. She was smaller than me, so the blow sent her flying. When she landed with a thud on the grimy cement, the man spat onto the floor at her feet.

"No girls in the pit," he declared.

His words stirred a fiery rage inside me, prompting me to scramble to my feet and fling the entirety of my weight into his gut. It only knocked him back a few steps, but his anger tripled. He came at me again, and this time, he didn't try to disguise his violence through pit-appropriate moves. Instead he took my shoulders in both hands, shoved me to the ground, and slammed the heel of his boot into my stomach. Air whooshed from my lungs as pain shot through my body like a lightning bolt. The man raised his foot to land another kick, and I curled into fetal position to protect myself.

Before the boot fell, someone burst through the crowd and

smashed a fist into the man's jaw. A pair of hands gripped me under my armpits and lifted me to standing.

"Are you alright? Are you hurt?" Donovan's voice met my ears, sending a wave of relief crashing over me. In a daze, I nodded. My eyes took a few seconds to process what was happening in front of me, but eventually the image pieced together.

Dante threw punch after punch into my attacker's face, and when the man managed to roll over and get a few blows in, Luca ran in and tackled him back down.

"Dono, get security," Luca shouted, struggling to keep the man pinned. "Let's get this piece of shit out of here."

Donovan nodded and pressed a kiss to my temple before pushing through the crowd towards the line of men in uniform at the front of the venue. Luca gripped the man's t-shirt and gave him a rough shake.

"Apologize to the ladies," he snarled through gritted teeth.

The man responded by spitting a glob of saliva in Luca's face.

Luca barely even flinched. He simply smiled an eerie, utterly merciless smile that sent a chill down my spine. Then his fists tightened, and he raised the man up a few inches before throwing him back down, smashing his head against the cement.

"Have at him, Dante," Luca said, rising to his feet and coming to stand beside me.

Like a rabid dog finally let off its leash, Dante tore in and returned to pummeling the man. Either he was deceivingly strong, or he dug into some unknown force deep inside him that gave his blows power. Within seconds, the man's face was bloody and battered, but Dante showed no signs of stopping. His eyes were typically glazed over, lost in a thought some-where, but now his gaze was locked on the present, narrowed and gleaming with ruthlessness. Painted with the lights from the stage and the blood dripping from his nose, he was a beautiful and horrifying angel of death.

The beam of a flashlight cut through the crowd, and the band onstage stopped their set. The houselights came on as security shouldered their way to the mosh pit. Everyone had stopped their brawling except for Dante. He continued his assault on the man, who was now sputtering garbled swears around a mouthful of blood. It took three security guards to drag the bassist off of him.

"That fucker was beating up women," Luca said, pointing to the man on the ground with one arm while protectively sliding the other around my waist.

Security nodded and expressed their thanks before lifting the man to his feet and hauling him towards the exit. I thought that was the end of it, but then they grabbed Dante by the back of his shirt and gruffly led him to the venue doors.

"Wait, what are you doing?" I yelled, leaving Luca's embrace to run after them. "He was defending me!"

"Doesn't change the fact he just beat someone to a pulp," a security guard replied, blocking my path. "We don't tolerate that shit here."

"That's stupid," I blurted, trying to push past him, but he stretched out his arm, barring the way.

"You want to get thrown out too?" he snapped.

"Fuck you," I muttered, ducking under his arm and jogging after the group.

When I exited the venue, I caught up to security just in time to see them chuck Dante to the pavement and return inside. I raced over and knelt beside his limp form, but when I rolled him over, I found him laughing.

"Fuck," he exclaimed, flopping onto the asphalt like he was making a snow angel. "What a rush!"

Puffing a relieved sigh, I sat back on my heels. "Are you ok?"

"Hell yeah, I'm ok." Dante sat upright, but despite his statement, he groaned at the effort. "Never better."

"You're bleeding."

He wiped his nose with the back of his hand and examined the blood smeared across it. "Looks that way."

"Is it broken?"

"Maybe."

"We should find you a paramedic."

"There's nothing they can do. I've had worse and survived. I'll be fine."

Dante scrambled upright and extended his hands to help me to my feet. I blinked in surprise at the gesture, but accepted.

"Feel better?" I asked.

"For now. Ask me again in an hour."

He turned and started towards the tour buses at the back of the venue, but I stayed where I was.

"Thank you," I called after him.

Dante stopped walking and faced me. "For?"

I gestured to the building. "What you did for me in there."

The bassist shrugged and glanced down at his battered knuckles. "We both benefited from that."

"Still." I shoved my hands in my pockets and shuffled my feet. "No one's ever done something like that for me. No one's ever… protected me."

I smiled in an attempt to distract from the sudden moisture pricking my eyes. Dante peeked up through the sweaty strands of black hair poking out from beneath his beanie, his piercing stare no doubt seeing right through my facade. Eventually, he shook his head and spun on his heel again, beckoning for me to follow.

"It was a good way to blow off steam."

Pushing my emotion back down to the painful well it usually slept in, I trailed after him. We rounded the venue, flashed our badges to the security guards stationed at the fence, and continued towards Legion's tour bus.

"You know," I mused, "maybe you should find some other ways to blow off steam that don't involve breaking bones."

Dante mumbled something I couldn't hear, so I picked up my pace to catch up with him.

"What was that?"

"I said it's either hurt myself or hurt someone else," Dante repeated.

My stride slowed to a halt.

Feeling my eyes on him, Dante sighed and turned around again. "Don't do that."

"Don't do what?"

"Pity me."

"I'm not."

"No?" Dante stomped forward and thrust his finger in my face. "What's that look then?"

I stared up at him, trying not to focus on the way my heart began to pound as another wave of vulnerability rose to the surface. "I think we might be able to help each other."

Dante's eyes narrowed, but I wasn't sure if the spark in them was suspicion or curiosity.

"You can't save me, angel," he muttered. "Trust me. People have tried."

"I'm not trying to save you."

"Then what are you trying to do?"

"Same thing as you. Find relief from the war in your mind."

Dante scoffed and leaned in close. "What would *you* know about war?"

"Plenty."

My body was shaking, either from my close proximity to Dante, or the way I was preparing to cut my soul open and share a piece of myself I'd rarely showed anyone.

"I have nightmares," I stated, focusing on the word *sinner* tattooed on Dante's cheek so I wouldn't lose myself in his knee-weakening stare. "One, mainly. It's always the same. Corn fields. A twig snapping. A scream. It's so simple, and for the longest time I couldn't figure out why it scared me as bad as it did."

I swallowed hard and tucked my shaking hands behind my back. "About two years ago, I started having the dream nightly. It got so bad I didn't want to go to sleep, and I started taking caffeine pills to stay awake. It affected my work, my relationship, my friendships. Eventually, I decided to see a therapist, who referred me to a colleague of theirs who specialized in hypnotherapy. I did a session and found out the nightmare was actually a memory of something that happened to me as a kid."

Dante's frown deepened. "What happened?"

I sucked in a shaky breath and shook my head. "I'm not ready to talk about that just yet. I've only ever told three people; my best friend, my ex, and my mom. My best friend handled it perfectly, but my ex treated me like a freak after, and my mom..." Emotion wedged itself in my throat, strangling my words. "Well, I don't talk to her anymore."

Dante continued to search my face, like the secrets I was keeping were hidden somewhere in its freckles and laugh lines.

"Anyway," I went on, "it was a lot to handle. Too much. So one night, I tried to kill the pain... By killing myself."

Dante didn't move. He didn't flinch, or back away, or offer his condolences. He just listened, watched, and understood.

And I'd never realized how erotic it was to be understood.

I finally dared to look Dante in the eye. "Why I'm saying all this is because I agree with you. Some people *are* broken, but that doesn't mean they're fragile. It just means they need to find pieces that fit with theirs."

Dante sniffed grimly. "My pieces'll cut you."

"And I told you I like pain."

Our stares remained locked. A muscle in Dante's jaw tensed while his fingers danced at his sides, itching for an outlet. Answering their prayer, I reached out and took his hand, slowly leading it upwards until the rough, calloused pads of his fingertips brushed my collarbone. I stepped closer, moving my throat into his palm.

"You don't have to hurt yourself, Dante," I said softly. "We could make the world quiet together. Just for a little while."

Dante's fingers tightened, making my breath catch, but not from fear.

"You don't know what you're asking, angel," he hissed. "You think you've seen my dark side? You haven't even scratched the surface."

"Then show me." My expression hardened, and despite Dante's firm hold, I managed to lift my chin. "All I've ever wanted is for someone to give me permission to be fucked up and dirty and damaged so I can find power in it."

"You wouldn't have power with me," Dante cut in. "I'm not Callum and Donovan. I'm not going to kiss you or hold your hand. I don't want your pleasure, I want the opposite."

His fingers tightened even more, increasing the pressure on the sides of my neck. It heightened every sensation, making me hyperaware of the way his words danced across my lips in hot puffs.

"I want you helpless," he continued, his voice low. Dangerous. "I want you desperate. I want to watch the tears stream down your face when I break you. How does that give you power?"

"Because I'm choosing this," I whispered. "No one's taking it from me. I'm the one giving it away, and getting off on it."

Dante's hand lifted, dragging me onto my toes. A gasp escaped me, but it still wasn't from fear. A hint of trepidation tingled my spine, but it was overpowered by a rush of exhilaration.

"You sure you're gonna get off on it, angel?" he whispered, his mouth maddeningly close. Blood still trickled from his nose, staining his lips red.

"There's only one way to find out."

A few heart-pounding seconds passed before Dante released me. My feet found the ground again, and I hungrily sucked in an unobstructed breath. When Dante finally spoke, his voice was a low rumble. Half question, half threat.

"Why are you still standing?"

My body understood before my brain could catch up, and my legs buckled, dropping me to my knees. Dante stepped closer, towering over me so I had to crane my neck in order to keep eye contact. My fingers were the ones twitching now, impatiently fighting the urge to slide up Dante's thighs and unfasten the belt slung low on his hips. The buckle was positioned at mouth-level, leaving me inches away from something I'd craved since the night I signed that contract.

"Last warning, angel." Dante's hand drifted down to caress my chin, his touch deceptively gentle. "Do you really want to see beneath the surface?"

I nodded without hesitation.

Dante snatched my jaw in a vice-like grip, his fingers digging into the skin so hard I flinched. "Use your goddamn words, fucktoy."

An eager, uncontrollable shiver rattled my body. "Yes."

An abrupt *clap* rang out, and suddenly my cheek was stinging.

Holy shit. That fucker just slapped me. *Hard.*

My mouth hung agape, too stunned to form words, but my clenching pussy let me know my true feelings on what had just happened. I slowly raised my eyes to meet Dante's. His face was a blank slate, but a brief glance at the steadily growing bulge in his jeans revealed how he really felt.

"Yes, what?" Dante asked.

Blinking away my surprise, I mumbled, "Um…Yes, please?"

Another slap.

I grit my teeth as the sting on my cheek intensified.

"Try again."

I exhaled a quivering breath, wracking my brain for an appropriate answer. When the word popped into my mind, it felt so at home, so right, I wondered why the hell I'd never thought to use it before.

"Yes, Sir."

One side of Dante's mouth tugged upwards. "Good girl."

I instantly beamed at the praise, but gasped when his palm connected with my cheek again. Prepared to scream every curse word I knew, I opened my mouth, but Dante cut me off.

"Say thank you," he demanded, his words holding such authority my rage instantly fizzled. "You thank me whenever I punish you."

My cheeks turned an even brighter shade of pink than they already were. Part of me wanted to bite back, to hit him with some sassy quip or indignant rant, but it was only a small part. The rest of me wanted to silence my mind, lay down my walls, and go along with anything and everything he presented to me. It wanted to dive deep into his darkness so it could be free to embrace its own.

I rid my mind of that final indignant block, and melted into complete submission. "Thank you, Sir."

Dante stepped closer, pushing his hips to my face so my lips were pressed against the hard outline of his length. My tongue eagerly pricked with moisture.

"Hands behind your back."

I obediently folded my arms behind me.

Dante reached down and tapped my cheek, far more gently than he had before. "Open."

My lips parted, and Dante angled his hips further forward. My mouth wrapped around the width of him, the fabric of his jeans the only thing keeping me from swallowing him whole. His fingers threaded through my hair and tightened, pulling a tiny whimper of pleasure and pain out of me.

"You want another taste, angel?"

With my mouth stuffed, my words came out muffled. Dante crouched so we were eye-level, freeing my mouth but keeping a tight hold on my hair, which he gave a taunting tug. Air hissed through my teeth at the pain, while my inner walls pulsed with desire.

"Say it again," he commanded.

"Yes, Sir," I panted. "I want another taste."

Dante chuckled darkly and shook his head. "God, you're such a desperate little whore."

He spat the words like insults, but each one was a flame that stoked the fire building inside me. Arms still folded across my back, I dug my nails into the skin so I wouldn't be tempted to reach forward and drag Dante's cock out myself.

"Yes, Sir," I whispered, my body quaking with anticipation.

Dante's lips curled into a smirk. Tightening his grip on my hair, he lifted his free hand to the blood flowing down his face, coating his fingers in crimson. "You want a taste? Then fucking taste me, whore."

He parted my lips with his bloodied fingers and drove them deep into my mouth, hitting the back of my throat. The tang of metal spread across my tongue, but my mind was too clouded with lust, adrenaline, and blissful surrender to be repulsed. I kept my stare locked with his, admiring the arousal written on his face. When he dug deeper into my throat, I stifled my gag with a moan, prompting him to hiss an expletive and pull his fingers free. I gulped in a breath, never breaking eye contact. Dante smeared the remaining blood across my lips.

"Thank you, Sir," I said earnestly.

Dante released a slow, shaky breath.

"Jesus-fucking-Christ," he mumbled, his gaze roving over my face like it was his first time seeing it. "I think our broken pieces do fit."

I couldn't control myself any more.

I jerked my head forward, pulling my hair from Dante's grip, and kissed him.

It was a quick peck. Innocent, tender, and over in the blink of an eye, but it still left him looking like he'd just seen a ghost. I immediately wilted at his expression.

"I... I'm sorry," I stuttered. "I didn't—"

Dante silenced me by dragging me up by my throat, throwing my back against the venue wall, and smashing his lips into mine.

I was no longer Jade Matthews. I no longer had any identity at all. There was no thought, no worry or fear. The only thing in the world was sex and lust, pleasure and pain, and I was merely a vessel for them. Dante's tongue explored my mouth with vicious, punishing strokes, while his grip around my throat alternated from violent embrace to passionate caress. I had no idea how long we were locked in our feverish dance, but eventually we noticed someone clearing their throat to get our attention.

Dante jumped back like my skin had just burned him and whipped his head to our left. Craig hovered nearby, hands awkwardly stuffed in his pockets and his gaze aimed at the night sky to give us privacy.

"Sorry," he muttered. "First band's finished and Phantom Spark just went on. It's time to start getting ready."

Dante cleared his throat and wiped the remaining blood from his nose with the back of his hand. His gaze lingered on me a few seconds before he whirled and started for the loading dock doors. "Clean yourself up. You're a fucking mess."

Suddenly insecure, I lifted the hem of my shirt to my face and wiped any remnants of blood from my lips. Sensing Craig's eyes on me, I prayed my cheeks weren't as red as they felt.

"He kissed you."

I froze at the statement. Craig spoke even more rarely than Dante did, so the sound of his voice was still foreign and a little jarring. His expression didn't reveal much, but a hint of surprise glinted in his eyes.

I swallowed, the taste of iron still a phantom on my tongue. "Well, I kissed him first, but… yeah."

Craig nodded slightly, watching me a few seconds longer before turning to go. "You know, when the guys first told me they were bringing you on, I said it was a terrible idea."

I bristled, but relaxed when Craig looked back at me and smiled, his eyes softening.

"I was wrong. Whatever you're doing, keep doing it."

He walked away, leaving me alone in the alley with my cheek stinging and my head spinning.

30

I smirked at the text and inwardly patted myself on the back for successfully playing cupid.

The two had been flirting up a storm in each other's DMs since I'd been on the road with Legion, and the more I got to know Vee, the more I thought she and Kayla would be a good fit. I'd been talking her up for the past hour, and my friend finally got out of her own way and decided to give Vee a chance.

Doing a little happy dance, I sent Vee's number off to Kayla and glanced at Luca. He sat across from me, scratching lyrics into his notebook, his broad shoulders laughably too wide for the vintage patio chairs we were seated in. An extensive Google search of "Best Coffee In Dallas" had led him here, an adorably quaint cafe not far from the venue. He'd attempted to come alone, but I felt especially ornery today and followed him no matter how many times he told me to turn around and go back to the bus.

Sitting in front of Luca was his usual double espresso, as

well as a steaming cup of peppermint tea with honey. Last night he'd sung with more angst and passion than usual thanks to the events in the mosh pit, and his voice was paying the price this morning. The tea might've helped if he hadn't paired it with a cigarette, which he held in his left hand while he wrote with his right. When his phone dinged and he checked the message, he tried to camouflage his irritation, but he was unsuccessful.

"What's up?" I asked, sipping at the mocha horchata latte I purposefully picked out so Luca would have to suffer the embarrassment of ordering it.

He ignored me, and instead took a long, pensive drag of the cigarette before firing off a text back.

I sat my mug down and leaned forward on my elbows. "Come on, tell me. We both know I'm going to find out eventually."

Luca raised his eyes to the sky. "For fuck's sake. Five minutes of silence. That's all I want."

"If you wanted silence, you shouldn't have begged me to get coffee with you."

"What the fuck? I didn't—" Luca's fury fizzled when he clocked my amused expression.

I arched an eyebrow to toy with him even further. "Regret spending that fifteen grand yet?"

"Yep. You're worth a hundred bucks, max."

"Joke's on you, I would've done it for free."

Luca rolled his eyes and returned to his lyrics, but a slight smile now tugged at one corner of his mouth. After a few seconds, he grunted in frustration, tore the page out, and crumpled it up.

"When did writing get so hard?" he muttered, rubbing his temples gingerly. "I used to be able to do this shit in my sleep."

"You should ask Donovan for help. I know he's been trying to write some stuff lately."

Luca scoffed and flipped to the next page in his notebook. *"Trying* being the key word there."

"How about you forget your stupid civil war for two minutes and give him a chance? You're a band, you're supposed to collaborate."

"That's not how we work. Me and Dante write the music, the other two just have to show up."

"And now you're all so fed up with each other that you're ready to throw in the towel, so maybe it's time for a change."

Luca opened his mouth to retaliate, but promptly shut it when his phone dinged again. Air puffed from his nose in exasperation as he snatched it up, his expression darkening when he read what was on the screen.

"The label again?" I asked.

"No." Luca dropped the cigarette to the cobblestones underfoot so he had both hands free to type.

"One of the guys?"

"No."

"Then who?"

Luca set his phone face-down on the table and glared at me over the top of his mug as he finished his coffee.

I sighed and lifted my own drink to my lips. "Alright, fine. Keep everything bottled up. That's clearly working so well for you all."

"I'm not going to sit here and cry about my feelings with you."

"Why not? You hired me to be an outlet for your feelings."

"Not those kinds of feelings."

"Well you're not indulging in *those* kinds of feelings either, so I'm trying to make myself useful."

"You know how you can be useful?" Luca leaned across the table and lowered his voice to a whisper. "By shutting the fuck up."

I matched his position. "Make me, asshole."

Quick as lightning, Luca's hand whipped out and grasped my chin, his thumb darting between my lips and pressing down on my tongue.

Jesus, I didn't expect him to actually *do it.*

For a split second I worried what other people would think if they looked over and saw me sucking a grown man's thumb, but all that disappeared when Luca pushed his face closer and grazed my nose with his. My stomach dropped all the way to the floor and my arousal flared, heating me from the inside out.

"I'm not in the mood today, angel," Luca purred, his words a silky caress that carried the intoxicating promise of danger. "Don't make me punish you."

He pulled his hand from my mouth, grabbed his notebook, and pushed away from the table. I was left too dumbfounded and turned on to do anything but blink at our empty cups.

He shouldn't have said that.

Now I was absolutely going to keep pushing his buttons.

"Holy shit, girl! You look amazing!"

I beamed at Kayla's face on my phone screen. "Really?"

"That's a joke, right? Look at you!"

I glanced at my reflection in the mirror and chewed my bottom lip. It was the most effort I'd put into my appearance since the night I signed the contract, and I felt pretty damn good. My hair was bouncy with voluminous curls, my eyes popped thanks to a shimmery smokey eye, and my legs looked a mile long in a mini skirt and thigh high boots.

"I don't look skanky?"

"Oh no, you definitely look skanky. But in a hot way."

I laughed and leaned a hip against the bathroom sink. The opening act was nearing the end of their set, the pulsing bass of their final power ballad making the walls of the venue shake all the way in the women's restroom. I practically had to shout for Kayla to hear me over video chat.

"I miss you! I can't wait to come home in a few weeks and see you. By the way, did you get a hold of Trent? He stopped blowing up my phone thank god, but now he's not responding at all when I ask for updates on Gracie."

"I tried calling him, but he's ignoring me too. I'll stop over there tomorrow after work and ring the doorbell. We'll call it a doggy wellness check."

"Thank you so much. I owe you one."

"It's all good. You just stay safe, ok? Take your birth control and sage your space."

"I will. Love you, Kay."

"Love you more, Jay."

I clicked the phone off, did one last fluff of my hair, then zipped my leather jacket up to the neck and exited the bathroom.

After making my way backstage, I bumped into Craig as he came out of the green room. He scanned my outfit.

"Damn. Ok, legs. What's the occasion?"

"Just thought I'd show everyone I clean up ok." I craned my neck to look over his shoulder. "Is Luca in there?"

"No, he's checking equipment for the fifteenth time." Craig jerked his chin towards the stage behind me. "Careful, though. He's on the warpath."

"Good."

"Huh?"

"Nothing. Thanks!" I spun on my heel and started for the stage.

"Jade."

When I stopped and faced Craig again, I found him watching me closely, a far-off look in his eye.

"I know these guys like the back of my hand," he stated. "Luca and Dante especially. I grew up with those two."

"You did?"

"Someone had to be the lookout while they played pranks on the nuns."

I chuckled at the image, and a smile crept onto Craig's lips too.

"What I'm saying is, I know how they tick even if they don't always realize it themselves." He folded his arms and nodded in Luca's direction again. "Your instincts are right. A woman's been making his life hell, so he could use one to show him a slice of heaven."

I smiled sheepishly and ducked my head. "Thanks. And thank you for the encouragement the past few days."

He patted my shoulder as he passed me. "Well, we all know how much you like praise."

I gasped and lightly smacked him as he retreated, his mischievous giggle following him all the way out to the merch tables. When he'd gone, I refocused on my mission.

It wasn't praise I was after tonight.

Tonight I was finally going to unleash the Beast.

I caught sight of him fumbling around in a trunk of gear at the side of the stage. He was already dressed and painted for Legion's set, his mask firmly in place. I came up alongside him just as Phantom Spark took the stage and burst into their first song.

"They're pretty good, huh?" I said as my greeting.

Luca glanced at me out of the corner of his eye, his gaze lingering on my bare legs before returning to the microphone cord he was coiling.

"If they were at a high school battle of the bands, then yes, this poppy bullshit might be considered good."

"Lead singer's pretty hot."

Luca remained silent, but the tendons on the back of his hands flexed as his grip tightened, and his rings flashed in the light as he looped the cable more aggressively.

"Think I should go for him?" I pressed.

"If you want him to die," Luca mumbled.

"What was that?"

Luca hurled the cord to the ground, undoing all the progress he'd made. "What the fuck do you want, Jade? I told you I'm not in the mood today. Dante's drunk, Donovan and Cal are having a lovers' quarrel, and everyone in the world wants something from me. So what? What is it?"

"I don't want anything. I'm just enjoying the music."

I faced the stage, unzipped my jacket, and slid it off my shoulders, revealing the Phantom Spark t-shirt Chase gave me. Verging on too small, it was stretched tight across my chest, and I'd tied up the front hem so it exposed a sliver of skin above my skirt. I kept my attention on the band playing so I couldn't see Luca's expression, but the rage rippling off him was so palpable it made my skin prickle. My adrenaline spiked, and the rebellious fire in my heart victoriously roared to life.

"What the fuck is that?" he spat.

I peeked down at my shirt, adopting a doe-eyed expression. "This? I'm showing my support."

A few seconds of silence passed before Luca latched a hand around my elbow and dragged me further into the wings, cloaking us in shadow. He released my arm, but cornered me against one of the gear boxes.

"I told you what would happen if I ever caught you wearing that," Luca hissed, the gold horns on his mask catching the multicolored lights spilling over from the stage.

"Did you?" I innocently batted my eyelashes up at him.

Luca blinked as he finally processed what it was I was doing. His eyes narrowed into furious slits. "You think I won't fucking do it?"

I laughed and leaned in so the words he once said to me would be clearly heard now. "I *know* you won't do it."

Luca shoved my back flat on top of the gear box, gripped the neckline of the shirt in both hands, and ripped. Crisp air hit my skin as the fabric tore down the center.

"Oh my god!" I cried, "What the—"

A hand clapped over my mouth, pinning me to the trunk. Luca leaned over me, so close that my nose puffed condensation onto the mask, while the upside-down rosary hanging from his neck tickled the skin between my breasts.

"You've been poking at me for weeks trying to break me down," he growled. "Well congratulations, you did it. The flood-gates have opened, now you're gonna suffer the consequences."

Fucking *finally*.

Even in the shadows, I had no doubt Luca saw the hungry gleam in my eyes. I reached for the waistband of his black joggers, but he caught my hands and slammed them back to the trunk I was splayed on.

"No. You're not fucking moving."

Luca bent and snatched up the microphone cable he'd thrown to the ground, then looped it around my wrists and tugged it tight. Air hissed through my teeth as the rubber dug into my skin, but I still eagerly wriggled my hips towards him. An ache, low and deep, formed inside me, pulsing frantically as I watched Luca thread the cable through the trunk's handle and tie it off. My heart pounded at the thought of someone seeing us, but I was too goddamn turned on to care. If I didn't have this man right here, right now, I was going to burst.

The Beast seemed to feel the exact same way. Unconcerned about who might be watching, he spread my legs wide and reached for my panties, which he tore apart with the same ferocity he had the shirt hanging around my torso.

"Is this what you fucking wanted?" Luca asked, shoving his fingers between my thighs and parting the lips of my pussy. I gasped out a moan as he pushed them inside me. Luca's hand moved at a punishing pace, and the whole world would have heard my embarrassingly wet sounds if it hadn't been for the band playing just a few feet from us.

Oh god, what if Chase looked over to this side of the stage? Were we shrouded in enough darkness, or would he witness our moment of weakness?

As if reading my mind, Luca's eyes flicked to the lead singer. "What would your little boyfriend say if he knew I was finger-fucking you to his song?"

"He's… He's not my… boyfriend," I stuttered, squirming against Luca's movements. It was teetering right on the edge of too much, but it was still making my knees quake from the pleasure.

"No, he's not. You want to know why?" Luca leaned over me again and pressed his forehead to mine. "Because you belong to *me*."

He ripped his hand away, leaving me panting, dripping, and desperate for more. He gestured for me to turn over with his arousal-slicked fingers, but I rebelliously stayed on my back.

"God-fucking-dammit," Luca snarled, hooking his elbows under my legs. "When are you going to learn to behave?"

In one tug, he hurled me onto my stomach, then added a solid, stinging smack to my ass as punishment. I yelped and tried to jerk away, but my hands were still fixed to the trunk by the cable. To add salt to the wound, Luca brought down two more slaps in the same spot he just hit. I grit my teeth to keep from crying out, but a smile spread across my face. Adrenaline roared in my ears, spurred on by the symphony of our building breath and the pulsating beat surrounding us.

I craned my neck over my shoulder to see Luca standing over me, looking half man, half ancient deity ready to rain down his wrath.

"Is that all you got?" I mocked.

Luca set his jaw and slammed his palm to my skin one last

time, making my back arch from the pain. I heard another tear, and part of the mangled t-shirt detached from my back.

"There's really no other way I'm going to get you to be quiet, huh?"

A ribbon of fabric whipped in front of me and wedged between my teeth like a horse's bit. I struggled against the gag, but Luca tightened his hold, dragging my head backwards. Something warm and velvety soft slid between my ass cheeks, moving down until it teased my center and made my core clench in anticipation.

Luca pressed his lips to my ear, the scrape of his scruff on my neck sending a shiver down my spine.

"You wanted this, angel," he hissed, "so fucking *take it*."

On the last word, he slammed his full length inside me, forcing me to buck at the intrusion.

My *god*, he was big. Almost *too* big. It would have been agonizing if he hadn't warmed me up with his fingers first. Still, my inner walls strained around him, and I had to shut my eyes tight and puff air through my nose as my body adapted to his size. But instead of waiting for me to adjust fully, Luca slid himself out and furiously rammed back in. My teeth gnashed at the fabric between them, muffling my cries, and I tugged against my restraints.

"You're not going anywhere." Luca's fingers threaded through the hair at the base of my skull and pulled tight. "You're taking every last inch."

He plunged in again and again, holding me steady so each thrust filled me to the brim. I moaned against the gag, my eyes rolling back in my head as my body finally acclimated, and any remaining discomfort melted into knee-weakening pleasure. With each thrust, I felt my arousal dripping further down my inner thighs, the tickling sensation only adding to the stimulation.

"God, look how wet this needy little pussy is," Luca said

through gritted teeth. "You were fucking aching for this cock, weren't you? Just a filthy little cumslut desperate to be filled."

My moans morphed into stuttering groans as tension settled low in my belly, amplifying each time Luca slid against my G-spot.

"Look at you. About to come already?" Luca huffed a breathless laugh. "God, you were fucking made to be used. Just a pretty little plaything ready to be fucked and filled."

Luca released his hold on the gag, letting it slip from my mouth. The fingers in my hair pulled, dragging me as close to standing as I could manage with my wrists still tied with the microphone cable. Luca slipped his free hand to my throat, applying pressure to the sides as he continued to hammer into me. The new position hit my inner walls even better than before, and my body raced towards a climax.

"Oh god," I cried.

"He's not here, angel. Just me, and I prefer to be called Master." Luca's mouth found my ear again, his gravelly words barely audible as the crowd burst into cheers when a guitar solo broke out. "You're mine, you understand? My property." He jerked his chin to Chase performing in the spotlight in front of us. "Not his, not anyone else's. Fucking *mine*."

I nodded, so close to my peak I could barely keep upright. Luca's grip around my throat tightened, and his thrusts increased to a brutal pace.

"Come for me, angel. Let that fucker onstage know who owns you."

"Oh fuck, Luca!" I shouted, my orgasm erupting at the same time the song finished, my words smothered by a roar of applause from the crowd. My body shuddered and twitched from overstimulation, but I received no mercy from the Beast. He held me steady, continuing to pound into me until his pants deteriorated into haggard gasps.

"Shit," he hissed, releasing my hair and neck to grab my hips with both hands. He pulled me flush with his skin, sheathing himself completely inside me, and a burst of warmth spread through my core as he released. When he'd finished, his body crumpled over the top of mine, pinning us both to the gear box as we caught our breath.

It took almost the entirety of Phantom Spark's second song, but Luca eventually slid out of me and tucked himself back in his pants. He bent and untied the cable from the trunk handle before unbinding my wrists, then shrugged off his black cloak and draped it over my shoulders. Without another word, he readjusted his mask and walked away, leaving me alone to slide to the ground, dazed, spent, and as much a mess physically as I was mentally.

31

I didn't stay to watch Legion's set.

Clutching the Beast's cloak tight to protect my modesty, I hurried back to the bus and changed into a hoodie and yoga pants before returning the garment to the green room. Not wanting to make contact with Luca, I left it hanging on the door-knob outside before hiding in my bunk for the rest of the night.

An influx of thoughts and emotions swirled in my mind, making it impossible to do anything but stare at the wall and listen to music in the hopes someone else's words could help me make sense of it all. Suddenly, Dante's ever-present headphones began to make a lot more sense. When my shuffle landed on "Poison & Wine" by The Civil Wars, I hit repeat on the soulful, melancholy duet and played it until my racing mind slowed.

The encounter with Luca was one of the hottest thing's I'd ever experienced. I'd fantasized about sex like that, read about it, watched it in porn, and in the moment, I was lust-drunk and blissed out. But now a weight had settled on my chest, and I felt strangely numb. I liked what we did, but my body was responding like I hadn't. Maybe I just needed someone to tell me that it was ok to like it. *I* knew that of course, but an outside voice confirming it might be nice too.

We didn't have to drive long after the guys finished the show. There was another day off wedged between the next date in Albuquerque, so it was decided we would get a hotel in Dallas that night and get back on the road tomorrow after we'd all had a good night's rest.

I shuffled into my hotel room, tossed my key card and duffle bag on the bed, then discarded my hoodie and headed for the bathroom. I was exhausted, but not remotely sleepy despite the clock pushing 1 AM. Hopefully a hot shower would relax me. The musk of sex still clung to my skin, and when I caught my reflection in the mirror, I discovered smudges of white paint on my neck from where Luca had grabbed me. I had no doubt there was more of it located on other body parts too.

When I reached for the shower faucet, I caught a glimpse of another trophy that was a result of my brush with the Beast; dark red marks encircled my wrists where the tightly wound microphone cable had cut into my skin. The sight of the marks invoked a twinge of arousal and a strange sense of pride.

A knock at the hotel room door snapped me from my thoughts. I glanced at my cellphone to check the time, then warily crept out of the bathroom and put my eye to the peephole. I blinked in surprise at who stood in the hallway, then slowly opened to door.

"Hey," Luca mumbled, readjusting his weight from one foot to the other. His hair was mussed, his voice hoarse, and he fiddled with something behind his back.

"Hey," I replied. "Everything ok?"

"Yeah. I just…" Luca trailed off and frowned. After a few beats, his arm moved out from behind him and he extended a rolled up t-shirt. "Here. To replace the other one."

It was a different color than the one he'd ripped off me, and when I took it from his hand and unfolded it, I discovered it wasn't Phantom Spark merch at all.

The logo belonged to Legion.

"If you're going to rep anyone's band, it's going to be mine," Luca stated firmly.

Instinct had me wanting to roll my eyes, but I was too tired to fight. I tucked the shirt under my arm and nodded. "Ok."

Confusion flickered across Luca's face at my lack of attitude, but he dipped his head curtly and began to walk away. I watched him for a few seconds, then moved to close the door.

"Jade?"

I peeked back into the hall. Luca had faced me again, his eyes fixed on the carpet as he absentmindedly spun one of his rings around his finger.

"Thank you."

I opened the door a little wider. "For what?"

"For the… *distraction* earlier." Luca's eyes lifted to meet mine. The furrow in his brow relaxed, and his eyes softened. "It helped."

A smile found its way to my lips, and the weight in my chest grew a little lighter. "I'm glad."

Luca politely bent his head again and stuffed his hands in his pockets as he turned to go.

"Do you want to stay the night?"

The words tumbled out before I even realized they were on the tip of my tongue.

Luca's surprised expression mirrored my own, and I quickly fumbled for a recovery.

"It just saves me a trip tomorrow morning. This way I won't have to track you down for our coffee run."

Luca sniffed. "*Our* coffee run?"

"You know what? Never mind." I backed deeper into my room. "I forgot you have to stay with Dante."

"Craig said he'd look after him tonight."

I froze with one hand on the doorknob. He stayed still too, his stare glued to my face.

"I, uh…" He cleared his throat. "I still need to shower."

"I've got one of those."

Another tight silence stretched between us. Finally, Luca slowly moved towards me. Once he'd crossed the hall and landed in front of me, I opened the door fully.

"Come on in."

My breath caught as Luca slipped by me. After our encounter earlier, I thought the pull of his body would be lessened, and I could finally stop being so distracted any time he was close. But the electricity between us remained, thickening the air as he passed.

I averted my gaze and gestured to the bathroom. "I need to shower too, but you can go first."

"You sure?"

"Yeah, you just played a show. You need it more than I do."

Although the scent of sex on my skin begged to differ.

"Alright, thanks." Luca hesitated a few seconds more before retreating to the bathroom. Once he was gone, I inhaled deep and let it out slow, trying to calm my racing heart as I wandered over to the bed. When the faucet squeaked on in the bathroom, I remembered the bag of toiletries packed away in my duffel and fished them out.

"Luca?" I called, wandering towards the sound of running water. "If you don't want to use the hotel stuff, I've got some body wash you can—"

I stopped in my tracks when I turned the corner and caught sight of the singer in nothing but his boxer briefs, his clothes discarded in a pile on the floor. I quickly looked away.

"Sorry."

"It's nothing you haven't seen before."

"I know, but you're usually covered in paint. Bare skin is so much more intimate." With flushed cheeks, I kept my eyes on the tile under our feet and held out the bag. "Here. You can use whatever you want. Just not my toothbrush."

A small chuckle puffed from Luca's lips as he took the bag from my hand. I began my retreat, but froze when his fingers latched around my wrist. I faced him, noting his somber expression. Luca's grip loosened, and he ran his thumb over the red welts on my wrist.

"Are you ok?" he asked, his voice as soft as his touch.

My stomach dipped at his uncharacteristic tenderness, but I responded with a casual shrug. "I wouldn't have let you in if I wasn't."

Luca nodded, a flicker of relief passing over him as he continued to trace the marks. "Next time I'll stick around to make sure you're taken care of."

"Taken care of how?"

This time, it was Luca who shrugged. "Check in with you. Hold you." His thumb stopped moving. "Kiss you."

Suddenly it became harder to breathe, like someone had siphoned all the air out of the room. As if being pulled by an unseen force, I stepped forward. Luca's hand traveled from my wrist to my waist, his touch still tender as he pulled me in close. At this moment, there were no walls between us. No cool facades or bitter defenses. We were just Luca and Jade. And somehow, that was just as erotic as what had happened earlier.

I lost myself in Luca's gaze, the bathroom light bringing out flecks of gold in his irises.

"You could take care of me now," I said softly.

"I was hoping you'd say that."

Luca slowly leaned in, but halted just before his lips met mine, leaving them tingling. Instead, he delicately nudged my nose, his voice lowering to a whisper.

"Are you sure you're ok?"

I gave him a small, grateful smile and nodded. "I liked it. A lot."

"Me too."

Only then did he close the distance between us, pressing his lips to mine with the same tenderness he'd used handling the marks on my wrist. It was a change of pace from our usual dynamic, but after how off I'd been feeling, I welcomed it. I melted into him, sliding my hands up his wide chest before draping them over the back of his neck. Luca's tongue swept into my mouth, entwining with mine using long, unhurried strokes. He tasted vaguely of spearmint and the lingering spice of tobacco, and I found myself craving more. I hungrily pulled him tighter, accidentally knocking him off balance, but he dragged me with him as he stumbled backwards into the shower. Steaming water connected with our skin, soaking my clothes, but doing nothing to deter us.

Luca's hands roved over my body, alternating between soft caresses and firm grasps, like he had to remind himself to be gentle. When my fingers wandered to the waistband of his briefs, all bets were off. He slammed my back into the shower glass, planting his palms on either side of me as he pressed the hard outline of his cock into the sensitive spot between my legs. I moaned into his mouth and ripped the fabric down his hips, letting the entirety of him spring free. He'd felt massive when I'd had him inside me, but I'd only experienced him, not actually seen him. When my eyes landed on his length, I gasped.

"Jesus-fucking-Christ," I muttered.

How the hell did I fit that thing inside me and walk away after?

As if reading my mind, Luca smirked and moved his mouth to my neck, dragging his lips across the tender skin. "Don't act like you can't take it. We both know you do it flawlessly."

A twinge of lust shook me from the inside out, propelling me into action, and I took Luca in both hands. My fingertips weren't even close to touching, making me anxious at the impossible concept of fitting him in my mouth. But I didn't need to worry, because Luca was the one who dropped to his knees, yanked my water-logged yoga pants to the shower floor, and shoved my legs wide.

"God, that's a pretty pussy," he muttered, shaking his head in disbelief as he ran his fingers up my thighs. Without waiting for my response, he buried his face in my heat and began devouring me like it was his job.

I smacked a hand to the glass behind me to brace myself as Luca's lips and tongue surged pleasure through my core. The soaked t-shirt stretched across my chest heaved up and down, a sight Luca kept his eyes glued to. Eventually, he reached up to take a breast in each hand, and I moaned my approval as he kneaded them in time with his swirling tongue.

"Fuck, that feels good," I breathed, using my free hand to rake my fingers through Luca's hair and out of his face. He looked damn good eating me out, and I wanted to thoroughly enjoy the view.

He kept his pressure steady, but sped up when my breaths grew quicker and more shallow. Eyes still focused on me, Luca lifted his lips just enough for me to hear him mumble, "You're going to come just like this, you understand?"

My insides eagerly twinged at the command, but I huffed a nervous laugh. "I can't just come on cue—"

Luca hauled my legs over his shoulders, suspending me in the air before diving back between my thighs. My yelp of surprise transitioned to a moan when his tongue circled my clit in rapid sweeps, drawing out a full body shudder.

"Oh my god," I groaned. "Fuck, Luca, just like that. Don't stop."

Luca lifted his face again. "Where's that word we always talk about?"

I rolled my eyes, but what Luca had been doing felt too perfect for me to risk him stopping.

"*Please* don't stop."

A satisfied smirk appeared on Luca's face before he dipped his head back down. He continued the same pattern as before, rocketing me right back into a state of bliss. The lapping of his tongue and the warm spray of the water had my body relaxed and my mind clear, allowing me to race to a climax. The pleasure peaked, my breath caught, and I gripped Luca's hair with both hands to ground myself. His fingers dug into my hips, holding me in place, as an orgasm tore through me so hard I saw stars.

When I'd finally come back down to earth, Luca shrugged my legs off his shoulders and let me slump against the glass to catch my breath. He rose to his feet and took my face in his hands, then kissed me deeply. The passion and intimacy in that kiss had me instantly ready for round two despite the way my knees where trembling.

I sunk to the shower floor and took his shaft in both hands. Staring up at him, I ran my tongue along the underside, top to bottom and back again. Luca shuddered, then clapped a hand to the shower wall above my head to brace himself when I took him into my mouth. My jaw stretched to its limit trying to fit him.

An appreciative groan rumbled in Luca's chest as he pushed his hips forward, shoving himself further into my mouth. "That's it, take it all."

I choked, but somehow managed to let him into my throat. Luca expressed his approval through a series of hissed curses before grabbing my arms and raising them overhead, interlocking his fingers with mine as he pinned my hands. He drove himself in and out of my mouth with increasingly rapid movements, pulling out just long enough for me to suck in a deep breath before he dove back in again.

"That's a good girl," he said through gritted teeth. "God, look at you taking that cock like a perfect little slut."

I gulped for air as he ripped himself free and hauled me to my feet, spinning me around so my chest was pressed against the glass. Something firm and warm nudged my entrance from behind while Luca's mouth found my ear.

"You want me?" he whispered, catching my earlobe in a nip.

I nodded frantically and wriggled my hips towards him so his tip stretched me open. "Yes. Please, *please* fuck me, Luca."

An animalistic growl rose in his throat. "Goddamn, you sound good when you beg."

He thrust himself inside me, making me cry out at the intrusion and puff a cloud of hot air against the glass. My body still struggled to adjust to his size, but it eased faster than it had earlier, and any sliver of discomfort soon melted away. Luca fucked me slower this time, sliding in and out with smooth, deliberate movements. He spread my cheeks apart so he could fit the entirety of his length inside, and I leaned my forehead against the glass as I relished the decadent tightness.

"Touch yourself," came Luca's command.

I obediently slid my hand between my legs and rubbed circles on my clit, my breath hitching as the tension amplified. Luca kept up his momentum, but began planting kisses up my spine until his lips connected with my neck. There he sunk his teeth into my shoulder, making me simultaneously wince and moan. Our pants huffed in tandem as our bodies fell in sync, moving in perfect harmony. One of Luca's hands slid around my waist to hold me steady, while the other slid around my neck to keep me close. I caught his eye over my shoulder, taking a moment to admire his rugged beauty and the raw emotion coloring it. He held my stare for a few seconds, then hauled me in for another passionate kiss as his hand around my waist dipped lower, overlapping mine between my legs.

"Come for me, angel," he murmured against my mouth. "I want you fucking dripping."

My insides constricted at his words, and tension coiled feverishly in my abdomen. With Luca's fingers helping me, I massaged my clit faster and faster until the pleasure burst. I cried out, but Luca muffled my sounds by smothering them with a hungry kiss. I was still shaking when Luca's breath caught and he pulled out just in time to release a warm spurt of cum on my ass.

With our bodies pressed together, we slumped against the glass to catch our breath, just like we had earlier at the side of the stage. Only this time, Luca didn't abandon me once he'd recovered. He slid out of me, grabbed the body wash that had started this whole thing, and lathered it over my body. I did the same for him, and together we washed the sweat and leftover paint from each other's skin until the water ran clear.

Luca shut off the faucet and stepped out, then grabbed a towel and held it open for me. I blushed a little, hoping he'd think the color was from the heat of the shower, and nestled in to it. A yelp leapt from my mouth when Luca suddenly scooped me into his arms and carried me out of the bathroom.

"What are you doing?" I shrieked, smacking his back. "You're gonna hurt yourself!"

"Please, you're light as a feather."

"I most definitely am not!"

"You are to me."

Luca hauled me over to the bed and set me down gracefully, and I ducked my head to hide the way my cheeks had flushed even more. Luca casually lifted the flap on my duffel bag and rummaged through its contents.

"Where would I find your pajamas?"

"Bottom left. Why?"

Luca pulled an oversized t-shirt and a pair of cotton shorts from the bag and faced me. "Arms up."

I squinted at him. "What is this?"

"I told you, I'm taking care of you."

Still watching him suspiciously, I lifted my arms overhead. Luca slid the shirt over my shoulders, then bent and shimmied the shorts up my legs and hips, planting kisses along my thighs as he went. I had to bite my lip to keep a giggle from escaping.

"Who are you and what have you done with Luca Serino?" I teased.

"Oh, shut up. I can be nice sometimes." Luca gave me a sharp rap on the ass as he stood.

Ah. There he is.

Massaging the spot, I watched him cross to the other side of the bed and pull back the covers. He was still naked, glistening from the shower and looking like a golden god thanks to the lamp in the corner that highlighted his body in orange light. Luca looked around the room for something to pull back the damp hair grazing his shoulders, and I handed him the hair tie from my wrist.

"Can I ask you a silly question?"

"Sure." Luca restrained his waves and clambered into bed, pushing back the blankets on my side so I could do the same. I crawled over to him.

"Did you really sell your soul to the devil for fame and fortune?"

Luca sighed and rolled his eyes like it was a question he'd been asked a thousand times. "You're still thinking about that?"

"Come on, just tell me." I nuzzled into the pillows and blinked up at him with wide eyes. "*Please.*"

Luca smirked, settled onto the mattress beside me, and propped his fist under his chin. "You want the truth?"

"Always."

"Fine. The truth is… I don't know."

Luca rolled onto his back to stare up at the ceiling and intertwined his fingers over his stomach. "Ten years ago, the four of us were stumbling drunk down Sunset Boulevard after a show at the Roxy. Callum came clean about why he and Donovan came over from England, and I admitted why me and Dante left San Diego. We realized our pasts were the one thing we had in common, and the fact we'd found each other in the City of Angels was eerily serendipitous. Donovan joked it was a sacred meeting ordained by the devil himself, and I said they should join me and Dante's band so we could pay homage to our dark lord. Then we wandered into a tattoo parlor, paid the artist a hundred bucks to let Callum borrow his tattoo gun, and he carved the word *sinner* into Dante's face to signify the occasion. It was stupid, drunken, 20-something behavior, but when we met up the next day to play together, we sounded good. Weirdly good. Like it was fate for us to come together. We got signed a month later, and the rest is history. So *did* we sell our souls that night? Maybe. But that's for people to decide on their own."

He angled his head towards me, scanning my face for a clue as to what was going on in my brain. "What do *you* think? Do you think our souls are damned?"

I considered the story, then answered honestly. "No."

"Why not?"

"Because if you were promised to the devil, you wouldn't be in the presence of an angel."

I popped a playful kiss on his cheek, prompting a smile to spread across his face. He rolled onto his side and draped an arm over my hips, dragging me close using a handful of my ass.

"That's a damn good point."

Exhaustion finally setting in, Luca's eyes drifted shut. I reached out a hand and lightly smoothed the furrowed lines on his brow until they relaxed and disappeared.

"Luca?" I said softly.

A sleepy "Mm-hmm" answered.

"What was it you four you had in common?"

Luca's body tensed, but he didn't open his eyes. He simply found my hand, brought it to his lips, and pressed a kiss to the welts on my wrists.

"We aren't good men, angel," he murmured. "But we'll be good to you."

He let go of my hand and flipped over so his back was facing me. I stared at the tattoos covering it, my gaze holding on one that looked like a snarling monster with curling horns and fangs dripping in blood.

I frowned and reached forward to trace the outline of the beast. "Luca?"

"Mm-hmm?"

"Did you hurt someone?"

A long, tense silence followed. After what felt like an eternity, I received a response.

"Go to sleep, angel. We've got a long day tomorrow."

I should have run for the hills, but instead I stayed in bed with the devil and fell asleep.

32

Stalks of corn.

The crack of a twig behind me.

A scream for help that no one was around to hear.

My eyes snapped open, and I shot upright in bed, blinking repeatedly to try and make sense of my surroundings. A lamp was on in the corner, my duffel bag lay open at the foot of the bed, and Luca was fast asleep beside me.

I was safe, and it was just a dream.

Breathing a sigh of relief, I fumbled for my phone in the front pocket of my bag. 4:37 AM the screen read.

Groaning, I sat back in the pillows and put a hand to my racing heart. There was no way I'd be falling back asleep any time soon. By the time I'd finally manage to pass out, Luca would probably be waking up for coffee, or Donovan and Callum would be hitting me up for our morning run.

I considered my options for a few minutes, then swung my legs over the side of the bed and tiptoed across the room, grabbing my room key on the way. Maybe the front desk had some over-the-counter sleeping pills I could purchase, or at the very least some allergy medication that would make me drowsy.

Checking over my shoulder to make sure I wasn't waking Luca, I turned the door handle and maneuvered it open, squinting as bright fluorescent light poured in from the hall.

Slipping out of the room, I carefully clicked the door shut, then turned in the direction of the elevators. I froze when I discovered someone seated on the floor just a few feet from my room, slumped with their back against the wall and a bottle of champagne in their hand. I relaxed when I caught sight of a familiar pair of headphones jammed over the figure's ears.

I wandered over and tapped Dante on the shoulder. He lifted his head, his bloodshot eyes taking a few seconds to focus on me before sparking with recognition. I sank to the carpet beside him as he hit pause on his music.

"Where's Craig?" I asked.

Dante lifted the champagne to his lips. "Craig sleeps like a log. When he babysits, I can do anything I want and he'll never know."

His slurred speech made me wonder how many of those bottles he'd gone through tonight.

I jerked my chin to the drink in his hand. "You gonna share, or what?"

Dante smirked and extended the champagne. "That's what I came here to do, but you were too busy to answer the door."

"Sorry, I was—"

"Fucking Luca, I know." Dante leaned his head back against the wall and shut his eyes as I took a drink. "Thank fuck *someone* finally is. Maybe now he'll stop making everyone miserable. Good for you, angel. You're really doing the Lord's work."

He chuckled grimly and tried to take the bottle back, but I angled away from him and chugged the rest of its contents. I'd expected him to get angry, but Dante just laughed.

"Damn, you trying to drown your sorrows too? Was Luca that bad?"

I wiped my mouth with the back of my hand and wedged the

empty bottle between us. "Is that what you're doing out here? Drowning your sorrows?"

The light in Dante's eyes dimmed and he averted his gaze. After a few seconds, he sighed and groggily rubbed his face. "Noisy."

I scooted closer, unsure I'd heard the muffled word correctly. "What was that?"

"It's noisy," Dante repeated, raising his index finger to his temple and tapping. "Too noisy."

"Ah." I glanced at the music paused on his phone. "So what's drowning out the noise tonight?"

Dante hesitated, but eventually lifted his headphones off his ears and hung them around his neck. Then he turned up the volume, restarted the song, and handed me the phone. The screen read "Paralyzed" by NF. Slow, somber piano chords played through the speakers, followed by melancholy vocals. The hallway echoed with lyrics about feeling numb and no longer recognizing who you were, and my heart tugged at one line in particular where the singer pondered if the person they once were disappeared at the same time as their faith.

I peeked at Dante out of the corner of my eye. He stared straight ahead, eyes glazed and shuttered, but his jaw clenched. He might look emotionless to someone on the outside, but the war waging inside was clear to anyone who knew him deeper. I wished I could take whatever pain was eating away at him, but I knew firsthand that nothing can save you from a dark place but yourself. All anyone else can do is be a light to guide you back home.

When the song finished, I searched the music library for another. I landed on "Carry You" by Ruelle and Fleurie and pressed play.

"You know this one?" I asked over the piano intro.

Dante shook his head and closed his eyes to take in the lyrics. Once the chorus hit, his frown was replaced with a sad smile.

"You should run, angel," he mumbled. "Run as far away from us as possible."

Despite his warning, he sunk further onto the floor and maneuvered himself so his head rested on my lap. My fingers found their way into his hair, where I began absentmindedly twirling the strands.

"I'm not going anywhere," I whispered.

Dante's breaths grew deeper and more drawn out, hinting that sleep was finally coming to claim him. Just before it did, his lips parted to speak.

"I have nightmares too."

Then he slipped away to face them.

I woke to someone gently shaking me.

My head angled to the side, and I discovered a hand decorated in an assortment of gold rings resting on my shoulder.

"Good morning," Luca greeted gently.

I blinked up at him, then at my surroundings. I was still seated in the hotel hallway, the empty bottle of champagne beside me and Dante's head still resting on my lap. He snored softly, looking uncharacteristically innocent in his vulnerable state, maybe even angelic.

"What time is it?" I mumbled, rubbing sleep from my eyes.

"Coffee time." Luca's head tilted as he watched Dante a few seconds longer. "You got him to sleep."

He sounded equally surprised and relieved.

I shrugged and stroked Dante's hair the way I had last night. "Not really. He was halfway there when I found him."

"He's halfway there a lot." A subtle smile found its way to Luca's face. "Pretty sure it was you."

He lightly kicked Dante's sneaker, causing him to jerk awake and sit upright. The man immediately clutched his head and miserably slumped against the wall.

"Wakey-wakey, sunshine," Luca chuckled.

"Fuck off," Dante groaned back.

I patted his thigh. "Come on. Some breakfast will help that hangover."

"Just bring me an energy drink and some ibuprofen."

"Best I can do is eggs and a latte." I stood and offered him my hands. "Let's go. It's coffee time."

Luca frowned. "I didn't say he could come on our coffee run."

I raised an eyebrow. "*Our* coffee run?"

Luca's mouth opened then promptly shut, his frown deepening. I bit back a giggle and helped Dante to his feet.

"Hurry up," Luca grumbled, spinning on his heel and stomping down the hall towards the elevators.

An hour later, the three of us were seated in a colorful cafe in the heart of Dallas. It wasn't the coffee shop Luca had originally wanted to go to, but I'd insisted the food options at this one would be better suited for someone dealing with a hangover, and he'd begrudgingly agreed on the location.

We sat in a cozy corner of the restaurant, Dante struggling with a cold brew and ham and cheese croissant, while I opted for a smothered burrito and raspberry truffle latte. Luca was still moping over his double espresso, but judging by the way he kept stealing bites of my food, I had a hunch he wasn't as annoyed by our company as he let on. When his phone dinged, though, a storm cloud seemed to form overhead. Luca's energy darkened as he read the text on the screen and tapped out a response.

"What's wrong?" I asked. "Is it the label asking about the single again?"

"Nah." Dante muscled down a sip of coffee and jerked his chin to Luca's phone. "When he acts like that, it's baby mama drama."

Luca glared at him and set his phone face-down. "It's private."

Dante shot me a look that said, *told you so.*

"What does she want this time?" he asked around a mouthful of croissant. "Fancy new car? Vacation in Mykonos? Two Gucci handbags?"

Luca sat back in his chair and crossed his arms. "What part of 'it's private' do you not understand?"

Dante tapped his ear. *"No hablo ingles."*

Luca kicked him under the table.

"I still think you should get a paternity test," I cut in. "There has to be some way to make it happen."

"Besides breaking into her house and stealing the kid's DNA, not one I can think of."

"We could do that," Dante offered, his eyes lighting up.

"No." Luca's phone dinged again. When he checked it, he sighed. "Ok, *now* it's the label. Have you gotten any farther on that chord progression, D?"

"I've got a sick bass line," Dante replied, "but Dono won't let me borrow his guitar to fuck around with melodies."

The bell on the cafe door dinged, causing the three of us to look over. Callum and Donovan strolled in, sweaty from their run but laughing and talking as they walked hand in hand.

"Speaking of *el diablo,*" Dante muttered, refocusing on his breakfast.

"Looks like they made up," I mused, smiling at the two as they came to a stop in front of the counter. Callum hugged Donovan from behind, perching his chin as his shoulder as they ordered smoothies from the peppy barista. Over ten years together and they still acted like teenagers falling in love for the first time. My heart tugged with longing for a connection like theirs.

"Ugh, *disgusting*. I don't want to see that," came a female voice. The Texas twang dripped with contempt, and when I looked for its owner, I found a middle-aged Southern belle at the table beside us who was busy glaring in Callum and Donovan's direction. A man with a mustache and cowboy hat sat with her, and when he followed her gaze, his face fell.

"I'll take care of it, honey," he stated, patting her hand and standing.

Luca shot up from his chair too. "No, you won't."

Missing the subtle threat behind Luca's words, the man tipped his hat and continued across the cafe. "It's alright, son. I'll handle this."

Luca set his jaw and followed him.

Cowboy hat arrived at the counter and tapped Callum on the shoulder. When the two men turned, he motioned to their proximity. "Gentlemen, there are places to do this, but it sure as hell ain't here."

Donovan's eyes narrowed, but he tilted his head in mock confusion. "Do what?"

"Just ignore him," Callum urged, tugging Donovan's elbow to try and pull his focus away.

"No, I'd like to hear what this guy meant too," Luca chimed in, looming behind the man like a phantom in the night.

Cowboy Hat glanced over his shoulder and raised his hands in defense. "Listen, I'm just saying they're making folks uncomfortable."

"I'm not uncomfortable," I stated, loud enough to capture the attention of the entire cafe. I stood and crossed my arms. "Seems to me you're the only bigot in here."

"This conversation doesn't involve you, miss," Cowboy Hat snapped. "Sit down."

Dante pushed back from the table and joined me on my feet. "I thought Dallas was supposed to be a liberal city."

The man clocked Dante's face tattoo and frowned, then pulled back his jacket to reveal a holstered revolver at his hip. "I don't want any trouble."

"Kinda seems like you do," Dante replied, shoving me behind his back.

The man placed his hand on his gun, making the customers in the cafe nervously murmur among themselves.

"Jesus," Callum exclaimed, tugging at Donovan again. "Come on, let's just go. It's not worth it."

Donovan looked ready to argue, but he was interrupted by Luca stepping in front of the gun and looking the man up and down.

"What the fuck are you gonna do, asshole?"

The man stubbornly lifted his chin. "It's within my rights to protect myself."

"Acting out a hate crime in broad daylight is considered protecting yourself?"

Luca took a threatening step closer, causing the man's finger to move towards the trigger. The cafe erupted in more anxious chatter, and several customers jumped from their seats to rush out of the building.

"I don't want to hurt you, son," the man warned.

"No, you'd prefer to hurt my friends, you homophobic fuck."

The click of the trigger made my breath catch, and I nervously clutched Dante's hand.

"Here's what's going to happen," Luca hissed, unphased by the line of danger he currently stood in. "You're going to keep that gun right where it is, you're going to apologize to the couple you just insulted, and you're going to walk away. And I'm sure you're thinking, 'I'm quick on the draw. I can get a shot in.' You're absolutely right. You'll be able to take me out, no problem. But that fucker over there?" He nodded to Dante. "He's fast.

Ungodly fast. He'll be on you before you have another one in the chamber. And that Draco Malfoy motherfucker?" He gestured to Callum. "He's scary strong. He'll break every bone in your hand before you can pull the trigger a second time. But god help you if the other guy gets his hands on you." Luca's eyes landed on Donovan. "That one's no stranger to bullet holes, and he won't hesitate to put one in you too."

The room was so quiet you could have heard a pin drop. Dante's fingers tightened around mine, and the muscles in his back flexed as he prepared to leap into action.

Finally, Cowboy Hat's finger eased off the trigger, and he slowly backed away. "Debbie, let's go."

The woman he'd been sitting with abandoned her coffee at the table and raced for the exit, the man not far behind her. Once they'd left, the barista, still quaking with fear, turned to Luca.

"I'm sorry, but I'm going to have to ask you to leave too."

Luca nodded, but before he could make for the door, Donovan intercepted him.

"We didn't need you to save us," he stated.

Instead of matching the ice in his eyes, Luca just shrugged. "I know. That one was purely for me."

The two stared at each other for a few tense beats before Donovan averted his gaze to the ground.

"Thank you," he mumbled.

Acting like he didn't hear, Luca jumped right back into his role of commander. "Bus call's in an hour. Don't be late."

He stomped out of the coffee shop, the rest of us following after him. I wasn't sure Dante realized that his hand remained glued to mine as we walked, but I didn't call attention to it.

Once outside, I reached my free hand out to squeeze Callum's shoulder.

"Are you alright?" I asked.

He smiled and slid his arm around my waist. "It's nothing we haven't experienced before."

I frowned and leaned into him, nestling my face in the crook of his neck. "I hate that."

"It is what it is." Callum planted a kiss on my temple. "Thank you for standing up for us, though."

I pulled back just enough for him to see the sincerity in my eyes. "Always."

He smiled again and pressed his lips to mine, kissing me deeply.

It should have felt strange holding one man's hand while kissing another, but for some reason, it was the most normal I'd felt since signing that contract.

33

The shows in Albuquerque and Denver went abnormally smooth. Luca kept his bossing to a minimum, and I even caught him and Donovan calmly chatting on a few occasions. Maybe I was just getting used to the rift, but I couldn't shake the feeling that something healed that day in Dallas, even if it was something small.

On the way to Salt Lake City, the atmosphere on the bus was the most bright and full of life I'd seen yet. Craig was spending time with Vee and the rest of the crew on the other bus, so it was just me and Legion gathered in the front lounge. Callum and Dante were involved in a heated match of Mario Kart, both playfully elbowing each other to throw the other off their game. I laid on the opposite couch with my legs on Donovan's lap as he absentmindedly strummed at his guitar. Over at the kitchen table, Luca tapped away on his laptop.

After sending off the text I'd been composing to Kayla, I admired Donovan's fingers moving along the strings of his guitar. "That's a cool melody. What song is that?"

"It's nothing yet," he replied. "I'm still messing around with the chords. I feel like they're not quite right."

"Try putting it in B-minor," Dante chimed in, frantically thumbing the joystick on his controller. "Fuck, fuck, fuck…"

"Ha!" Callum raised his own controller in victory and pumped a fist overhead. "I win!"

"Best three out of five?"

"Nope. Pay up, asshole."

Dante sighed and rummaged around in his pocket. "How the hell do you keep winning every bet we make?"

Callum snatched the twenty dollar bill out of Dante's hand and winked. "Just lucky, I guess."

"B-minor," Donovan mused, adjusting his fingertips. The chords he'd been working with transformed into a dissonant yet beautiful tune.

"Ooo," I exclaimed, sitting upright. "I like that a lot."

My words made Luca look up from his computer. "I missed it, play it again."

Donovan hesitated, frowning at Luca's commanding tone, but a flicker of insecurity passed over his face too. "You won't like it. It's a ballad."

"Let me hear."

After a few tense beats, Donovan took a deep breath and strummed the series of chords again. Luca nodded slowly as he listened, the look in his eyes growing distant. When his guitarist finished, Luca grabbed the notebook next to his laptop.

"Again."

Donovan glanced at me and rolled his eyes at the demand, but he played the melody again.

Luca flipped through the notepad until he landed on a passage he'd been chipping away at over the past few days. "Again, please."

Callum turned to Dante and whispered, "Did he just say *please*?"

Eyebrows arched in surprise, Dante nodded.

Donovan played the notes again, this time more confidently.

Luca hummed along with it, then traced his index finger along a sentence.

"Fire… twisted choir…" he muttered. He thought a few seconds longer before closing the notebook and leaning back in his seat. "There might be some potential there. We'll play with it."

Donovan shrugged cooly, but I could feel the pride rippling off him. I reached out to squeeze his arm in congratulations, and he smiled back at me.

An abrupt buzzing pulled our attention back to Luca as his phone lit up on the table beside him. He checked the number and lifted it to his ear.

"This is the Beast." He listened intently to the voice rattling off on the other end, his expression darkening. "Wait, slow down. What do you mean the Salt Lake date is cancelled?"

The rest of the band stopped what they were doing to eavesdrop.

"We've had protests in every city, why do we care now?" Luca sighed and rubbed his eyes. "A human barricade? Why are they suddenly so riled up? …Wait, *what* rumor?"

He wedged the phone between his ear and shoulder so he could freely type at his computer. I stood from the couch and joined him as he clicked on an article with this morning's date. The headline read, "Satanist Rock Band Sacrifices Virgins, According to New Reports."

My stomach dropped at the memory of the confrontation on the steps in Cheyenne. I'd told that woman something similar to mess with her head, and now I wondered if she was exactly who these "new reports" were referring to.

"So the show's cancelled?" Callum asked, the joy on his face waning.

I scanned the article and nodded. "Looks like it. This says there's a huge crowd circling the venue. They're not letting anyone in, and cops aren't doing anything to break it up."

"Of course not," Donovan mumbled, setting aside his guitar. "So what now?"

Luca raised his finger, signaling for us to be quiet, and listened a few seconds longer. "There's nothing we can do at all? … Goddammit. Alright, I guess it is what it is. Refund the tickets and we'll head straight to Vegas to kill a few days before the show there. It's Sin City, there's no way that one'll get shut down."

He hung up the call and released a sigh that carried the weight of the world before barking up to the driver. "Randy, change of plans! We're headed to Vegas."

Donovan and Callum high-fived, but Dante pulled out his headphones, jammed them over his ears, and sunk deeper into the couch, all signs of his previous good mood gone.

By the time we got to Nevada and checked into our hotel overlooking the strip, night had fallen, and the city had come alive. I was thoroughly prepared to spend the night in, thinking I'd enjoy the sights and sounds tomorrow during our day off, but when I got out of the shower and heard a knock at my door, my plans changed.

I opened the door to find Donovan and Callum standing in the hall. Callum's hair was slicked back, and he looked stylish in Doc Martens, black jeans, and a half unbuttoned shirt displaying his intricate chest tattoos. Donovan had touched up the pink in his hair, and was effortlessly cool in a white muscle tee, slacks, and a tangle of necklaces.

Donovan whistled appreciatively as he admired the water dripping from my hair into my cleavage. "While I'd prefer to keep you just like this, we need to get you dressed, darling."

"Why? What's wrong?"

"Nothing's wrong." Callum sauntered into the room and

began helping himself to the mini bar. "We have a Las Vegas tradition, and we're taking you with us."

"What tradition is that?"

Donovan leaned a hip against the doorframe, eyes still glued to my curves. "You got anything you can wear dancing?"

An hour later, I was strolling hand-in-hand down the strip with both men, dressed in my thigh high boots and the Legion t-shirt Luca had given me. It was just long enough to cover my ass, which occasionally peeked out to show a sliver of my silky black panties.

"Fucking hell," Callum hissed through his teeth, checking me out for the hundredth time. "You make our band look good, angel."

"She certainly does." Donovan gave me a twirl and finished it by planting a sloppy kiss on my lips, making me burst into a fit of giggles. Up until tonight, I'd only seen the two men touch alcohol a handful of times, but now they were tipsy, boisterous, and their joy was contagious.

"So you guys go to this club every time you're in Vegas?" I asked when Callum peeled me away from Donovan.

"Yep," he replied, continuing to lead with a hand glued to my backside. "We're the epitome of health for all of tour except Vegas. Tonight we get to be naughty."

He squeezed one of my ass cheeks to drive his point home.

"But don't worry, darling, we'll keep it mild for you," Donovan assured me.

I pouted. "What? Why?"

The two men exchanged looks.

"Well…" Callum chewed his bottom lip as he considered his words. "Usually we play a little game."

"What kind of game?"

"A sexy game," Donovan answered, his pace slowing as we neared a flashing neon sign emblazoned with an arrow pointing into a darkened alley. "And it's not necessary tonight because we have *you* to entertain us."

We turned into the alley, and I playfully smacked his shoulder. "Come on, don't leave me hanging. What's this sexy game?"

The men shared another look as we halted in front of a bouncer standing in front of an unassuming metal door. They both leaned in close so I'd be able to hear their whispered words over the thumping beat in the distance.

"Cal and I look for someone we both find attractive," Donovan explained. "When we do, he goes over and does his thing."

"And Dono watches," Callum added, seductively nuzzling the side of my neck. The hairs there prickled as my stomach fluttered with butterflies.

"I see." I angled my head to face him, my lips tingling at their proximity to his. "And how far does this rendezvous go?"

"It depends. Sometimes just kissing. Sometimes we go somewhere private for a little more."

"And sometimes we bring them back to the hotel with us and take them at the same time," Donovan said, his fingers grazing my thigh near my shirt's hem. "But like I said, we have you for that."

I eagerly pressed my knees together at the image. I hadn't fooled around with the two of them since Montana, but I'd thought about it every day since, and often those fantasies involved having them both inside me at once. The picture alone heated my blood and had my insides quivering.

Trying to compose myself, I inhaled a shaky breath and nodded. "I'd like that."

"That's our girl." Donovan popped a kiss on my cheek and stepped up to the stone-faced bouncer, clapping him on the shoulder. "Good to see you again, Jimmy."

"You as well, Mr. Davies." Jimmy opened the door and dipped his head to Callum. "Mr. Sherwood."

I followed the guys through the doorway, which opened to a staircase leading down into a dark abyss of industrial techno and flashing lasers. I kept one hand on Donovan's shoulder as I descended the stairs, while the other gripped Callum's bicep beside me. I'd never had a clubbing phase, but with Donovan and Callum with me, I felt surprisingly at ease. When we arrived on flat ground, I laughed as the two men grabbed my hands and dragged me to the dance floor, twirling and swaying until I joined in. Eventually, I melted into the music and lost myself in the provocative melody, entranced even further when Callum glided behind me to grind against my backside. His hands slid around my waist and roved over my torso, his face buried in my neck.

Donovan watched us with adoration in his eyes, his stare drinking in every touch. He shook his head in disbelief.

"Fuck, you two are beautiful."

I smiled and curled a finger at him, beckoning him closer. He happily obliged and maneuvered between my legs, rolling his hips forward and back in time with Callum's. I draped my arms over his neck to bring him even closer.

"How come you like watching so much?" I asked, holding back a moan of appreciation as Donovan's movements grazed the sensitive area between my legs.

"I've never really thought about it," he replied, his gaze alternating between me and Callum. "I guess it's like looking at art in motion. You're not allowed to touch it, but the more you look at it, the more you want to."

"It's another game," came Callum's voice in my ear.

I leaned my head back to rest on his shoulder. "Show me."

Both men stopped dancing.

"Yeah?" Donovan said, his eyes sparking with lust.

I nodded. "Play your game. I want to play with you."

Callum chuckled, his lips finding my neck once more. "You're full of surprises, angel. Game on."

A rush of adrenaline shot through me as we surveyed the crowd. "Man or woman?"

"Hmm…" Donovan jerked his chin towards the bar. "How about her, Cal? Mesh shirt and eyebrow ring."

I followed their gazes to a girl with long dark hair accepting a martini from the bartender. I looked up at Callum. "I think she's cute. Do you?"

"Of course." He glanced at me and winked. "She looks like you."

He pushed through the crowd towards her, leaving me blushing in his wake. As Callum wove through the dance floor with the intensity of an animal locked onto the scent of its prey, Donovan moved behind me and encircled his arms around my waist.

"How do you not get jealous?" I asked.

He began slowly moving us back and forth to the beat as Cal neared his target.

"I know how he feels about me. Adding someone else isn't going to change that. Plus, I like him to feel good, and selfishly, I feel a sense of pride when people want what's mine."

At that moment, Callum made contact. He slid his hand to the girl's lower back and whispered something in her ear, making her head jerk up in surprise, but she beamed when she saw the attractive stranger standing before her.

"Looks like she likes him," I mused.

"Of course she does. Our boy is a fucking god."

My stomach dipped. "*Our* boy, huh?"

Instead of expanding on the comment, Donovan nodded to Callum taking the girl's hand. "We've got movement. Now comes my favorite part."

I nestled further into his chest as Callum led the girl out to the dance floor. The two began swaying to the beat, their hands flying over each other's skin.

"Are *you* getting jealous?" Donovan asked, his breathy words tickling the outer shell of my ear. I searched my soul for the truth.

"I don't know if jealous is the right word. I don't feel anything negative towards her, but I definitely wish it was me in her place."

"Embrace that feeling." Donovan's hands sunk lower, gripping my hips as he moved us to the steadily increasing pace of the music. "Watch everything Cal does, and imagine it's you on the receiving end."

I obeyed, letting my focus drift back to Callum and his dance partner. The flashing lights made their bodies look like they were moving in slow motion, the sight truly a piece of moving art like Donovan had described before. Callum's hands moved down the woman's back, drifting towards her ass, and my body warmed as I imagined him doing the same to me. As if reading my mind, Donovan's hands mirrored Callum's and cupped my backside.

Across the dance floor, Callum's eyes lifted, meeting mine through the crowd. His lips twitched upwards in a subtle smile, and he spun his partner so she was facing us. Keeping his stare locked with mine, he traced both hands up the woman's torso towards her chest. Lust and longing twinged in my core, the sensation tripling when Donovan copied Callum's movements and began caressing my breasts. I uttered a soft moan and relaxed into him, still keeping my attention on the couple in the distance. An erotic game of follow-the-leader commenced, each copycat move building the fire in my blood and the moisture between my legs. A firm bulge had grown in Donovan's trousers too, and it ground against me every time his hips thrust forward. I wondered if Callum was just as turned on as we were, but judging by his heaving chest and parted lips, the answer was yes.

By the time the game reached its finale, I was so goddamn turned on I thought I might explode, and Donovan's cock was so swollen I feared he might rip a seam. Eyes burning with passion, Callum dipped a hand between his companion's legs, making her head toss back in ecstasy. My clit was already screaming for contact, so when Donovan slipped his fingers up the hem of my shirt and down my panties, I could have cried from the burst of pleasure.

"Oh my god," I exclaimed, clapping a hand over my mouth so as not to draw attention to myself.

"It's alright, darling," Donovan murmured, nipping my earlobe. "Let it out. No one's going to judge you here."

My fingers dropped as Donovan's pushed inside of me. I shut my eyes to savor the sensation and reached up to clasp his neck in order to ground myself.

"So wet already," Donovan remarked, his voice husky. "I think it's safe to say you like watching too, huh?"

"Yes," I breathed.

My words caused his cock to twitch against my ass.

"Fucking hell, I can't leave you two alone for five minutes," a familiar voice interrupted.

I peeled my eyes open to find Callum standing in front of us, his dance partner nowhere to be seen.

"What...what happened to your friend?" I stuttered, still distracted by Donovan's fingers rubbing slow, sensual circles around my aching clit.

Callum stepped forward so our faces were close and reached down to catch Donovan's wrist. Keeping eye contact, he pulled the hand from my panties and raised it up, the flashing lights illuminating my glistening arousal on Donovan's fingertips.

"She's not you, angel."

His lips parted, and he pulled Donovan's fingers into his

mouth, primal hunger flaring in his eyes. A rumble of appreciation rolled in Donovan's chest, vibrating into me from behind. When Callum had finished every last drop of me, Donovan removed his hand, and Cal hauled me into a claiming kiss, the tang of my musk still on his tongue.

When he pulled away, I was left panting for more.

"Take me back to the hotel," I demanded. "*Now.*"

Needing no further bidding, the men each took a hand and dragged me through the crowd.

34

We stumbled back into my hotel room, our bodies locked in a frenzy of passion.

Everything was a blur.

I was kissing Donovan. Then Callum. They were kissing each other as I kissed their necks. They were both kissing me. Soon sweat and saliva formed a sheen across our skin, it's heady scent only heightening our lust. I dragged the two men towards the bed, frantically pawing at the shirts that had been on for far too long. When they were freed of their clothing, they turned on me, with Donovan tracing his tongue down my thighs on his way to unzip my boots, while Callum peeled my top overhead and planted kisses along my collarbone. I shivered at the stimulation, so aroused I could barely string words together. Luckily, our bodies were the only ones that needed to do the talking.

Donovan lifted me off the ground and carried me over to the bed, Callum trailing behind us as he finished disrobing. The English gentleman disappeared as Dono tossed me onto the mattress and flipped me onto my stomach with the ferocity of a starved animal.

"Ass up," he demanded, landing a stinging smack to one cheek.

I sucked in sharply at the burst of pain and arched my back, pushing my hips to the sky. I was greeted by Dono's groan of appreciation, followed by his hands gripping the flesh of my backside and spreading me apart before burying his face in my heat.

I moaned into the comforter as Donovan's tongue lapped me up and down. The mattress dipped as Callum crawled beside us, and when I peeked up at him, I discovered his cock stiff and ready. On instinct, I moved forward and took him into my mouth, humming appreciatively at his taste. Cal tossed his head back, his lips parting as I worked his shaft.

"Jesus," he breathed, his hand entwining in my hair. "That's the sexiest thing I've ever seen."

"You should see it from my angle," Dono mumbled. His mouth moved off of me as he stood, making me grunt in protest at the absence of his tongue. I was promptly silenced by his cock pressing into me.

"Oh my god," I gasped, slumping against Callum's torso. He chuckled and brushed the hair from my face.

"Does that feel good, sweetheart?"

I nodded feebly and shut my eyes to savor Donovan's long, deep thrusts. Callum guided my hand to his own length so I could stroke him, then reached between my legs to massage my clit. I could have cried at the overwhelming burst of pleasure.

"God yes," Donovan hissed through his teeth. "I can feel her clench around me when you do that."

"Yeah?" Callum's fingers moved faster. "How would it feel if I made her come?"

"We better find out."

Dono's thrusts increased in speed and ferocity. I tried to keep pumping Callum, but as the tension coiled inside, it became harder and harder to keep the momentum. As if reading my mind, Cal nuzzled my neck.

"Come on, you can do both. I know you can."

Eager to please and too turned on to think for myself, I obeyed. Callum bit his lip and nodded in approval as I stroked him. He picked up the pace between my legs, making me whimper as his fingers found the perfect spot that tripled the pleasure.

"I think she's close, Cal," Dono said, landing another smack to my ass. "Keep doing that."

"Yes, please keep doing that," I panted. "Fuck, I'm gonna… I'm gonna…"

One final thrust from Donovan broke through the boundary to bliss, toppling me over the edge into a climax. Cal held me tight to his chest as I came, kissing my cheeks and hair until I'd finished riding the waves of pleasure.

"That's our girl," Dono muttered. He pulled himself out of me, knelt to the ground, and buried his face in me a second time. I whimpered as he sucked at the overly sensitive skin, then migrated upward to swirl his tongue around my asshole. I tensed as something pressed against the ring of tight muscle, but relaxed when I realized it was just his finger.

"Are you going to fuck me there too?" I asked. The idea was daunting, but I couldn't deny it got me wet.

"Not tonight," Donovan replied, pushing his finger in to the knuckle while continuing to trail his tongue along the outside. "But eventually I will. We'll need to work you up to that, though. Would you like that?"

A moan of appreciation leapt from my mouth as he eased a second finger in.

"I think that's a yes," Callum laughed.

"Yes," I confirmed. "I want to be able to take you both at the same time."

Cal dragged my leg over his hips so I straddled him. "We can arrange that."

Before I knew it, his cock had pushed inside me, dragging a gasp from my lips. He fucked me with slow, deliberate strokes, while Donovan kept his fingers and mouth dedicated to my second entrance. It was unlike anything I'd ever felt, and it had my eyes rolling back in my head at the pleasure.

"Such a good little slut for us," Donovan praised, rising to his feet. He slid his fingers out and spent a few moments watching Callum and I kiss and grind against each other. "Jesus. How did I get so lucky?"

His earnest words had me blushing, and I craned my neck to smile at him over my shoulder. "I'm asking myself the same thing."

Donovan grinned and took hold of his cock, moving forward so that he could run the head along the outside of my sensitive pucker. Apprehension still tugged at me, but it was overpowered by lust, and I attempted to wriggle my hips closer.

"I thought you weren't going to fuck my ass."

"I'm not," Donovan replied. "I'm just teasing you, darling. Have you learned nothing about me?"

Antsy with need, I tried to maneuver him in, but he remained just out of reach, toying with me.

"I promise I can handle it," I insisted.

"We said not yet," Callum reprimanded, wrapping a claiming hand around my throat to immobilize me. He slammed into my pussy, reminding me who was in charge. It may have put me in my place, but it didn't stop my desire from escalating into desperation.

"Please," I begged. "I want you both. I *need* you both."

A wry laugh met my ears.

"Darling, I said I wasn't going to fuck your ass. I never said you weren't getting us both tonight."

The head of Donovan's cock slid down and notched at my

pussy, blocked by Callum's shaft still pumping in and out of me. Realization crashed into me, hitting me with a wave of arousal tinged in fear.

"I… I don't know if you both will fit," I murmured.

"We will if you're wet enough. And I think Cal did a good job at that." Donovan reached between my legs to swipe his fingers across my clit, his touch sending shockwaves through me. "Oh, yeah. You're fucking dripping."

He pushed himself forward just an inch, stretching me wider. It was uncomfortable for a split second, but pain soon made way for pleasure.

"Fuck," I whimpered, collapsing onto Callum's chest.

"Too much?" he asked.

"No, it's amazing. Just go slow please."

"Hear that, Dono?"

"I heard." A kiss of encouragement pressed against my shoulder. "We've got you, angel. You have your safe word. Say it and we'll stop. Promise."

I nodded and readjusted myself on Callum's cock. "Ok, I'm ready. More, please."

Donovan clicked his tongue. "Look at those good manners."

There was another twinge as my pussy stretched wider, allowing more of Donovan to glide inside. I sucked in a breath and buried my face in Callum's neck.

"Good?" Donovan asked, restraint making his voice tremble. I could tell it was taking everything in him not to jam himself in all the way to his hips.

"Good," I answered.

And I *was* good.

I was trembling with need and aching for more, so much so that I drove my hips backward, plunging both men further into me. Donovan smacked a hand to my back to hold me in place.

"Easy," he gasped.

I bit my lip in frustration and forced myself to be patient.

Donovan pressed in further, and after one final stretch and a fleeting moment of discomfort, he fit inside me entirely. The fullness caused a dance of pressure and pleasure that made my body sing.

"Oh my god," I exclaimed, slumping further into Callum and grappling at the sheets under us.

"Fucking hell, that's tight," he groaned. He planted a kiss on my shoulder, then lifted my face to look him in the eye. "You good, baby?"

I nodded groggily, my mind foggy with lust. I'd been pushed to my limits and was loving every second, riding a high so addictive I could already tell I'd never recover. I smothered Cal in a kiss, then looked back at Donovan. Holding my stare, he began to thrust, slow at first, then increasing when my moans informed him of the building pleasure. He and Callum pumped in time, their puffs of breath syncing with the beat of my racing heart. Each stroke felt better and better as I adjusted to their combined size, the stretch heightening each pulse of my inner walls.

"Damnit, you feel too good," Donovan said through gritted teeth. "You're going to get me so fast."

The statement had Callum increasing his speed, causing Donovan to hiss an expletive.

"That's not helping."

"I know," Callum replied, eyes glinting with mischief.

Donovan growled and leaned forward, sandwiching me between the two of them as he glared down at Callum. "Don't play a game you can't win."

Cal's confident smirk was the sexiest expression I'd ever seen. "But I *am* winning. I can feel you both getting close."

He wasn't wrong. Donovan's pulsating cock gave him away, and my insides had begun to shudder and tighten with the promise of an orgasm.

"You're going to come with us then," Donovan countered,

matching Callum's speed with firm thrusts of his own.

Both Callum and I gasped at the sensation. No one cared about winning anymore; the moment consumed us all, and we lost ourselves in the intensity clouding us. I had no idea who gave in first, but all at once it was warm and tight and I was hurtling into a climax stronger than any I'd ever had as two pairs of arms clutched me tight.

The three of us collapsed in a breathless heap, so drunk on adrenaline and dopamine that we couldn't stop giggling. Donovan carefully slid out of me, followed by Callum, and we all burrowed into the bed. Exhaustion crept in and tugged my eyelids shut, and soon I was dozing off between two sweat-slicked, softly snoring men.

Suddenly, a crash echoed through the hallway, prompting us all to sit up in alarm.

"What was that?" I asked, instinctively clinging to Donovan.

Callum pressed a finger to his lips, angling his ear to the door. We could faintly make out two voices, one a hushed whisper and the other loud and intoxicated. Recognition dawned on me, and I clambered out of bed.

Donovan reached for me. "Where are you going?"

I dodged him and picked my t-shirt up off the carpet, shimmied it over my head, and tip-toed across the room. Cautiously, I eased the door open and peeked my head out. Two familiar faces came into view.

Luca stumbled down the hall, grunting with effort as he supported a half-unconscious Dante, who slurred nonsense as they headed for their room. A toppled-over room service cart lay behind them, collateral damage in the wake of Dante's drunken stupor.

Luca's eyes lifted from the carpet to meet mine, the expression on his face transitioning from worried to hardened. He lifted his chin as much as he could with Dante's arm slung around his shoulders and donned a charming smile.

"Viva Las Vegas."

His act would have fooled anyone but me.

Gently closing the door behind me, I stepped into the hall, took the spot on the opposite side of Dante, and nestled into the crook of his arm to share his weight. Luca pressed his lips together and stared at the ground, refusing to look at me. From the outside looking in, it would appear he was furious. But from where I was standing, I could see the shame glinting in his eyes.

We trudged forward, passing door after door until we reached their room at the end of the hall. Luca fumbled a key card out of his pocket and tapped it to the door, which beeped and lit up green.

"I can take it from here," he mumbled.

I pretended I didn't hear him and shuffled inside. Together, Luca and I made our way over to the bed and carefully lowered Dante onto the mattress. He muttered something incoherent, then rolled over and tucked his knees to his chest. Within seconds he'd stilled, and a soft snore reached our ears.

I lowered onto the edge of the bed to catch my breath, but Luca immediately got to work removing Dante's shoes and placing a glass of water on the nightstand for him to find in the morning. I watched him as he worked. His expression was grim, his movements methodical and familiar. He'd done this too many times.

Eventually, Luca came to sit beside me. Neither of us said anything for god knows how long. We simply stared at the thin, worn carpet beneath our feet and listened to Dante's breath. The sound was strangely comforting; it proved he was experiencing a rare moment of peace.

"We play San Diego in two days."

My gaze shifted to Luca. Even though he'd spoken, he refused to look at me and kept his eyes downcast as he gestured to the figure curled on the bed.

"He always gets like this before the hometown show."

I sneaked a peek at Dante. His brow wrinkled as he met some unseen foe in the astral plane, confirming he was just as tortured in sleep as he was in life.

"Is there anything I can do to help him? Or you?"

Luca twirled one of his rings, lost in thought. After a stretch of heavy silence, he hung his head, took a deep breath, and let it out slow. "I've been asking myself the same thing."

My heart ached at his vulnerability, and before I could second guess myself, I slid my hand into his. His arm twitched like he was about to wrench it away, but he allowed me to thread my fingers through his.

"You're a good friend to him," I said earnestly.

Luca glanced back at Dante, his hardened expression cracking to reveal a glimpse of the sadness buried underneath. "Not good enough, apparently."

My heart tugged again, and I squeezed his hand. "Do you want me to stay with you?"

At that, Luca ripped his hand from my grasp and straightened his shoulders. "I'm fine."

"Would you admit it if you weren't?"

He froze, several tense seconds passing before he stood. "Good night, Jade. I'll see you tomorrow."

I stayed there a few moments longer, trying to catch a glimpse of the softness I'd just seen, but his defenses had walled up again. I sighed and stood too, weighing my words before gesturing to both men.

"You two don't have to face things alone if you don't want to. There are people who care about you, no matter how much you push them away."

When Luca didn't look up at me, I reached out and squeezed his shoulder, then headed for the door. "Good night."

I left the room, went back to my own, and snuggled up in bed between Donovan and Callum. But for the rest of the night, our thoughts remained with the two at the end of the hall.

35

The next morning, I managed to convince Cal and Dono to cuddle in bed and watch TV instead of going for our normal run.

Donovan had tutted and called me a bad influence, but he'd promptly shut his mouth when I turned on Attack on Titan. We spent the morning watching anime, talking, and fucking until the clock struck noon, before Donovan finally insisted he and Cal needed to spend at least *some* time at the gym or else he'd lose his mind. I elected to stay behind and attempt to get some work done.

When they'd gone, I pulled out my sketchbook and added finishing touches to the monster pierced by arrows. It was a horrible, vicious looking thing, with curling horns and a forked tongue hanging limp from a wide mouth full of fangs. It was so vile-looking that the fiery barbs that had taken its life felt like a triumph. I lifted the notebook up and examined the piece, happy with how it looked, but not quite satisfied. It didn't feel right yet.

I stared at it for ten minutes, still not content, but I was blanking on how to fix it. Finally, a lightbulb went off. It started slow at first, just a spark of an idea sprouting like a seed at the back of my mind and growing larger the longer I stared at the paper. By the time I flipped to the next blank page in my sketchbook, the idea had enveloped me, blocking out any and all thought except for this.

My pencil flew across the page in frantic sweeps, forming the same image I'd drawn before. Only this time, instead of a monster lying in a pool of blood, burning arrows in its back, there was an angel. He was tall and strong, with short curly hair and beautiful, statuesque features. One feathery wing covered his manhood while the other hung bent and broken at a nauseating angle, his bright but tortured eyes staring up at the heavens, silently begging his god for a release from the torment. A bloodied hand decorated in rings was outstretched to the sky to further his plea, but his mouth was bitterly pressed shut like he expected it to go unheard.

I held the two drawings up to each other and scanned my work. They looked like identical moments on two different timelines. I was unsure what I wanted to do with the piece, but for the time being, I was happy.

I set the sketches down when someone rapped at the door. Dono and Callum had taken my extra key card to the gym, so it couldn't be them. Confused, I stood and padded over to peek out the peephole. When I saw who was on the other side, I pulled it open.

"Hey," Luca muttered.

"Hi." I caught myself nervously smoothing the front of my sundress and quickly tucked my hands behind my back. "What's up?"

He shifted his weight from one foot to the other, then extended a paper coffee cup. "Here."

I cautiously accepted the beverage and arched an eyebrow in silent question. Luca stuffed his hands in his pockets and shrugged.

"It's creme brûlée something or other. The barista recommended it. It's not bad, actually. It's not as sweet as I thought it would be."

I blinked in surprise. "You tried it?"

Luca frowned, and I could have sworn a hint of color rose in his cheeks. "That sugary shit's all you ever get, I had to see what the fuss was about. I'm not going to order it, but… Yeah. It's not bad."

I nodded and took a sip to hide my smile. The drink *was* good, but I could tell that Luca had asked them to add an extra shot of espresso to cut the sweetness.

"Thank you."

"No problem."

I expected him to walk away, but Luca's feet stayed planted.

"How did you sleep?" I asked.

"I didn't."

"How's Dante?"

"Normal." Luca swallowed and lowered his gaze to the floor. "So… Not great."

An ache formed in my chest at his honesty, and how it clearly pained him. I gently touched his arm, and unlike last night, this time he didn't flinch.

"How about you take some time for yourself today?" I suggested. "I'll keep an eye on Dante. You could relax at the pool or—"

"Write," Luca interrupted, meeting my gaze again. "I want to write. I'm finally feeling inspired."

"It must be one of those days."

Our eyes remained locked for a half second more before Luca cleared his throat, fished around in his back pocket for his room key, slid it into my palm, and curled my fingers around it.

"Thank you," he said, giving my hand a long, firm squeeze. I got the feeling that the gratitude he expressed wasn't just in reference to this.

I smiled and peeled myself away before I became lost in his

orbit like I had so many times before. We watched each other for the entirety of my walk down the hall, and only when I touched the key to the door and it beeped open did Luca turn away and shuffle towards the elevators.

When he'd disappeared from view, I slipped into his room and quietly closed the door behind me. I immediately caught sight of a figure at the window, silhouetted by the afternoon light as they smoked a cigarette and stared out over the Las Vegas strip.

"Hey." I set my coffee down and eased closer like he was a wild animal primed to attack.

Dante didn't move, but a cloud of white smoke puffed from his mouth. I eased onto the bed and stared at his back as the cigarette repeatedly returned to his lips, burning shorter with each pull. We sat in silence until nothing remained but a nub.

"These windows don't open."

Dante's abrupt statement made me jump.

Keeping his eyes on the world outside the hotel, he snuffed out the cigarette on the glass and let the butt fall to the floor. "They seal them shut so people don't commit suicide."

He turned and looked at me for the first time.

"You're lucky, you know," he said, wry amusement in his voice.

"How so?"

"Your dreams. You said they're memories you'd forgotten."

Unsure where this was headed, I nodded.

Dante's fingers twitched at his side like they were in search of something. Violence, another cigarette, anything to provide a release. "It must have been nice to forget the thing that broke you."

I buried the part of me that wanted to ask what it was that broke *him*. Instead, I leaned back on the bed, bracing my hands on the mattress.

"It was. For a little while, at least. Until I realized I still felt like shit, I just didn't know why."

I lost track of how long we sat in silence. When Dante finally spoke, his voice was barely above a whisper.

"I don't want to feel like shit anymore."

A ball of emotion wedged in my throat, but I managed to speak around it. "What can I do?"

Another agonizing silence stretched. The air grew tight, the way it does before lightning strikes or a volcano erupts. The world hung in the balance for a split second, teetering on a taut string that Dante's next words snapped in half.

"You can get on your knees."

A strange sense of calm washed over me, and I obediently sank to the floor. Dante neared, his footfalls landing with each beat of my heart. When he stopped in front of me, my body hummed. There was no shame anymore, no guilt or fear or nerves or panic. It wanted this. *I* wanted this, and I had for a long time. With that acceptance came peace.

I lifted my eyes to Dante towering over me. His fingers inched towards the buckle on the belt around his hips.

"Do you remember your safe word?"

"Yes, Sir."

"Good. You're gonna need it."

The belt whipped from his jeans with a snap, and suddenly the thick black leather was around my throat. It tightened, cutting off airflow, but arousal bloomed where fear should have.

Dante crouched so we were face-to-face and jerked the belt to pull me closer. "There you go. You don't need to breathe, you just need to be a brainless little plaything for me to use and abuse."

My body buzzed with desire while my head went dizzy from lust and lack of oxygen. My eyes began to flutter shut, but the belt loosened before they closed entirely. I gasped in a breath, experiencing a spike of adrenaline with the burst of air.

"Breathe," Dante murmured, stroking my hair with his free hand. "Breathe."

The contrast of violence and softness had me trembling. I was putty in his hands, ready to be molded however he wanted.

Dante searched my face, smiling slightly at the complete and utter submission written across it. His hand shifted from my hair to my jaw, and he gave my face a taunting shake.

"Such a filthy little whore. You love this shit."

"Yes, Sir," I panted, squeezing my knees together to combat the ache there.

Dante yanked the belt tight again and jerked his chin to my legs. "Keep them open."

I jumped to obey. The belt relaxed again, and I gulped in another lungful of air.

Dante released his grip on my face and slid his hand to the sensitive area between my thighs. In one quick move, he pushed the hem of my dress past my hips, dragged my thong aside, and pushed two fingers inside me. A moan leapt from my lips at the intrusion, but I was silenced by another tug from the belt.

"Look at this greedy cunt," Dante tisked. His fingers slid in and out, slowly increasing in speed. "Already a fucking mess."

Again, all I could do was nod.

Dante's pace was punishing now, and another firm tug from the belt forced me to press my lips together to muffle my stuttering groans. My arousal dripped down my thighs, which quaked so bad it was hard to stay upright. Just when I thought I couldn't take anymore, Dante pulled his hand away, allowing me to slump forward, breathing heavily. I only had a few seconds to recover before he jammed his slick-covered fingers into my mouth, driving them so far down my throat I retched violently.

"Don't get sick on me now, angel," Dante chuckled. "We're just getting started."

He stood abruptly and gave the belt a jerk, motioning for me to follow him. I crawled after him on my hands and knees like a pet on a leash.

"Such an obedient little slut for me," "Dante mused, wrapping the belt tighter around his fist.

My pussy pulsed at the praise, and I picked up my pace in an attempt to please him more.

When we arrived at the window, Dante switched places with me so my back was to the glass and he was looking out.

"Arms clasped behind you," he ordered.

When I'd obeyed, he kept one hand on the belt while the other unfastened the button on his jeans, then the zipper. My mouth watered as the waistband of his boxer briefs came into view, stretched tight across his swollen cock.

Clocking my gaze, he nodded to the outline. "You want it?"

"Yes, Sir."

"Beg for it."

"Please, let me taste you," I pleaded, the words tumbling from my mouth like my tongue was possessed. "*Please*, Sir. I'll do anything you want. "

"Yes, you will." Dante hooked his waistband with his thumb. "Open."

My jaw dropped, and I impatiently sat in wait as Dante dragged his underwear down and released what I was after. His length was flushed with blood flow, its tip slick with pre-cum. Without waiting for my response, he slapped the head of his cock against my outstretched tongue and thrust his hips forward. He slid into my mouth, nudging the back of my throat and inciting another gag. A swift palm to my cheek followed, the stinging clap it made against my skin echoing throughout the room.

"Come on, you can take it," Dante urged. "You've done it before."

Squeezing my eyes shut, I forced the muscles in my neck to relax, allowing Dante full entry. His cock slid all the way in, surpassing my gag reflex as it reached into the depths of my throat.

Dante's hand fondly stroked my hair. "That's it. Take it all."

Lungs stinging for air, I moved to pull him from my mouth, but the leather around my neck went taught as Dante tightened his grip to keep me in place.

"You're not done yet," he snapped. "Fucking choke on it, slut."

The muscles in my throat fought against the object hindering them, triggering another desperate pulse of my gag reflex. I dug deep and muscled down the sensation by focusing on the appreciative groan grating from Dante's mouth. His cock ripped from my mouth, leaving me heaving. His chest rose and fell same as mine, while his cock dripped a string of my saliva to the floor.

"Again," he demanded.

He pinned me against the window and shoved himself back in, repeatedly slamming his cock into my mouth and knocking the back of my head into the glass with each thrust. My fingernails dug into my skin as I fought to keep my hands behind me, the effort forcing moisture to spill out the corners of my eyes. I took the pounding until the contents of my stomach began to rise, and I hurriedly smacked my hands to Dante's thighs and pushed him back.

"I'm sorry," I panted. "I had to."

In response, Dante latched a hand around my ponytail and yanked upwards, dragging me to my feet. I cried out in pain, and Dante tossed me to the bed, where I landed in a shivering heap. He snapped his fingers and pointed at the edge of the mattress, prompting me to wriggle closer. My heart pounded in anticipation, creating a deafening drum in my ears. It was so loud I almost didn't hear Dante as he lined himself up at my entrance.

"Eyes on me, angel."

He thrust forward and began hammering into me with such ferocity, I clawed at the sheets in an attempt to move away. But Dante snatched up the leather strap still hanging around my neck and yanked it taut.

"Where do you think you're going? This pussy's mine, I'll fuck it how I want."

As he pounded into me, he held the belt so tight I struggled to breathe. It amplified each sensation, making the world disappear. I squeezed my eyes shut as Dante smashed into the most tender parts of me, creating knee-weakening pleasure and toe-curling pain.

A solid slap landed on my cheek.

"I said eyes on me," Dante hissed.

With tears streaming down my face, I peeled my eyes open. His palm made contact again, this time with my breasts.

"Say thank you."

"Thank you, Sir."

"You're fucking welcome."

I choked on a sob as the overload of sensation swelled towards a climax. Another slap landed on my tits.

"Sounds like the slut wants to come."

"Yes, Sir. Please, let me come."

"I don't think you've earned it yet."

Dante slid out of me and flipped me onto my stomach. I was a quivering, pitiful mess, but my needy cries were ignored. With another rough tug of the belt, Dante lifted my face off the bed.

"Ready to use that safe word yet?" he asked, the head of his cock teasing my entrance. My pussy clenched in anticipation, and I swallowed hard.

"No."

"No?" Dante's palm found my ass cheek, the stinging slap making me grit my teeth.

"No, Sir," I ground out.

Dante's fingers wrapped around my wrists and pinned them to my back so I couldn't get away even if I wanted to. He pushed his length inside again, the new position bringing with it another wave of unfathomable pleasure. The more he plunged into me, the more my moans deteriorated into frantic whimpers. Soon, I was shaking as I teetered on the edge of my peak.

"Oh my god," I gasped. "Fuck! Please, Sir, can I come?"

The tension on the belt eased, letting my head fall forward on the pillow in front of me. Dante brushed the hair from my face before giving me two firm raps on the cheek.

"Say it again, slut. Beg like a good little fucktoy."

"*Please*," I wailed, the pressure in my core dangerously close to exploding. "Please let me come! I'll do anything! *Please!*"

"Goddamn, you're pretty when you cry," Dante growled. He slammed into me fast and hard, over and over again. "Come for me, fucktoy."

"Oh, god!" I buried my face in the pillow to smother my scream as my orgasm erupted.

Wave after wave of bliss tore through me, leaving me used up and trembling in its wake. Dante continued fucking me even after I'd come, and I was so spent that I could do nothing but lay limp and relish the sensation.

"Thank you," I murmured listlessly. "Thank you, Sir."

Dante responded by pulling out of me and kneeling near my face, his fingers sinking into my hair and tugging so I was looking up at him. His free hand rapidly stroked his cock as his breaths deteriorated into gasps.

"Open," he demanded a third time.

My lips parted and I stretched out my tongue as the muscles on Dante's abdomen flexed and his body went rigid. A guttural moan escaped him as he released in my mouth, his cum spurting across my tongue and spilling down my chin. Keeping my eyes glued to Dante's, I swallowed, licked my lips at the musky taste of him, then used my finger to swipe up the excess and suck it from my fingertips.

Still breathless, Dante huffed a stunned laugh and carefully removed the belt still hanging from my neck. His thumb gently skated across my skin.

"Shit. Looks like you may bruise a little."

"That's ok." I beamed up at him. "I like them."

Dante sniffed. "Yeah? You like getting marked by the devil?"

"You could say that."

He watched me a few seconds longer before shaking his head and flopping onto his back beside me. "You're fucking unreal, you know that?"

I frowned. "In a good or bad way?"

"Obviously good." He reached out and grabbed a pack of cigarettes off the nightstand. "Looks like we really are the same brand of fucked up."

I propped a fist under my head and watched as Dante pulled a cigarette from the carton with his teeth. His lighter clicked, and he took a long, appreciative drag, before letting a wisp of smoke swirl from his mouth.

"Maybe that makes it not so fucked up," I mused. "Maybe your dark side recognizes mine, and they come together to make something beautiful."

Dante nodded pensively. "That would make a good song lyric."

Exhaustion was setting in fast, and I found it difficult to keep my eyes open. I nuzzled further into the pillow, scooting a little closer to the man in the bed with me.

"Dante?" I mumbled groggily.

"Hmm?"

"Will you hold me?"

Dante tensed. "Cuddling's not really my thing."

"Oh. Never mind, then." My heart sank, but I pushed aside my disappointment and shut my eyes. When something touched my hand, they snapped back open, but I calmed when I realized it was only Dante threading his fingers through mine.

"How about this?" he asked hesitantly. "Is this ok?"

I smiled and squeezed his hand. "This is great."

It wasn't cuddling, but it was what he could give, and in that moment, it was everything.

36

The only sounds in the green room came from Phantom Spark playing in the distance and Dante throwing up.

Oddly enough, it wasn't from alcohol. He hadn't touched a drop since Vegas. Even at the show in Phoenix, he'd only consumed energy drinks. Earlier, after he'd run to the bus bathroom for the fifth time, I'd suggested to the others that he might have caught a nasty stomach bug, but they assured me this was standard Dante behavior before the San Diego date.

I was in the process of transferring my sketches to a digital illustrator app on my iPad, but I set it aside and crossed to the figure hunched over the trashcan in the corner. As he retched, the wings on the back of his leather jacket shuddered like their painted feathers had come to life.

"Gum?" I asked, pulling a stick of spearmint from my back pocket. "You don't want to be stuck with puke breath inside that mask."

Dante looked up, the bags under his eyes the darkest I'd seen them. Too exhausted to put up a fight, he spat into the trash one last time before unfolding the gum wrapper and popping it in his mouth.

"Thanks," he mumbled, sliding the Lucifer mask back into place.

I turned and strode back to my spot on the couch, feeling Luca's eyes on me the entire way. He'd been a statue in the corner for the past hour, holding a steaming cup of tea and watching Dante like a hawk, his brow furrowed with worry. Now his face was half-covered with the gold ram mask, but his clenched jaw and pursed lips showed his concern remained.

"It's going to be weird not having you around for a week," Donovan said, giving Callum's back a pat as he finished smearing white paint across the skin. "What are we supposed to do with ourselves?"

"Maybe we should take you home with us," Callum added, shrugging on his studded vest and winking. "You could keep our bed warm while we're out riding the waves."

"And when we get back, you can ride *us*," Donovan added.

I smiled and tucked my knees to my chest. "As lovely as that sounds, I'm going to be spending the week getting all the puppy snuggles I can."

"Damn." Dono leaned over and planted a kiss on my forehead. "This is the first time I've ever been jealous of a dog."

I chuckled and checked my phone for the thousandth time. I'd sent five consecutive texts to Trent asking when I could come see Gracie, but my messages had gone unanswered. Kayla hadn't been able to get ahold of him either, and when she'd gone to my apartment to check on Gracie, she'd discovered her spare key didn't work anymore. If I never received an answer, I'd decided to go over, scale the balcony, and climb in through the window. No amount of changed locks or cheating exes were going to keep me from my dog.

"Bring the pup to the beach," Callum offered, pulling his drumsticks from his back pocket and absentmindedly twirling them. "I bet she'd like having all that open space to run."

"She would." I smiled at the thought of him and I jogging on the sand as Gracie chased us. "Maybe all five of us could get together for a beach day."

Donovan and Luca exchanged glances, their frowns communicating their feelings on spending unnecessary time together.

"We'll have to check our schedules," Dono muttered.

"Please?" I pressed. "I want you all to meet Gracie."

"We'll see," Luca stated. But judging by his tone, it meant, "Not likely."

The finishing notes of Phantom Spark's set reached our ears, and the crowd exploded in cheers.

"That's our cue." Donovan stood and grabbed his devil mask off the coffee table. "Everyone ready?"

Though the question was spoken to the whole room, it was clearly directed at Dante. But the bassist didn't answer. Instead, he yanked the door open and headed for the stage.

I started gathering up my belongings as everyone filed out of the room. Callum hung back and waited for me.

"Hey," he said, lowering his voice and checking over his shoulder to make sure the others were out of earshot. "I wanted to ask… Is he doing ok?"

"Who?"

"Dante."

"How should I know?"

"You spent the day with him in Vegas."

"Yeah, but we didn't really talk much. He mostly napped."

"I didn't know he was physically capable of sleeping."

I smirked and lead the way out of the room. "If you're worried about him, you should just talk to him."

Callum scoffed and fixed his fang mask over the bottom half of his face. "He doesn't talk to me."

"Have you tried?"

Callum's pace slowed, and his brow furrowed. "No, I guess I haven't. It's hard to reach out to someone when you know it's not wanted."

"You don't know it's not wanted."

"Yes, I do. But luckily we have you to extend a hand to him."

My cheeks heated. "You don't know he'd want that from me either."

Callum's eyes crinkled with a smile, and he took hold of my hand. "Yes, I do."

"What's the hold up?" a familiar voice barked further up the hallway. Its owner stormed into sight soon after.

"Let's go," Luca snapped, jerking his thumb over his shoulder. "Check your kit."

"Marcus already checked my kit," Callum grumbled, but realizing arguing was pointless, he released my hand and shuffled towards the stage.

When he'd gone, Luca turned to me. "Where were you headed just now?"

"Vee mentioned she could use some help at merch—"

"I need you to stay."

I blinked. "You what?"

Luca took a step forward, making the hair on my arms prickle at our proximity, and his voice lowered. "I need you to stay with us during the show. Stand onstage with us, in the wings. Specifically on Dante's side."

"I don't want to be in the way—"

"He needs you there, Jade." Luca swallowed and averted his gaze. "*We* need you. Please."

Pain coated his words, on top of a hint of embarrassment and desperation. All his defenses, those usual thorns and unaccessible walls, were laid bare for the very first time. With how foreign vulnerability was to him, it was clear it required significant courage. My heart ached at the realization, and I nodded.

"Ok, I'll stay."

Luca's shoulders slumped like a weight had just been lifted off of them. "Thank you."

"Of course."

Our stares lingered a few seconds longer before Luca spun on his heel and headed back towards the stage. In the distance, the crowd was already starting to get uneasy, chanting Legion's name and erupting in whoops and hollers to hurry the band out. The volume amplified as we walked closer, and when we arrived side stage, it was a dull roar in our ears.

Luca led the way up the ramp into the darkened wings, falling into place beside Dante while I hovered in the shadows.

A hiss met our ears as the fog machines hummed to life, blasting a dense cloud of white onto the stage for Legion's opening song. Sensing what was coming, the crowd went wild. When the stage had filled with thick mist and the house lights blinked out, Luca crept onto the stage, moving slow so as not to disturb the swirls of fog and alert the crowd to his presence. I hesitantly took his place beside Dante. The bassist's body was taught, like he was coiled tight, ready to explode at any moment. He was so focused on the activity onstage that he didn't notice me at first, and when he did, he jerked in alarm. I offered him an encouraging smile and refocused on Luca.

The beginning notes of Legion's first song rang out, and the crowd went wild. But instead of being energized by the reaction, Dante inhaled a sharp, shuddering breath. On instinct, my hand whipped out and latched around his. He flinched again, but didn't pull away. Instead, his eyes lowered to our joined hands, his brows wrinkling like it was a sight he'd never seen. The mask slowly lifted to look me in the eye. I offered it a reassuring smile and tightened my grip. Dante's fingers squeezed back.

There was no need for words. In that brief interaction, we said more than we had all of tour.

As Luca neared the first chorus, Dante took a deep breath, lifted his chin, and stepped onto the stage. I anxiously wrung my hands as I watched him, mentally sending him all my strength as the the spotlight hit him. I puffed a relieved exhale as the crowd roared at his presence, and he came alive as a performer. An uncontrollable smile stretched across my face as I watched him not just going through the motions, not just surviving, but shining bright.

A sudden presence at my side made me jump.

"Relax, it's just me," Chase laughed. Still sweaty from his performance, he mopped his brow with a small towel and directed his attention to the show in front of us.

I refocused on Dante. I caught the white Venetian mask periodically angling my way, letting me know he was looking for me in the shadows.

"You've gotten close to them."

It was a simple statement, but for some reason, Chase's words hit my ears like nails on a chalkboard. I glanced at him and raised an eyebrow.

"Yeah, I have."

Chase's eyes stayed glued to the stage, his expression eerily calm. "Super close, it seems. With them *and* their crew."

Something in my gut twisted with unease. "Yeah, we're a tight knit group."

"Clearly."

I faced him fully. "Why do I get the feeling there's something you're not saying?"

Chase huffed a condescending laugh. "You're a perceptive one, aren't you? Well, so am I." He finally faced me, his cool expression twisting into a snide smirk. "I understood fucking the lead singer, but after Montana, I couldn't for the life of me figure out why you were hanging on one of the roadies. But the more I thought about it, the more it made sense."

My stomach dropped, but I forced my face to remain blank. "I don't know what you're talking about."

"They're both crazy protective of you, they're the same height and build, and that tech always seems to disappear during live performances. In fact, half their crew disappears when they step onstage. Pretty big coincidence, don't you think?"

Heart hammering in my chest, I turned back to the show, praying I didn't look as panicked as I felt. "Cute conspiracy theory, Chase. It's almost as good as the one that said they're sacrificing virgins."

"Go ahead and deny it all you want. But my eyes are open now." He chuckled and shook his head. "Man, I'm going to have some fun with this. Tour just got a hell of a lot more interesting."

He clapped me on the back as he walked away, his fading laughter creating a roar in my ears so loud it drowned out the music. A sense of dread chilled my blood, and it only worsened when my phone buzzed with a text. I slipped it from my pocket, expecting a response from Trent, but the message was from someone else.

> MOM: The Lord spoke to me and told me you would come back to us

My hands began to shake so violently I could no longer see the words on the screen. Legion's first song neared its climax, the complex riffs, thundering beat, and powerful vocals blasting through the venue and rattling the foundation of the building. The melody tore through me, flooding my soul with strength and fiery rage.

I lifted my phone, swiped open to the text thread full of countless unanswered messages from my mother, and typed a response.

> God lied.

Then I blocked that bitch, turned off my phone, and lost myself in some good old fashioned rock and roll.

37

"Still no answer?"

I sighed and set my phone down on the kitchen table. "Nope. Maybe he changed his number on top of changing the locks."

"No, he's just being a dick."

Kayla puttered around the kitchen, checking the pancakes on the stove and scooping scrambled eggs onto a plate in front of me. For the five days I'd been home from tour, she'd entered full-blown mother hen mode. She made us breakfast every morning, gave me a manicure, and was doing everything in her power to help me see Gracie, something that Trent was making impossible.

"Maybe I deserve it," I mumbled, spinning my fork in circles on the countertop. "I did sort of abandon her."

"You broke up with a narcissist and are crashing with a friend whose lease doesn't allow dogs, and then you went on vacation. You didn't abandon her. And besides, it's not like you dumped this huge burden on him. She's his dog too."

I rolled my eyes. "He paid half the adoption fee, but that's about it. I fed her, took her to vet appointments, walked her, bought her food and toys. He only really did something for her when I asked him to."

"Oh, then fuck that guy." Kayla tossed a pancake in the air and caught it perfectly in the skillet. "He can pull his weight for a little bit."

I chewed the inside of my cheek, not entirely convinced.

Knock. Knock. Knock.

My head swiveled to the front door.

"Could you grab that, Jay?" Kayla asked, transferring the pancakes to the stack warming in the oven. "I'm expecting a delivery."

"On it."

I slid off my stool and shuffled across the apartment, hauling open the door to smile at the UPS man on the other side.

"Hi. Delivery for Kayla Vaughn?"

The guy frowned and checked the box in his arms. "No, I'm looking for Jade Matthews."

"Huh?"

The man rechecked the name. "Jade Matthews?"

"Yeah, sorry. That's me, I just don't remember ordering anything." I signed the man's notepad and accepted the box, closing the door behind me.

"Did you black out and online shop again?" Kayla called from the kitchen.

"Not that I know of."

I checked the return address, but the only thing in its place was a drawing of a smiley face with devil horns. My heart leapt, and I tore open the box with the giddy excitement of a kid at Christmas. Inside, I found a sealed envelope and two individual parcels wrapped in black tissue paper and shiny red ribbon.

"What is it?" Kayla asked, standing on her tiptoes and craning her neck to see the box from the stove.

"It's from the guys."

I was smiling so big my cheeks hurt as I ripped open the

envelope and pulled out a handwritten note, several polaroids dropping from the folds of the paper in the process. When I picked them up, I couldn't help the delighted squeal that leapt from my mouth.

It seemed Donovan and Callum had held an impromptu photoshoot in the bathroom of their Malibu home, with Donovan being the photographer and Callum the increasingly undressed muse. The final two photos were of Callum fully naked in the shower, washing the sand from his skin, and a closeup self-portrait by Donovan. *That* polaroid had "U Should B Here" written across the bottom in sharpie with an arrow pointing to his outstretched tongue.

I bit my lip and peeled my gaze away from the sexy images to focus on the note.

> *Darling angel,*
>
> *Your demons miss playing with you. Here are a few things you'll need for when we get our claws in you next.*
>
> *Your sweethearts,*
> *C + D*
>
> *(P.S. Feel free to send photos back)*

Kayla whistled, looking over my shoulder. "Goddamn, that's some good spank bank material."

I immediately hid the photographs from view. "Kay! You're not supposed to see what they look like!"

"Girl, you think I was looking at their *faces*?" She winked and returned to rummaging through the cabinets for maple syrup.

While she was distracted, I tore into the rest of the packages. In the first, I discovered a red lingerie set made up of a balconette bra, thigh high stockings, a garter belt, and a pair of lacy panties. The second present contained a velvet pouch, and when I loosened the string and peeked inside, my cheeks warmed.

A set of jeweled stainless steel anal plugs lay inside, their sizes varying from cute and manageable to holy-shit-how-is-that-going-to-fit-inside-me. It was daunting yet thrilling, and the image of using them while I was with Dono and Cal had my insides clenching eagerly.

Gathering up my spoils, I dashed to the bathroom. "I'll be right back, Kay. Go ahead and start without me."

Once inside, I whipped off my t-shirt and maneuvered the bra on. The boys did damn good. The skimpy design shaped and lifted my chest perfectly, but it was still comfortable thanks to the buttery soft lace.

I raised my phone and snapped a selfie of my tits, then fired it off to the gift-givers.

Got your present 😘

I received an immediate response back.

> CALLUM: Oh...my...GOD

> DONOVAN: I'm hard

> CALLUM: Me too. Fucking hell. You're devastatingly delicious, you know that?

> DONOVAN: I'm going to photograph you in that and then rip it off with my teeth

I blushed and pulled my shirt back on. My phone dinged again. I figured Callum and Dono hadn't gotten all their compliments out yet.

What I didn't expect was someone else's name to pop up on my phone.

LUCA: Coffee?

I blinked a few times to make sure I was actually seeing the text correctly. When I'd processed it was real, I swiped opened the message.

What about it?

LUCA: Do you want some? I'm in your neck of the woods.

I chewed my bottom lip as I thought.

Yes, but on one condition.

LUCA: And what might that be?

I slid into the passenger seat of Luca's car and extended a Tupperware container full of pancakes.

"Compliments of the chef."

Luca took the box and examined its contents like he was a judge on a baking show. "You know, most girls just do bottomless mimosas. I've never heard of Pancake Saturday before."

"All the popular brunch spots get too crowded on weekends. And I never said Pancake Saturday didn't have mimosas."

I suggestively waggled my eyebrows, forcing Luca to crack a smile.

"Uh-oh. Did my car just turn into a drunk bus?"

I laughed. "No, I just had two. But seriously, Kayla wants your opinion on those as payment for stealing me away."

Luca set the box in the backseat, put his car in gear, and pulled away from the curb. "Alright, but you should warn her I'm a harsh critic. I'm a pretty damn good cook myself."

"And incredibly humble too."

Luca let out a small laugh. "I wish I could take credit for it, but it's all my Nonna. Without her recipes, I'm nothing."

I noted the way his eyes grew distant, and a fond smile tugged at the corners of his lips. "It sounds like you two are close."

"We used to be." His face iced over again.

I settled in my seat and turned my attention to the palm trees passing by the window. "Well, you'll have to cook for me sometime."

"You free tonight?"

I arched a brow in his direction. "You're stealing me for the whole day?"

Luca shrugged, keeping his eyes glued to the road and honking at another driver. "Wasn't planning on it, but if you've got nothing going on, I've been craving Nonna's bolognese. Plus, I gave Dante some lyrics to put a tune to, so after working all day, he's gonna be hungry."

My heart did a giddy little flutter at the idea of spending time with the two of them. Not that it ever included anything but Luca and Dante bickering, but part of me missed the chaos.

"Sure, I'm down. I was going to try and stake out my old apartment so I could see my dog, but I could go for some pasta instead."

"Wait, back up. What's going on?"

"It's my ex," I sighed. "He's ignoring my calls and texts, so I can't come get any of my stuff or spend time with my dog. And he changed the locks so I can't get in either."

I yelped as the car swerved to the side of the road and screeched to a halt in front of an empty parking meter. Luca threw the stick shift in park and faced me, his calm expression a stark contrast to his driving.

"This is the same man who cheated on you?"

Heart still racing, I nodded. "I think he's punishing me for ignoring his texts after we broke up. I didn't talk to him until the night I left for tour, when I found him with a woman in our bed. *Again.*"

A muscle in Luca's jaw ticked, but otherwise, his face remained expressionless. "Change of plans, angel. I'm not feeling coffee anymore."

The engine revved, and we sped off down Ventura Boulevard.

"What's your address?" Luca asked, eyes narrowed on the road ahead as he zipped around traffic.

"Why?"

"Address, Jade."

The warning in his words made my blood run cold.

I swallowed and pointed to an upcoming stoplight. "Turn left up here."

The rest of the ride was spent in silence, except for me timidly offering directions. Something about Luca's energy kept my typically sassy tongue behind my teeth. He wasn't his usual self. He was dangerous now. Maybe he always had been, and I'd never cowered in fear because I trusted him enough to keep the Beast tamed. But now it was free, and it was fucking terrifying.

When we pulled up to the curb outside my apartment, Luca's face was still blank. I wanted him to smirk, bark an order, purr something seductive in my ear, do anything to prove he was still inside this cold shell of a man, but no such luck. He simply reached into the backseat and dragged a backpack forward. After tugging the zipper open and rummaging around inside, he pulled out the gold ram mask he usually wore onstage.

"Come on," he commanded, jerking his head to my building and exiting the car.

I followed. "What are you doing?"

But he only gestured to the callbox, demanding the passcode. I warily punched it in. When the door buzzed, Luca ripped it open and stormed inside.

"What apartment number?"

"2D."

He walked with determined strides, forcing me to jog in order to keep up with him.

"Luca, please tell me what's going on."

"Do you want to see your dog or not?"

"Of course."

"Then let me handle it."

We arrived at my front door, and I raised my fist to knock, but Luca caught my wrist. He put a finger to his lips and motioned for me to step out of the eyeline of the peephole. When I was safely out of sight, Luca rapped at the door, keeping his face angled to the ground.

"What's your ex's name?" he whispered.

"Trent Walden."

Scuffling came from the other side of the door, followed by a female voice. "Yes?"

It shouldn't have surprised me that fucking Stacy was there, but it did, and suddenly I was filled with such rage that it made me nauseous. Whatever Luca had planned, I was 100% on board.

"Yes, ma'am," Luca said, adopting a convincing Southern accent. "I've got a delivery here for Trent Walden? I'll need a signature."

"Ok, hang on," the female replied.

More scuffling, followed by low murmurs as two people conversed. Then the deadbolt clicked, but before the door opened far enough for Trent to see who was on the other side, Luca raised his foot and slammed it into the wood. The door blew open, knocking Trent backwards and eliciting a scream from Stacy. Frenzied barking started up somewhere deep in the apartment.

Luca slid on his mask before anyone could get a good view of him and stomped into the apartment. I cautiously peeked in the doorway just in time to see him straddle my ex, grip him by the shirt, and give him a rough shake.

"You're a real piece of shit, you know that?"

"Take anything you want," Trent blurted, raising his hands in defense, "just please don't hurt us!"

"Where's the dog?"

Trent's brow furrowed. "The… the what?"

I rounded the corner. "My dog, asshole."

My ex's eyes widened. "Jade? What the fuck! You psycho bitch, I'm calling the cops—"

He was silenced by Luca's fist to his jaw. After attempting to fight back, he received another blow, this one dazing him.

I stepped over his body and followed the sound of panicked barks towards the bedroom, passing Stacy cowering on the couch.

Once again, the bitch was wearing my clothes.

When I entered the bedroom and found Gracie locked in her crate, her barks of fear were replaced by yips of excitement.

"Sweetie, why are you locked up?" I knelt in front of her cage and tore open the door. Gracie leapt into my arms, whining and licking my face like she'd thought she would never see me again. I lifted her into the air and walked back out to the living room.

"You've been keeping her in the crate even when you're home?" I snapped. "When was the last time you let her out?"

"We let her out to eat," Stacy offered from her spot on the couch.

I whirled on her, my eyes narrowing into an icy glare. The woman balked and shrunk further into the couch cushions. Nothing would have made me happier than doling out the same punishment Luca gave Trent, but that would require setting Gracie down, and nothing could make me let go of my girl. Instead, I jerked my chin to the vintage t-shirt stretched across Stacy's tits.

"That's mine."

Stacy blinked. "What?"

"That's my shirt. I want it back."

"Um… Ok. Sorry. Let me go change—"

"No, I want it now. Take it off."

Stacy's gaze darted to Luca. I stepped in front of her, blocking her view.

"Don't worry about him, he's an ass man." Keeping one arm around Gracie, I extended the other. "Shirt. Now."

Stacy gulped as her trembling fingers found the hem and yanked it over her head. She hurriedly dropped the shirt in my outstretched palm and hugged herself, shielding her chest from sight. I took a moment to look her up and down like she was a piece of meat, basking in her discomfort, then spun on my heel and headed for the door. Only when me and Gracie had exited the apartment did Luca climb off of Trent, but not before giving him one last punch that knocked him out cold.

The door slammed shut behind us, and Luca removed his mask as he fell into step beside me.

"Thank you for noticing," he said.

"Noticing what?"

"That I'm an ass man."

38

"Are you sure Gracie can stay with you guys for a few days?" I asked. "It would just be until I can get her set up at a kennel."

Luca reached a hand across the car to Gracie, who sniffed him cautiously but eventually gave his fingers a lick of approval. "As long as Dante's cool with it. We'd do a hell of a better job than that douchebag back there."

Gracie nestled into me, the motion of the car already lulling her to sleep. I gently stroked her head.

"Thank you, Luca," I murmured. "You didn't have to do that for me."

"Yes, I did. No one fucks with my girl."

I froze, the word echoing in my ears. I sneaked a glance at him out of the corner of my eye. "What did you just say?"

"I said no one fucks with my friends."

"No, I don't think that was it."

"It wasn't?" Genuinely confused, Luca frowned. "What did I say then?"

"Nothing." I smiled to myself and refocused on the dog in my lap. "Probably just a Freudian slip."

We drove in silence for another fifteen minutes before Luca

turned onto a winding road that led into a sleepy, middle-class neighborhood. The houses were modest and charming, idealistic for families and newlyweds but difficult to picture a couple of rockstars living in. But sure enough, Luca pulled into a driveway at the end of the cul-de-sac and parked in front of a modern single-family home. The garage door was already open, revealing a sleek black Yamaha motorcycle stationed inside.

"You guys live here?" I asked, still scanning my surroundings.

"You sound surprised."

"It's just not what I expected."

"What did you expect?"

"I don't know. A high-rise penthouse or bachelor pad in the Hollywood Hills?"

Luca chuckled and unfastened his seatbelt. "Not our style. After the madness of tour, all you want to do is come home. We wanted ours to feel like one."

I followed him out of the car and set Gracie on her feet. She immediately pranced over to the lawn and began rolling in the grass, forcing Luca to crack a smile.

"Somebody's making herself right at home."

I whistled, and Gracie immediately jumped up and ran to my side. "Come on, Gracie girl. You don't own the place."

Luca led the way into the garage and entered the house, kicking off his shoes in the mudroom before hanging his keys on the hook on the wall. Gracie blew past us and padded down the hallway, sniffing every square inch of the place.

"Welcome to our humble abode," Luca said, stretching his arms out wide as he trailed after her.

My steps slowed as we passed a row of photos hung on the wall. There were early pictures of the band, with the boys playing on old equipment in their garage and wearing home-made masks. Their platinum records hung next to the images, encompassing just how far they'd come. Further down the wall were even older photos. Luca and Dante in soccer uniforms holding a trophy, them as children sipping sodas on the beach, as well as the same family photos that Luca had pinned in his bunk on the tour bus.

"Is this your Nonna?" I asked, stopping in front of the photo of the old woman making pasta.

"That's her." Luca came up behind me to look at the picture over my shoulder. "Whenever I think of her, that's what she looks like. Covered in flour and smiling until you tried to steal a taste of the sauce before it was ready. Then you'd get a smack to the knuckles with her vicious wooden spoon."

He smacked my ass to drive his point home, my yelp of pain transforming into a giggle.

"There's another photo you keep in your bunk. Your Nonna and another woman, with a man behind them."

The joy in Luca's eyes vanished, and he continued on through the house. "My mom and dad."

I followed after him. "You don't talk about them much."

"Nope."

"Why?"

"Dad was an abusive piece of shit, mom put up with it for too long."

I froze. "I'm so sorry—"

"Don't," he interrupted. "Don't do that. Everyone always acts like it's such a big deal. It's not. I got through it, and it made me stronger. Now no one will ever fuck with me or the people I care about ever again."

My own past tugged at me. I wished my heart could be as cutthroat and untouchable as Luca's was, instead of this miserable, panic-stricken thing that raced whenever it remembered the pain. Oh, to be the person who could look their demons in the eye and say, "You won't hurt me." If *I* faced mine, I'd probably just freeze like a deer in the headlights, or curl into a ball and cry like I did all those years ago in that cornfield.

Shaking the thoughts from my mind, I refocused on my surroundings. We'd entered into a living room, the open floor plan showing the kitchen beyond. A modern black leather sectional took up most of the room, its color coordinating perfectly with the chrome furnishings and abstract art on the wall. A familiar figure appeared in the doorway across the room, dressed in dark gray jeans, a black hoodie, and his signature headphones around his neck. Gracie stood at his side, staring up at him with her tail wagging.

Dante pointed to her. "Why is there a dog in my house?"

"Sorry, that's Gracie," I said. "She got away from us."

I whistled for my dog to come, but her paws stayed planted, and she remained hyper-focused on Dante.

"Forgot to mention I was bringing two girls over." Luca headed straight for the kitchen and began washing his hands. "How's the song coming?"

"Alright. I'm stuck on the first verse." He suspiciously eyed Gracie and started for the garage. "I'm gonna take a break and go for a ride, see if that sparks anything."

Luca shut off the faucet and shook his hands dry. "How about you take Jade with you?"

"I thought we were making pasta?"

Luca smirked. "I said *I'm* making pasta. Never said that process involved you. You'll just get in the way."

"Rude."

Luca shrugged and shifted his attention to Dante. "Keep her entertained while I'm working, will you?"

"Um…" Dante shuffled his feet and stuffed his hands in his pockets. "I don't think she should come with me."

"Why not?"

"I'm going to see Celia."

The sound of another woman's name on his tongue caused an irrational twinge of jealousy to cut through my chest. Luca, however, was unaffected by the comment and shrugged.

"My statement still stands. Take Jade with you."

Dante hesitated, chewing the inside of his cheek as he considered. Finally, he sighed and faced me.

"I drive fast." His clipped words were as much a challenge as they were a warning.

"I'll hold on tight," I replied simply.

Air puffed from Dante's nose in exasperation, and he jerked his chin for me to follow. "Fine. But if I hear one peep about speeding, I'm leaving you on the side of the road."

"That means he's excited," Luca called after him.

He received a middle finger in response and Dante disappeared down the hall.

"You sure I can't help?" I asked Luca.

He looked up from the pile of ingredients he'd stacked on the counter and smiled. "You already are. He needs you more than I do right now."

His words made my heart swell with pride. "Well, I look forward to sampling what you've cooked up when we get back, chef."

"You're going to get addicted."

I shuffled after Dante and lowered my voice so Luca wouldn't hear me when I mumbled, "I think I already am."

When I found Dante in the garage, he extended a helmet with a tinted visor by way of a greeting.

"Put this on. When we're going around a slow turn, lean in the opposite direction of the bike. Otherwise, just lean with it."

I squinted. "Lean which way when?"

"Just follow my lead. One last thing."

Dante pointed to a small bluetooth headset clipped to the side of my helmet. "I've got one of these too. It's hooked up to the Spotify on my phone, but you can also use the intercom to talk to me. With the wind in our ears, we won't be able to hear ourselves otherwise."

"Got it."

Dante grabbed his own helmet and jammed it over his head before swinging his leg over the bike and settling in with practiced ease. His energy immediately calmed the second he twisted the key in the ignition. The engine rumbled to life, and Dante jerked his chin to the space on the seat behind him.

"Hop on."

I shuffled over and awkwardly climbed onto the slightly raised end of the seat, leaving as much room between me and Dante as possible.

"Ok, I'm ready," I said, lightly resting my hands on his shoulders.

Dante sighed, abruptly accelerated, then smashed the brakes, jolting me forward in the seat so I was pressed against his back. I yelped and threw my arms around his waist to hold on for dear life.

"That's better," Dante stated, a hint of a smile in his words.

He slammed his visor down, tapped the bluetooth on his helmet, and "The End" by Zero 9:36 blasted into our ears at full volume as Dante peeled out of the garage. I had to bite my tongue to keep from screaming and tightened my hold instead, probably squeezing all the air from Dante's lungs. He didn't seem to mind, and quickly changed gears to further increase our speed. We were going dangerously fast for a residential area, but Dante's calm confidence gave me courage. By the time we pulled onto the main road and neared the freeway exit, my heart was still racing, but it was more from excitement than fear.

When we hit the highway, all traces of trepidation were gone, and I was thoroughly able to enjoy the thrill of Dante effortlessly weaving in and out of traffic. The pounding of my heart and the whistling wind blended with the beat of the music, making the perfect soundtrack for a ride that felt more like flying.

"Doing ok back there?" Dante's voice cut in over the intercom.

I raised a finger to my headset and pressed the circular button at its center.

"I thought you said we were going to go fast."

A dark laugh followed. Then Dante changed gears again, the engine roared, and I regretted everything I'd just said. The bike hurtled forward, reaching a truly terrifying speed that had me wanting to shut my eyes and scream bloody murder. We were going too fast to swerve in and out of the cars on the road anymore, so Dante veered the bike onto the shoulder and used it as his personal fast track. I didn't know much about motorcycles, but I was 99% certain it was illegal. I would have yelled at him over the intercom for it if I wasn't too scared to loosen my hold.

Suddenly, a siren whooped, followed by red and blue flashing lights, but Dante was undeterred by the cop now tailing us. He maneuvered back into the flow of traffic, causing a barrage of furious honks from other drivers on the road before rocketing down the nearest off-ramp. The police car was unable to take the exit in time, leaving us free to speed through side streets until we were certain we'd lost him. When Dante ran two red lights in a row, I'd had enough.

Forgetting the intercom, I repeatedly smacked his shoulder to signify I wanted him to pull over. Dante checked for any sign of the cops before guiding the bike to a neighborhood street and stopping not far from a woman selling flowers on the corner. We both slipped off the bike, my legs feeling like jello when I set foot on the ground. Still, I managed to give Dante a rough shove.

"What the fuck was that?" I shrieked. "We could've been killed!"

Dante's shoulders shook, and I assumed it was from contained rage, but soon muffled laughter reached my ears. His visor lifted to reveal his green eyes squinted with merriment.

"Don't you feel alive?" he asked breathlessly. "Goddamn, there's nothing like it!"

He spun on his heel and strode for the merchant on the corner.

"Where are you going?" I barked. "I'm not done yelling at you yet!"

But Dante was already in the process of flagging the woman down.

"*¡Hola, Rocío!*" he called, waving his arms overhead.

The woman looked up from her buckets of bouquets, the wrinkles around her eyes crinkling as she beamed. "*¡Hola, Dante!*"

Not wanting to be caught at the scene of the crime, I abandoned the motorcycle and jogged over to join them.

The woman's head tilted curiously as I ran up. "*¿Quién es la mujer bonita?*"

Dante winked. "*No le tengas celos.*"

The woman, Rocío, clicked her tongue and batted him away. "*¿Por qué eres tan travieso?*"

Dante chuckled. "*¿Cómo está tú familia?*"

"*Están bien. ¿Quieres lo de siempre?*"

"*Si. Gracias.*"

Rocío bent and pulled two gorgeous bunches of red roses from one of her buckets, then nodded to me. "*¿Flores para tú amiga también?*"

"No," Dante stated, his typical frown returning.

Rocío grunted her disapproval but handed over the flowers. Dante slipped her a one hundred dollar bill. She frantically shook her head.

"*Para tú familia,*" Dante insisted.

Rocío sighed in exasperation, but gratitude shone in her eyes, and she clasped his hand in thanks. Dante smiled and dipped his head, then turned and started back towards the bike. I politely waved goodbye to the woman and hurried after him.

"I didn't know you were fluent in Spanish," I mumbled when I'd caught up.

Dante arched an eyebrow. "You hear Vee yell at me in Spanish all the time."

"Yeah, but you always act like you don't hear her."

"I do that with a lot of people. Doesn't mean it's true."

We arrived at the motorcycle, and Dante tucked the flowers under his arm and patted the bike seat.

"I'm told I look more like my dad," he explained as I wiggled into place, "but my mom's Mexican. She moved to the states as a kid and insisted we hold onto our culture."

"What happened to your dad?"

Dante shrugged and slid onto the seat in front of me. "Who fucking knows. He ran off back to Orange County when my mom told him she was pregnant."

He turned the key in the ignition and handed me the two bouquets over his shoulder. "Hold onto these, will you?"

I took the flowers and laid them in my lap, trying not to crush the petals as I wrapped my arms around Dante's waist again. Thankfully, he drove at a much more manageable pace this time as he turned into the neighborhood. Quaint stucco houses passed us by, their manicured yards filled with happy families enjoying the beauty of September in Los Angeles.

The bike rolled to a stop in front of the largest house on the block, and Dante shut off the engine. He climbed onto solid ground and held out his hands. I offered him the flowers, but he rolled his eyes.

"No, silly," he muttered, "that's not what I was doing."

He reached forward, grabbed me around the waist, and lifted me off the bike like I weighed nothing. I let out a squeak of surprise, my cheeks flushing bright pink as he planted me in the driveway. Dante motioned for me to follow him.

"Come on."

We both pulled off our helmets and made our way towards the front door. Instead of knocking, Dante dug into his pocket, pulled out a set of keys, and jammed them into the lock.

I had no idea what would be waiting for us on the other side. A girlfriend? A secret family?

The last thing I expected was a cheery yellow room filled with sunshine, and a woman in hospital scrubs shuffling over with her arms outstretched.

"*¡Que sopresa!*"

She hurled herself into Dante and gave him two fierce kisses on each cheek. He flinched against them, but not out of disgust. More like a child being smothered by a loving aunt or grandmother.

"*Hola, Celia,*" he greeted, patting her back. "*Como estas?*"

"*Muy bien. Y tú?*"

"*Estoy cansado.*"

"*Y como sigues de tú mente?*"

"*Ruidoso.*"

"*Sigue luchando.*" The woman, Celia, pulled away and gestured to me, her warm brown eyes lighting up even more. "*¿Quién es ella? Tú novia?*"

Dante scoffed. "*¡Ni madres!*"

Celia tutted and lightly smacked Dante's shoulder. "*¡Cuidado lo que dices!*"

Dante smirked, pulled the flowers from my arms, and handed one bouquet to the woman in front of him. "*Mi empleada.* Jade."

"Hello, Jade." Celia took the roses Dante offered and smiled at me like she knew a secret I didn't.

"Hi." I extended my hand for her to shake. "You must be Celia."

"I am. It's nice to meet you."

"You too. Dante doesn't talk about his family much, it's nice to have a face with the name."

Celia chuckled. "Oh, I'm not family."

"You're not?"

"Yes, she is," Dante cut in, wandering deeper into the house.

Celia followed behind him. "Not technically. You could say I'm an honorary member."

I padded after them, taking in the array of cozy furnishings and family photos on the wall. Many of them included a green-eyed little boy with pale skin, black curls, and a bright smile that dimmed as the years went on. When I finally peeled my eyes from the pictures and rounded the corner, I froze.

Stationed in the living room was a hospital bed.

It faced a window that overlooked a luscious garden alive with hummingbirds and butterflies. Tucked in the sheets and draped in a homemade quilt, was a woman.

She had dark hair streaked in gray, and brown eyes that were half-lidded and glazed as they stared into the distance. She looked to be in her fifties, but it was difficult to tell with the IVs, oxygen tubes, and beeping monitors blocking my view. I didn't need to see her face to know who she was, though. When Dante placed the flowers in a nearby vase, kissed her forehead, and lowered into the chair beside her bed, it was clear.

"*Hola, Mamá,*" he whispered, taking her hand and gently stroking it with his thumb.

Celia appeared at my side, watching the scene with a melancholy smile. "Jade, meet Marcela. Dante's mom."

"Oh," I breathed. "I… I had no idea."

"No, I'd expect not." Celia's face fell, and she lowered her voice. "He doesn't like to talk about her much. He feels too guilty."

I glanced at Dante out of the corner of my eye. He was mumbling to Marcela in Spanish and pointing to a pair of finches nibbling at the bird feeders hanging outside the window.

"Why does he feel guilty?"

Celia fiddled with one of the blossoms in her bouquet. "Something happened a few years ago… It's not my place to go into details, but one night, Marcela received a call that something had happened to Dante while he was on tour. He was in the hospital. On the way to see him, she was hit by a drunk driver. She wasn't even supposed to make it through the night, but she's a fighter. They both are. She's made wonderful progress since then, but she'll never be the same."

While Celia had been talking, involuntary tears formed along the edges of my lashes. I quickly averted my gaze and blinked them away. Something deep in my gut knew the evening she was referring to was the night Dante had tried to take his life, and all of a sudden his self-hatred made a lot more sense.

"Can I meet her?" I asked, my voice hoarse with emotion.

"Yes," Dante replied from across the room.

Of course he'd been pretending he couldn't hear.

I inhaled deep and let it out slow, then crossed to the bed overlooking the garden. Marcela made no move to look at me, her eyes remaining fixed on the greenery outside. Still, I sat down beside Dante and smiled.

"Hi, Mrs. Ramos. I'm Jade. It's an honor to meet you."

"Jade es la novia de Dante," Celia added before darting into the kitchen.

Dante sighed and rolled his eyes. *"Celia habla demasiado, Mamá."*

I stifled a laugh and returned my attention to Marcela. "Your son is very talented, Mrs. Ramos. He amazes me every day."

Dante sniffed. "Don't lie."

"I'm not."

Our eyes met and held for a few moments, but I forced myself to refocus on the woman in the bed. "You said you two didn't look alike, but you do."

Dante's gaze softened as he scanned his mother's features. "You think?"

"Yeah. I can't put my finger on what it is exactly, but it's there. Something beautiful." I dared to look his way again, and found him already looking at me. I cracked a grin to break the tension. "All she's missing is the face tattoo, and you'd be twins."

To my surprise, Dante tossed his head back and laughed out loud, prompting his mom to shift in her bed.

"*Dios mío*," Celia grumbled, puttering out of the kitchen carrying a platter of cookies. "I've told him to get that thing removed a hundred times. They have lasers that can do that now."

"*Yo ya sé, Celia.*"

Celia set the plate of goodies down on my lap and motioned for me to eat. "Don't let the attitude fool you, Jade. He's a good boy."

Dante started to roll his eyes again, but Celia smacked the back of his head.

"I'm serious! Not many children would make sure their parents are taken care of the way you have. Jade, did you know he spent his life savings to buy this house so she could be close to him? And when he's home from tour, he always brings her favorite flowers and sings her favorite hymns."

My brows arched. "Hymns as in church hymns?"

Celia nodded and fluffed Marcela's pillows. "She only smiles when he sings them. Not when they're on the radio, not when I sing them, only when *he* does."

Dante grabbed a cookie off the platter and rotated it between his fingers. "Yeah, well. Sometimes you do things you don't want to for the people you love." He peeked up between the strands of dark hair that had fallen in front of his face, catching me staring at him. "Don't look at me like that."

I hurriedly averted my gaze.

"I have an idea!" Celia eagerly clapped her hands and wandered over to an acoustic guitar sitting in the corner. "Dante, how about you play us something?"

He frowned. "I don't think Jade—"

"*Por favor?*" Celia carried the guitar over and winked at me.

"Dante's been giving me lessons, but I think Marcela is probably tired of hearing my pathetic attempts at 'Wonderwall.'"

Dante sighed in defeat and stretched out his hand. "Alright, fine."

Celia beamed and handed over the instrument. Dante cleared his throat and put the guitar into position, testing the tone and tightening the strings to adjust it.

"Don't look at me like that either," he murmured.

This time, I didn't look away. "How am I looking at you?"

"Like this somehow changes who I am."

His fingers moved into place, and he strummed a chord, followed by another, then another. It was a tune I'd never heard before, slow and haunting, filled with passion and longing. Marcela moved in her bed again, her lashes fluttering.

"That's beautiful," I mused. "What is it?"

"Just a little something I was working on today," Dante replied. "It's not finished yet."

"Well, keep playing it," Celia urged. "I think your mom likes it."

Dante and I glanced at Marcela. A faint smile tugged at the corners of her mouth, which made Dante's face light up.

"*¿Te gusta, Mamá?*"

She muttered something incoherent, but it may as well have been glowing praise. Dante radiated joy from the inside out and played the rest of the verse and chorus, then transitioned into an array of different song ideas he'd been toying with.

We stayed there for another hour, listening to music, watching the birds in the window, and eating cookies, until Celia informed us it was time for Marcela to wash up for bed. We said goodbye, and on the way out, Celia pulled me into a warm, lingering hug that gave me more comfort in ten seconds than my own mother had given me in the past two years. I eventually pulled away and busied myself with adjusting my helmet so no one would see me getting emotional. I was still able to hear the conversation happening between Celia and Dante as they said their farewells.

"*Te amo, Dante.*"

"*Te amo también.*"

Celia cupped his face in her hands, forcing him to look her in the eyes. "*Me encanta Jade.*"

"*Yo también.*"

"*Ella es muy especial.*"

"*Sí, ya sé.*"

Celia nodded and kissed Dante's cheek one last time before shooing him towards the motorcycle in the driveway. She stood on the doorstep and waved goodbye until we'd disappeared in the distance.

We took the long way home along Mulholland Drive so we could watch the sunset from the crest of the Hollywood Hills. There, I confiscated Dante's phone, changed the music to Zella Day's dreamy cover of "Wonderwall," and decided now wasn't the time to remind him of what I'd told the band the night I signed my contract.

I'd told them I graduated from college with two degrees.

They knew about the first degree, graphic design.

But the second?

Spanish.

I'd understood everything that had been said today.

And in regards to Dante and Celia's final words, I felt the same way:

I really liked him, and thought he was pretty damn special too.

---

*Spanish to English translation located after the Epilogue

39

When we got back to Dante and Luca's house, we were hit by an aromatic cloud of garlic and butter the moment we walked in the door.

"Smells amazing," I said, wandering over to the man puttering around the kitchen. The sleeves of his henley were rolled up to the elbows, the tattoos on his arms dusted with flour as he rolled out dough across the granite countertops using a large rolling pin.

"Sauce is simmering," Luca replied, keeping his eyes glued to his work. "We should be ready to go in about an hour or so."

I hovered over the fragrant pot on the stove and reached for the lid. "Can I have a taste?"

Luca dropped his rolling pin and smacked my knuckles, making me yelp. "Not until it's ready."

I looked to Dante for support, but he shrugged helplessly.

"Sorry, angel. His tyranny doesn't stop at the stage." He leaned a hip against the counter and looked around the kitchen. "Where's Gracie?"

"Outside chasing squirrels." Luca wiped a strand of hair from his eyes with the back of his hand, leaving a smear of flour behind on his cheek. "I gave her some bites of meat from the bolognese, I hope that's ok."

I pouted. "So my dog can sample your cooking but I can't?"

Luca finally looked up, eyes shining mischievously. "She's a good girl. Can't say the same about you."

At the hint of a game, my blood heated. I tossed my hair and strolled across the kitchen, swinging my hips a little more than usual. When I came to a stop behind Luca, I pressed my chest to his back and let my hands drift lower, nearing the curve of his ass. He tensed at my touch, but kept his focus on the pasta.

"I could be good for you," I purred.

Luca scoffed. "That'll be the day."

"I will, I promise." I raised to my tiptoes and grazed the side of his neck with my nose. "You just have to do something for me first."

Luca's hands flexed as he gripped the edge of the countertop, but he still didn't look at me. Dante did, though. I could feel his stare boring into me as he moved across the kitchen and pulled a beer from the fridge.

"What do you want, angel?" Luca asked, his voice low and husky.

"It's simple." My hand slipped into his back pocket and pulled out his phone. I reached around and slid it onto the counter in front of him. "I want you to ask Cal and Dono to come have dinner with us."

Dante's beer paused halfway to his lips.

Forgetting the meal he was cooking, Luca faced me and arched a brow. "What?"

"You heard me. We have more than enough food for everyone."

Luca glanced at Dante, who shrugged. "They wouldn't come."

"You don't know that," I countered.

"Yes, I do. You've seen how we operate, angel. Those guys aren't a part of this band for anything other than the money."

"And maybe the music," Dante mumbled into his drink.

"*And* the people who make the music," I insisted. "They wouldn't have stuck around so long otherwise." Snatching Luca's phone, I held it out to him, refusing to back down. "I know you're tired of how things are. You've been fighting for a long time, but you haven't given up yet. That means something. You're still making music, you're still pouring your hearts out in performances, you all still want this. I know you do. Distracting yourselves with sex isn't going to solve your problems. "

"Says the woman currently trying to distract me with sex."

"I'm trying to bribe you with sex, there's a difference."

A stifled laugh came from the other corner of the kitchen. Luca and I peeked over at Dante. He shook his head, took a pull from the beer bottle, and licked his lips.

"Fuck it. Text 'em."

Luca's gaze returned to mine, and he set his jaw. "Fine. But you have to do something for me tool, angel."

"Name your price."

A devious smile spread over Luca's face. "Tonight, you behave for once."

I laughed, but Luca didn't flinch.

Oh my god. He was being serious?

"You don't talk back," he continued, "and you obey every command I give you."

I raised an eyebrow. "This sounds suspiciously like I'm your slave for the night."

"Exactly why you'll call me Master."

I sighed and rolled my eyes, but it was just an act. In reality, my core twinged at Luca's words, and I was practically salivating at the thought of being at his mercy.

"Fine," I stated, extending my hand. "It's a deal."

Luca's fingers closed around mine. "Pleasure doing business with you."

Dante finished his beer and grabbed another from the fridge. "You two are a match made in freaky heaven."

"Heaven has room for everyone, Lucifer," I cooed. "You want to be called Master tonight too?"

"You know what you're supposed to call me."

His voice was a seductive warning that immediately had me fighting the urge to fall to my knees in submission. I swallowed hard and averted my gaze.

"Yes, Sir."

"That's better." Dante popped the bottle cap off and lifted the beer to his lips. "Looks like I can command your slave better than you can, Luca."

The singer irritably sucked his teeth, but a competitive gleam flashed in his eyes. He stole his phone back and began tapping out a message, but not before grabbing my face with a flour-dusted hand and snapping a photo.

"Proof you're the instigator of this," Luca explained.

I smirked and wiggled out of his grip to saunter over to Dante. His eyes tracked me as I plucked the beer out of his hand and took a sip.

"You're on one today, angel."

"Am I?" I moved to take a second drink, but Dante's hand whipped out, caught the bottle, and dragged me closer. My breath hitched as his lips stopped an inch from mine.

"If I didn't know better, I'd think you were purposefully trying to rile us up."

I coyly batted my lashes. "And why would I do that?"

"Because you're a hopeless little cumslut whose holes have been empty for too long."

A carnal twinge shot through my core, and I bit my lip. "Your words not mine."

"Sent." Luca tossed his phone aside and braced his hands on the counter behind him. "Where were we?"

I started to turn towards him, but Dante caught me by the neck and spun me back around.

"He didn't say you were done here."

"No, I did not." Luca plucked the cork from a wine bottle beside the stove and took a pull. "You two give me an appetizer. Show me what I have to look forward to."

Heat pooled in my sensitive areas.

"Hear that, fucktoy?" Dante patted my cheek, his raps growing increasingly firm. "Show him how well you obey when you want to."

I nodded, my mind flipping the switch to that delicious place of surrender it always found its way to with Dante. When he pushed me to my knees, I went eagerly.

"What a good slut," he praised, taking a sip from his beer with one hand while loosening the button on his jeans with the other. "You want a taste?"

I was already salivating. "Yes, Sir."

Dante maneuvered his jeans down his hips, allowing his length to spring free. He hiked up the hem of his hoodie, exposing his torso, and tipped the beer bottle so a trickle of liquid spilled down his abs into the sprinkling of pubic hair at the base of his shaft.

"Drink," he demanded.

I obediently leaned forward and stuck out my tongue, lapping at the malty liquid as it trickled down his manhood and onto his balls. Dante's hand landed on the back of my head and pushed me further into him, smashing my nose into his skin. His salty musk enveloped my senses and caused an involuntary moan to escape me.

"You missed a little, angel," Luca called.

Dante let me lift for air and glance at the man across the

kitchen. Luca beckoned to the floor, and I followed his gaze down to a small puddle of beer that had formed on the tile.

"You're absolutely right," Dante chuckled, balling a fist in my hair. "We can't have her getting sloppy, can we?"

He gruffly shoved my head towards the floor, but I didn't struggle. I'd loved seeing him kind and gentle today, but I'd missed this side of him, this darkness. I'd missed my own too.

Humiliation and arousal formed an addictive cocktail as my cheek smashed into the beer-splattered tile, and Dante's foot came to rest on my head.

Luca wandered across the kitchen and landed a stinging slap to my ass as he crouched beside me. I grunted at the pain but instinctively lifted my hips skyward.

"What a good little slut," he crooned, rubbing tender circles on the area he'd just struck. "Face down, ass up, ready to be used." He tilted his head to look me in the eyes. "Do you want to be used, slut?"

"Yes, Sir."

Another slap made contact with my ass, this one harder than the first.

"That's not what you call me. What's my name tonight?"

I pressed my lips together, fighting with myself on whether to act up or not. I got a sick high from testing Luca's patience, but the shoe pressing into my skull complicated things. With Dante here, I felt inclined to be on my best behavior, even if it meant biting my tongue with Luca.

A third slap landed when I took too long to reply, forcing me to grit my teeth. "Yes, *Master*."

"Don't make the mistake again." Luca dipped his chin to the puddle under my cheek. "Now drink."

I held his stare and stuck out my tongue. Even though my cheeks heated with embarrassment as I slurped up what beer I could, I pretended like it was the most fun I'd ever had just to get a rise out of him.

Luca smirked. "Don't think I can't see the attitude, angel."

"Then maybe you should fuck it out of me," I mumbled into the floor.

Dante dug the heel of his shoe deeper. "What was that, fucktoy?"

"Nothing."

The two men exchanged glances.

"I think someone's craving a little pain," Luca mused. He slapped my ass a fourth time to drive his point home, causing an ache that straddled the line of too much. I bit my lip and embraced the discomfort.

"We can make that happen," Dante said, removing his shoe and crouching to grab a fistful of my hair instead. One firm tug, and I was forced to lift my chin.

"Remember your safe word?" he asked.

"Yes, Sir."

"Good. Now show us what that mouth is capable of."

Before I could offer a rebuttal, Dante took hold of his cock and jammed it between my lips.

I gagged as he invaded my throat, but dug deep and held him there until he groaned his appreciation. He slid himself out and thrust back in, then again and again until my eyes were watering. Just when I thought I couldn't take anymore, Dante ripped free.

"What a good fucking girl," he growled, rapping at my cheek before smothering me in a vicious kiss. When he pulled away, he gave my face a gruff shake. "Go show your Master the same treatment."

I obediently turned to Luca, but he rose and backed away as I reached for the button on his jeans.

"Come," he demanded, curling his finger at me.

I moved to stand up, but he shook his head.

"*Crawl.*"

His command sent a pulse through my core, further fueling

my adrenaline and arousal so I was practically vibrating as I crossed the kitchen on my hands and knees. By the time I arrived at Luca's feet, he was back at his spot from before, leaning against the counter and casually sipping from the bottle of wine. He motioned to my clothes with a flick of his wrist.

"Undress."

Had he always sounded this sexy barking orders?

Kneeling before him, I slowly peeled my shirt over my head, revealing the balconette bra I'd snapped photos in earlier. When he caught sight of it, Luca's fingers tightened around the neck of the bottle.

"Goddamn," he murmured, his eyes roving over my breasts.

I teasingly trailed my fingers along the red lace. "It's a gift from Dono and Cal."

"Yes, it is." Luca set aside the wine and reached down to stroke my hair. "Remind me to write them a thank you card."

"You can thank them yourself when they come over tonight."

Luca's lips curled into a smile. "You know, that mouth is doing a lot of talking when it should be doing something else."

My gaze lowered to the large bulge in his jeans, which caused an eager pulse of my inner walls. Luca unzipped, hooked his thumbs in the waistband of his briefs, and tugged them down, releasing his stiff cock. I immediately took it in my hands and teased the sensitive skin with my lips and tongue, making sure to keep my eyes locked with Luca's. He braced his hands on either side of the counter behind him, his chest rising and falling faster the more I toyed with him.

"Such a tease," he huffed, shaking his head in wry amusement. "But you were supposed to show me the same treatment you showed Dante. D, is this how you fuck that pretty face?"

Dante wandered over and smacked my ass so hard I almost screamed. "Nope. Your slave is being lazy. We can't have that."

A gasp leapt from my mouth as he looped his arms through mine, yanked them behind my back, and dragged me to my feet.

I tried to wriggle free, but he held me flush to his chest, making it impossible to move an inch. Luca stepped up and yanked my pants down to my ankles, then used one hand to cup my breasts while the other slipped inside my lacy panties. I groaned and leaned my head back on Dante's shoulder as my hips instinctively rolled in time with Luca rubbing circles on my clit.

"Am I going to have to punish you," the singer asked, "or are you going to do what you're told?"

Before I could answer, he dipped two fingers inside me, drawing out a moan. After a few delicious strokes against my G-spot, his pace quickened and his movements grew more forceful. Soon the kitchen filled with the wet slaps of his hand working me.

"Answer me, angel," Luca snapped, "before you make another mess on my floor."

I was quivering so bad my knees gave out, and I sank all my weight into Dante. Each stroke was an explosion of sensation so powerful I could barely string together words.

"Y-y-yes... I'll... *fuck*... I'll behave!"

Luca ripped his hand free, leaving me limp, and smashed his arousal-slicked fingers into my mouth so deep I choked. "Now let's try this again, shall we?"

Dante loosened his hold and bent me over so I was face-to-face with Luca's cock again. I took him all the way into my mouth, muscling down my gag reflex as he thrust into my throat. My legs shook so badly I could barely stand, but it became less of an issue when Dante grabbed my hips to hold me upright. My panties slid to the side, and something warm and velvety slipped between my ass cheeks before spreading the lips of my pussy. Before I fully realized what was happening, Dante plunged his length inside me, my following cry of surprise muffled by Luca's cock. I moved to spit him out, but a tattooed hand landed on the back of my head and forced me back down.

"Uh-uh," Dante scolded. "You're staying right there. You can take it."

He started up his typical punishing pace, and Luca matched it on the other end. Their soundtrack of growls and groans kept me going, turning me on too much to tap out. A trail of saliva dribbled down my chin, and tears squeezed out the sides of my eyes as they fucked me from both ends. After one last deep stroke, Luca pulled himself free, leaving me gasping for air. With Dante still pounding into me from behind, Luca pushed me upright and smothered me in a passionate kiss.

"Thank you, Master," I blurted when he pulled away, my words bouncing with Dante's thrusts.

A genuine smile stretched across Luca's face as he brushed the strands of sweat-drenched hair from my eyes. "That's my girl."

He reached down to the sensitive area between my legs and found the aching bead at its center. Applying the perfect amount of pressure, he flicked his fingers up and down, shooting bursts of pleasure with every swipe.

"Oh my god," I moaned. "You're gonna make me come like that."

Dante's hands moved from my hips to my hair, hauling it into a ponytail and yanking my head back. "That's right, angel, you earned it. Come all over that cock."

But it wasn't just *his* permission I needed.

My attention shifted back to Luca.

"Please, Master, can I come?" I whimpered, desperation strangling my voice.

"Yes, angel, you can."

It was the final thing I required to hurtle over the edge. More tears squeezed from my eyes as I came, and an influx of emotion exploded with the tension in my core. I rode the waves of bliss until every particle of energy was depleted from my body, and I could no longer stand on two feet. But the men weren't finished with me yet.

After one last slap to my ass, Dante slid out of me, spun me around, and passed me off to Luca. I was as limp as a rag doll, and he wrapped both hands around my throat to keep me propped upright as Luca lifted my hips and slid into me. Even though I was more than warmed up, I still groaned at his size.

"You're not done yet, fucktoy," Dante said. He nodded to his cock, still glistening with proof of my climax.

I obediently took him in my hands and stroked him while Luca pumped into me from behind. He fucked me slow at first, but gradually increased his tempo. My speed on Dante's length followed suit.

"Am I doing good, Sir?" I panted, looking up at him through my lashes.

Instead of replying, his grip around my neck tightened, cutting off airflow completely, but I just smiled up at him. I'd learned to trust his brand of violence.

"Open your mouth," Dante demanded. When I obeyed, he spat onto my tongue, then gave me a gruff shake. "Swallow it."

Despite his hold around my throat, I managed to gulp, then stuck out my tongue for more. A slight smile tugged at Dante's lips.

"Such a filthy little whore. I fucking love it." His fingers loosened, allowing me to gulp down a lungful of air before they clamped back down again. "After Luca fucks you stupid, you're going to get on your knees and beg for my cum on this pretty face. You understand?"

I nodded just as stars began to scatter across my vision. Seeing my eyes go glassy, Dante immediately stopped choking me and pulled me in to rest on his chest as I recovered. Tingles spread from my head down to my toes, heightening the pleasure of Luca's toe-curling drives into me. His fingers tightened around my hips as his breaths grew sporadic, and after a few more pumps, he pulled out and released on my back with a groan. Dante immediately shoved me to my knees and pumped his length in time with his heaving chest. A few strokes later, a line of cum spurted across my tongue. Still breathless, Dante swiped a missed droplet from my chin with his thumb and shoved it between my lips. Our stares held while I sucked at his finger. When it popped free, I licked my lips and moaned my appreciation.

"Thank you, Sir."

Dante huffed a laugh and shook his head. "Jesus Christ. You're something else."

I grinned and glanced over my shoulder at Luca. "So when's dinner? I'm starving."

He smirked and readjusted his jeans. "Why? You just ate."

I rolled my eyes and gratefully accepted the hand Dante extended to help me up. A buzz drew our attention to the counter.

Luca shuffled over and picked up his phone, his eyes narrowing at the screen. "Huh. Will you look at that. Dono and Cal are on their way."

40

I'd be lying if I said the meal wasn't awkward at first.

The guys seemed quiet and uncertain upon Callum and Donovan's arrival, acting more like strangers at a cocktail party instead of bandmates having dinner together. But after enough glasses of wine, everyone seemed to relax. I only got one glass into Donovan, but after enough of my prodding, Cal had a few too many, and soon his cheeks were flushed and his boisterous laugh was echoing through the house. Dante overindulged as usual, but not enough to get sloppy. He and Cal were at the same level of intoxication, and I sat back to watch the two of them reminisce about the past and geek out on various drummers in other bands.

It was an odd sight, witnessing two of the more reserved members of Legion happily chatting the night away. Odd, but not unwelcome. Donovan seemed surprised at Callum's extroverted behavior, but he still watched him with admiration in his eyes like he always did. On the other hand, Luca stared at Dante like he was an alien, but once he noticed the rare smile making frequent appearances on his friend's face, he eased. Luca and Donovan eventually talked among themselves too, discussing mundane topics like the weather and traffic at first before delving into band-related matters like streaming numbers, marketing, and the recent protests.

"I just worry about the next leg of tour," Luca muttered, holding out his wine glass for a refill as I made a pass with the bottle. "I can see places like Alabama and Mississippi canceling shows if the opposition gets loud enough."

After dinner, we'd migrated from the dining room table to the sectional in the living room, where Gracie was taking turns searching each of us for any remnants of bolognese.

Donovan nodded as he considered Luca's words. "It's a realistic concern. I think we should amp up our social media presence the next few weeks. Make sure the fans we do have in those states show up in full force."

"Good idea. Can you get some more photos up on our page?"

"I could, but I'm running out of content. We need to do another shoot."

"There's some cool old churches in the South," Dante chimed in. "What if we sneak into one of those and shoot footage there?"

Donovan blinked. "That's… not a bad idea, actually."

"No, it's not." Luca frowned, but his eyes were more alight with joy than I'd ever seen. "You've been full of good ideas lately. Where've you been hiding all this?"

Dante shrugged and patted his thigh, beckoning for Gracie to climb into his lap. She eagerly did so, and gave his chin a loving lick before curling into a ball and tucking her nose under her tail.

"Wait, what other ideas have you had?" Callum asked.

"He's working on a new song," I offered, plopping in between Luca and Donovan. The latter slid his hand into mine at the same time Luca laid a hand on my thigh. When the two realized, a crackle of competition electrified the air between them, but I pretended like I didn't notice and inwardly basked at their simultaneous touch.

"A new song?" Callum perked up. "What new song?"

"Luca gave me some lyrics to play with," Dante replied. "It's not finished yet."

"He played me a piece of it today," I added. "It's beautiful."

"It's just a silly idea," Dante countered. Maybe it was just from the wine, but it looked like he was blushing.

"I want to hear," Callum chirped. He poured himself another glass before chanting, "Play it, play it, play it!"

"Maybe you should ease up on the drink, Cal," Donovan cut in. "If you keep going at this rate, you're not going to be coherent for tomorrow's run."

I pouted. "Come on, he can skip one day, can't he? This is a special occasion. When was the last time you all hung out like this?"

"Years," Luca muttered.

"What do *you* want, Cal?" Dante asked, pulling the bottle from Callum's hand and topping off his own glass. "You call the shots for once. Do you want to keep having fun, or do you want to have a stick up your ass like usual?"

Donovan bristled, but I caught his hand and gave it a reassuring squeeze. "Babe, relax. He's not trying to be an asshole, he's just having fun."

Dono opened his mouth to argue, but froze, and wry amusement replaced the anger in his expression. "Did you just call me babe?"

I blinked in surprise. "Did I?"

"You did."

"Is… that ok?"

"That's perfect, darling." He planted a kiss on my cheek, his previous irritation now forgotten. He didn't even seem to mind when Dante continued to prod Callum for an answer.

"Come on, Cal, what's it going to be?"

The drummer glanced from Dante to Donovan and back again, a slow smile making its way across his wine-stained lips.

"I'll make you a deal. Show me the new song, and I'll do shots with you 'til morning."

"Seriously?" Dante's eyes gleamed, but I wasn't sure if the excitement in them was from the mention of alcohol, music, or spending time with Cal.

"I'm dead serious."

"Fuck yeah, let's do it." Dante scooped Gracie off his lap and set her on the sofa so he was free to stand. She let out an indignant huff at the disturbance and came to snuggle Luca instead.

Dante returned from his room gripping the neck of an acoustic guitar and plopped down beside Callum. His fingers twitched nervously, but calmed when they found the instrument's metal strings.

"Leave the lyrics out," Luca blurted just before Dante plucked the first chord. "They're not ready yet."

"Neither is this. I don't have a chorus."

"Please," Luca insisted.

Dante sighed in defeat. "Whatever." He returned his attention to the guitar in his hands. "So I know we don't really do ballads, but... I don't know. This felt right for some reason."

He took a deep breath, shut his eyes, and strummed the same pattern of chords he'd played at his mother's bedside. It was still as beautiful to me now as it was then, and I leaned forward, immersing myself deeper in the music. It was a melody that seemed plucked out of another world, full of lust and longing, magic and wonder. I desperately wanted to know the lyrics that had inspired Dante, but he obeyed Luca's command and kept his demonstration purely instrumental.

I subtly glanced around the room to see the others' reactions. Unable to control himself, Callum's hands quietly rapped on his thighs, creating a beat to accompany the song. Donovan's eyes remained fixed on Dante's chipped black nail polish, making mental note of which chords he played. And finally, when I peeked at Luca beside me, I caught him slowly nodding to the beat, his gaze distant. A faint smile adorned his lips, an unreadable emotion written on his face.

The music crescendoed, and just before the climax, Dante stopped playing and sat upright. "That's it, that's all I've got."

"Holy shit," Callum blurted. "I fucking love that!"

"Yeah?" Dante asked. The surprise and hope in his words made my heart swell.

"Yeah! Dono, what do you think?"

"I want more," Donovan chuckled. "But it was sick, mate."

In unison, we all looked to Luca. He was still nodding like the melody continued to echo in his ears. After what felt like an eternity, he lifted his chin.

"That's good. Damn good."

I beamed at Dante, who looked like he'd been waiting a lifetime to hear those words.

"It's still a work in progress," he mumbled, ducking his head and setting the guitar aside. "A song is nothing without a good chorus."

"What about…" Donovan began, but he hurriedly shook his head. "Never mind."

"What?" I urged.

He glanced warily at Luca. "It's nothing, it's just… You were playing in B minor, yeah?"

"Yeah."

Donovan considered, then briefly looked to Callum and then me. "What about that bit I played on the bus not long ago? Would that fit in the chorus?"

Dante raised his eyes to the ceiling as he racked his brain for the memory. Eventually, he extended the guitar to his bandmate. "Remind me how it goes again?"

After another cautious glance in Luca's direction, Donovan grabbed the instrument and slid his fingers into place. The familiar tune rang out, just as compelling as it had been that day. He and Dante's pieces blended seamlessly, like they'd once shared a home in the vast realm of wonder, magic, and world-shattering love they paid homage to.

Callum, Luca, and I sat captivated by every note. I inhaled a shuddering breath, suddenly overwhelmed by the beauty of the piece, the moment, and the men around me. Things were far from perfect. *We* were far from perfect. But right now, suspended in time under the canopy of a song, we were one.

And somehow, that made me feel closer to God than I ever had in a church.

41

I laughed at the photo attached to her text and showed Dante, who was locked in another heated Mario Kart battle with Callum. He briefly glanced at the screen and cracked a wide grin at the picture of Gracie perched on his pillow with her paws crossed in front of her like a dainty princess.

"I think she misses you. Kayla says she's barely left your room the past three days."

She'd barely left his side the night we all had dinner too. Even after I passed out on the sofa, sandwiched by Callum and Dante, she forced herself into the pile and wedged herself under the arm Dante had draped over my waist. Luca and Donovan had stayed awake talking while we all slept, but Dono managed to snap a photo of the cuddle puddle, and the image now lived on my phone's lock screen.

When Luca had asked me if Kayla could housesit for them during the second half of tour, watching over Gracie in the process, my best friend and I had gone to brunch and had a serious discussion about my emotional investment in the guys.

"You're an employee," Kayla had reminded me. "You have a contract, which is going to end. So don't get attached."

It was good advice, and I'd tried to keep it in mind, but for some reason I couldn't shake the feeling that there was something here. I'd been noticing it for weeks during the first half of tour, in fleeting moments that seemed to stop time and intimate connections that felt deeper than they should have. The guys seemed different too, especially now that we'd started the eastern leg of tour. They'd still grated on each other's nerves during the last three shows, but their bickering had lessened, and they'd been spending more time together. Even now, while Dante and Callum played video games on the bus, Luca and Donovan were huddled together with a guitar on the opposite couch, brainstorming the final portion of lyrics for the ballad they'd pieced together the other night. Sure, they'd periodically get heated, with Luca passionately raising his voice while Donovan's anger flared in defense, but they had more patience with each other this time around. And call me crazy, but now it actually seemed like they enjoyed each other's company more than they didn't.

Maybe I was delusional. Maybe I was just setting myself up to get hurt. Or maybe I was right. Maybe *this* was right.

Us.

All of us.

Together.

I shook the thought from my mind. That was crazy. An idea like that was nothing but fanfic fodder I read about in dirty books. That stuff didn't happen in real life.

… Did it?

I looked around the bus, my heart aching at the idea of giving it all up. Laughing with Donovan and Callum, grabbing coffee with Luca, listening to music with Dante… All of that nothing but a memory. The thought hurt so much more than it should have, and I quickly returned my attention to my phone so no one would see the tears welling in my eyes.

"Hey guys?" Craig wandered out of the back lounge, phone in hand and his expression grim. "Can I talk to you all for a second?"

"Hell yeah, I win!" Dante cheered, hurling his controller to the sofa and stabbing his middle finger in Callum's face. "Suck it!"

Callum rolled his eyes and batted Dante's hand away. "You act like that's not your first win in days."

"It's the start of a winning streak, my friend. I can feel it."

"Uh-huh, sure." Callum set his controller aside and leaned forward. "What's up, Craig?"

Legion's tour manager sighed and rubbed the back of his neck. "I've got some not-so-great news."

At that, Luca sat upright. "What's wrong?"

"We've got another Salt Lake City on our hands."

"Shit," Donovan hissed, setting aside his guitar. "The Montgomery date was cancelled?"

"It's not just Montgomery. Religious fanatics have been camped out in front of venues across the South for days. We lucked out with New Orleans, Nashville, and Atlanta, but Orlando, Charleston, and Raleigh have all cancelled and refunded tickets."

Callum groaned and buried his face in his hands. "Fucking hell."

"What about Richmond?" Luca asked, sounding strangely hopeful.

"Richmond is still on the books. For now, at least."

Air puffed irritably from Luca's nose as he slumped in the couch and crossed his arms. "Wonderful."

"There has to be something you guys can do," I said, looking to each man individually. "What if you contact the local law enforcement before each city and ask them to create a perimeter around the theater?"

"The cops are probably in on it," Donovan muttered. "Who do you think they're more likely to support? A bunch of God-fearing, hard-working American folk, or a band of virgin-sacrificing devil worshippers?"

"Good point." I mirrored Luca's deflated position. "So what now?"

"Like I said the other night, we should try to get as many of our fans excited about the remaining shows as possible. Create positive buzz to combat the negative. Ideally, we drop a surprise music video or something like that."

"We don't have a music video," Dante mumbled. His eyes had that far-off look in them that hinted he was at risk of disappearing into himself. I scooted closer to him to offer silent support.

"Dono's got his camera," Callum offered. "At the very least, let's make a teaser. We can use a lesser-known song off the old album, and do what Dante suggested at dinner the other night and find a cool location to shoot some content. We have plenty of time to kill now."

"What's the point?" Dante murmured, hauling himself off the couch, pushing past Craig, and shuffling back to his bunk. He climbed in and jammed his headphones over his ears. A heavy metal breakdown began blaring from the speakers, loud enough for us to hear all the way in the front lounge.

Watching Dante's emotional deterioration in real time caused Luca's hardened expression to crack, revealing a sliver of sadness and gut-wrenching worry. When he caught himself, he wiped his face blank and faced Callum again.

"I'll research locations. There has to be something around here that would make a good backdrop for a shoot. An old graveyard or abandoned sanatorium or something like that.

We'll use the track Reign of Darkness off the most recent album. Sound good?"

"How about a video message to fans explaining the situation?" I added.

Luca nodded as he considered. "We've done that in the past. The Beast posted a message thanking everyone for helping us go platinum. I used a voice changer to disguise my voice. I could do that again."

"How about each of you say something in the message," I pressed. "If no one's seen the other members speak before, it would be buzz-worthy."

"I love that idea," Callum exclaimed, popping a kiss on my cheek. "Good thinking, baby."

My stomach flipped at the word "baby," but the fears from before came rushing back in. Did that word mean something to him, or was it just something said in the heat of the moment? And why, god, *why* did I care so much?

Luca frowned as he weighed my suggestion.

Donovan rolled his eyes and picked up his guitar again, plucking at the strings to disguise his grumbling. "A group video message would require our lead singer actually sharing the spotlight for once."

Luca's eyes flashed, and he opened his mouth to offer a scathing response, but I beat him to speaking.

"Dono, please. Cutting each other down isn't going to help us find a solution. Let's all have an open mind." I looked pointedly at the lead singer. "Right?"

Luca sighed in exasperation, but nodded begrudgingly. Donovan followed suit.

"You're right," the guitarist conceded. "I'm sorry, that was out of line."

I brightened and pushed down the urge to say, *see how easy it is to get along*? Instead, I grabbed Luca's laptop off the kitchen table and slid it into his lap.

"So it's decided. Luca, look up locations to film at. Donovan, write a message with four separate parts for each member to say. Dante, get everyone's masks and stage clothes together so you're ready to shoot."

At first I thought Dante hadn't heard my command, but he grunted, rolled out of his bunk, and began to fumble through his duffel bag.

"What about me?" Callum asked.

I smiled. "I want your opinion on some artwork."

42

"I'm obsessed."

Beaming, I lifted my iPad eye-level and examined me and Callum's collaboration. Over the past two hours, while the guys had been busy with the various chores I'd assigned them, I'd been showing Callum the drawings I'd been working on over the course of tour. He'd lit up when he saw the near-mirror images of the monster and the angel studded with arrows, immediately praising my artistic talent more than any employer, friend, or cheating ex-boyfriend ever had. I'd asked if it might work for a t-shirt design, and that immediately got his creative wheels churning. We played with the idea of the monster's image on the front and the angel's image on the back, a notion we loved, but we soon decided the images weren't quite complete. My style didn't quite match Legion's, so Callum helped me tweak certain details to transform my design into something that blended seamlessly with their current merchandise.

"You really like it?" I asked, flipping back and forth between the front of the shirt and the back. "I feel like it's still missing something."

Callum laughed and slid his arm around my waist, pressing his lips to my temple. "Such a perfectionist. You sound like Luca."

I glanced at the man in question. He was pacing the bus's length, mumbling his lines to himself and periodically checking his phone. Someone had been continuously texting him, and by the way his mood had been souring, I had a good feeling who it was.

"Does the mother of his child ever give him a break?" I whispered to Callum.

He sighed and eyed the lead singer. "Sometimes if she's silent, you have to worry more. It means she's plotting something."

I frowned. "God, I hate that he has to worry about that."

"Welcome to fame, sweetheart. There's always going to be someone trying to get something from you. Imagine how much worse it would be if people actually knew our identities."

My stomach sank as his words brought to mind the last conversation I'd had with Chase at the San Diego date. I'd purposefully avoided him during the past three shows, and he'd made no effort to seek me out. I hoped that meant the final words he'd said to me were nothing but empty threats he had no intention on following through with, but the hollow feeling in my gut argued against it.

"We're almost there," the bus driver Randy hollered from the driver's seat.

"I've got to get ready," Callum said, craning his neck to plant a kiss on my lips before standing. "But seriously, I love it."

"Thanks, baby."

Goddammit, there was that word again, flowing effortlessly from my mouth like it belonged there. I needed to get a handle on this. If it ended up meaning nothing, I wasn't sure my heart could handle it.

The bus lurched back and forth as it turned onto a bumpy

rural road. I clung to the couch to keep myself steady, but Luca seemed unaffected and continued his frantic pacing like an animal trapped in a cage. He'd found a location to shoot at within twenty minutes of me handing him his laptop, and since then, he'd transformed into his gruff, controlling, pre-show persona, whose intensity was only heightened by the barrage of texts tormenting him.

Territorial hackles raised on the back of my neck at the thought of someone taking advantage of Luca. This woman had every right to demand that the father of her child pull his weight, but there was a way to do it that didn't involve siphoning every dollar from the man's bank account and slowly pecking away at his sanity. We still didn't even know for sure if Luca even *was* the dad. I wanted to assume this woman was earnest, but what if she was lying? What if she saw an opportunity, and was now making my man's life hell?

I flinched and shook my head. *My* man? Jesus, Kayla was right. I was way too emotionally invested in this. I needed to detach, and fast. I'd already had one heartbreak this year, there was no way I could handle four more.

Deciding now would be a good time to retreat so I could attempt to get a grip on my mental state, I disappeared into my bunk while the guys finished changing and drenching their bodies in stage paint. When the bus lumbered to a stop and the door popped open, Donovan grabbed his camera and devil mask from where he'd laid them out on his bed.

"You coming?" he asked. "It's a beautiful location, perfect for snapping a few shots of my gorgeous muse."

I smiled even though my heart ached. "No, I'm a little tired. Gonna try to nap a little."

It was easier to lie than to tell the truth. What was I supposed to say? *No thanks, I'm struggling with the realization that you all mean more to me than I anticipated so I'm getting a head start on the pain of saying goodbye?*

I wasn't sure that would make sense to anyone but me.

Donovan smiled back and playfully knocked me under the chin. "Alright, darling. See you in a bit."

He and the rest of the guys filed out of the bus, and the door banged shut behind them, leaving me in deafening silence. I tried to tolerate it, but when my thoughts roared too loud, I decided to take a page from Dante's handbook and fumbled for my headphones.

I stuffed my earbuds in place and hit shuffle on my Spotify, then settled into my pillow and closed my eyes. Ironically, the first song that came on was "I Think I'm in Love" by Taylor Acorn. I only made it to the end of the first chorus before I grunted in exasperation and sat upright. Exchanging my phone for a sweatshirt, I made for the door.

The setting sun was teetering on the horizon, bathing the world in molten gold. We'd parked on the side of a rural road, where the lush forest opened into a large clearing. Moss dangled from the branches of gnarled trees while thick vines twisted around their roots. At the center of the clearing stood a massive cathedral, its spires and pointed arches once impressive but now decrepit as nature took back the land. The majority of the stained-glass windows were busted out, and graffiti marred the decaying wood door hanging off its hinges. I could see why Legion chose this place for their shoot; the Southern Gothic scene was as eerie as it was beautiful.

Scanning the area for any sign of the band but finding none, I figured they must be inside the building. I stuffed my hands in my pockets and started towards the church, making sure to watch where I stepped in case there were any snakes basking in the final rays of daylight. The chirps of cicadas and crickets filled the humid air around me as they eagerly greeted the coming night, and a handful of lightning bugs already blinked in the depths of the forest. It was so peaceful, it was almost enough to make me forget the war raging in my heart.

I made my way up the mossy steps and entered into the cathedral's crumbling interior. I couldn't see the guys yet, but their words echoed around me, carrying from somewhere deeper in the church.

"Dante, shift your body more to the left. More. More. Too far."

"Jesus Christ. It doesn't matter. None of this fucking matters."

"What is that supposed to mean?"

"Why are we even trying to get people excited about us if this is the end?"

I halted behind a cracked pillar and angled my ear towards the voices speaking on the other side. Donovan spoke next.

"How do you want to go out? With a fizzle or with a bang? I personally want to go out in a blaze of glory."

"So it's official, huh? You guys are done?" Bitterness coated Luca's words.

Several tense beats followed, and I imagined Donovan and Callum exchanging glances, communicating in that silent way they do.

"Don't act like you didn't know this was coming," Donovan said, an edge developing in his voice to combat Luca's. "It's the whole reason you brought Jade on."

"And she's been loads of fun," Callum added quickly. "But… I don't know if we've had enough fun to go another round. We've been through too much shit over the years."

"Why the fuck did you just look at Dante?"

"Come on, mate. You know why."

"Don't 'mate' me. Jesus, I'm sick and tired of this holier-than-thou attitude you two have taken on. It's just you two against the world, isn't it?"

Callum laughed out loud. "God, that's rich coming from you. Me and Dono are always on the outside, and we always have been. We were even the last ones to hear that Dante tried to commit suicide, for fuck's sake!"

"I told you never to mention that."

"Exactly! Since we've known you, it's just been you defending him and pushing everyone away, no matter how hard me and Dono have tried to connect. We bore our souls to you two that night we met. We shared the darkest part of ourselves, every detail, but all we got from you were vague explanations and half truths."

"So this whole thing is me and Dante's fault because ten years ago we didn't go into nitty gritty detail the way you two did?"

"No, this is *all* our faults because there's been a serious lack of trust from the beginning and we've let it fester until it's destroyed us."

"What do you want, Cal? An apology?"

"No, I want—"

"The truth," I said, stepping out from behind the pillar.

Startled, Legion whirled to face me. With their costumes against the backdrop of the church ruins, the group looked straight out of a horror movie.

"Tell the truth," I repeated. "Lay everything on the table. Right here, right now. No more games, no more masks, just the truth. We deserve that." I swallowed hard, my heart wrenching in preparation of what I was asking. "We *all* deserve that."

"Go back to the bus, Jade," Luca snapped, pointing in the direction I'd just come from. "This conversation doesn't involve you."

"Well, maybe it should." I stubbornly lifted my chin. "Clearly, you're incapable of having civil conversations with each other. There's too much pain there, so let me help you."

"No," Luca stated, his eyes icing over.

I fought the urge to stomp my foot in exasperation. "Just give me a chance—"

"You think you can just barge in here boss us around?" Luca barked, storming over to me. Refusing to give him the satisfaction of intimidating me, I stood my ground. "We're not taking orders from a—"

"A what, Luca?" I bit back.

He stood with his face inches from mine, our eyes locked in a silent challenge. Finally Luca sniffed, looked me up and down, and articulated his words so they'd sting as much as possible.

"A hired hole."

Humiliation and rage heated my blood, roiling it into a fiery frenzy until it had no choice but to bubble over. My patience snapped. I was done with uncertainty, done with the games, done with pining after someone if they didn't want me the way I wanted them. I was worth more than that.

I stepped back from Luca and spun to face the others. "Is that what I am to all of you? Just a body? And after this tour you wash your hands of this and never see me again? Or..."

My voice broke as my emotions got the better of me. Tears sprung to my eyes, blurring my view of the men. Not seeing them was strangely helpful, and made it possible for me to ask the question I'd been dreading the answer to.

"Or is this something more? Tell me honestly." I pointed at Donovan and Luca. "Drop the egos..." Then to Callum. "Don't try to people-please..." Lastly, to Dante. "And don't you dare disassociate. I deserve to know if what I've been feeling is real or if you're all just damn good actors."

I'd never heard silence so loud. Each second that ticked by carved the pit in my stomach deeper. Attempting to hold onto whatever was left of my dignity, I swallowed hard, blinked back my tears, and forced a smile.

"Well, now I know."

Defeated, I turned to leave.

"Jade wait," Donovan blurted.

I paused, keeping my face angled away from the men so they

wouldn't see my bottom lip quivering. Rubble cracked as Donovan uncomfortably shifted his weight from foot to foot.

"We don't know what you are. You're definitely not *just* a body. Any bit of emotional intimacy you've felt, we've felt too."

A spark of hope ignited in my heart. Slowly, I turned around. Donovan pulled off his mask, revealing his bright eyes shining with sincerity.

"We sure as hell didn't expect it when we brought you on," he continued, "but you've left your mark on us. Where that leaves us, though? I have no idea. Everything's up in the air right now. We're not sure what our next chapter of life is going to be, or who's going to be in it." He looked pointedly in Luca's direction. "But I know I speak for me and Cal both when I say I don't want the last day of tour to be the last time we see you."

The spark of hope burned brighter, fighting off the shadow of despair threatening to close in.

I wiped my nose with my sleeve and averted my gaze to the ground. "I'd... I'd like to hear Cal say that for himself, if that's ok."

"Oh, angel," Callum breathed, pulling his mask down so I could see him smile. "You've had me in a chokehold since that first kiss. There's no way I can say goodbye yet."

My heart swelled, but only halfway. I still needed two more answers.

My gaze flicked to Dante. His hands were stuffed in his pockets, the Lucifer mask locked on my face the same way it had been the night we met. I jerked my chin in its direction.

"What about you?"

Another painful silence passed, so long even Dono and Cal got antsy. But eventually Dante cleared his throat.

"I don't let anyone meet my mom."

He didn't say anything more, and didn't have to. It was the same confirmation I'd gotten from Callum and Donovan.

I wasn't crazy. There was something here. Something *real*.

All of our heads swiveled to the final member, who faced away from us, watching the last of the sunset shoot multi-colored beams of light through the remaining stained-glass windows.

"Luca?" I asked hesitantly.

Slowly, he turned. His jaw was clenched, his lips a tight line. His face betrayed nothing, but I knew. Deep in my soul, I knew the truth. And he did too. He felt it in our trips to get coffee, he felt it when he kissed the bruises on my wrists, he felt it when he defended my honor and stole me and Gracie away with him. I know he did. I just needed him to admit it.

Hope choked the breath from my lungs as Luca's lips parted to answer.

"You're nothing to me."

A strange peace washed over me as I stared at him, like the quiet calm at the eye of a storm. I scanned his hardened features, seeing the walls he'd built up to protect himself as clear as day. I huffed a grim laugh and shook my head.

"You're such a fucking coward."

Luca's eyes darkened. "Run."

I balked, the hair on my arms prickling with apprehension. "I... I'm sorry?"

Luca's words were measured, his voice low. It was the hiss of a snake, the growl of a wolf, a born predator's threat of violence.

"There's only so much disrespect I'm willing to take," Luca continued. "After that, there are consequences. And you just crossed the line."

He was joking. He had to be joking.

I narrowed my eyes, calling Luca's bluff. "I'm not afraid of you."

"You should be." He whirled to face the other band members, stretching his arms wide. "Second question! Boys, what did we discover we all had in common the night we met? What brought us together that night on Sunset Boulevard?"

Callum, Donovan, and Dante all stiffened.

"Come on," Luca urged. "Everyone wants the truth, right? So here we go. What made us all seek sanctuary in the City of Angels?"

Still, the men remained silent.

My gaze connected with Callum's. A glimmer of fear shone in his eyes as he hurriedly shook his head.

"Please don't make us answer that, Jade," he whispered, his voice hoarse.

My heart picked up speed. "What did you do?"

"Jade, please," Donovan said, reaching out to me.

I took a wary step back, unsure why I was starting to feel less like a woman and more like prey. "Answer the question."

Callum looked ready to throw up.

Donovan looked like he was fighting tears.

Luca chuckled under his breath like a madman.

But it was Dante who finally spoke up, his chilling words making my blood run cold.

"We killed someone."

43

A ringing started in my ears.

I must not have heard correctly. It almost sounded like they said—

"We killed someone," Luca repeated, his lips curling into a terrifying grin. "Multiple someones, actually."

"It was an accident," Callum blurted.

A grim laugh echoed from behind Dante's mask. "Maybe yours was."

It felt like someone had pulled the floor out from under me. I stumbled backwards, blinking rapidly in the hopes this was just another nightmare. But the four men in front of me didn't dissipate back into my subconscious with the morning.

The world started spinning, and I locked onto a pair of amber eyes to try and ground myself. They did nothing to comfort or seduce me like the usually did. Now looking at Luca was like staring into the eyes of the devil himself.

"Are you afraid now?" he sneered.

I took another step back, my breath graduating to panicked gulps. Dono reached out for me, but I dodged him.

"Don't touch me!" I shouted, my voice bouncing off the

crumbling cathedral walls as I hurled my index finger at him like it could somehow keep a killer at bay.

"We told you we weren't good men," Callum mumbled, mainly to himself.

"No one can know, Jade," Donovan persisted, his hands raised in defense as he took another wary step towards me. "Not our crew, not Vee, no one. Swear to us you won't say anything."

My mouth dried up, and my lips repeatedly parted and closed like a fish out of water. Shock had taken over, paralyzing my tongue and filling my legs with lead. Every instinct in my body screamed run, but I remained frozen in place.

Frozen, that is, until Luca shrugged off his robe, craned his neck from side to side, and cracked his knuckles.

"You know what they say, boys. Curiosity killed the cat." His gaze met mine, and for the first time since that miserable day in the cornfield all those years ago, I felt true terror.

"Start running, angel," Luca demanded. "If we catch you, no god will be able to save you."

Suddenly my feet had wings, propelled by an animalistic sense of self preservation. I hadn't run fast enough twenty years ago, but I'd be damned if I wasn't fast enough now.

I tore through the entrance of the cathedral and sprinted across the clearing, my pounding heart matching the slamming of my sneakers against the earth. Shouts rang out behind me, growing increasingly loud and panicked, but I forced my eyes to stay on the path ahead of me.

I couldn't go back to the bus. My only option was to disappear in the surrounding forest, then find the nearest town to call Kayla to come and save me.

With this new goal in mind, I blew past Craig and the driver Randy as they puffed on cigarettes outside the bus.

"Everything alright, Jade?" Craig shouted after me.

But I barely heard him, already too far into the thickening woods where all sound was suffocated by the moss and trees.

Branches grabbed at my clothes as I ran past, but in my mind they were demons trying to claw me to hell. I grit my teeth against the pain and pushed myself harder, the tang of adrenaline on my tongue making way for the sweet taste of freedom that grew stronger with every step.

Something solid collided with my back, and suddenly I was careening towards the forest floor. I landed with a thud and a grunt in a bed of damp leaves, their earthy aroma overtaking my senses as my face smashed into the ground. Dazed and disoriented, I rolled over. In the final shards of daylight poking through the trees, I caught sight of a white Venetian mask hovering over me.

"Where do you think you're going?" Dante hissed.

On instinct, I jerked a knee to his groin, causing him to groan and crumple over me. Seizing my chance, I frantically wriggled out from under him to continue my escape, but just when I'd crawled to my feet, Dante recovered and tackled me back down again.

"No!" I shrieked, hitting and kicking and fighting harder than I ever had in my life. There was no rational thought, no compassion for this man I'd grown to care for. My only concern was survival.

Impervious to my struggle, Dante caught my wrists and pinned them at the sides of my head.

"Help!" I screamed, so loud my throat burned. "Somebody help me!"

"Jade?" a familiar English accent called.

Sticks and leaves crunched, and Callum's face appeared over Dante's shoulder. His presence did nothing to calm me.

"Help!" I screamed again, struggling even harder against my captor. He released one of my wrists to clap his hand over my mouth.

"Shut up!" Dante snapped.

I took the opportunity to close my fist and swing a solid left hook to the side of his face, knocking his mask off-kilter.

"Goddammit!" he barked, latching his fingers around my arm again and slamming it back down to the forest floor. "Cal, will you fucking help me please?"

Callum obediently knelt at my side.

"No!" I screeched, squirming frantically.

Cal cupped my face in his palms. "Baby! Baby, it's ok! Stop screaming."

I jerked my head to the side and attempted to bite down on his fingers.

"Jesus!" Callum exclaimed, yanking his hand out of the way in the nick of time.

"Alright, that's enough," Dante growled. In one swift move, he rolled onto his side and swept me into a headlock. My screams died out as his arm tightened, cutting off airflow. Terror was swallowed by dread as my helplessness hit me like a ton of bricks. Tears squeezed from the corners of my eyes as I realized my fate, and my movements slowed. Callum caught my flailing arms and held them to my chest, his brow furrowing in concern.

"For fuck's sake, don't hurt her."

"She likes being hurt, remember?" Dante grunted, keeping his grip steady. "That's why she started playing with us demons in the first place. How's that going for you, angel?"

I gaped for air, stars scattering across my vision.

Callum's eyes tracked the tears spilling down my cheeks. "Ok, that's enough. She can't breathe."

"She's good at not breathing," Dante taunted in my ear, the cold porcelain mask coming to rest in the crook of my neck. "You get off on it, don't you? Remember my belt around your throat while you gagged on my cock, angel? Remember how fucking wet that made you?"

Jesus. The sick fuck was enjoying this.

I tried to hurl my heel into Dante's shin in one final attempt at a fight, but my limbs felt miles away from my body. I finally went limp, and my lashes fluttered shut.

"Goddammit, I said that's enough!" Callum yelled, tackling Dante off of me.

The pressure around my throat eased, and I gasped in a desperate breath and rolled to my stomach. Coughing and sputtering, I glanced over my shoulder to find Callum gripping Dante by the shirt collar and throwing a fist into the Lucifer mask. A crack rang out as the porcelain split near Dante's cheek.

I refocused on the forest ahead. My arms and legs were too weak to push myself upright and continue running, so I dragged myself across the forest floor, eyes set on freedom. I was chased by the sounds of another crack and a pained grunt.

My hair clung to the sweat on my forehead and tears blurred my vision, but when a pair of hands caught me and shoved me flat to the ground, my shallow breaths deteriorated into hysterical sobs.

"No!" I wailed, attempting to jerk away. "No, let me go!"

"Jade, relax," Callum urged, straddling my legs and pinning my arms behind my back. "I'm not gonna hurt you."

I struggled, but Callum held me so tight that I barely moved an inch. I froze as a maniacal laugh reached my ears. Out of the corner of my eye, I could barely make out Dante rising from the ground and brushing the leaves from his clothing, his mask in shards at his feet and a cut on his face bleeding into a Cheshire-cat grin.

"No one's coming to save you, angel," he sneered, stretching his arms wide. "You wanted the real us, here it is. You dug your grave, now you get to lie in it."

"You're insane," I croaked.

"He's scared," Callum countered, still keeping a firm hold on my arms as he leaned over to speak in my ear. "We're all fucking scared, ok?"

"*You're* scared?"

"Just let me explain. Please."

Realizing I had no choice, I attempted to wrangle my hysteria and pressed my lips shut. Air puffed from my nose, rustling the leaves in front of me, and I begrudgingly nodded.

"Alright. It's… it's not something me and Dono like to talk about. Hell, I don't even like to think about it. It's our biggest regret, and it's eaten away at us every day since." Callum inhaled a shuddering breath, his grip easing on my wrists ever so slightly. "We were seventeen when Dono's sister found us in that coat closet after a sermon one Sunday. She ran and tattled to the minister, and after that, she and Dono were no longer welcome there. The only reason I got to stay was because my Nan made a generous donation to the church, and signed me up for counseling with the youth minister every week. I wasn't allowed to see Donovan anymore, but I'd skip school to hang out with him at the guitar shop he worked at."

A clack drew our attention to our left, where Dante was kicking the fragments of his mask into the nearby bushes.

"She doesn't want to hear your sob story, Cal. She wants to know why there's blood on your hands. Hurry up."

"I'm trying." Callum huffed a heavy sigh. "As the months went on, we'd talk about what happened and how angry it made us. The week of my eighteenth birthday, we were out getting piss drunk at a local pub, and I jokingly mentioned I wanted to make the minister pay for kicking Em and Dono out of the church. Teach him a lesson, you know? So Dono and I figured, why not stop by and wreak a little havoc? Paint some graffiti, or some other stupid teenage shit like that. But we were drunk and riled up… So it escalated to us making a Molotov cocktail. We thought, it's the middle of the night and no one's inside, so what the hell? Why not burn the whole fucking place down? They had enough people like my Nan in the congregation willing to throw money at them, so the parish would be rebuilt in no time."

The hands around my wrists loosened, leaving enough space that I might be able to fight my way out.

But I didn't. I stayed, and listened.

To his story, the earnestness in his words, and the way my foolish heart begged me to give him a chance. Those warning bells in my mind screaming *run* were drowned out by a desperate sliver of hope that kept me flat on my belly with tears in my eyes.

Callum cleared his throat, but it did nothing to diminish the strain of emotion on his words. "We smashed a window, threw the thing in, and the place went up in flames. In that moment, it was a vision of victory. But in the morning when we saw the news, it became a nightmare." Cal's voice broke. "What we hadn't realized the night before, was that there was a facilities manager who cleaned the sanctuary after Sunday night service. She was still finishing up when we set the fire, and she didn't make it out in time."

My stomach hollowed.

Callum held himself together, but his anguish was palpable.

"When we realized, Dono just screamed and screamed and screamed. I spent the next hour retching over the toilet. We knew we should go to the police and turn ourselves in, but we couldn't. Our lives were just starting. It was selfish, but… we left. We grabbed our passports and fled the country, then headed to America. We got odd jobs here and there, trying to survive long enough that we didn't have to go home. On our third day in Los Angeles, we met Dante and Luca, and another night of getting piss drunk changed our lives forever."

I could feel Callum's body shaking on top of me. I instinctively reached out to comfort him before realizing my hands were still trapped behind my back. Tears stinging my eyes, I shifted my attention to Dante hovering nearby. His smile had disappeared, and his stare had adopted that distant sheen.

"And what about you?" I asked. "What's your excuse?"

Dante's lips pressed into a tight line.

"They don't like to talk about theirs either," Callum answered for him. "They never have. All they've ever told us is that they killed—"

"A priest."

Cal and I both jumped at Dante's voice.

He blinked a few times, and the far-off look in his eye disappeared, taken over by something cutthroat and merciless. "It was a priest we grew up with. We broke into the parish one night, and Luca held him down while I smothered him with a pillow."

A small gasp leapt from my mouth, prompting Dante's gaze to flick to me.

"Trust me, he deserved worse. And unlike Callum, I don't regret it. I fucking enjoyed it, and I'd do it again. Happily."

Unable to contain my emotions anymore, a choked sob tore from my throat. Callum leaned forward and brushed the hair from my face.

"This is all so fucked up. But you know us, Jade. You have to know we would never hurt you. You have to trust us, just like we're trusting you with this now."

"That's the problem," I whispered. "I do trust you."

My breaths deteriorated into hiccuping sobs as fear, anger, confusion, and shame came to a head and tore my soul in half.

"It doesn't make sense. I *shouldn't*. I should run as far away from you as possible, just like I should've done the night we met, but I *can't*. I feel fucking crazy! I *know* better! I *know* this is a suicide mission, but the idea of leaving hurts just as bad, and I hate myself for it. I *want* to run. I want to be normal, but—"

"You're not."

Dante's interruption shocked me into silence. His shoes appeared in front of my face, and I slowly lifted my gaze to meet his as he crouched down to my level. His expression was hard to read. It wasn't callous like it had been before, but it wasn't blank either. Instead, Dante seemed to stare right into every mixed-up corner of my mind.

"You're not normal, and you never will be." His hand slid to the back of my neck and tightened around the hair at the base of my scalp. With a tug, he lifted my head off the ground. "You've known it from the beginning. You kept saying you weren't an angel, and we didn't believe you. But you're right. You're just as fucked in the head as we are."

With my bottom lip quivering and tears streaming down my cheeks, I finally accepted the truth, calmed the war in my heart, and nodded.

Dante's grip tightened, tearing a pained gasp from my throat, but he silenced it by smashing his lips into mine.

Even if I hadn't been pinned, the sheer shock of Dante's kiss was enough to keep me frozen in place. It was like I was looking down on myself from above, watching a strange stage play of familiar characters acting out a jarring plot-twist. But I rocketed back to my body as fast as I'd left it, and I was present again, caught in the pull of Dante's gravity. His tongue rolled with mine, the taste of iron still on his lips from the blood dripping down his face. I was so lost in him that I completely forgot we weren't alone, and only remembered when the body straddling my back shifted its weight.

I broke away from Dante's kiss to crane my neck and look at Callum over my shoulder. There was a question in his eyes, asking if this was *really* who Jade Matthews was.

And for the first time in my life, I knew the answer and wasn't ashamed.

"I want this," I stated. "I want *you*. The good, the bad, and the ugly. I see you, and I see *me*, and I'm not running. I'm yours."

Keeping my wrists pinned, Callum leaned forward to graze his lips against the shell of my ear.

"Say it again," he whispered, sending a shiver skittering down my spine.

"I'm yours."

His nose trailed down the sensitive skin of my neck at the same time Dante's grip tightened in my hair. "Again."

"I'm yours."

Callum sank his teeth into my shoulder, mixing pleasure with pain and making me gasp out a moan. I was immediately silenced by another kiss from Dante. His tongue danced with mine as Cal continued to nip at my neck and back, both men's movements growing quicker, more determined. I tugged against the hands restraining my wrists, desperate to touch and explore the way Dante and Callum were, but they kept me immobilized. I was completely at their mercy, a realization that unsettled me as much as it turned me on.

When Callum's hands moved to the waistband of my jeans, I angled my hips up to help him slide them off, then groaned as he ripped my panties aside and buried his face between my thighs. Dante moved his grip to my neck to keep me propped up and watch the pleasure manifest on my face. Callum lapped and sucked with a vigor I'd never experienced from him, causing my legs to shake in record time.

"You're going to get off just like this, angel," Dante declared, his thumb skating across my bottom lip. "Then you're going to ride me until you see God. Understand?"

"Yes, Sir," I panted, attempting to grind in time with Callum's tongue using what little mobility I'd been granted. Dante's fingers around my throat tightened as I inched closer to a peak, his eyes never leaving mine. My head began to feel floaty, intensifying the pressure coiling deep and low in my abdomen. A few more persistent strokes from Callum's tongue and the tension snapped, sending me hurtling into heaven for an extended moment of bliss.

When I came back down, Dante hauled me onto his lap, tearing at his jeans to release himself. In one swift move, he laid down and slammed me onto his cock, making me cry out at the intrusion. A familiar presence came up behind me and kissed my neck.

"Are you ok?" Callum asked earnestly.

I managed to nod amidst Dante's punishing thrusts. Callum had never seen how Dante and I were together, didn't recognize how our demons liked to play. I tossed my head back and moaned with pleasure to show him how ok I really was, and he pressed another kiss to my neck to communicate he understood. He started to retreat, but I lifted my arm to grip the back of his neck and hold him close.

"Stay," I said, leaning my head back onto his shoulder. "Please stay."

Callum's arms slid around my waist, his fingertips tracing shiver-inducing lines up and down my stomach. "That's not entirely up to you, baby."

I looked to Dante beneath me and slowly ground my hips forward and back, driving his cock deeper. The intimacy and restraint of the slower pace was unusual for him, but judging by the way his eyes shuttered and his lips parted, he enjoyed it.

"Can I have you both?" I asked.

His gaze flicked to the man behind me. "I want her fucking dripping."

"Me too," Callum replied.

Dante gripped my jaw and dragged my face down to his. After a nip of my bottom lip, he pressed his forehead against mine. "Then yes, angel, you can have us both."

A rush of excitement washed over me, the adrenaline making my teeth chatter. Callum's nails raked down my back as he better positioned himself behind me.

"Have you been using the gift Dono and I bought you?" Callum asked, pressing his thumb against my asshole and massaging it gently.

"Yes."

"Good girl."

Every night on tour so far, I'd sneak to the bathroom and secretly try out out the anal plugs I'd received back in LA. At first I could only do the smallest one, but after relaxing into the sensation, I'd graduated to the larger sizes and grown obsessed with the feeling.

Callum spat a glob of saliva onto the sensitive puckered skin, then pulled his cock from his jeans and used it to prod my back entrance. He swirled the tip around the area the same way he'd done with his finger, but after a few seconds, he cautiously pushed forward. The tight muscles gave way slightly, allowing his tip entry. The pressure was a different sensation than I was used to, but the farthest thing from unpleasant. When he was sure I was alright, Callum eased forward even more.

I hissed an expletive and shut my eyes at the overwhelming tightness as he slid in fully.

Dante slapped my cheek to keep me focused. "Come on, you can take it."

I puffed a few calming breaths to relax, my discomfort making way for a delicious new sensation. I was completely and utterly full, able to feel Callum and Dante pressed up against each other inside me, putting knee-weakening pressure on my G-spot.

"That's so tight," Callum exclaimed, pressing his forehead to my shoulder blade. "Jesus-fucking-Christ."

"Goddamn, you look pretty with all your holes filled," Dante muttered, pushing me upright so he could see me fully. His words made my pussy pulse, forcing both men to groan.

"Fuck, you're gonna feel good when you come," Callum panted.

Dante thrust upwards, driving himself deeper into me, and I gasped out another moan. Callum followed suit, his strokes slower and more gentle than Dante's. The contrasting movement had me whimpering.

"Oh my god," were the only words I could manage to speak,

and I stuttered them over and over as the men pumped into me. My holes began to ache from being stretched so wide, but pleasure overpowered the sensation and that familiar tension began to build.

"Such a good girl," Callum breathed, his praise warm against my ear. "Look how well you're taking us."

"She's the perfect little fucktoy," Dante added. "Do you want to come, fucktoy?"

I nodded frantically. "Yes, Sir."

"Of course you do." He pounded into me so hard I saw stars. "Such a greedy whore, wanting two cocks at once. You fucking love it nasty like this, don't you?"

I held onto Callum to anchor myself. "Yes, Sir."

"Yeah, you do. You know why you like it dirty and fucked up? Because it's just like you."

Callum planted kisses along my spine, the tender gesture mixing with Dante's erotic cruelty and spiking my lust. The tension in my core raced towards the finish line.

"Oh, fuck!" I screamed, latching onto Callum for dear life as my inner walls tightened. My orgasm exploded, tearing through me with the ferocity of a hurricane and ravaging my body in its wake. My release was inspiring enough to topple Cal over the edge too. His cock repeatedly pulsed, and sudden warmth spread through my ass as Callum crumpled over top of me. Dante wasn't far behind us. After a few more punishing thrusts, he grunted and dug his nails into my thighs. I felt him twitch inside me and moaned my appreciation as he released.

Gradually, Callum enveloped me in his arms and held me to his chest as he slowly slid out. I shakily maneuvered off of Dante and slumped to the ground between him and Cal.

While we'd been preoccupied, the night had swept in entirely and the sky burned bright with stars.

44

We lay on the ground until our sweat dried and our breathing returned to normal.

With its gnarled trees and chittering nocturnal creatures, the dark forest would have felt menacing if it weren't for the fireflies lighting up the air around us. I smiled up at them and rested my head on Callum's chest. On my other side, Dante softly hummed his appreciation as I threaded my fingers through his hair and toyed with his curls. Once the adrenaline had died down, I was left deliciously spent, and I would have fallen asleep if it weren't for Craig's voice in the distance calling our names.

Cal craned his neck to kiss my cheek. "We should probably head back."

I nodded drowsily and let him guide me upright and reassemble my disheveled clothes. When I was fully dressed, he gave my ass a playful squeeze and started in the direction of the bus. I followed after him, sliding my hand into Dante's to steady myself as we fumbled through the dark. He made no move to free himself.

"Sorry about your mask, mate," Callum called from up ahead.

A dry chuckle followed as Dante gingerly dabbed at the cut on his cheek. "It's alright, I have a spare."

We trudged on in silence, and I began to replay everything that had happened that night, my mind lingering on Dante and Callum's confession. I peeked at the bassist out of the corner of my eye, still trying to process the disturbing callousness he'd shown when describing what he'd done to an old man in his bed. The only way I could imagine doing something so cruel was if it was someone who's done something truly terrible to me—

I stopped dead in my tracks as the realization hit me.

Something about Dante had always felt familiar. We'd never met before that night backstage, but there was a connection between us, something unknown and unspoken that I'd locked onto the moment he pulled off his mask. There was a common thread between us, but I'd never known what it was until now.

I turned to face the man beside me. His features were hidden in shadow, but his eyes occasionally glinted with the reflection of the fireflies. It was beautifully haunting, similar to the thread of pain that tied our souls together.

"The priest," I said.

Dante tensed. "What about him?"

"He hurt you, didn't he?"

Twigs crunched as Callum slowed to a halt.

Dante was quiet for a long time, so long I worried he'd slipped into that place in his mind where the past still had a hold on him. The same place I'd lost my memory in as a child in order to forget my own.

Eventually, a shuddering exhale puffed from Dante's mouth, which was answer enough.

I tightened my grip on his hand. My heart ached for him, all too familiar with the pain it carried.

"Was it just you and Luca?" I asked softly.

Callum continued to stand still, his head angled to hear us better.

Dante cleared his throat. "It didn't happen to Luca. Luca never shut up. If you want to keep a secret, you target someone you know will stay quiet. I fit the profile, so…" He trailed off.

I had no words, and couldn't have spoken them even if I did. A nauseating mix of painful familiarity and righteous fury had carved a hole in my chest, robbing the air from my lungs. I could do nothing but lift Dante's hand to my lips and press a kiss to his knuckles. He immediately ripped them away.

"Don't," he snapped. "Don't fucking pity me, Jade."

"I'm not," I whispered, cautiously sliding my hand back into his. "I've always felt there was something connecting us, Dante, but I could never put my finger on it. Until now."

The weight of Callum and Dante's stares was palpable. I opened my mouth, but the words were trapped at the tip of my tongue. I hadn't said them aloud since the day I'd stopped talking to my mom. I'd spoken the truth and been stabbed in the back, prompting my pain to lock itself away and claim it would never be caught vulnerable again.

Dante understood the battle, had fought it himself countless times, and he nodded in recognition.

"You too?" he asked.

My heart cracked, and a single tear escaped down my cheek. Dante reached up with his free hand to brush it away.

"Who?" he pressed. His words carried the subtle threat of violence, like he was planning the end of whoever had hurt me. Hell, he probably was.

I looked up through the trees at the sprinkling of stars that had taken their places in the night sky. "My stepdad."

Leaves rustled behind me as Callum stepped closer. "That's why you don't talk to your mom?"

I nodded, still lost in the cosmos above. It looked wonderful up there. Blissfully calm, and so far removed from the war within. I envied those stars, and imagined myself floating among them. Words tumbled from my lips, but they sounded distant.

"By the time I was ten, I'd started thinking that maybe what he was doing to me wasn't ok. That maybe it wasn't normal. I'd always felt that, but I was too young to know exactly what was happening, and too afraid to disobey. So I started finding any reason I could to stay away from him. My favorite place to hide was the neighbor's cornfield. I'd stay out there from morning to night because he'd never find me. Except one day, he did. The things he'd done before had never been especially violent. But this time… I think he was scared. He saw himself losing control, and worried 'our little secret' was going to get out."

I was shaking so hard my teeth chattered, but I barely registered it. My eyes were still on the sky, making everything around me seem like a distant dream, even Callum sliding his arms around my waist to support me. I wasn't on earth. I was swimming in a vast expanse of nothing, dancing with nebulous clouds and glittering galaxies where the past couldn't hurt me.

"I remember crying," I murmured, my words muffled in my ears. "And screaming. But no one heard me. I don't know how I got home, or what I said to explain the cuts and bruises to my mom."

"Come back." Dante's voice was a far off echo.

Fingers gripped my chin and tugged my face away from the stars, hurtling me back to reality. I blinked a few times, finally processing the earnest green gaze in front of me.

"Come back, Jade," Dante repeated softly. "Disappearing won't fix it. Running only makes it easier for a little while, but it won't make it go away. I would know."

My heart cracked even further, causing a flood of bitter tears. Callum tightened his hold around me and buried his face in the crook of my neck.

"Stay here," Dante urged, cupping my cheek. "Stay with us. You're safe."

I forced myself to nod, and dragged out the words stubbornly clinging to my tongue. "My mind blocked out what he did. I forgot most of my childhood for a long time. But two years ago, I remembered, and when I told my mom, she said I was lying. I brought up all the times she saw her husband's hand on my knee or caught him sneaking into my bedroom. She acted like she'd forgotten too, and said I was just trying to damage the reputation of a Godly man. So I left, and never looked back."

"Good," Dante stated. "Fuck 'em."

A laugh of surprise puffed from my lips at his blunt words. Then another laugh tumbled out, along with another barrage of tears. But these weren't from the pain anymore; they were a flood of relief from the sensation of feeling seen, heard, and understood.

"I'm so sorry," Callum mumbled into my neck, his hold on my waist unwavering. I wondered if he'd ever let go. "I had no idea either of you went through something like that. If I'd have known—"

"You'd have treated us differently," Dante cut in. "And that's exactly what we don't want."

Cal nodded, considering. "I get that. But I think Dono and I would have had more patience for you if we'd known. We just thought you were a piece of shit for no reason."

This time it was Dante's turn to laugh. The rare sound was so beautiful, it planted a seed of light in my soul, ever so slightly easing the ache that had been there for as long as I could remember.

"Asshole," Dante chuckled, punching Cal's shoulder before stepping past us and starting for the bus again. We followed, with Callum keeping one arm around my waist the whole way.

"There's a boxing gym by our house that Dono and I go to," he called ahead to Dante. "We picked up the sport a few years ago. It's a good workout, but sometimes it just feels nice to punch something every once in a while. You should come with us sometime."

"Sounds therapeutic," I mused.

"It is."

Dante was quiet for a few seconds before nodding. "Yeah, maybe I will."

I smiled and laid my head on Callum's shoulder. He was right. I *did* know these men. I'd seen them at their highest and their lowest, witnessed their passion and their pain, and throughout it all, my soul had only ever said, "I'm home." Home wasn't judgment and betrayal, or tiptoeing around me like I was some fragile creature on the edge of collapse. Home was understanding, patience, and love that lit up the dark like the dawn. And somehow, despite their demons, these men had always felt a little like sunshine.

When we reached the church, Donovan, Craig, and Randy were milling around the front of the bus, silhouetted by the headlights as they anxiously puffed on cigarettes. Even Dono had one wedged between his lips, which he immediately threw aside when he caught sight of us.

"Fucking hell, where were you? I've been worried sick!"

He stormed past Dante and intercepted me and Callum.

"We're fine," I said, squeezing his hand. "We were just working through a few things."

Donovan frowned, but when his gaze moved to my hair, his eyes lit up with amusement. He pulled a twig from the tangled strands and waggled it in front of me. "Working through some things, huh?"

I blushed and ducked my face into Cal's shoulder.

"So does that mean…"

Callum nodded and kissed the top of my head. "Our girl is staying."

Air puffed from Donovan's mouth like he'd been holding it this whole time. "Oh, thank god. I thought we'd lost you."

"Never." I beamed up at him, and he responded by leaning forward and smashing his lips to mine.

"Hold your horses," came a gruff voice dripping in a Southern twang.

We looked over to see Randy stomping towards us, sucking the last bit of tobacco from his cigarette before grinding the butt into the dirt with the toe of his boot. Craig followed him.

"Give us a moment with the young lady," Randy insisted, shooing Callum and Donovan away.

Confused, I followed him and Craig a few paces from the others.

"A'ight, be honest," Randy demanded, checking over his shoulder to make sure the guys couldn't hear him. "You ok? You were runnin' like a bat outta hell. If one of those dip-shits hurt you, just say the word and we'll leave 'em behind so we can get you somewhere safe."

"We'll get you on the first flight home," Craig added.

"I'm ok, I promise." I glanced back at Donovan, Callum, and Dante hovering close by and smiled. "I'm not going anywhere."

"You sure?" Randy pressed.

I laughed and squeezed his arm. "Yes. But thank you for looking out for me. It means more than you know." I turned to Craig. "Where's Luca?"

Craig's face fell, and he jerked his chin to the bus. "He and Dono got into it. Last I saw, he was nursing a bloody nose in the back lounge."

My head swiveled back to Donovan. Looking at him closer, I could make out a bruise forming around his left eye and a small slit in his bottom lip. Sensing my eyes on him, Dono looked up and offered me a reassuring smile. I motioned to his eye, and he simply shrugged and mouthed the words, *I'm fine.*

Craig came up alongside me. "Take care of your other boys tonight, Jade. Luca needs some time to get his head right."

I nodded and slid into Craig's side to give him a hug. He hesitated a moment, then draped an arm over my shoulder to pull me close.

"Thank you, Craig," I mumbled. "You're a good friend."

We broke apart, and I made my way over to the trio gathered in the headlights. Nodding to the cuts on Dante and Donovan's faces, I took both of their hands in mine.

"Come on. Let's get you two cleaned up."

45

We didn't see Luca for the rest of the night.

He remained locked in the back lounge, while I tended to Donovan and Dante's wounds using the first aid kit Randy kept stashed under the driver's seat. He didn't even make a sound when the bus started off again and we headed for Richmond, where we would spend our unexpected string of days off.

We were all drained from the events of the evening, so after everyone had washed up, we crawled into our bunks and turned out the light. Sleep found everyone except me, it seemed. I tossed and turned every time we hit a bump on the road, and while the hum of the engine was typically a lullaby, tonight it may as well have been nails on a chalkboard. After a third pitiful attempt at counting sheep, I sighed and reached for my head-phones, hoping music would drown out the world enough for me to sink into unconsciousness.

Just as I was putting in one of the earbuds, I froze as something like sharp, shallow puffs of air reached my ears. I turned my head to scan the bus around me. Craig, Callum, and Donovan were all peacefully asleep, and the back door of the lounge was still shut tight, sealing Luca inside. When my gaze landed on the bunk diagonal from mine, I discovered the source of the sound.

Miraculously, Dante was sleeping, but his mind clearly hadn't found rest. His lashes fluttered as his eyes moved wildly beneath his lids, and his brows were pinched together in a concerned expression. His chest rose and fell rapidly like he was having a panic attack, but he remained trapped by the confines of his unconscious mind.

I knew that place he was drowning in, had been there too many times myself. It led to waking in a cold sweat, disoriented and haunted by images that hung on until morning. Taking it upon myself to save him from that fate, I crawled from my bunk, raced to Dante's side, and shook him awake. His eyes snapped open, and he sucked in a breath and sat upright, his gaze darting all around him.

"Shhh, it's alright." I clutched his hand and squeezed it. "It was just a dream. You're ok."

Dante gulped air, trying to calm himself, but it barely helped. I continued to hold his hand, gently stroking his knuckles with my thumb, until he leaned over the side of his bed, reached down to grip my hips, and hauled me up into the bunk with him. The space was barely enough for one person let alone two, but I didn't mind the cramped quarters. All I could focus on was the pounding of Dante's heart as he pulled my head to his chest.

"We're ok," he muttered.

"We're ok," I repeated.

And for the first time in a long time, I believed it.

My lashes fluttered open, and Dante's face slowly came into focus. He was still out cold, his expression peaceful and his breathing slow and heavy. I smiled and carefully lifted my hand to brush a strand of hair from his eyes. He stirred in his sleep but didn't wake. Wanting to keep it that way, I carefully maneuvered out of his bunk and tiptoed back to my own. Craig, Donovan, and Callum were all still asleep, but when I passed the back lounge, the door was cracked and the room was empty.

I scanned the bus for any sign of Luca. He wasn't in his bunk, the bathroom, or curled up on one of the couches in the front. When I realized the bus wasn't moving, I immediately slipped on my shoes and padded towards the door.

The fresh chill of morning hit my cheeks as soon as I stepped out. The sky was just lightening with the promise of dawn, making it possible to see the rural motel we'd stopped at. The quaint, log-cabin style building was nestled beside a field of wildflowers, their white and yellow petals swaying in the slight breeze. A figure sat hunched at the edge of the meadow, looking out over the landscape with his hood pulled up over his head to ward off the cold. I tightened my sweater around me and made my way over to him.

Luca glanced up as I wordlessly lowered onto the ground next to him, but I kept my attention on the field ahead, prompting him to do the same. He didn't say anything until a ray of light appeared on the horizon, beaming gold in a sea of green.

"Is Dante still sleeping?" Luca asked, his voice so soft it was almost drowned out by the chorus of insects chirruping around us.

I nodded and plucked a nearby blade of grass, absentmindedly tearing it apart between my fingers.

"He only does that when he feels safe."

I finally met Luca's gaze. The sunlight hit his eyes at just the right angle to make them look like they were glowing from the inside out. A ghost of a smile haunted his lips.

"You know he's falling in love with you, right?"

My heart skipped a beat, and a wave of emotions flooded me at once. But the most prominent emotion was relief, like my heart was breathing a sigh as it whispered, *thank god I'm not the only one.*

"How do you know?" I asked.

Luca shrugged and looked back out over the field. "Trust me. I know that man better than I know myself."

Another beam of sunlight appeared, turning his skin golden. His stare grew distant, as if a memory danced on the horizon with the morning.

"When we were kids," Luca began, his bleak expression a stark contrast to the brightening sky, "I made it my mission to be his protector. And not just his. Mine, my mom's, anyone I cared about. I was going to be so strong that no one could hurt us ever again." He cleared his throat and dropped his gaze to the grass at our feet. "But over the years, that shield I put up became so hard that nothing got through, and if anything ever tried, that shield morphed into a weapon. I'm sorry you've had to get caught in its path."

Those amber eyes flicked to me, making my breath catch in my throat. "But the truth is, Jade... You *did* get through."

My heart skipped another beat.

"My whole life I've had control, but suddenly you walked in and changed everything." Luca loosed a shaky breath and ran his fingers through his hair. "You can build me up or ruin me with nothing but a smile. You don't run when I push you away. And when I close my eyes at night, I can't stop seeing yours. Do you know how terrifying that is?"

"Yes." I swallowed hard. "Because I feel the same about you."

Luca stilled. He remained quiet for a few breathless seconds where time was suspended.

"It doesn't make you want to turn and run the other way?" he finally murmured.

I considered his words, my pounding heart, and the truth

curled deep in the base of my soul where it had been hiding all along.

"I've been running as long as I can remember," I admitted, "searching for a place I could really be myself. Somewhere that will embrace and celebrate all that I am; the good and the bad. The messy and the broken. And for the first time in my life, I feel like I've found it."

A single tear dripped from my lashes and trickled down my cheek, but I made no move to wipe it away.

"I'm done running, Luca," I whispered. "I'm finally home."

"What if you get hurt?"

Something told me his question wasn't directed at me as much as it was him.

I gently slid my hand into his. "You pray that you won't, but trust you're strong enough to survive it if you do."

Luca sniffed wryly. "Sounds like you're telling me to have a little faith."

"I guess I am."

"I've never been good with faith."

"Me either. But there's a first time for everything."

Luca nodded, his gaze shifting back to the sunrise and his fingers threading through mine as he sucked in a shaky breath.

"Well if you're the god I'd worship, I think I could get on board." He looked back to me, the caution and cold melting from his face.

There he was. *That* was the man without the mask. Fiercely loyal and protective. Passionate and hardworking. Broken, but not damaged beyond repair.

"Jade," Luca began, clasping my hands in his. "I'm nothing but a lowly sinner begging for the forgiveness of a heavenly being. I don't deserve her mercy or her grace. I'm not perfect, and I never will be, but for what it's worth, if it's worth anything at all… I'm yours."

Blinking back the threat of more tears, I slid my hands free to cup Luca's face. "Perfect's overrated."

I hauled his lips to mine, sinking into his embrace as he clutched me with such intensity it felt like he'd been waiting his whole life to do it. He peeled himself away just enough to mumble against my lips.

"I'm still the boss though, ok?"

"Only in the bedroom."

"Deal."

I laughed as he dragged me back in and swept his tongue into my mouth. I eagerly climbed onto his lap so I could drape my arms around his neck and feel him as close physically as I did emotionally.

A chorus of whistles and hollers made us break apart and look over at the bus. Donovan, Callum, and Dante had their heads poking out the door, their hair still ruffled from sleep but their faces alight.

"Get a room!" Callum called, his cheeky grin so wide it crinkled his eyes.

"Or come back in and share!" Donovan added.

Dante just smiled.

Smooching noises accompanied us as Luca grabbed my ass and hauled me up with him as he stood.

"Back off, boys," Luca demanded, carrying me back to the bus. "She's mine."

"Wrong," Dante corrected, holding the door open. "She's ours."

God, I liked the sound of that.

46

"I think that's the fifth time Luca's checked the gear."

With the Charleston and Raleigh dates cancelled, we had an extra day off in Richmond. I'd killed time in the morning with a jog as well as me and Luca's coffee run, which the rest of the guys joined us on. Things were still strained between Donovan and Luca, but the blood they'd spilled with their fists seemed to be a much-needed release, and tensions had eased considerably. Whoever said violence is never the answer clearly never met Legion.

I sipped at the remnants of my spiced maple latte while observing Luca through the window of the bus. All morning, he'd been antsy and uncharacteristically quiet. When he wasn't on his phone texting, he was obsessing over equipment or anything else that was within his control.

Callum slid his arm around my shoulders and followed my gaze outside. "He always gets like this in Richmond."

"Why?"

"His baby mama lives here," Dante mumbled around the cigarette between his lips. His lighter clicked and lowered, and a wisp of smoke curled out of his mouth. "She gets worse than usual when we're in her city."

I frowned. "Does he have to see her?"

"She comes to the shows and stands front row." Donovan snapped a photo of Dante as he puffed a smoke ring into the air. "She does it just to fuck with him."

My blood boiled. "Does she at least bring his son so Luca can see him?"

"Nope. Leaves the kid at home with a sitter. It's fucked."

"Yeah, it is." I chewed my bottom lip, trying to control the obscene amount of rage I felt towards someone I didn't know. "It makes me wonder."

"Wonder what?"

"It's just…" I sighed. "How can we be sure she's not just using him? If I was confident in who my son's father was, I wouldn't feel the need to torment him at every turn to get what I want. It just seems like very manipulative, insecure behavior to me."

Donovan lowered his camera and considered my words. "You've got a good point. It does seem like overkill."

I nodded and nestled into Callum's side. "If only there was a way to find out the truth once and for all."

Cal kissed the top of my head. "You're sweet to care so much, angel. I'm sure Luca would appreciate the thought, but it is what it is."

"Is it?

Dono, Callum, and I turned to look at Dante. His stare was distant and his brow furrowed as he took a long drag of the cigarette and released the smoke through his nose.

"We're a bunch of criminals," he continued. "I'm sure we could figure something out. It wouldn't necessarily be legal, but that's never stopped us before."

Donovan set his camera aside. "We're not kidnapping a kid."

"I wasn't suggesting we kidnap the kid."

"We're not abducting a grown woman either," Callum added.

"No matter how tempting it sounds," I muttered.

"I wasn't at that. All we need is the kid's DNA. If we get into that bitch's house and grab some, we could buy a paternity test at CVS and have an answer in 6-8 weeks."

Callum scoffed. "You want to break into someone's house and steal their DNA?"

Dante shrugged. "I've broken in somewhere and committed a crime before, and so have you. Should be second nature to us now."

My stomach lurched at the reference to their dark pasts, and judging by the way all the color drained from Callum's face, he felt the same.

"Come on," Dante pressed, leaning forward with his elbows on his knees. "I can get Luca his answer, I just need a distraction and a lookout. Which one of you is it gonna be?"

I sat upright. "I'll be your lookout."

Dante grinned and blew a wisp of smoke out the side of his mouth. "Good girl."

Donovan and Callum exchanged glances, communicating in their silent way. I'd grown to know them well enough that I could interpret. Callum was on board, but Donovan wasn't convinced. But eventually, Cal faced us, his jaw stubbornly set.

"I'm in."

"Fucking hell," Dono grumbled, smacking a hand to his forehead. "Fine. I am too, but just so I can make sure you all don't get arrested."

"Great." Dante stubbed out his cigarette and stood. "Let's go commit a felony."

I hadn't expected the house to be so charming.

Quaint, historical, and set on a wooded plot of land on the

outskirts of the city, it was so adorable that casing the joint like a burglar felt dirty. But our minds were set, and there was no going back now.

"Alright, listen up," Dante whispered, ducking back behind the bush we were all huddled behind. "I don't see any security cameras, so we should be good to go. Callum and Dono, you go up and knock, then give us the signal when she opens the door. We'll run around back and go in through the window. Any questions?"

Callum raised his hand. "What do we do if she shuts the door on us?"

"You two can charm anybody, you'll be fine."

Donovan clicked his tongue. "Was that a compliment? Is Dante going soft on us?"

"Fuck off."

I stood, brushing leaves from my pant legs. "Everyone ready?"

"Ready." Callum looped his arm through Donovan's. "Godspeed, everyone."

After giving them both a kiss for luck, I turned and followed Dante towards the back of the house while the Brits headed for the front door. When everyone was in place, I peeked around the corner of the house to nod at Dono and Cal on the porch. They nodded back, then Callum rang the doorbell.

I looked back at Dante hunched under the window to my left. "Alright, we're moving."

He raised to his toes and peered through the glass. "Coast is clear here. Just need the signal."

I peeked my head around the corner again just as the front door opened. I couldn't see the person on the other side without risking blowing my cover, so no matter how badly I wanted to see the woman who'd been making Luca's life hell, I stayed where I was.

"Good afternoon, miss," Donovan greeted her, his words

dripping in a fake Southern accent. "We're so sorry to disturb you, but me and my husband here are in the process of buying a house nearby, and we're wantin' to talk to a few of the kind folk who live 'round here so we can get a feel of the neighborhood. Could you spare a few minutes of your time?"

"It's alright if you're busy," Callum added in a similar Southern-gentleman twang. "We understand this is a little unorthodox. As you can see, so are we."

I chuckled under my breath. If the music thing didn't work out, the guys could make a killing as actors.

"Aw, you two are so cute," a female voice cooed. "I'd be happy to! I'd invite you in, but I just put my son down for a nap, so we'll have to stay out here."

Goddamnit, I hated how kind she sounded.

"That's actually perfect." Donovan's eyes flicked to me as he leaned in and popped a kiss on Callum's cheek.

I whirled to Dante. "Alright, they just give the signal. Let's go."

He tried the window, but it didn't budge.

"Shit," I hissed. "We didn't consider it would be locked!"

"No problem." Dante stooped and grabbed a fist-sized river rock from the ground.

"Dante, no! The kid is—"

Crash!

"—Sleeping."

Shards of glass fell from the window as Dante used his elbow to smash the rest of the pieces through the hole he created. "If we see the kid, we'll tell him we're Santa."

With a grunt, he hoisted himself into the opening and wriggled inside.

I warily checked over my shoulder for prying eyes and followed.

A shake, then a wiggle, and I was awkwardly tumbling through the window. Dante caught me just before I hit the linoleum floor and set me on my feet. We'd landed in a kitchen, with a stack of sippy-cups in the sink and the makings of a peanut butter and jelly sandwich still on the counter.

Dante raised a finger to his lips and jerked his head towards the hall. Glass crunching beneath our feet, we crept across the wood floor like it was a field of landmines, wincing every time we hit a creaky plank that threatened to expose us. When we arrived at the first door and peeked inside, relief washed over me at the discovery of a bathroom. Toys lay in the bathtub, and a step stool led to a vanity with a child's toothbrush on the sink.

"Bingo." Dante reached in and snatched the toothbrush, then slipped it in a plastic baggy we'd brought along for this exact purpose.

"Find a hairbrush too," I insisted, checking over my shoulder again. "We've only got one shot at this, I want to make sure we get a good sample."

Dante slunk further into the bathroom and began rummaging through the cabinets. When he straightened, he had a tiny blue comb in his hand. He raised it in victory at the same time a child's cry hit our ears.

"Fuck." Dante shoved the comb into his pocket with the plastic bag. "Run!"

I spun and sprinted down the hall, no longer concerned about stealth. Our escape was the only thing that mattered, and it lived in a kitchen that felt light years away.

In the distance, the front door creaked open, and I heard Callum frantically exclaim, "Wait! How's the school district? We're hoping to adopt."

"I'm sorry, I hear my son calling for me. I have to go. It was nice meeting you two. I hope to see you around."

Dante and I reached the kitchen just as the front door closed. The cries from the child in his bedroom grew louder. I scrambled up into the busted window and received a firm shove from

Dante that toppled me out the other side. The sound of footsteps accompanied him as he dove through after me.

"What the fuck?" shrieked a woman's voice. I assumed she'd just seen the glass on the floor, or maybe Dante's Nike's disappearing through the window frame.

Dante gripped my hand and hauled me upright, then dragged me across the yard at a breakneck pace.

"Let's go!" he shouted at Dante and Callum. They took one look at the panic on our faces and bolted after us.

We tore down the street like we were being chased by hellhounds until the house was nothing but a speck in the distance. Then Donovan and Callum started whooping and hollering like schoolboys on the run from the principal, and before I knew it, we were all laughing and howling like maniacs and punching our fists into the sky.

I'd never felt so alive.

We were still riding the high when we got back to the bus. We'd stopped at the pharmacy on the way, and now a crumpled brown paper bag in Donovan's hand held the answer to a question Luca had been asking for the past three years. It was closure he hadn't asked for, and I worried that might make him lash out worse than he ever had before. When we found him scribbling out lyrics in the back lounge, I held my breath in anticipation as I knocked on the wood paneled wall to get his attention.

He looked up and surveyed the four of us crowding the doorway. "Hi?"

"Hi," I answered.

He blinked at me expectantly, waiting for me to say more, but I was unsure where to begin. Eventually, Luca closed his notebook.

"Do you need something?"

I looked to the men around me for support, inspiring Donovan to come to my aid. He tossed the brown paper bag onto the cushion beside Luca.

"Got you a present."

Luca's brows pinched together in confusion. Warily, he reached into the bag like whatever was inside might bite him. When he pulled out the paternity test, rage flashed across his face.

"What the fu—"

Dante tossed the plastic bag with the samples onto Luca's lap, promptly shutting him up. The singer slowly lifted the comb and toothbrush eye-level, staring at them with an expression that was difficult to read.

"Is this what I think it is?"

I nodded. "We thought you could use some closure. This way, you'll at least have a little peace of mind."

Luca shook his head. "How… how did you get this?"

"It's probably best if you don't know," Callum chuckled. "You might be getting an angry phone call pretty soon, and the less you know about it, the better."

Luca's gaze shifted from the items in his hand to his guitarist standing sheepishly at my side.

"Why?" Luca asked, his words hoarse. Almost pained.

Donovan shrugged. "We're sick of you taking all your shit out on us."

Luca averted his gaze, something resembling guilt washing over his features.

"And…" Donovan cleared his throat and slipped his arm around my waist to pull me close. "You got us a fantastic going away gift, so maybe we wanted to return the favor."

A few more seconds of tense silence passed before Luca set aside the samples and stood. He stepped in front of Donovan, holding his gaze.

"I don't deserve this."

"No, I'm not sure you do."

A shaky exhale left Luca's mouth, and he extended his hand for Donovan to shake. "Thank you."

Dono sniffed and hauled Luca into a firm hug instead. "We're a team. It's what we do."

They clapped each other on the back and pulled apart, putting on their toughest faces to disguise their emotion. I, however, was smiling like an idiot. Luca clocked my expression and smirked.

"Let me guess. This was *your* doing?"

"It was a group effort, but Dante spearheaded it."

Dante stuffed his hands in his pockets and whirled to exit. "I don't know what she's talking about."

I laughed and followed after him, Callum behind me, but when Donovan made to leave, Luca caught his arm.

"Wait. I'm almost done with this song. I could use some help on the final lines if you're not busy."

There was a pause, and in the silence, I could practically feel Donovan's heart soar.

"Let me grab my guitar."

47

Luca and Donovan stayed hunkered in the back lounge for the rest of the night, writing, rewriting, laughing, fighting, and singing. I'd never heard Donovan's voice except for when he was purposefully singing off key in the shower to make Callum laugh. In reality, he possessed a clear tenor that harmonized perfectly with Luca's raspy baritone and Dante's growling bass. The latter joined their writing session around dinner time, offering a few tweaks to their choices here and there. When Cal and I left to go pick up pizzas for everyone, we half expected the trio to have murdered each other by the time we got back, but they were still enraptured by the music when we all sat down to eat.

The songwriting continued into the evening until one by one we each fell asleep on the couch. We stayed there even after we woke up in the morning, and decided to have coffee and breakfast delivered while we continued the Attack on Titan marathon me and Donovan had wrangled the others into. After a few episodes, Callum was the only one still complaining.

"Can we *please* watch anything else?" Cal whined. "There's a Friday the 13th marathon on—"

"Shhh," Donovan hushed, readjusting his head on my shoulder. "We don't speak when Captain Levi's onscreen."

On the other side of me sat Luca, who absentmindedly grabbed my left hand and intertwined our fingers. "Is it just me, or does Captain Levi put off some serious Dante vibes? Just give him a face tattoo and amp up the pained expression and they're basically twins."

"I can see it," I laughed.

From his spot lounging on the floor, Dante nestled further between my legs. "Levi's a fucking badass, so I'll take that as a compliment."

"God, this is my nightmare," Callum mumbled.

A knock on the front door of the bus gave him an escape, and he scrambled out from under Donovan's arm.

"Food's here! Let's pause this while we eat."

"No way," Luca said, protectively snatching up the remote as Callum reached for it. "This episode's just starting to get good."

Callum grunted and shuffled towards the front of the bus. "If this becomes a habit, you're gonna need a new drummer."

"You secretly love it!" Donovan called after him.

He received a middle finger back as Cal descended the steps to the front door. The lock clicked and the hinges squeaked, followed by a shout from Callum. The four of us in the back lounge sat up in alarm as Chase came tearing onto the bus.

"I fucking knew it!" he panted, hurling a finger in our direction as he stomped towards us. "Crew members, huh? You really expect people to believe that?"

Luca, Dante, and Donovan leapt to their feet, while shock froze me in place. Callum sprinted back onto the bus, his features twisted with rage.

"He got the jump on me and barged in, I couldn't stop him." He gruffly grabbed Chase by the shoulders. "Let's go."

"No," Chase snapped, shrugging him off. "*I'm* the one giving the orders now. You wouldn't want your little secret to get out, would you?"

Cal balked at the threat, his eyes darting to the rest of the band. They were helpless for the first time since I'd known them, and the longer the silence stretched, the more I could sense their growing panic.

Finally, Luca stepped forward.

"What do you want?" he asked, his voice a low growl.

"I think the real question is how much are you willing to give?" Chase individually sized up everyone in the group, a proud smile twitching at his lips. "I know a lot of news outlets that would kill for this story. How bad do you want to keep your names and faces out of the spotlight? Pretty bad, I'd assume. Otherwise, all these theatrics over the years would have been for nothing."

"What the fuck do you want?" Luca spat.

Chase's gaze landed on me. "I want the same deal you have with Jade."

My stomach dropped, and my blood turned to ice in my veins.

"Sorry," Donovan muttered, shaking his head. "I'm not sure I heard you right."

"Oh, you heard me just fine." Chase grinned and scanned my curves. His attention may have been flattering once, but now it did nothing but make my stomach turn. I instinctively pulled a blanket over my tank top and shorts to inhibit his view.

"$25,000," Chase continued, stubbornly folding his arms over his chest. "I want $50,000, half your merch sales, and Jade alternates nights with me and my band on our bus. That shouldn't be a problem for you guys, right? Clearly you're good at sharing."

I could barely breathe I felt so sick. For a few earth-shattering moments, I thought the guys would agree, and I'd be passed off like property to the highest bidder. Every choice I'd made leading up to my signing that contract flashed across my mind, followed by a river of regret that threatened to drown me.

But then something moved out of the corner of my eye, and before I had time to realize what was happening, Luca had lunged at Chase and punched him square in the nose. A sickening crack rang through the bus, and Chase stumbled backwards into Callum's hold. Blood poured from his nostrils in streams.

"You sick fuck!" Luca snarled, fists balled tight and primed for violence. "You're not even worthy of *looking* at that woman let alone fucking her!" He threw another punch, this one into Chase's stomach, knocking the wind out of him. "There's not enough blackmail in the world that will make her touch you, you hear me?"

Callum let Chase slump to the floor. Dante crouched to his level and jerked his chin towards the exit.

"Get up, get out, and get off our tour. If you're not packed and gone by soundcheck, a broken nose will be the least of your worries."

Chase shakily clambered upright. "You can't kick us off two weeks before the run ends."

"Just did," Donovan said, tapping at his phone. He hit one last button, then read aloud. "We regret to inform you that due to irreconcilable differences, Phantom Spark will no longer be performing at the remaining tour dates. We apologize for any inconvenience." He looked up and shrugged. "Posted to Legion's two million followers. It's official. You're out."

Chase scoffed and swiped his sleeve across his nose, his glare shifting to me. "Jade, if you let them do this, they'll be fucked."

I swallowed my fear and rose from the couch, holding my head high. "We've survived worse than you."

Several tense beats passed, but eventually, Chase whirled and stormed out of the bus. The bang of the door echoed in our ears long after he left.

A hand alighted on my arm.

"You ok?" Dante asked softly.

I nodded and sank into his side. "I feel like this is all my fault. I'm so sorry."

"Stop," Luca interrupted, still glaring at the door like a guard dog on watch. "You didn't do anything wrong. That fucker is the problem, not you."

Donovan wandered over to me and Dante and pressed a reassuring kiss to my cheek.

"No one touches you except us," he murmured. "Promise."

I nodded, the relief from his words washing the guilt from my soul. "What are you going to do if Chase says something?"

"We'll cross that bridge when we come to it." Callum motioned us all back to the couch. "Come on. We were having a great morning, let's get back to that. Let's experience normal while we still can."

A small, grim chuckle huffed from my lips as I curled back in my spot at the center of the sofa. "Nothing about this is remotely normal."

Callum slid onto the cushion beside me and dragged my legs onto his lap. "Maybe it could be."

As the others settled in around us, I ruminated on his words, and desperately hoped they were true.

48

Phantom Spark's departure was unexpectedly peaceful.

Craig ensured us he'd handle everything on the professional end, but dread still hung over us like a raincloud. The Richmond show was an unusual one, wrought with anxiety and an earlier stage time now that the tour only had one opener. But as usual, all of Legion's problems seemed to disappear the moment that first note played.

The Baltimore, Philadelphia, New York, and Boston shows went off without a hitch, and slowly, we began to relax. We settled into that new normal again, spending the drives between each city laughing, fooling around, and living in a world all our own. The clashing personalities had found harmony, and all the pain finally had a safe space to heal. I saw Luca and Dante smile more in those days than I had the entirety of tour, while Dono and Cal blessed everyone with their company instead of pairing off on their own.

Everything was pure bliss until my nightmares started again.

The first one was after the show in Buffalo, the second during a nap on the drive to Pittsburg. The closer we came to Ohio, the more my subconscious recognized the landscape and reminded me of the past. Only this time around, my dreams were interrupted halfway through by Callum shaking me awake, Dante dragging me into his arms, or Luca kissing my forehead until my lashes fluttered open. If I was afraid to fall asleep, Donovan would stay up late with me and we'd watch anime in the back lounge, with Dante joining us more often than not.

By the time we reached Cincinnati, I was still on edge, but the support system the guys had built around me helped me function somewhat normally. Me, Dono, and Cal had our morning run, which Luca and Dante joined us on. After that, Luca and I found a cozy bistro to enjoy coffee at before grabbing breakfast to go for the guys. I'd managed to convince Luca to try some of my peppermint mocha latte, and despite the fact he gagged when he first drank it, he spent the walk back stealing sips until it was finished.

"Come on, admit it!" I pressed. "You like it!"

"No, I don't," Luca insisted, finishing off the remaining coffee and tossing the empty cup into a nearby trashcan. With his hand now free, he reached for mine and wove our fingers together. "It's terrible, I'd never drink a full one."

"You basically just did," I laughed. "I think I got four sips in."

"I don't know what you're talking about." Luca stared straight ahead, but he couldn't hide his mischievous smirk. A buzzing drew his attention to his side, and he released my hand to dig his phone out of his pocket. The way his expression darkened informed me who was on the other end.

"Is it her?" I asked.

Luca nodded solemnly. He hesitated for a few seconds before taking a deep breath, hitting the decline button, and shoving his phone back into his jeans. "She can wait. I'm busy."

He took up my hand again and pressed a kiss to my knuckles, sending a wave of butterflies through my stomach.

As we neared the venue, a dull roar reached our ears, growing louder with each step.

"What is that?" I asked, looking around. The streets were populated with typical passersby going about their day, revealing nothing about the source of the sound.

Luca's head cocked to the side as he listened. After a few beats, he frowned. "I think I know."

We rounded the corner to the venue and halted at the scene in front of us.

"I was right," Luca mumbled, motioning to the slew of protesters camped out in front of the venue, hollering scriptures with their picket signs wielded overhead like weapons. "They just can't mind their own fucking business, can they?"

He tightened his grip on my hand and gruffly pushed through the crowd towards the police line blocking the religious fanatics from rushing the buses in the parking lot. Flinching at their deafening shouts, I ducked my head and huddled close to Luca as he led the way through the masses.

"Jade?"

In the midst of the chaos, that one word stopped time.

The people around me blurred, sound evaporated, and I was that little girl in the cornfield again, unable to move, unable to breathe, unable to do anything but feel like the world was caving in around me.

"Jade," the male voice repeated, more firm this time. "Jade Matthews?"

I turned in slow motion. Keeping my eyes on the ground, I saw a woman's shoes first, then a pair of men's cowboy boots beside them, the scuffs on the toes all too familiar.

"It *is* you," a female voice cried, and suddenly I was wrapped in an embrace so tight it squeezed the remaining air from my lungs. "Oh, praise God! It's a miracle!"

I swallowed even though my mouth had gone dry. "Hi, Mom."

The woman pulled away and cupped my cheeks in her hands. Petite and blonde, she was everything I wasn't. We had nothing in common except for a deceivingly angelic face.

"Oh, honey," she breathed, "I knew the Lord would bring you back to us!"

Us.

I finally registered the man's voice that had said my name, and the boots standing beside my mother. With a pit in my stomach, I lifted my gaze.

The source of my nightmares loomed overhead. He was an old man now, with withered skin, brown teeth, and scraggly hair, but the monster still lived underneath. I recognized that evil glint in its eyes regardless of the way its mask had changed.

I stumbled backwards out of my mother's grip, feeling like the ground was being ripped out beneath me. I could have cried with relief when a pair of strong hands caught me, the rings on their fingers digging into the flesh of my waist.

"Are you ok?" Luca asked.

I threw my hand to his and gripped it like my life depended on it. My mother blinked at me and Luca before drifting down to his tattoos and crew lanyard. Her expression twisted into one of shock and horror.

"Jade, don't tell me you're *with* these heathens!"

I finally managed to turn away from my parents and urgently clung to Luca.

"Get me out of here," I begged. *"Please."*

Luca leapt into action at the desperation in my words. He threw his arm around my waist and barreled through the crowd, dragging me with him. My breath finally returned, coming in frantic, gasping gulps as we flew past the barricade and rushed towards the bus. When we exploded through the front door, I collapsed on the couch in the front lounge, wrecked by a fit of uncontrollable sobs that sprung from the well of pain deep inside me.

"What happened?" Callum shouted, hurrying over to lay a comforting hand on my back. Donovan joined us, lowering onto the couch in front of me and swiping the hair from my tear-streaked face.

"Baby, what's wrong?" he whispered.

I shook my head and continued to shudder as sobs racked my body. Dante emerged from the back lounge, his brow furrowed with concern. He took one look at me before realization washed over his face. He knew this place all too well, and instantly placed the root of the cause.

Dante's eyes darkened. "Was it him?"

I retched and held onto Donovan for support, which was enough of an answer.

Dante's jaw clenched, and his gaze shifted to Luca. "Do you remember what he looked like?"

Luca glanced at me, then Dante, then back again, finally grasping who I'd just come into contact with. His eyes briefly widened before narrowing into vengeful slits. With one curt nod, he spun and stomped back out the front door, Dante on his heels.

"It's going to be ok," Callum assured me, rubbing circles on my back.

"It's not," I gasped, wrangling in my emotions enough to form a coherent sentence. "They'll kill him. You know they will."

"Kill who?" Donovan asked.

I couldn't say the name, but the tears welling in my eyes helped Donovan put together the puzzle. His expression hardened at the same time as Callum's. The latter dipped his head in silent confirmation, and Donovan leaned forward to plant an earnest kiss on my lips. When he pulled away, he pressed his forehead to mine.

"I told you no one touches you."

He rose from the couch and followed Callum out of the bus, leaving me alone. The solitude gave me time to rein in my emotions and gain control of my breathing, but the pit in my gut stayed put. When the roar of the protestors outside graduated into shrieks of alarm, the sensation only worsened.

I hauled myself upright and stumbled down the bus steps. When I opened the door, I blinked at the blinding daylight, trying to locate the commotion. When my eyes adjusted, I saw a disturbance in the crowd, with onlookers darting away in fear while police officers rushed towards the melee.

"Jade!" a female voice shouted.

I turned to see Vee and Craig running over from the crew bus.

"What the hell is going on?" Vee asked, her face wrought with worry.

Craig craned his neck to see into the crowd, then hissed an expletive and sprinted for the mob.

"Where are the guys?" Vee pressed.

I miserably pointed to the chaos in front of us.

Vee's eyes went round. "Oh, shit."

She slid her arm around my shoulders for support, and together we helplessly watched until the horde had calmed. Craig emerged from the masses and lumbered back to us, the guys nowhere to be seen.

"Where's everyone else?" I asked, wringing my hands as I surveyed the dispersing crowd behind him. "Where the hell are my boys?"

"They're fucked, Jade," Craig sighed. "They just got arrested."

49

"I should've been out there with them," Marcus mumbled. "I'm supposed to protect them, and I didn't."

Hunched forward in the passenger seat, he had his head in his hands, while me, Craig, and Vee sat crammed in the backseat. We'd slipped our Uber driver an extra $20 to get us to the police station as quick as possible, and he didn't disappoint. We zipped around the Cincinnati streets so fast it made me viciously carsick, but it was a price I was willing to pay in order to get to my boys quicker.

I reached forward and patted Marcus's shoulder. "It happened too fast, you couldn't have known."

"What exactly *did* happen?" Vee asked, staring out the window and anxiously gnawing on her lip piercings.

I shivered at the memory of the ice in Dante and Luca's eyes, and the determination in Callum and Donovan's strides as they followed after them. They hadn't said what their intention was, but their mission had been clear.

They'd been out for blood.

"I got there right as the cops were breaking it up," Craig said, furiously scrolling through a Google search on his phone entitled

Best Lawyers in Cincinnati. "All I saw was Dante beating the shit out of some old dude. The others were fighting off anyone who tried to step in."

A strange mix of guilt and pride swelled in my chest. If it wasn't for me, they wouldn't have taken it upon themselves to make my stepdad pay. But god, did it feel good to have someone fight for you, especially when I wasn't able to fight for myself.

The Uber swerved into a parking lot and skidded to a halt in front of a modern building with rows of cop cars parked out back. After thanking our driver, we jogged towards the entrance, clutching our jackets tight against the autumn wind.

We burst through the front doors, taking a moment to adjust to the flurry of activity in the waiting area before finding the front desk.

"Hi," I greeted the male police officer stationed there. "We're looking for information on our friends."

The man looked up, his expression weary and jaded. He was my age or a little older, with both arms covered in tattoos, one of them a photo-realistic depiction of Jesus on the cross.

Great.

"What are their names?" the officer muttered, clicking onto the computer at his side.

"Luca Serino, Dante Ramos, Donovan Davies, and Callum Sherwood. They were brought in after a riot at a concert venue downtown."

"Ah." The man nodded knowingly. "The devil-worshippers."

"They're not devil-worshippers."

"That's not what the folks pressing charges said."

I groaned and ran my fingers through my hair, wracking my brain for a way out of this mess. "Who's pressing charges?"

"I'm not at liberty to say."

"Is it Phil and Donna Matthews?" My stomach churned just saying the names.

"I told you, I'm not at liberty to—"

"I'm their daughter," I cut in, pulling my license from my pocket and handing it to him. "See? Same last name. Please, let me just talk to them."

The cop raised an eyebrow and glanced between me and the ID. "They're filling out a report right now. You can talk to them after."

"I had a better vantage point," I lied. "I could help them give a more accurate statement."

The man considered my words, then grunted and stood. "Fine. But your friends stay behind."

I nodded and faced Vee, Craig, and Marcus.

"I'm going to fix this," I said, lowering my voice. "The guys fought for me, now I'm going to fight for them."

Vee squeezed my hand for encouragement. I backed away and trotted after the policeman leading the way into the back.

"Thank you," I said when I'd caught up to him. "I really appreciate it, Officer…" I glanced at his nameplate. "Collins."

"Mm-hmm," Officer Collins replied. "You from around here?"

"I grew up in a town about an hour away."

Collins nodded. "Figured. You've got that Midwestern thing about you. Sweet and wholesome."

I almost snorted.

"It just seems like you might've gotten mixed up with the wrong crowd."

We stopped in front of the closed door of a private interview room.

"Not everything is what it seems, Officer Collins. Sometimes you have to look past the mask."

The man considered my words a few seconds before grunting, twisting the handle, and pushing the door open. I took a deep breath, lifted my head high, and walked inside to face my demons.

For years I'd fantasized about seeing Phil bloodied and

broken, and it was one of the most beautiful sights I'd ever witnessed.

Crumpled in a chair in the corner, he held an icepack to his left eye, which was swollen shut. The rest of his face was covered in bruises and cuts, his nose was crooked, and it looked like he was missing a few teeth. Dante had been disturbingly brutal, a thought that had me fighting a smile.

My mom looked up from the papers she was filling out on my stepdad's behalf. Her eyes were the same shade as mine, and they narrowed into furious slits at the sight of me.

"I'm heartbroken, Jade." Her voice wavered like she was on the verge of tears, but I knew her too well to buy into the act. "Truly. I'm horrified by the people you've chosen to surround yourself with."

"Likewise," I muttered, looking pointedly at Phil. He quickly averted his gaze.

My mom choked on a fake sob. "This isn't the daughter I raised. I can't believe how far you've strayed."

"You can't?" I sat down at the table across from her and folded my arms over my chest. "I poured my heart out to you about something traumatic that happened to me, that *your husband* is responsible for, and you acted like it was nothing. You don't think that might push someone away?"

My mother dropped the emotional facade and straightened. "I don't entertain cruel lies made up to discredit a good man."

"Why would I lie about this, mom? It's not like this is something I'm proud of and want to go around promoting on a t-shirt."

My mom dismissed the comment with a wave of her hand. "Only God knows your heart."

I rolled my eyes and sneaked another glance at Phil. His presence still made me nauseous, and I'd been shaking like a leaf since I walked in the room, but now that the initial shock had worn off, he was so much less terrifying in real life than in my dreams. His guilt hung over him like a blinking neon sign, evident in the way he couldn't meet my gaze, the way he kept sinking lower and lower into his chair, and the way he fidgeted nervously the longer I watched him.

He was a monster, yes. But he was also just a man, and I wasn't powerless anymore.

I returned my attention to my mom. "You want to know what's in my heart? I'll tell you. Consider this my confession."

At that, my mom looked up from the police report, a glimmer of hope softening the ice in her eyes.

I took a deep breath. "I'm so unbelievably angry. I'm angry that my innocence was stolen from me by a sick, selfish man. I'm angry that when I think of my childhood, I think of *him*, and every happy memory is tainted with my abuser's face. But the thing I think I'm most angry about is the fact it took me so long to realize that you have absolutely no maternal instincts."

My mom opened her mouth to argue, but I raised a hand, stopping her.

"A mother is supposed to protect and fight for her children, but for reasons I can't even fathom, you hear about my trauma, can see it in my face, and you have the fucking audacity to tell me it's not true. That makes you just as fucked up as your husband, and if heaven is filled with people like you, I'll happily take the pits of hell."

I pushed back from the table. "If you're filing a police report, then I am too."

My mom scoffed. "A police report for what? We were the ones who were attacked."

"It's not for today." I went to the door and knocked. "Officer Collins?"

A few seconds later, the policeman entered the interview room. "All done here?"

"Not quite." I lifted my chin. "I'd like to report a sexual assault on a minor."

"What are you doing?" Phil blurted, bolting upright.

My mom stood too. "Relax, honey. She's just being dramatic."

Officer Collins studied her and then my stepdad before turning back to me. "When did the assault take place?"

"A little over twenty years ago, about an hour from here."

"That's not in your jurisdiction, is it?" Phil asked, trying to sound casual and failing miserably.

"It doesn't matter. You're innocent," my mom insisted.

But Phil ignored her.

"It's out of your jurisdiction, right?" he pressed, taking a step closer. "And it's so long ago, I assume there's nothing they could do."

Collins shrugged. "Actually, there's no statute of limitations for sexual assaults in the state of Ohio. A rapist can be prosecuted any time after the incident."

All the color drained from Phil's face.

"I have some powerful friends, too," I added. "You met a few of them earlier. I've seen them cost people their careers with a single sentence on social media. Imagine what kind of backlash you'd get if they posted your picture and a copy of the report detailing exactly what you did to me."

"*Allegedly*," my mother snapped. "Officer, isn't this blackmail?"

"No, ma'am. Police reports are public record. Anyone has access."

Phil looked ready to be sick.

I shook my head and clicked my tongue. "Imagine what your church would say if news like that started circulating."

"It's your word against Phil's. Obviously they're going to believe—"

"We'll drop the charges."

My mother gasped in surprise and outrage, her head whipping to her husband. "What?"

Phil's expression was stoic, but he was the one shaking now. "The Bible says when someone harms you, you're to turn the other cheek. So that's what we're going to do, Donna. We'll be good Christians, and show these Satanists the grace our Lord and savior shows us."

A slow smile spread across my face. "How selfless of you, Phil."

He still couldn't look me in the eye.

"You can't be serious," my mom shrieked, practically vibrating with rage. "You want them get away with this?"

"Sometimes bad people get away with bad things," Phil muttered, grabbing his jacket and slinging it on.

I kept my eyes glued to his face as he skulked towards the exit. "Couldn't have said it better myself."

My mom watched her husband go, her mouth agape. After a few seconds, her head swiveled back to me. Tears shone in her eyes.

"I love you, sweetie. And I want you to know I forgive you for this."

I nodded. "I love you too, mom. And I always will. But I'll never forgive you."

My mom sniffed and stomped out the door, taking a massive weight from my heart and soul with her.

When she'd gone, Officer Collins lifted the police report from the table.

"Did you know it's legal for police to lie to you?" he asked casually. "We do it all the time to get information or make someone confess."

A loud rip echoed through the room as Collins tore the stack of papers in two. "There *is* a statute of limitations in Ohio, unfortunately. You just surpassed it, so you wouldn't be able to prosecute. But those motherfuckers didn't need to know that."

I blinked in surprise.

Collins wandered over to a trashcan in the corner and

dropped the paper scraps inside. "One of my favorite quotes is by Ghandi. It goes, 'I love your Christ, but I hate your Christians. Your Christians are nothing like your Christ.' I've always liked that."

Collins caught me curiously eyeing the religious insignia inked on his skin and smiled. "We're not all bad."

"Christians or cops?"

He chuckled and beckoned for me to follow him out. "Both."

Thirty minutes later, I sat on the front steps of the police department with Craig, Marcus, and Vee, anxiously chewing my nail beds to nubs. Every time the door opened behind me, I perked up, only to be let down when it wasn't them.

"What's taking so long?" I grumbled. "Shouldn't they be out by now?"

"I don't know," Vee sighed. "I have no idea how jail works. Maybe there's paperwork and stuff."

Craig checked his phone. "We've already missed soundcheck. At this rate, there's no making the show. Looks like we're going to have to cancel."

"You're not cancelling shit," barked a familiar gravelly voice.

I leapt to my feet and spun, my heart soaring at the sight of my band of misfits shuffling out the front doors of the police station. I ran up the steps two at a time and threw myself into Luca's arms, nearly crying from relief and joy at the safety I felt there. Fatigue shadowed the guys' faces, but their smiles mirrored my own.

"Are you alright?" I asked when Luca set me on my feet again. I cupped Donovan's cheeks in my hands to search for injuries, then moved to Callum. They were all relatively unscathed, but when I got to Dante, it was a different story. He had a split lip and the makings of a black eye, but he looked worlds better than his victim had. Gratitude swelled in my chest, the beautiful ache finally pushing me over the edge. The tears that had been on the verge of releasing overflowed, and I leaned in to graze a kiss across the ink under Dante's eye before pulling him close.

"Thank you," I whispered.

His arms tightened around my waist, saying so much without saying anything at all.

"The real question is are *you* alright?" Callum asked, rubbing my back tenderly. "I heard you stood up to your family."

I pulled away and beamed up at him. "They're not my family. My family's right here."

Donovan planted a kiss on my cheek. "Proud of you, darling."

"Me too." I slid my hand into his and pulled him towards Luca, who was already jogging down the steps towards the street. "Now come on. We have a concert to get to."

50

We got to the venue with minutes to spare.

Craig and Marcus rushed backstage to prime the instruments, and I was put to work mixing the body paint while the guys threw on their stage clothes. By the time they were finally ready and stationed backstage, the crowd had grown antsy and raised a chant for Legion's appearance. I stood between Luca and Dante in the wings, adrenaline buzzing through my veins at the crowd's energy. Opposite us, Donovan and Callum were clearly experiencing the same excitement as they eagerly bounced on their toes and craned their necks side to side.

"Ready?" I asked the men on either side of me.

Luca chuckled wryly. "Baby, we were born for this."

At that moment, the venue lights blinked out, and the crowd went wild. Donovan struck a single chord, then nodded to Luca. The lead singer made to move onto the stage, but froze like he'd forgotten something. Then he spun, slid a hand to my neck, and dragged me forward to claim me with a fervent kiss.

"This is for you, angel," Luca declared when we broke apart.

Then he turned and strode to the center of the stage.

The spotlight hit him, illuminating his body in a golden glow, and the roar of the crowd swelled so loud it shook the ground beneath our feet. When the first notes poured from his lips, it was just as magical as it had been the first night I heard them. An exhilarated chill broke out across my skin as the other band members took the stage. They were just as enraptured by their dark siren song as the fans in the crowd, and in that moment I knew, without a shadow of a doubt, that I was in love.

I stayed for the entire show, watching from the sidelines with my heart so full of pride and joy it almost hurt. I didn't want to think about what might happen when the tour came to a close. I couldn't. This had been an unexpected chapter of my life, but I wasn't finished reading yet.

As the final encore ended, I shuffled to the side and pressed up against an amp box so the guys would have room leaving the stage. When they didn't pass after a few seconds, I peeked out again, confused.

They were still onstage, with Luca at the center motioning for the crowd to quiet down.

"Thank you," he said into the microphone when the venue was silent. "Thank you very much. I, uh… I don't usually do this sort of thing. I'm a singer, not a speech-giver."

Light laughter rippled through the crowd.

"But I just wanted to take a moment to let you know how much we appreciate you all. It's been an interesting tour to say the least. The odds seemed stacked against us, and we faced adversity at every turn. But *you*, our fans, have continued to show up for us, and that's kept us going. You're why we do what we do."

Applause erupted, but Luca waved it down again.

"We've had the time of our lives tonight, and we have you to thank for that. But we also have someone else to thank."

His eyes softened and flicked to the side of the stage.

To *me*.

"We would have crashed and burned on day one without this

person," he said earnestly, "and we want them to know what they mean to us. We've been working on something new, and tonight we're going to share it with you."

Deafening cheers and whistles exploded through the room, making my ears ring. Luca's gaze shifted to Donovan, who stepped up to the microphone beside him, strumming a familiar tune.

"My friend Diablo here is going to help me sing it."

A dissonant bass chord reprimanded him, and Luca chuckled.

"So is Lucifer."

I laughed along with the crowd while Luca dragged the microphone between him, Donovan, and Dante.

"Oh, and by the way…" Luca looked my way again. "This is a love song."

The lights on the stage dimmed as Donovan plucked out the opening notes of the song I'd heard them toying with over the past few days on the road. Now it had grown into a polished piece, so full and evocative it cast a spell over the entire room.

Luca pressed his lips to the microphone and shut his eyes.

I've done some bad things, yeah I've done them well

They all sing my praise in the depths of hell

A liar and a killer, I'm a sinner not a saint

Drown my sorrows in a bottle so the pain drifts away

I'm dying here, it's been a long time coming

Please God, all I want is to fade into nothing

I'm taking a bow, this is my curtain call

Then came a spark in the night, and I watched an angel fall

Her eyes pierce my soul, they burn like fire

She dances with demons in a twisted choir

A hint of heaven still shines on her face

I fear this girl will be my saving grace

. . .

One man's loss is another man's gain
  The hosts of heaven turned away from her pain
  Bleeding and broken, shattered heart, tattered wings
  Now a light in the dark that can make a man sing
  One dose and I'm hooked, I'll never recover
  Drunk on her poison, I won't ask for another
  The devil repents, he's changing his tune
  Dear God, don't take me from my angel too soon

Her eyes pierce my soul, they burn like fire
  She dances with demons in a twisted choir
  A hint of heaven still shines on her face
  I pray this girl will be my saving grace

If demons are angels that fell to the ground,
  Then leave me in hell, I don't want to be found

Her eyes pierce my soul, they burn like fire
  She dances with demons in a twisted choir
  A hint of heaven still shines on her face
  Thank God this girl is my saving grace

The crowd roared with applause as the song ended, and I watched with tears in my eyes as Legion stepped up to the front of the stage, draped their arms around each other, and took their final bow. The cheers chased them offstage, and didn't die down even after they joined me. The guys were sweaty and breathless, but that didn't stop me from hugging and kissing each one of them.

"That was beautiful," I whispered, my body trembling from the emotion coursing through it.

Callum slid his arms around me from behind, the warmth of his skin instantly soothing me. Luca pressed a kiss to my lips.

"It was all true," he murmured against my skin. "Every word."

I pulled away so I could stare deep into those golden eyes. "We saved each other."

The intimate moment was interrupted by a blurted expletive from Donovan. He'd set his guitar aside and was checking his phone, the blue light of the screen reflected in the Diablo mask still on his face.

"What's wrong?" Dante asked, setting down his bass and wandering over.

Donovan slowly lifted his phone to the group, revealing the headline of a news article open in the browser.

Legion Revealed: The True Identities of Rock and Roll's Bad Boys.

"Chase leaked it," Donovan croaked. "Pictures of our crew lanyards were posted on Reddit. It's everywhere. The band's Instagram is blowing up with mentions."

Callum's arms went slack around me, air whooshing from his mouth like someone had punched it from his lungs.

"Fuck!" Dante shouted, kicking a nearby gearbox so hard it toppled over.

Trying to keep my panic under control, I turned to Luca and searched his gaze. "What do we do?"

His face solemn, Luca stood as still as a statue as he searched for an answer. After an unbearably long silence, he took a deep breath, squared his shoulders, and lifted his chin. "I don't know. But whatever happens, we'll get through it."

His hand slipped into mine and squeezed.

"Together."

The Malibu sun beat down on my skin, warming me from the inside out. I angled my face to the sky to bask in its rays, absent-mindedly running my fingers through Gracie's fur as she dozed on the towel beside me. A ding from my phone made me open my eyes. I checked the screen and smiled at the text from Vee. It was a photo of Kayla ice skating at the rink in Pershing Square, a cup of cocoa in her hands.

When I'd heard what the two had planned for their third date, I'd demanded picture updates from both of them, and so far, they hadn't disappointed.

A revving engine drew my attention behind me. A sleek black sportbike pulled into the driveway of the townhouse at the edge of the sand. I smiled and waved, then patted the snoozing dog beside me.

"Gracie girl, look who's here!"

Gracie groggily lifted her head and looked around the beach. When she caught sight of the rider dismounting his bike, her tail wagged and she let out an excited yip.

"Go get him," I urged.

She immediately bolted towards the townhouse, barking

eagerly. He'd barely removed his helmet before Gracie leapt into the rider's arms and smothered his face in kisses, nearly crushing the bouquet of roses he held.

"Oh, good. I don't need a shower anymore," Dante laughed, squinting as Gracie repeatedly licked the tattoo under his eye. He trudged through the sand and flopped down on the towel beside me. Gracie happily curled up between us.

"Hi," Dante greeted, leaning in to press a kiss to my lips and slide the flowers onto my lap. I lifted them to my nose and inhaled deeply.

"How was your visit with your mom?"

"Good. Celia and Rocío say hi."

"Aww." I grinned and set the flowers aside. "Tell them I say hi back. Did you get a chance to drive by the boxing gym like you wanted?"

"Yeah, it looks cool. I'm gonna try it out the next time the guys go. I think it'll be fun."

"They'll love that." I leaned back on my elbows and gazed out at the ocean where Callum and Donovan were currently riding a wave into the shore. "As the weather gets colder, they might not want to surf as much."

Dante laid down and wrapped an arm around my waist, nestling into my side. "I talked to my therapist today too."

"Oh, that's right! I'm so happy she made time for you. How was it?"

"It sucked." Dante opened one eye to peer up at me. "But it was helpful."

I nodded and combed my fingers through his hair. "Healing is painful sometimes, isn't it?"

"Yeah. But it's worth it."

We fell silent, relaxing into the symphony of the crashing surf and the calls of hungry gulls in search of dinner. The thought of food made me sit upright.

"Will you keep an eye on Gracie for a bit?"

"Mm-hmm," Dante mumbled, already nodding off.

I kissed his forehead and scooped up the flowers, then jogged for the townhouse. When I arrived at the patio, I brushed the sand from my legs and wiped my feet before entering through the open French doors. The smell of garlic, onion, and butter immediately hit my nose. I followed the scent trail to the kitchen, where a burly figure was simultaneously stirring a pot of sauce and taking the temperature on a roast chicken.

"Anything I can do to help, chef?" I asked, placing the roses on the counter before coming up behind him and wrapping my arms around his waist.

"Nope, I'm good."

"It's hard to mess up stirring, you know."

Luca hesitated, then begrudgingly extended his wooden spoon. "Ok, but keep it constant, and don't stir too fast, and make sure to scrape the sides, and—"

"Luca. I got it."

Realizing what he was doing, Luca winced and nodded. "Right. My bad." He bent and kissed my cheek in thanks before refocusing on the chicken. "We're less than ten minutes out, is Dante back yet?"

"Yep, he just got in."

"Ok, then we need to flag down Cal and Dono and—"

"They're already on their way." I squeezed his arm. "Relax. It's a holiday."

Luca grumbled something under his breath as he basted the chicken and pushed it back in the oven. I rolled my eyes and lifted the sauce spoon to my lips.

"What are you doing?" Luca blurted, snatching it from my hand. "It isn't ready yet!"

"I want to taste what you've been slaving over for hours!" I whined.

"And you *will*. In ten minutes."

I frowned, then rethought my tactic. Sidling up to him, I

pressed my bikini-clad chest to his body and widened my eyes into a doe-eyed stare.

"*Master*," I cooed, "may I *please* have a naughty little taste?"

Luca irritably puffed air from his nose, but his cock twitched in his jeans.

"Fine." He dipped the spoon into the sauce with one hand, while the other cupped my jaw. "Open."

I obediently stuck out my tongue. Luca leaned in and sucked it before raising the spoon high. Just before it touched my lips, he changed directions and popped it in his own mouth. I gasped and smacked his shoulder.

"You asshole!"

Luca laughed and shooed me away from the stove. "Get out of here with your feminine wiles. You have to wait like everyone else."

"I'm gonna make you pay for that tonight," I called over my shoulder. "You're about to meet the brattiest sub of your life."

"Can't wait."

I made my way to the dining room and began laying out five place settings. Gradually, a flurry of laughter and barks neared, and soon Callum, Donovan, and Gracie rushed in. The guys had abandoned their wetsuits outside and had towels wrapped around their hips, which Gracie was currently trying to catch the hem of. Dante trailed after the group, a look of genuine joy written on his face.

"She's trying to get me naked!" Donovan wailed, gripping his towel tight as Gracie took a corner between her teeth and gave it a firm tug. "She's just like her mother!"

Callum scooped my dog into his arms and calmed her with a few scratches behind the ears. "No nudity before dinner, Gracie. We've talked about this."

Dante appeared beside me and kissed my bare shoulder. "Can I help with anything?"

"Could you grab some wine glasses?"

He nodded and headed to the kitchen. When he returned, he only had four in his hands.

"You're not having any?" I asked.

"Nah, I don't really feel like it. I'll steal a sip of yours."

"Ok." I gave him an earnest smile, which he returned.

"Alright, everybody," Luca shouted from the other room. "It's time! Find your seats."

"Do we have time to change?" Callum asked.

"No!" Luca barked.

"I'm changing," Cal murmured, darting for his bedroom. Donovan remained behind.

"You need any help, mate?" he shouted towards the kitchen.

"No!"

"Are you lying?"

"... No."

I sighed. "Dono, could you—"

"On it." Donovan readjusted his towel and padded into the kitchen. The sounds of he and Luca squabbling filled the entire house, but when the two of them reappeared, Donovan was proudly carrying the roast chicken on a platter.

"Where did Callum go?" Luca snapped, setting a bowl of pasta on the table and glaring around the room.

"Right here!" Cal jogged back in wearing sweats and a t-shirt. He smacked my ass as he ran past.

"You're pushing it, Sherwood," Luca muttered.

"Take it out on Jade," Callum quipped, sliding into a seat. He got to work pouring the wine while the rest of us followed his lead and took our places. Luca and Dante sat on either side of me, while Cal and Dono sat opposite. With her tail wagging, Gracie wove in and out of our legs, already searching for scraps.

"Right." Donovan eagerly rubbed his palms together. "Let's eat."

"Wait," Dante interjected. "There's something Luca wants to say first."

"Like a toast?"

Luca frowned. "Not quite."

A tense silence settled over the room as Luca raised his eyes to the ceiling, searching for the right words. Eventually, he cleared his throat.

"I want to apologize."

Donovan gasped in mock horror, prompting Callum to burst out laughing. I nudged them both under the table with my foot, and they quieted.

"I'm sure you've all noticed how tightly wound I am today," Luca continued. "But it's not because I wanted to make everything perfect. I did, but that's not what was stressing me out."

I slid my hand into his. "What's wrong?"

He inhaled a shuddering breath. "I got an email today... The results of the paternity test are in."

"Oh, shit," Callum mumbled. "What did it say?"

"I don't know yet. I wanted to wait until you guys were here. I... I needed the moral support."

"Of course, mate," Donovan said. "We've got you."

"Thanks." Luca offered him a smile and took turns looking to everyone in the room individually. "I just want you all to know how much I appreciate what you did for me. The unknown was eating me alive, and now I'll finally have an ending. And..." He swallowed hard, his brow furrowing. "And no matter what happens, that was my kid for the last three years. In my heart, he was my son. So no matter the outcome, I still want the trust fund I set up to go to him. If he's not mine, it'll just be a generous gift from an anonymous rockstar."

I tightened my hold on Luca's hand. "That's really sweet of you."

The others murmured in agreement.

Luca nodded curtly and loosed a heavy sigh. It looked like he'd been holding it in all day. "Alright. Let's do this."

He pulled out his phone and swiped it open, then clicked on his inbox. His brows inched together at what he saw.

My heart was practically beating out of my chest. "What does it say?"

"I haven't looked yet." He paused, his head angling to the side. "I just got an email from Craig."

"Our Craig?" Dante asked.

Luca nodded, his eyes tracking the words across the screen. "He says the label loves the new song, and he has a tour lined up in the new year if we want it. Only this time, we'd be playing stadiums." He looked up from the phone. "Stadiums in Europe."

Donovan and Callum exchanged glances.

"We've never done a European tour," Dante mused, scooping Gracie onto his lap.

"Exactly why Craig says it'll be successful." Luca sat back in his chair and began twirling one of his rings, his stare glazing as he lost himself in his thoughts.

"We'd play London," Donovan said, still looking at Callum, whose face had drained of color.

"We'd play everywhere," Luca corrected. "London, Paris, Milan, Berlin. Every major city."

"You'd need a bigger crew," I mused. "You'd have to let more people in, which means more people will find out your identities. Even with the band's social media posts saying it was fake information, that Reddit leak is still going around. I'm not sure you'd be able to escape that. Either way you look at it, you can't keep doing things the way you have been."

Luca nodded, then turned his attention to Callum and Donovan. Their eyes were still locked, a secret conversation happening within their silence.

"What do you think, boys?" Luca asked. "You want to give it another go? Or should we call time on this? On us?"

Several agonizing seconds passed before the two men faced forward.

Callum braced his elbows on the table and clasped his hands in front of him. "We could be persuaded to stay, but on one condition."

"What's that?"

"Jade comes with us."

I sat up straighter, unsure I'd heard them correctly. The words finally processed when Donovan winked at me.

"You got a passport, darling?"

I huffed a stunned laugh.

"We need an artist to design a new backdrop," Dante said, watching me out of the corner of his eye and fighting the smile trying to sneak onto his lips. "A graphic designer told me that the old one is too simple. It wouldn't cut it on a flashy arena tour."

I shook my head in disbelief. "Are you being serious? You're not serious... *Are* you serious?"

"We're serious, angel." Luca pressed a kiss to my hand. "Now say yes already."

My head was spinning, but my heart felt at risk of soaring out of my chest.

"Of course I'll come with you!"

Gracie barked her approval.

Luca beamed and raised his wine glass high. "In that case, I *would* like to propose a toast."

We all mirrored his motion with our drinks, except for Dante, who lifted Gracie like she was Simba from The Lion King. When we'd all stopped laughing, Luca continued.

"To Legion's next chapter."

"To more madness and mayhem," Donovan threw in.

"To more memories," Callum added.

"To healing," Dante said under his breath.

"To family," I finished, clinking our glasses. "Merry Christmas, everyone."

ENGLISH TRANSLATION OF CHAPTER 38

"Don't you feel alive?" he asked breathlessly. "Goddamn, there's nothing like it!"

He spun on his heel and strode for the merchant on the corner.

"Where are you going?" I barked. "I'm not done yelling at you yet!"

But Dante was already in the process of flagging the woman down.

"Hello, Rocío!" he called, waving his arms overhead.

The woman looked up from her buckets of bouquets, the wrinkles around her eyes crinkling as she beamed. *"Hello, Dante!"*

Not wanting to be caught at the scene of the crime, I abandoned the motorcycle and jogged over to join them.

The woman's head tilted curiously as I ran up. *"Who's the pretty woman?"*

Dante winked. *"Don't be jealous."*

The woman, Rocío, clicked her tongue and batted him away. *"Why are you so naughty?"*

Dante chuckled. *"How's your family?"*

"They're good. Do you want the usual?"

"Yes. Thank you."

Rocío bent and pulled two gorgeous bunches of red roses from one of her buckets, then nodded to me. *"Flowers for your friend too?"*

"No," Dante stated, his typical frown returning.

Rocío grunted her disapproval but handed over the flowers. Dante slipped her a one hundred dollar bill. She frantically shook her head.

"For your family," Dante insisted.

Rocío sighed in exasperation, but gratitude shone in her eyes, and she clasped his hand in thanks. Dante smiled and dipped his head, then turned and started back towards the bike. I politely waved goodbye to the woman and hurried after him.

"I didn't know you were fluent in Spanish," I mumbled when I'd caught up.

Dante arched an eyebrow. "You hear Vee yell at me in Spanish all the time."

"Yeah, but you always act like you don't hear her."

"I do that with a lot of people. Doesn't mean it's true."

We arrived at the motorcycle, and Dante tucked the flowers under his arm and patted the bike seat.

"I'm told I look more like my dad," he explained as I wiggled into place, "but my mom's Mexican. She moved to the states as a kid and insisted we hold onto our culture."

"What happened to your dad?"

Dante shrugged and slid onto the seat in front of me. "Who fucking knows. He ran off back to Orange County when my mom told him she was pregnant. Haven't heard from him since."

He turned the key in the ignition and handed me the two bouquets over his shoulder. "Hold onto these, will you?"

I took the flowers and laid them in my lap, trying not to crush the petals as I wrapped my arms around Dante's waist again. Thankfully, he drove at a much more manageable pace this time as he turned into the neighborhood. Quaint stucco houses passed us by, their manicured yards filled with happy families enjoying the beauty of September in Los Angeles.

The bike rolled to a stop in front of the largest house on the block, and Dante shut off the engine. He climbed onto solid ground and held out his hands. I offered him the flowers, but he rolled his eyes.

"No, silly," he muttered, "that's not what I was doing."

He reached forward, grabbed me around the waist, and lifted me off the bike like I weighed nothing. I let out a squeak of surprise, my cheeks flushing bright pink as he planted me in the driveway. Dante motioned for me to follow him.

"Come on."

We both pulled off our helmets and made our way towards the front door. Instead of knocking, Dante dug into his pocket, pulled out a set of keys, and jammed them into the lock.

I had no idea what would be waiting for us on the other side. A girlfriend? A secret family?

The last thing I expected was a cheery yellow room filled with sunshine, and a woman in hospital scrubs shuffling over with her arms outstretched.

"What a surprise!"

She hurled herself into Dante and gave him two fierce kisses on each cheek. He flinched against them, but not out of disgust. More like a child being smothered by a loving aunt or grandmother.

"Hello, Celia," he greeted, patting her back. *"How are you?"*

"Very good. And you?"

"I'm tired."

"And how's your mind?"

"Noisy."

"Keep fighting." The woman, Celia, pulled away and gestured

to me, her warm brown eyes lighting up even more. *"Who is she? Your girlfriend?"*

Dante scoffed. *"No way in hell."*

Celia tutted and lightly smacked Dante's shoulder. *"Careful what you say!"*

Dante smirked, pulled the flowers from my arms, and handed one bouquet to the woman in front of him. *"My employee. Jade."*

"Hello, Jade." Celia took the roses Dante offered and smiled at me like she knew a secret I didn't.

"Hi." I extended my hand for her to shake. "You must be Celia."

"I am. It's nice to meet you."

"You too. Dante doesn't talk about his family much, it's nice to have a face with the name."

Celia chuckled. "Oh, I'm not family."

"You're not?"

"Yes, she is," Dante cut in, wandering deeper into the house.

Celia followed behind him. "Not technically. You could say I'm an honorary member."

I padded after them, taking in the array of cozy furnishings and family photos on the wall. Many of them included a green-eyed little boy with pale skin, black curls, and a bright smile that dimmed as the years went on. When I finally peeled my eyes from the pictures and rounded the corner, I froze.

Stationed in the living room was a hospital bed.

It faced a window that overlooked a luscious garden alive with hummingbirds and butterflies. Tucked in the sheets and draped in a homemade quilt, was a woman.

She had dark hair streaked in gray, and brown eyes that were half-lidded and glazed as they stared into the distance. She looked to be in her fifties, but it was difficult to tell with the IVs, oxygen tubes, and beeping monitors blocking my view. I didn't need to see her face to know who she was, though. When Dante placed the flowers in a nearby vase, kissed her forehead, and lowered into the chair beside her bed, it was clear.

"Hello, Mom," he whispered, taking her hand and gently stroking it with his thumb.

Celia appeared at my side, watching the scene with a melancholy smile. "Jade, meet Marcela. Dante's mom."

"Oh," I breathed. "I… I had no idea."

"No, I'd expect not." Celia's face fell, and she lowered her voice. "He doesn't like to talk about her much. He feels too guilty."

I glanced at Dante out of the corner of my eye. He was mumbling to Marcela in Spanish and pointing to a pair of finches nibbling at the bird feeders hanging outside the window.

"Why does he feel guilty?"

Celia fiddled with one of the blossoms in her bouquet. "Something happened a few years ago… It's not my place to go into details, but one night, Marcela received a call that something had happened to Dante while he was on tour. He was in the hospital. On the way to see him, she was hit by a drunk driver. She wasn't even supposed to make it through the night, but she's a fighter. They both are. She's made wonderful progress since then, but she'll never be the same."

While Celia had been talking, involuntary tears formed along the edges of my lashes. I quickly averted my gaze and blinked them away. Something deep in my gut knew the evening she was referring to was the night Dante had tried to take his life, and all of a sudden his self-hatred made a lot more sense.

"Can I meet her?" I asked, my voice hoarse with emotion.

"Yes," Dante replied from across the room.

Of course he'd been pretending he couldn't hear.

I inhaled deep and let it out slow, then crossed to the bed overlooking the garden. Marcela made no move to look at me, her eyes remaining fixed on the greenery outside. Still, I sat down beside Dante and smiled.

"Hi, Mrs. Ramos. I'm Jade. It's an honor to meet you."

"*Jade is Dante's girlfriend,*" Celia added before darting into the kitchen.

Dante sighed and rolled his eyes. "*Celia talks too much, Mom.*"

I stifled a laugh and returned my attention to Marcela. "Your son is very talented, Mrs. Ramos. He amazes me every day."

Dante sniffed. "Don't lie."

"I'm not."

Our eyes met and held for a few moments, but I forced myself to refocus on the woman in the bed. "You said you two didn't look alike, but you do."

Dante's gaze softened as he scanned his mother's features. "You think?"

"Yeah. I can't put my finger on what it is exactly, but it's there. Something beautiful." I dared to look his way again, and found him already looking at me. I cracked a grin to break the tension. "All she's missing is the face tattoo, and you'd be twins."

To my surprise, Dante tossed his head back and laughed out loud, prompting his mom to shift in her bed.

"*Oh my goodness,*" Celia grumbled, puttering out of the kitchen carrying a platter of cookies. "I've told him to get that thing removed a hundred times. They have lasers that can do that now."

"*I know, Celia.*"

Celia set the plate of goodies down on my lap and motioned for me to eat. "Don't let the attitude fool you, Jade. He's a good boy."

Dante started to roll his eyes again, but Celia smacked the back of his head.

"I'm serious! Not many children would make sure their parents are taken care of the way you have. Jade, did you know he spent his life savings to buy this house so she could be close to him? And when he's home from tour, he always brings her favorite flowers and sings her favorite hymns."

My brows arched. "Hymns as in church hymns?"

Celia nodded and fluffed Marcela's pillows. "She only smiles when he sings them. Not when they're on the radio, not when I sing them, only when *he* does."

Dante grabbed a cookie off the platter and rotated it between his fingers. "Yeah, well. Sometimes you do things you don't want to for the people you love." He peeked up between the strands of dark hair that had fallen in front of his face, catching me staring at him. "Don't look at me like that."

I hurriedly averted my gaze.

"I have an idea!" Celia eagerly clapped her hands and wandered over to an acoustic guitar sitting in the corner. "Dante, how about you play us something?"

He frowned. "I don't think Jade—"

"*Please*?" Celia carried the guitar over and winked at me. "Dante's been giving me lessons, but I think Marcela is probably tired of hearing my pathetic attempts at 'Wonderwall.'"

Dante sighed in defeat and stretched out his hand. "Alright, fine."

Celia beamed and handed over the instrument. Dante cleared his throat and put the guitar into position, testing the tone and tightening the strings to adjust it.

"Don't look at me like that either," he murmured.

This time, I didn't look away. "How am I looking at you?"

"Like this somehow changes who I am."

His fingers moved into place, and he strummed a chord, followed by another, then another. It was a tune I'd never heard before, slow and haunting, filled with passion and longing. Marcela moved in her bed again, her lashes fluttering.

"That's beautiful," I mused. "What is it?"

"Just a little something I was working on today," Dante replied. "It's not finished yet."

"Well, keep playing it," Celia urged. "I think your mom likes it."

Dante and I glanced at Marcela. A faint smile tugged at the corners of her mouth, which made Dante's face light up.

"Do you like it, Mom?"

She muttered something incoherent, but it may as well have been glowing praise. Dante radiated joy from the inside out and played the rest of the verse and chorus, then transitioned into an array of different song ideas he'd been toying with.

We stayed there for another hour, listening to music, watching the birds in the window, and eating cookies, until Celia informed us it was time for Marcela to wash up for bed. We said goodbye, and on the way out, Celia pulled me into a warm, lingering hug that gave me more comfort in ten seconds than my own mother had given me in the past two years. I eventually pulled away and busied myself with adjusting my helmet so no one would see me getting emotional. I was still able to hear the conversation happening between Celia and Dante as they said their farewells.

"I love you, Dante."

"I love you too."

Celia cupped his face in her hands, forcing him to look her in the eyes. *"I really like Jade."*

"Me too."

"She's very special."

"I know."

Celia nodded and kissed Dante's cheek one last time before shooing him towards the motorcycle in the driveway. She stood on the doorstep and waved goodbye until we'd disappeared in the distance.

We took the long way home along Mulholland Drive so we could watch the sunset from the crest of the Hollywood Hills. There, I confiscated Dante's phone, changed the music to Zella Day's dreamy cover of "Wonderwall," and decided now wasn't the time to remind him of what I'd told the band the night I signed my contract.

I'd told them I graduated from college with two degrees.

They knew about the first degree, graphic design.

But the second?

Spanish.

I'd understood everything that had been said today.

And in regards to Dante and Celia's final words, I felt the same way:

I liked him, and thought he was pretty damn special too.

ACKNOWLEDGMENTS

First off, I want to thank *you*, reader. If you got this far, I am eternally grateful. This was a personal and therefore very difficult book for me to write, and you taking the time to see it through means the world to me. Thank you for giving these band boys a chance, putting up with their rough edges, and seeing their good hearts beneath it all. This may not be the last we see of them; there *is* another tour on the horizon after all, and now that everyone has worked through some trauma, I think they're all primed to have *a lot* more fun in the future.

Shoutout to Sleep Token, Bad Omens, Motionless in White, and Bring Me The Horizon, whose musicality and theatricality were an inspiration, and their songs the soundtrack I spent many a late night writing to.

I also have to say thank you to the friends who banished my self doubt and insisted I write the book I was terrified to touch. And a particular shoutout to my brother-in-law and my lovely friend Erwin P. for helping me with my Spanish.

ALSO BY IVY BRANNON

THE VEIL SERIES

In Brannon's debut New Adult Romantasy trilogy,
a human woman in search of her Changeling brother stumbles
into the Fae realm, where steamy love affairs, heart-pounding
adventure, and a war between good and evil await her

AVAILABLE ON AMAZON, BARNES & NOBLE, AND WATERSTONES

RESOURCES FOR SURVIVORS

U.S. RESOURCES

Rape, Abuse & Incest National Network + Hotline - https://rainn.org/

Enough Abuse Campaign - https://enoughabuse.org/get-help/survivor-support/

National Suicide Hotline (phone, online chat, and Español available) - https://988lifeline.org/ (988)

National Institute of Mental Health - https://www.nimh.nih.gov/health/topics/suicide-prevention

Substance Abuse and Mental Health Services Administration - https://www.samhsa.gov/ (800) 662-4357 (free and confidential)

CANADIAN RESOURCES

Ending Violence Association of Canada - https://endingviolencecanada.org/sexual-assault-centres-crisis-lines-and-support-services/

List of Canadian Sexual Assault Centers - https://www.reescommunity.com/resources/

Kids Help Phone (Child Sexual Abuse Hotline) - (800) 668-6868

Canadian Centre for Child Protection - https://protectchildren.ca/en/resources-research/understanding-child-sexual-abuse/

9-8-8: Suicide Crisis Helpline (Available 24/7) - (988)

Hope for Wellness Help Line - (855) 242-3310 (toll-free) - Online chat available or text WELLNESS to 741741

The Canadian Centre on Substance Use and Addiction - https://www.ccsa.ca/

Families for Addiction Recovery - https://www.farcanada.org/resources/

U.K./EUROPEAN RESOURCES

Victim Support Europe - https://victim-support.eu/

Rape Crisis England & Wales - https://rapecrisis.org.uk/

Rape Crisis Network Ireland - https://www.rcni.ie/

European Women's Network Against Sexual Violence - http://reactagainstsexualviolence.org

Addiction Center - Europe - https://www.addictioncenter.com/addiction/addiction-in-the-eu/

International Suicide Hotlines - https://blog.opencounseling.com/suicide-hotlines/

International Association for Suicide Prevention - https://www.iasp.info/suicidalthoughts/

AUSTRALIAN RESOURCES

1800 Respect - National Domestic Family and Sexual Violence Counselling Service - https://www.1800respect.org.au/

Sexual Assault Crisis Line - (1800) 806 - 292

Australian Childhood Foundation - Counseling for children affected by abuse - https://www.childhood.org.au/ - (1800) 176-453

Beyond Blue - Mental Health Support - https://www.beyond
blue.org.au/

Lifeline - https://www.lifeline.org.au/

National Alcohol and Other Drug Hotline - 1(800) 250 015

457